PRAISE FOR THE NOVELS OF
Jasmine

"Deliciously erotic and completely...
—Susan John...   ...thor

"An erotic, emotional adventure of discovery you don't want to miss."
—Lora Leigh, *New York Times* bestselling author

"So incredibly hot that I'm trying to find the right words to describe it without having to be edited for content . . . extremely stimulating from the first page to the last! Of course, that means that I loved it! . . . One of the hottest, sexiest erotic books I have read so far."
—*Romance Reader at Heart*

"Sexy."   —*Sensual Romance Reviews*

"Delightfully torrid."   —*Midwest Book Review*

"More than a fast-paced erotic romance, this is a story of family, filled with memorable characters who will keep you engaged in the plot and the great sex. A good read to warm a winter's night."
—*Romantic Times*

"Bursting with sensuality and eroticism."   —*In the Library Reviews*

"The passion is intense, hot, and purely erotic . . . recommended for any reader who likes their stories realistic, hot, captivating, and very, very well written."   —*Road to Romance*

"Not your typical romance. This one's going to remain one of my favorites."   —*The Romance Studio*

"Jasmine Haynes keeps the plot moving and the love scenes very hot."
—*Just Erotic Romance Reviews*

"A wonderful novel . . . Try this one—you won't be sorry."
—*The Best Reviews*

Berkley Books by Jasmine Haynes

FAIR GAME

UNLACED
(with Jaci Burton, Joey W. Hill, and Denise Rossetti)

SHOW AND TELL

THE FORTUNE HUNTER

OPEN INVITATION

TWIN PEAKS
(with Susan Johnson)

SOMEBODY'S LOVER

FAIR GAME

Jasmine Haynes

HEAT | NEW YORK

THE BERKLEY PUBLISHING GROUP
Published by the Penguin Group
Penguin Group (USA) Inc.
375 Hudson Street, New York, New York 10014, USA
Penguin Group (Canada), 90 Eglinton Avenue East, Suite 700, Toronto, Ontario M4P 2Y3, Canada
(a division of Pearson Penguin Canada Inc.)
Penguin Books Ltd., 80 Strand, London WC2R 0RL, England
Penguin Group Ireland, 25 St. Stephen's Green, Dublin 2, Ireland (a division of Penguin Books Ltd.)
Penguin Group (Australia), 250 Camberwell Road, Camberwell, Victoria 3124, Australia
(a division of Pearson Australia Group Pty. Ltd.)
Penguin Books India Pvt. Ltd., 11 Community Centre, Panchsheel Park, New Delhi—110 017, India
Penguin Group (NZ), 67 Apollo Drive, Rosedale, North Shore 0632, New Zealand
(a division of Pearson New Zealand Ltd.)
Penguin Books (South Africa) (Pty.) Ltd., 24 Sturdee Avenue, Rosebank, Johannesburg 2196, South Africa

Penguin Books Ltd., Registered Offices: 80 Strand, London WC2R 0RL, England

This is an original publication of The Berkley Publishing Group.

PRINTING HISTORY
Heat trade paperback edition / June 2009

Library of Congress Cataloging-in-Publication Data

Haynes, Jasmine.
    Fair game / Jasmine Haynes.
        p. cm.
    ISBN 978-0-425-22759-6
    1. Sexual dominance and submission—Fiction.   I. Title.
    PS3608.A936F35 2009
    813'.6—dc22
                                            2008055289

PRINTED IN THE UNITED STATES OF AMERICA

10 9 8 7 6 5 4 3 2 1

To Dee S. Knight

ACKNOWLEDGMENTS

Thanks to Jenn Cummings, Terri Schaefer, and Kathy Coatney for always being there to keep me straight. To my agent, Lucienne Diver, and my editor, Wendy McCurdy. I'd also like to thank the people at Graniterock, especially Don Roland, for all the time he spent showing me around the Quail Hollow Sand Plant. What a great tour guide! Any adjustments to the actual workings of a sand plant were made for the sake of expediency.

FAIR GAME

1

KYLE Perry was running late. He could have jogged the five miles across San Francisco from his home to the office faster than he'd been able to drive it. In fact, that's often what he did when he was in town, except that today he had a morning meeting at the office, then a trip up to the Santa Rosa quarry in the early afternoon. Mondays were always a bitch. He was either catching a flight out, driving to a site, or prepping for endless meetings.

He made it into the garage elevator just before the doors closed on the cramped car, and ducked around a delivery man to hit the button for the thirty-fifth floor. At lobby level, there was a mass exodus and an equal influx.

Kyle moved to the rear, allowing room for the crush of new arrivals. Backing into him, a young woman knocked his knee with her notebook PC case. She turned her head enough to apologize, and he got an impression of green eyes and pink lipstick. She dragged the computer case in front of her to avoid hitting him again.

In the pack of overheated bodies, she smelled damn good. Not perfumy, but fresh, like flowers or fruits, something natural and outdoorsy. Dark hair grazed the collar of her black suit jacket, curling softly. A tantalizing patch of nape peeked through. Some women were incredibly sensitive right there. A flick of the tongue, a light kiss, even a warm puff of breath could make them a little crazy.

Kyle loved women, he loved sex, and he enjoyed the occasional flight of harmless fancy about a complete stranger a man might see on the street. Or in an elevator. The top of her head was level with his nose, her scent tantalizing his mind as he drew in the sweetness. That sliver of skin just above her collar made him hard.

The car jolted to a stop a couple of floors up, throwing her off balance and right into him, his cock gliding along the base of her spine. He didn't move, didn't speak, didn't breathe, waiting for her to jerk away.

Instead, she remained perfectly still. The crush in the elevator eased by two, but she didn't add even an inch of distance between them.

He closed his eyes a long moment and dragged in a deep breath of her, filling himself with her sensual fragrance. He felt her shift slightly, her backside caressing him. Or was that only in his mind? Hell no, that was her ass cradling his balls, her body rubbing his cock. One, two, three times. It was no accident.

Kyle dared to lay two fingers on her hip, just at the waist of her slacks, his touch hidden from view by her jacket. Everyone watched the tick of floors going by, waiting for theirs to come up. No one noticed where he'd placed his hand.

Except her. When the car stopped once again, she was flush up against him. He could hear his heart beating in his ears, feel the heat of her body seeping through his fingertips straight to his chest.

And he scented her. Like a lion scenting his mate's heat, something feminine and musky. He'd bet the world that her panties were damp beneath the staid black suit.

More floors, the press of her body increasing against him. Then he felt the unmistakable slide of her hand between them. He was hard as a pylon. She cupped him, fit his cock into her palm, held him, gave a gentle squeeze. His eyes drifted shut as he relished her touch, her stroking him, taking full measure of him. He was ready to taste her, ready to take her, caught up in a fantasy of going to his knees and flicking his tongue between her legs. She would taste sweet, and her moans of pleasure would bring him to the brink. As she cried out in orgasm, he'd lift her up against the elevator wall, thrust inside her, high, deep, and come harder than he ever had before . . . The elevator stopped.

Her body heat faded. She didn't even turn around to see exactly whose cock she'd touched. She merely exited the car and turned right down the hall. Disappearing as the doors closed, she left him alone with six other people who didn't have a clue what she'd just done to him.

Turned his world upside down. Shattered his equilibrium. Damn, it was hot. He'd never see her again. Never know exactly what she looked like, just dark hair, green eyes, pink lipstick, black business suit; her fresh scent; and a hand that had the potential to take his cock to heaven.

As the elevator stopped yet again, Kyle realized he'd missed his floor. He had to laugh. A day that had gotten off to a bad start was suddenly looking up.

HEH. Well. That was sweet. Josie smiled to herself as she pushed through the double doors of SMG Industries' high-rise San Francisco headquarters. Inside the lobby lay a gleaming black tile floor leading to a waist-high receptionist's desk, the blond girl seated behind it almost hidden by her computer monitor.

Josie had started off the morning commute in a really bad mood. Ernie Masters, her boss and the head of Program Management at Castle Heavy Mining, had called her cell on the way into the city this morning and told her he wasn't going to make the meeting with SMG. No way, no how. She'd have to handle it on her own. Which was fine, except that Ernie had all the hard copies of her presentation. Dammit, she knew she should have taken care of the packets. You want it done right, do it yourself. It pissed her off to no end that he'd cancelled at the absolute last minute; otherwise, she could have gone into the office early and printed more. SMG Industries was a first-time customer for Castle, and this project was a major machine upgrade for SMG's Coyote Ridge Sand Plant, one of their quarries out in the Santa Cruz Mountains. Being Castle's lead program manager on the quarry project, Josie wanted to make a good impression.

Because of that, her blood had been running high when she stepped into the elevator. Maybe that was the reason she'd done it. Or maybe it was because she was damned horny, not having had sex in at least two weeks. Whatever the reason, when she'd felt his hard-on at her back, she couldn't resist touching. She'd caught a glimpse of his face when she stepped on the elevator. Short brown hair, blue eyes, older, late thirties she'd say, with a body she wouldn't mind climbing. Not that she was into casual sex with strangers. She preferred casual sex with men she knew.

He'd just felt so damn good. A hot, hard male. She couldn't help herself, and he'd been pretty damn impressive in her hand. Ooh, baby.

Maybe she'd see him again on the way out. Nice thought. The final result, though, was that she'd lost her ire with Masters. Whatever. He wouldn't make it. Fine. SMG was her most ambitious project to date, and now the meeting was all hers. She'd get to shine.

Setting her PC case on the reception desk, she smiled down at the girl.

Rolling her chair away from her monitor, the blonde adjusted her headset and returned Josie's smile. Her bright blue sweater matched her eyes, and the fuzzy glittering white snowflake on it showcased her chest. Cute sweater. Except that it was August, not December. Josie read her nameplate. Kisa Korsakov. Kisa? She stifled an inappropriate laugh. Perhaps back in Russia it was cold in August. "Hi, I'm Josie Tybrook. I've got a nine o'clock meeting."

"Vould you please sign our visitor's log?" the girl said with a thick yet understandable accent as she pointed to the clipboard on the counter. "And your meeting vas vith whom?"

Before Josie could answer, the lobby doors opened once again and Kisa turned all sloe-eyed and sultry, her husky voice somehow managing to drop another sexy octave. "Good morning, Mr. Perry." She flipped her waist-length blond hair over her shoulder. "Vhat a magnificent tie you are vearing too-day."

Josie turned in the direction of the magnificent tie. She hadn't noticed the tie—which was a simple red-and-black stripe—on the elevator, only the hot body. And the hard cock. Oh shit. That was Mr. Perry?

"Thank you, Kisa." He said it with the slightest edge of indulgent laughter, his gaze on Josie as he spoke.

Kisa glanced down at her small yet perky breasts beneath the white snowflake. "And I'm vearing your favorite sweater too-day, too." She batted her eyelashes.

"So you are." The edge of his mouth kicked up.

Josie had to hang on to the counter to keep from falling over with laughter, both at the interesting little exchange and at herself. Kyle Perry. Wouldn't ya know the guy she copped a feel off of in a crowded elevator would turn out to be the very man with whom she was meeting? She could hear her mother's voice: "I don't know how you get yourself into these messes, Josie." Well, hell, she'd been out to impress, and she certainly had.

She didn't introduce herself. If he had any intelligence, he'd already figured out she was his nine o'clock appointment, the program manager on the Coyote Ridge project. She'd be working with him for the next three months while the new equipment and systems were installed, tested, and qualified.

So. Just how would he handle the meeting after their elevator interlude? She couldn't wait to find out.

AS Josie Tybrook flipped to another screen in her presentation, Kyle leaned back in his chair, stacking his hands behind his head.

At the conference room's sideboard, Todd Adams, the sand plant's superintendent, poured himself another cup of coffee, drinking in every word Josie said. He closed the blinds against a glare that played across the screen, then took his seat at the big oak table.

Seated next to Todd, Will Stevens, head of Machine Maintenance for the quarry, relaxed in his chair, one booted foot propped on his knee. He gave off his usual air of nonchalance, but the guy had an almost photographic memory. Show him a diagram once, and he could practically redraw the thing blindfolded. His genius was machinery.

Josie appeared to impress them both. When he'd first heard she was the daughter of one of Castle's board members, he'd had his misgivings. Connor Kingston had assured him she was good, and gave an extraordinary attention to detail. The purpose of this meeting was to update the SMG team on subcontractors and outside suppliers to be used, scheduling, installation, training, debugging—

especially for the new ticketing system—and a host of other particulars Josie was in charge of coordinating. Castle Heavy Mining would do the major portion of the equipment manufacturing, but on a project of this magnitude, there were myriad components that had to come from outside.

Listening to her, Kyle now agreed with Castle's CEO; Josie was *very* good. And in ways he was sure Connor Kingston didn't even know about.

"We've chosen Wilson Products for all the electronics, including the depth finder and the electronic eyes on both the load-out system and the weigh station," she was saying. "We used them on the Dominican project last year with excellent results."

She had a low, sweet voice, perfect for whispering dirty words in the dark of the night. Or over the phone. She'd apologized for her manager's absence without casting blame and didn't twitch or flush when Kyle introduced himself. For all her acknowledgment of it, or lack thereof, what happened in the elevator might have been nothing more than his flight of fancy about a pretty woman. She knew her stuff, too. She'd learned the ins and outs of SMG's silica mining, researched the suppliers best suited for the company's machine upgrade designs, and set up an aggressive yet manageable timetable. She wasn't merely a pretty face or the daughter of a board member.

And he wanted her. After that hot little elevator episode, when he saw the woman in the lobby, his heart kick-started. He'd had to enter with his suit jacket buttoned to hide his cock. Kisa, their receptionist, didn't miss a thing, and she'd have thought the hard-on was for her and her snowflake sweater. He'd complimented the garment once. She'd started wearing it at least twice a month after that and pointed it out to him every time she did. Or perhaps she was pointing out her breasts.

All he'd really had eyes for in the lobby this morning was Josie

Tybrook. Smart, confident, understated, primly suited up in black business attire. Yet he could still feel the phantom press of her hand on his cock.

Todd said something Kyle didn't catch. Coyote Ridge extracted a bottle-grade sand that was also good for fiberglass insulation. The deposit had been harvested since the seventies and much of the plant's equipment was outdated. Kyle, Todd, and Will had worked with the Castle engineers for three months on a new design utilizing existing machinery while incorporating new technologies. They'd also spent considerable time with Castle programmers flowcharting the in-house ticketing system that would tie the customer order to the truck making the haul, record both tare and heavy weights, issue the government-required ticket, and feed it all into the billing system. If it worked well, they'd install it in their other plants, paying Castle a licensing fee, and Castle would have a new product line. It was a win-win for both companies.

Josie flipped through a chart in front of her, pointing when she found whatever she'd been looking for. "We've got the operators scheduled for two days of training the week before we start bringing the new systems online for testing and qualification." Ah, so Todd's question had been about the complexity of the new operations protocol.

Todd rubbed a hand round and round his bald pate. Kyle had worked with him for almost ten years, but even back then, at thirty-five, the guy had been bald, with the same habit of rubbing his head.

"Seems like the training should be done simultaneously, in case there are any hiccups." It was a bit of a juvenile comment, but Kyle figured Todd was testing Josie. That was Todd's style.

She took the question at face value, shaking her head, her dark hair brushing her shoulders. "You're going from manual operation to computer controlled and making a lot of upgrades all at once.

Your guys need to know what every flashing light, signal, or warning means *before* they start making product."

Will Stevens popped Todd lightly on the arm with his fist. He was a head shorter, twenty-five pounds lighter, and ten years younger than Todd, but he never missed an opportunity to give his boss crap. They actually had a damn good working relationship. "Yeah, dude," he said, "it's like all those little warning lights in your Beemer. You gotta take it down to the shop to figure out what they mean." Will then glanced keenly at Josie. "What about my guys?"

Josie pointed to the same chart with an unpainted fingernail. In a world with silicon breasts, fake nails, and dyed hair, she seemed the genuine article. "Machine maintenance personnel," she said, "require three days total training time."

Will crossed his arms, rocking slowly in his chair, then nodded. "Makes sense."

It wasn't just the equipment itself, but, as Will had alluded to, the electronics required to run it all. Their guys would now have to troubleshoot at a whole new level. What they'd get in return for the capital outlay was significantly higher efficiencies in production and loading, which translated to improved gate-to-gate times. Gate-to-gate was a key factor. The shorter the amount of time a hauler was inside the gate, the more customer orders could be filled in a day.

"What's our downtime going to be?" It was the first Kyle had added to the conversation, letting his team get their questions out there before his. He already had a good estimate, but he wanted to see what she'd come up with.

The lady didn't hesitate. "We've arranged the various installations to coincide with your production schedule. Once you've filled the silos"—the silos housed the glass sand—"we'll remove the dryer for the new coating and install the temperature automation at the same time. It'll be back online before the silos are empty." She flipped to another screen on her presentation. "This schedule shows each installation and indicates that total downtime will be less than two days."

The timetable was better than he'd expected. "We'll hold you to that."

She met his gaze head-on. "I'm sure you will." A lick of heat flashed in her eyes, giving a whole separate meaning to the exchange.

Damn. He started getting hard all over again. Now, however, was not the time.

"I've got the charts on hard copy for you," she went on, focusing once more on Todd and Will, "which I'll have couriered over to you this afternoon."

She'd obviously forgotten to bring them with her. Then again, her boss, Masters, had been a no-show. Perhaps he'd had them.

"No need to courier it to me," he said. "Just e-mail it, and I'll have Kisa print it off."

The corner of her mouth quirked. Ah, she'd obviously noticed the little byplay in the lobby this morning.

"Same for us." Todd slid his business card across the table. "An e-mail's fine. We'll get a couple of copies printed up."

That settled, she continued with her presentation. Kyle enjoyed the way she moved, sometimes resting her hands on the table, ass thrust out slightly, or pacing to the screen to highlight an item with her pen. She strode, not so much with gracefulness as with efficiency, an economy of movement.

Despite his fascination, his mind didn't wander again, and the meeting was concluded with her same proficiency, all questions answered, and a plant tour scheduled for the following afternoon, Tuesday. He found it amazing how much she'd accomplished without even visiting the site yet, though with her résumé of projects—

Connor Kingston had furnished the list, including dates and duration—she'd become familiar with most types of mining operations. In her eight or so years since college—he guessed her age at about thirty—she'd accomplished a helluva lot at Castle.

After Will and Todd left, Kyle took the extra minutes as she shut down and stored her computer, shoving yellow pad and papers into the case's front pocket, to discuss some final points.

"I'll walk you out," he said when she was done.

"There's no need." She lifted her lips in a polite smile. "Thank you, but I can find my way."

Hell, yes, there was a need. Just inside the door, he stopped her when she would have left him in the dust. "I'd like to see you again."

"I'll be seeing you tomorrow at the plant."

He smiled. She was being difficult. "Personally, not professionally."

She blinked, then pressed her mouth into a flat line. "First, I don't date clients. Second, I don't date, period. In case you haven't noticed, I have a very demanding job."

"I've noticed. Let's skip the dating part, then, and get right to the sex."

Her eyes widened, her lips parted, then she huffed out a breath of air. Finally she found her voice. "I can't believe you just said that."

He chanced a step closer to her and lowered his voice. "I couldn't believe you'd rub my cock in a crowded elevator. But you did, and I would say that bears further exploration."

"If I'd known you were my client, I wouldn't have done it." She straightened her shoulders, standing slightly taller. "I don't mix business with pleasure."

"And I'm not going to pass up a wonderful opportunity simply because I happened to meet you at work." He smiled to take the bite out of anything he said. "We're both adults and perfectly capable of separating business and pleasure." Tipping his head, he let his gaze travel across her face, then back to meet her eyes. "Besides, we met personally first, business came later."

She huffed again, and her cheeks flushed. "I wouldn't call that *meeting*."

Her indignation amused him. "I'd call it intimate, which is even more important."

"I'm not going to argue with you." She stepped back, gave a longer-than-necessary look. "The answer is no."

Kyle studied her a moment, saying nothing, then finally raised his hands. "I go down in defeat."

Josie was almost sorry. A tiny part of her wanted him to try harder. She liked that he called what happened between them an opportunity. Somehow it took his proposition out of the realm of sleazy and into intriguing. Tantalizing. In today's careful business atmosphere, where a man's compliment could be construed as harassment and therefore men simply stopped complimenting at all, she liked that he was a person who asked for what he wanted.

She still wasn't going to screw up her career for a . . . screw. No matter how handsome Kyle Perry was. The guy somehow came out to be more than the sum of his parts. Tall, a couple of inches over six feet, toned physique, clean-shaven face with decent bone structure and a strong jaw, all of it coming together in a rather devastating package. Not to mention how big and hard he'd felt in her hand.

All through the meeting, she'd been really, *really* thinking about how good he would be, but she had to get that idea out of her mind. Since they'd be working together, the man was off-limits.

"Perhaps you should try Little Miss Snowflake," she quipped, giving him a big, toothy smile. "She seemed quite eager." Damn. Did that sound like jealousy?

"Little Miss Snowflake?" Kyle laughed, then cut himself off, but his blue eyes still sparkled. "No."

"Well, then"—Josie raised her hand—"gotta go. No need to walk me out. Honest."

"Tomorrow."

She'd turned, on her way out the door for the second time. "Tomorrow?"

"The sand plant tour. I'll pick you up at your office at two thirty."

Jeez, that sounded idiotic, forgetting about the plant tour. "I can drive myself." She cocked a hip. "Is this another come-on?"

He smiled. "I like the way you smell."

He could have made an excuse. Instead, the honest comment sent heat rolling through her body.

"I won't touch," he added.

She almost hoped he'd break the promise.

She'd known her share of persistent guys. But he was so low-key about it, it was enticing. She was a girl like any other girl, and it was nice to be desired. She found his attention flattering. She could also easily find herself wanting more of it, which was *not* good in this particular situation. "Okay, two thirty." So why was she agreeing?

"Wear a short skirt."

She narrowed her eyes at him. "Cool your jets. No means no." But God, she liked it. She liked *him*. He was intelligent, confident, authoritative, and exceptionally hot in suit and tie. A lethal combination. She liked a man who dressed up well.

"No means no," he agreed, "unless a woman has already put her hand on my cock."

Which she had. That robbed her of all arguments. "I'll e-mail you the presentation package and see you tomorrow at two thirty. No need to come in, I'll be out in the parking lot." Then she beat a hasty retreat. Was that him laughing as she passed down the hall?

She stopped in the ladies' room before heading out. The mirror revealed the telltale flush on her cheeks. The guy got her motor running. But really, this was a huge job. Her boss was Ernie Masters, but it was Connor Kingston she wanted to impress. He wasn't just family, being Faith's husband and all; he was CEO of Castle Heavy Mining. Faith's father, Jarvis, would retire soon, and then Connor would be chairman. He'd given her a big chance to make good with this project. She wouldn't let him down by having a fling with the lead client contact.

Leaving the stall, she washed her hands, then dried them. It wasn't *just* Connor. Business and pleasure did not mix in any way, shape, or form. Especially if the man had any power over you. He's in charge, you're the one who gets screwed. And not in a good way. Been there, done that, got the T-shirt to prove it. Granted, she might be judging Kyle harshly based on a college love affair gone sour, but hot as he was, casual sex wasn't worth taking the risk, not where her career was concerned. She had a couple of good guy friends to take care of those needs.

That was it. She was just horny. She needed a little roll in the hay to get Mr. Kyle Perry out of her system.

2

BY the time she got back to work, Josie had managed to move Kyle Perry to the back of her mind and was now ready to read Ernie Masters the riot act for ditching her. It was the principal of the thing. Even if he was her boss, he shouldn't have left her in the lurch without the presentation package. She would have tackled him right away, too, if she hadn't gone to her cubicle first to check her voice mails. The most significant was Connor, saying he wanted to see her ASAP when she got back. The slightest edge of tension laced his tone. Kind of odd for Connor, since nothing seemed to muss up his calm.

She left behind the hubbub of FI&T—Furnish, Install, and Train—of which Program Management was only one department. The cubicle arena housed not only her group, but the buyers, installers, instructors, et cetera. The phones never stopped ringing, and the voices rose to fever pitch as the day progressed and nerves frayed. A program manager was the center of a customer's attention. When the crap rained down, it rained right on the project leader's head. Yet Josie loved every minute of it. It was her job to make sure everything came together on time and on budget. If she screwed up, okay, not so pleasant. But when it all went right, she was a hero.

Her noisy, frenetic, predominantly male work environment was in marked contrast to the relative quiet along the executive row hallway leading to Connor's office. She'd always felt as if she needed to genuflect, which was a holdover from when Jarvis Castle was running the whole shebang. Now the old man only came in two or three days a week. He spent a lot of his time with Faith and three-and-a-half-month-old David. The way old Jarvis gloated over the baby, you'd think no one had ever had a grandkid before.

Connor was on his cell phone, feet propped on his desk, ankles crossed. Open folders lay strewn across his desktop, a ring from his coffee mug seeping through a couple of papers, the messiness uncharacteristic of him. There was something about his smile that said he was talking to Faith. Josie couldn't adequately describe that smile, except to say that it made her heart beat faster. She wasn't used to good marriages—her own parents' relationship was akin to walking through a minefield—but Connor and Faith, that couldn't be anything other than love and total commitment. The forever kind. See, sometimes marrying the boss's daughter worked out.

Josie tapped lightly on the doorframe.

Glancing up, he said into the cell, "Josie's here. Gotta go." He waved Josie in. "I'll be home on time"—he paused, sighed—"and yeah, some TLC would be in order. Love you, baby." Then he punched the end button and slid the phone onto his desk.

"You guys are sickening," Josie quipped, because that amount of gushing love made her nervous, even if she was on the outside looking in.

Connor grinned, then slapped his feet onto the floor, sat up straight, and toyed with his tie. His suit jacket hung on a coatrack by the door, and he'd rolled his shirtsleeves to his elbow.

She sensed the stress beneath the grin as she slid into the chair opposite his desk. His dark hair was messed up, too, as if he'd run his hands through it.

"Find a replacement VP yet?" she asked. "Because if you haven't, I'm still willing to take the job." A little levity might help, because obviously *that* was a joke.

Connor was acting head of FI&T since their VP resigned a couple of weeks ago. FI&T was a massive undertaking, and she knew she wasn't ready for that responsibility. She didn't have the managerial skills yet. What bugged her, though, was that she wasn't getting them with Masters standing in the way. The guy had no ambition and no desire to climb the ladder. How was she supposed to move into his job and get the experience she needed if he was never going to give it up? Not only that, his work had been on a downhill slide lately.

And here she was getting herself all pissed off again because he'd blown off that meeting.

Connor wasn't getting the levity in her comment. In fact, the grin died on his face. "No VP yet," he said. "And I wanted to tell you that we're also losing Ernie Masters as well."

Yes! Woohoo. She had a shot. Just when she thought life was a bitch.

Then she thought about the phrasing Connor had used, *We're losing Masters.* "Are you firing him?" She might be pissed, but she didn't want him fired. The guy had two kids he was putting through college.

Connor gathered a few of the papers on his desk, frowning at the coffee stains. "No. He's going on medical leave." Then he glanced up. "He won't be coming back."

He wasn't coming back? Ever? Josie felt her jaw drop. Enough to catch flies. She couldn't believe it. "Why not? What's wrong with him?" She felt idiotic, like a middle school kid who couldn't get fractions, but with that seemingly simple sentence, Connor had ripped the rug right out from under her.

"He's got cancer." The muscles of Connor's face flexed, stressed, and suddenly the strain she'd heard in his voice made sense. "Pancreatic," he added. "He has months, at most."

The air in the office felt so harsh it burned her throat as she dragged it in. When Connor said Ernie was leaving, in her own mind, she'd cheered. Her first thought had been about taking Ernie's job.

Jesus. Even if it was only to herself, all she'd done for months now was bitch and moan about the guy's slacker habits, how it affected her, that he was standing in her way, yadda yadda. What about how angry she'd been this morning? Ernie hadn't made it to the meeting because he was busy telling Connor he was dying. God. She started remembering how haggard he'd looked over the last few weeks and months, how tired. Yet he came to work every day, and she'd never even asked if he was okay. Good Lord, the man was only fifty-two, almost her dad's age.

"He thinks you're the best candidate for his job."

Good God, Ernie was recommending *her*. She was *such* a fucking selfish bitch.

"You should meet with him this afternoon so he can turn everything over to you. He also said you can call him any time you have a question."

Oh man. She wasn't a crier. Not even after what happened in college. But dammit if her eyes weren't burning right now. Connor was giving her the job, yet it felt like stepping over Ernie's dead body.

"It's not your fault, Josie. He didn't tell anyone what was going on." Connor wasn't that much older than her, thirty-five to her thirty, yet in a lot of ways he was so much more together than she was.

She was afraid if she opened her mouth, she would start crying. About work stuff she was generally emotional, volatile, and outspoken. Her mom said she was like a bull in a china shop when she wanted her way. For the very first time, she realized it really meant that she was all about me, me, me.

"Why don't you take an hour or so, go get a soda, sit in the sun." Connor tipped his head slightly to meet her eyes. "Then you can talk to Ernie."

What she wanted to do was talk to Faith. Funny. They were second cousins, and honestly, they'd hardly spoken until after Faith married Connor last May, yet Faith had become the closest thing to a best friend she'd ever had. There was Trinity, too. They wouldn't make her feel better, but at least they listened when she said she felt like shit.

Yet she needed to get her act in gear right here, right now. "I'm fine. I don't need a soda break." She managed a deep breath. "I'll talk to him now."

Connor nodded. "Good. But before you go, why don't you tell me about your meeting at SMG?"

She realized he was giving her a few extra minutes to compose herself. "It went well. I'm doing the tour tomorrow. They had a few suggestions for the plan's improvement, but for the most part we agreed on everything."

"What'd you think of Kyle Perry? Is he going to make the job easier or prove to be a pain in the ass?"

Kyle Perry. For the last five minutes, she'd forgotten all about him, yet the moment Connor said his name, warmth spread through her. "He seems like a knowledgeable, stand-up kind of guy, and I think he'll be cooperative." He'd be far more than cooperative if Kyle had his way.

"Good. I got the same impression." Connor had worked with Kyle when first securing the SMG project. He'd been involved in the engineering stages as oversight—Connor's background was finance— and as acting FI&T VP, he'd given final approval to her project plan.

Josie rose. "Well, if that's all, I'll go see Ernie."

Connor stared at her a beat. "You'll do fine, Josie." He wasn't referring to the job.

She nodded her head, but she wasn't so sure. Like her mom said, she was a bull in a china shop, and she didn't know how to talk to a guy who was dying. She knew she'd say the wrong thing.

At the door, she turned. "Thanks for having confidence in me to take his place." In her shock, she wasn't sure she'd said that earlier.

Connor had fought for her right from the beginning, getting old Jarvis to give her a shot at the Dominican project. If he hadn't, she'd still be treading in Ronson's steps, and *he* would have gotten Ernie's job. Ronson was a decent program manager, but he had a tendency to hold everything close to his vest. Hence, when a project got out of control, no one had any warning and the cleanup was that much harder.

Now it was going to be up to her to manage that particular problem of his.

Connor nodded and smiled, but the tension around his eyes was back. She figured he had his own difficult feelings about Ernie's illness. At least he had Faith and the baby to go home to for his shot of TLC. Even big CEOs needed it sometimes.

For a brief moment, she thought of how it would be to have someone to call when the chips were down. Someone to whom she could confess that she was utterly terrified to walk into Ernie's office. Someone who was more than a best friend. A lover, a man who knew her inside and out. Someone to put his arms around her and say, *Hey, baby, it's okay to cry, I won't tell anyone.*

Her distress over Ernie was making her feel unusually needy. Then again, maybe she'd been so focused on her career—and, admittedly, herself—that she'd missed the forest for the trees, so to speak. She hadn't noticed her boss was dying right before her very eyes.

What the hell else was she missing in her life?

GETTING out of the city was a crawl, but at least the Golden Gate moved at the speed limit. Being on the road so much of the time was beginning to wear Kyle down. As director of West Coast Operations, the regular travel dose was high—two and a half weeks out of four—but because he was divorced with no kids, he was often sent on other missions that were not strictly his venue. He needed to find another job. He made a damn good salary, but at thirty-nine he was more than ready for the challenge of a vice presidency. The opportunities, however, weren't opening up at SMG. Upon completion of the Coyote Ridge upgrades, finding a new position would become his priority.

Today, however, the drive up to Santa Rosa gave Kyle time to reflect. He didn't have to attend the quarry tour tomorrow. First of all, the sand plant was over an hour and a half south and the trip would chew up half the day—and that after he'd just been thinking how tired he was of traveling. Second, Todd was perfectly capable of conducting a tour of the facility he'd been in charge of for ten years.

The simple fact was that Kyle wanted to go because of Josie. She was, therefore, correct—that constituted mixing business with pleasure. It was a slippery slope. Yet his instincts said she was worth it, and he could keep his head about him.

Contrary to what Josie implied, he didn't indulge willy-nilly in office liaisons. Case in point: Kisa. She'd obliquely offered. He'd pretended he hadn't understood the signals she was sending out. It was the only polite way to handle it. No sense hurting the girl's feelings.

However, of all the women that could have stepped onto that elevator, it was Josie. He wasn't a new age freak, but he did believe people came into your life for a reason. There was also a reason she'd played with him in the elevator. Why him? Why her? She was forward, but it was a good thing. He loved a woman who felt comfortable with her own sexuality. He had a gut-deep need to explore it with her.

Life could change in a flash, or it could transform itself with a slow degradation. He'd been divorced for five years, and the last two years of his seven-year marriage had been hell. The painful breakup hadn't soured him on women or relationships in general; it had soured him on *bad* relationships. Josie, it seemed, wasn't looking for a commitment. She had her career to build. They could come to a mutually satisfying personal agreement with no strings attached, and for now that would be great. Whatever the outcome in the long run, though, this thing with Josie Tybrook was a compelling opportunity he'd regret missing if he failed to act on it.

He'd use the drive on Tuesday to convince her she didn't want any regrets, either.

JOSIE closed Ernie's door behind her, then slipped into the chair across the desk from him. The office was fairly small, with only the one extra seat. "I'm sorry I didn't notice something was wrong."

"I didn't want to admit anything was wrong myself." He leaned back, his chair creaking. The bags under his eyes were darker, and there was a deep sadness in his gaze she'd never noticed before.

Correction. She'd never bothered to look closely enough. "I apologize for being such a snarky bitch lately."

"You've been the same as always."

Yeah, she was probably always a snarky bitch, but she knew Ernie didn't mean it derogatorily. "I was even going to read you the riot act about not making the meeting today."

"And I deserved it."

"No, you didn't. But I wish you'd told me so I wouldn't have been making such an ass of myself so much recently."

"You're always hardest on yourself, Josie, expecting the most out of yourself. And you've been just fine to me, even lately, so forget about it."

She swallowed with difficulty. "Isn't there some treatment or something?"

He held up his hand, and she noticed the wrinkles in his palm, as if he'd stuck his hand in water for too long. "Don't make me talk about it, okay?"

That was the thing; nobody liked to talk about dying. All she'd wanted to do was get in here and get it over with. "God," she sighed, "that's actually kind of a relief." Then she heard how it sounded, and . . .

Ernie grinned, a real honest-to-God one. "That's what I've always liked about you, Josie. You just say it like it is."

"Bull in a china shop, according to my mom."

"Your mom could take lessons."

Everyone knew her mom. Dora Tybrook, who was a board member of Castle only by virtue of marriage to Josie's father,

Preston, never missed a board meeting or an expense write-off if she could help it. Of course, she'd gotten her dander up last year when Connor said her spa was not a business expense.

But was Ernie complimenting her or her mom?

"Thanks for recommending me for the job." She didn't say *his* job.

"I think you'll be the best at it." He'd had four other program managers to choose from.

It was her dream. Oh, not just managing the department, but moving up in Castle, being VP of FI&T, then CEO. Why not? She could do it. Not now, of course, but eventually, with experience, starting with department manager.

"Thanks, Ernie." He'd never really expressed his confidence in her before. She just wished it wasn't coming this way.

"I'll call a meeting tomorrow to tell everyone. I want to get through today first."

"That's fine." She could understand how hard it must be. "You want to go over the open projects now or save that for tomorrow, too?"

The poor guy was probably wiped. She was noticing all sorts of other things about him, such as how thin his skin seemed, like parchment paper, his veins blue and prominent beneath the surface. He'd never been a body builder type, always on the thin side, tall but gaunt, yet now, he seemed a shadow of a man. How could she have missed that something was terribly wrong?

"Let's do it now." He tapped a folder on his desk. "We need to start recruiting to fill your position, plus decide who's going to take over your projects."

Kyle's was the biggest, the most important. "I can pass on the other stuff, but I'd like to keep SMG. All the setup work is done, now it's just coordination. And it's local, so it shouldn't be a problem. Giving it to someone else at this point would be counterproductive and mess up all the continuity." She realized she was making too many excuses. Plain and simple, she *wanted* the project. It was her baby, the biggest opportunity to come her way. She couldn't just give it away.

"That'll probably work," Ernie agreed.

"Cool."

She didn't want to give up Kyle, either. Without allowing herself a moment to think, her gut said to keep him. It. The project. She didn't know where the whole thing might be heading, but just as Kyle had said he didn't want to miss a wonderful opportunity, she wasn't ready to let go. Maybe it had something to do with the shock of Ernie's leaving. The why of it, she'd think about later. Right now, she had a new skill set to learn.

Of course, the three hours she was in Ernie's office with the door closed raised plenty of eyebrows around the bullpen. An unnatural quiet settled over the cubicle area when she walked out at about four thirty. Whispers buzzed like angry hornets when Ernie locked his office door and left. Ernie never went home before five. She ignored the flashing question marks in the gazes of her coworkers. Ernie wanted to do the meeting tomorrow. It wasn't her place to say anything today.

She hadn't had the courage to ask how his family was taking it. One thing she did know—Connor was a stand-up guy, and whatever the company could do to help Ernie and his family, Connor would get it done.

Her first order of business was to let Kyle know her change in status wasn't going to affect her dealings with his project. She didn't want him to hear it on the grapevine and think she was giving him short shrift.

It wasn't an excuse to talk to him, of course. She'd give the same courtesy to any customer.

He hadn't returned her call before the end of her workday,

which was normally somewhere close to seven if she wasn't out at a project site. By staying late she could catch up on her spreadsheet work after most people had left for the day. Then she recalled the meeting Kyle had up in Santa Rosa, which was why they'd had to schedule their meeting in the San Francisco office. He probably hadn't come back to work.

Her cell phone rang on the way home. Stopped for a light, she glanced at the number and didn't recognize it. That wasn't unusual since she used the cell for work as well as personal and most of her minutes were work-related. Tapping her Bluetooth, she said hello.

"Congratulations on the promotion."

Kyle. Her heart actually started to beat faster. "Thank you. The announcement will be made tomorrow, but I wanted to give you a heads-up." She didn't tell him why she'd gotten it. She couldn't talk about Ernie now.

"That was a big sigh. Something wrong?"

She hadn't even heard herself. "Everything's fine." Except that she felt like she had one foot on Ernie's back when he was down. It wasn't right. She couldn't be happy with it. This time she managed to keep the sigh out of her voice. "I look forward to the challenge of the new position."

He waited a beat, as if deciding whether to let it go or not. "Since you're not my program manager anymore, we can date."

Obviously he wasn't willing to let go of the sex thing. She hadn't anticipated the impact his voice would have on her over the phone, like buttercream frosting sliding over her tongue. Sweet, leaving her wanting to lick another dab off her fingers. She followed the flow of traffic through the light. "I said in my voice mail that I was still going to manage the project."

"No, you said that Castle was still going to provide the same level of expertise despite the change in management."

She wasn't usually so obtuse, but yes, that's how she'd phrased it. "Well, what I meant was that *I* would be providing the same level of expertise."

"So no casual sex?"

She laughed. "And no dating." Why didn't she find his persistence annoying? Duh. She liked the attention. "That would be unprofessional."

"Don't worry. I wouldn't let your sexual performance affect my judgment about your professional performance. You fuck up this project for me, and your bosses will hear about it in no uncertain terms."

It was a challenge. Even if he didn't mean it that way. He could control his emotions, split himself in half, but was she capable of doing the same? Damn straight, she was. That wasn't the point, however. "No matter how it shakes down, it's my job on the line, not yours. I think you're better off with Little Miss Snowflake."

"You know," he said, "she does have this hot pair of thigh-high leather boots she wears with the shortest damn skirt she can get away with."

"Then go for it. You'll have her eating out of your hand." Yet there was an odd little hitch in her chest even contemplating the two of them together.

"I appreciate the vote of confidence."

She smiled. "Any time." Somehow, she'd slipped into an easy familiarity without even realizing it. It didn't bode well for keeping him at a distance.

"But," he added, "somehow I don't think Kisa could separate business from pleasure."

And she could? As in, she came off as more heartless? Or . . . Why in tarnation did this man make her question everything? She *was* heartless and glad of it. She'd had her heart trashed once, and thankfully it wasn't something she ever had to put herself through again. Besides, Ian, her college lover, was also her professor, and she'd learned hard and fast about the rule regarding mixing business with pleasure. He'd stolen her senior project, called it his own, and published it in a trade journal. When she confronted him, he actually said most of the work had been his, and he *believed* it. She could have sued him, but it was easier to let it go, move on, start over.

"Dump the project," Kyle said, voice low, seductive. "Give it to someone else."

"I can't." She wouldn't. She'd put her blood into getting everything together on Coyote Ridge. No way was she going to let someone else screw it up. Nor was she going to risk losing everything again and having to start over.

He paused long enough for her to think they'd lost the connection. "You're right," he said. "Unfair of me to ask."

"Don't worry." She might think dirty thoughts about him, fantasize, but she was *not* crossing that line. But the dirty thoughts were oh-so-fun. She could handle it, handle *him*, keep her thoughts separate from the job. After all, no one had to know about her little fantasies, not even Kyle.

"I'll pick you up tomorrow, as planned." He paused. "And don't forget the short skirt."

She huffed out a breath. "I am not wearing a skirt and heels to a quarry."

"You don't need heels. Wear your steel-toed boots with the skirt." She was sure that was a groan from his end. "Now that would be really hot. Girlie, yet dominant."

"Forget it. I'll get dirty and dusty." Since when had dirt and dust bothered her? His idea made her hot all over.

"Just do what I tell you, Josie." This time the dead air was real.

He was getting to her. Letting her imagination go wild, she fantasized about all the sexy things she could wear to give him heart palpitations. It left her with an odd, giddy sensation fluttering in her chest.

If she didn't watch herself, Kyle Perry just might make her break her own rules.

THAT was asinine. Kyle shut down his computer and started packing up his briefcase. Why the hell had he asked her to give up the project? Way out of line. It sure as hell didn't sound like keeping business and pleasure separate. Where was his head?

Oh yeah. In his pants.

He shut off the lights and locked his office door. The meeting in Santa Rosa had run late, and the commute traffic sucked, but he'd needed to get back into the office to check a few things. And he'd listened to her voice mail. There'd been something in her voice, both in the message and later, on the phone. He could have sworn she wasn't happy about the promotion. But why? She was all about the job, her career.

Damn, but his whole body revved up when he'd thought she wasn't going to manage the project. Which made her free.

Then he'd compromised himself, and her. They both had a job to do. What went on outside of those parameters was fine. But he'd asked her to take herself off the project. After all her prep work and all the knowledge she'd gained, losing her was bound to affect the scheduling. He hadn't cared.

It was a lesson. She was afraid of being compromised, and he'd make sure nothing happened that would put her in jeopardy. Any fraternization between them would occur outside of work hours and off business property.

Totally separate.

Which was why it was a damn good thing that by the time he was driving her back over the hill from the quarry tomorrow, it would be after five. Because he had plans for her.

3

LYDIA Gomez started crying. Her eyeliner smudged beneath her eyes, and she leaned forward until her long, dark hair fell across her face, hiding the tear streaks on her cheeks.

Standing beside her, Ernie patted her shoulder. He'd called the meeting for nine thirty Tuesday morning because Andrew Ronson had a long drive from Tracy and didn't get in early. They'd gathered in the conference room. Two of the program managers were present, Eastman and Ronson, with the other two, Jenkins and Walker, on speakerphone, since they were on site in West Virginia and Washington state, respectively. Then there was Lydia, the group's admin. No one had taken a seat. Silent, tense, they'd suspected something was going down after the amount of time Josie had been in Ernie's office yesterday.

Lydia, twenty-five and highly emotional in the best of times, burst into tears when Ernie said he'd be going out on medical leave and not returning. *Ever*, he'd added, when Lydia had pressed him.

They'd all known what it meant.

Lydia's crying made it easier to ignore that there wasn't a dry eye in the house. Josie handed the girl a box of tissues from the coffee counter.

Then Ernie clapped his hands. "Okay, well, so . . ."

He sucked in a deep breath, and Josie felt his pain at having to deal with it all. She knew Connor had offered to handle the meeting for him, but Ernie refused. This was his job, his responsibility, his department, his *family*. Josie's admiration for him and her guilt rose in equal degrees.

"I've discussed it thoroughly with Connor, and we're promoting Josie to take over the department." Nobody said a word. Ronson, however, shot a harsh breath out of his nose as Ernie went on. "We've looked over her existing projects and farmed them out appropriately, and this morning I submitted a requisition to Human Resources for a senior level program manager. Connor's signed off on it for immediate activation."

He paused. No one argued. Josie didn't expect congratulations. Under the circumstances, she didn't want them.

"Any questions?" Ernie asked.

Lydia raised her hand.

"You're not in school anymore, Lydia, you can just ask." For the two years she'd worked at Castle, Ernie had treated Lydia like a charming little girl. Or like one of his daughters.

"When are you . . . leaving?"

Josie's stomach clenched, and her eyes ached again.

"Today, I think." He didn't say he was tired or that he'd been hanging on by the thinnest thread, though Josie knew that's how it must be for him. He didn't ask for pity.

Lydia sniffed and applied the tissue beneath her eye to capture another tear.

"Anyone else?" he asked.

Out of respect for him, no one dared. Whatever fallout they'd experience, nobody was going to make Ernie deal with it.

"Well, then, it's been great. You're a good group. I wish you all the best of luck." He smiled as if he was off to a bigger, better opportunity instead of . . . "I'll just pack up a few things, then I'll stop by to see each of you individually." He leaned into the speakerphone. "Jenkins, Walker, I'll give you guys a call, too, okay?"

"Sure thing."

Josie wasn't sure which of the two had spoken. She didn't make everyone stay after Ernie walked out the door, nor did she schedule a meeting to discuss new assignments. She'd wait until tomorrow for that, after they'd all had time to wrap their minds around the fact that Ernie was gone.

Dammit, not *gone* gone, but out of the building. Oh Lord. This sucked. It didn't get any better when Ernie walked out the department door for the last time, a banker's box of personal effects in his hands.

When she climbed into Kyle's car at two thirty, she was damn glad she'd worn a skirt with her steel-toes. His glance along the length of her knee-high black boots set her nerves jangling.

It was just what she needed.

"THEY sure as hell don't make steel-toes the way they used to." Kyle rested one hand on the steering wheel, the other on the key in the ignition.

Josie fluffed her hair in the visor's pull-down mirror. The hard hat she'd worn for the tour had squashed it. The red marks left by the safety goggles were only now beginning to fade. He handed her a shop rag from the backseat to wipe the sand from her boots and the hem of her skirt. Even in a slight breeze the dust billowed up from the quarry floor.

Though dust covered the black leather, those boots were fucking hot. Two-inch waffled soles, three-inch man-sized heels, and tight lacing all the way up to her knee, which supposedly gave good support to the calf when one was walking in sand. Support, his ass, the outfit was sexy as hell. "I thought I told you to wear a short skirt."

She glanced down at the camel-colored, below-the-knee length. "I'm wearing a skirt. That's all you get."

He liked that she didn't just roll over to do whatever a man said.

Glancing at his watch, he noted they had five minutes until quitting time. Starting the engine, he pulled out, waiting at the gate a few moments as it rolled on its track.

When it was open, he pulled out. "Get everything you need out of the tour?"

She shoved her legal pad into the outside pocket of her computer case, then slipped it behind her seat, out of the way of her feet. "I'm not afraid of questions. If I'd needed something, I would have asked for it." Then she smiled, her eyes masked by her sunglasses.

He figured she wouldn't be so flippant with a regular client. He was special. That's why she was getting snarky with him.

At the bottom of the quarry drive, he turned left onto the road heading back up into the mountains.

She pointed over her shoulder. "Aren't we supposed to go that way to get out to the highway?"

"It's rush hour. The traffic will be a bitch."

"We'll be going opposite the commute."

True. Highway 17, the main road through the mountains, was primarily northbound traffic into San Jose in the mornings and a southbound rush hour in the evenings. "I feel like a nice drive on rural roads."

She didn't laugh, but a pretty smile tipped up her lips. "This is business."

"It'll be after five o'clock soon."

"My day goes until seven."

He quirked a brow. "Do you get paid for overtime?"

"No."

"Then technically you're only on the clock until five." He flipped his wrist. "Oh, look at that. It's after five. Now it's time for pleasure."

As he guided the car deeper into the hills, the foliage grew denser, redwoods lining the road, huge oak branches hanging over, creating natural arbors.

She slid her gaze to him.

"Open the glove box," he said.

"What for?"

"You ask too many questions. Just do it."

"You're awfully dictatorial." She leaned forward to pop the box. And stared. Then she took off her sunglasses, setting them aside. "You've got to be kidding me."

"Not at all. Take it out."

She held the vibrator dangling between thumb and forefinger, eyes wide, a sparkle in their green depths. "Is this what I think it is?"

"Pretty hard to mistake it for something else."

"But *if* it's a vibrator, what's it doing in your glove box?"

"It's a present for you." He'd picked it up on his way home last night. One day of her scent filling his mind, and he'd already been planning how to get round her rule about business versus pleasure.

She arched one brow, a shade darker than her hair. "I already have a vibrator, thank you very much."

"Yes, but your vibrator isn't here in the car."

"Why would I need it in the car?"

"Because I want you to use it."

She shot out a shocked breath. "Here?"

"Here."

"Now?"

"Now."

All she did was laugh.

He turned his head long enough to capture her gaze. A split second of mind-to-mind communication.

"Just because you're driving and not touching me and it's after five and we're off the clock, that does not mean my masturbating for you with a vibrator isn't mixing business with pleasure."

Damn. She had him pegged. "That's convoluted plus a double negative."

She shook the slim-line, no frills, leopard-spotted vibrator at him. "I am not doing it."

"You're afraid."

"Afraid?" Her pitch rose, and she tipped her chin up. "Of what?"

He figured her for a woman who would never admit to an ounce of fear. "Of exposing yourself."

"Well, I sure wouldn't want to get arrested if a cop's driving the other way."

A lone green-and-white sheriff's sedan had passed in the other direction a couple of minutes ago. "He wouldn't see you. Besides, I meant metaphorically exposing yourself."

"I don't care how you meant it. I'm not doing it."

On a straightaway, he allowed himself a long, studied look at her. "But you want to." Then he turned back to the road.

He scented her in the car, the sweet flowery aroma from yesterday, and something else, something elemental, womanly, hot. He saw her swallow and knew he had her close.

He wanted her to take him up on it. After pondering the whole thing on the drive back from Santa Rosa, he'd come up with this. It appealed to his kinky nature. It was something he'd never done before—not watching a woman masturbate, but doing it in a car with someone he'd known only twenty-four hours. It was not, in the strictest literal sense, having sex with her. But more than all that, he wanted to see how far he could push her, how adamantly she meant that word he didn't want to hear: *no*.

"Do it," he murmured.

He could almost hear her thinking, considering; her desire, excitement, fear.

Then she shifted in her seat, putting her back against the door. "I'm only doing it this one time. Then we're never doing it again. Back to all business, no pleasure."

He resisted the urge to pump his fist in the air.

"But do *not* get in an accident."

"I will retain full control of the car."

"I'm not sure how you'll even be able to watch me," Josie grumbled.

"I'm good at glancing, plus I can hear you"—Kyle shot her a look—"and smell how aroused you are."

She felt his gaze like a lick. It was a crazy idea, and that's why she wanted it. She was hot, wet, horny, and fidgety in her seat after being around him for three hours. Then he went and said things like that. Dammit, she should have called one of her buddies for some hot nookie last night and gotten this itch out of her system.

Too late now. She'd already lost control. Kyle kept looking at her boots, long perusals, brief glances, sometimes a shift of his gaze from the leather way up to meet her eyes. His own were burning hot. Josie could only hope Todd and Will hadn't caught on during the plant tour. Kyle had told her to wear a skirt, and she had, though the length wasn't what he'd intended. She'd known that, too, and chosen this relatively staid outfit to show him she was her own woman.

Obviously it had also revealed that she wanted to play. No man had ever made such a wild move on her. Insane as it was, she had to have it.

She pulled her left knee up on the seat, effectively spreading her legs beneath the skirt, yet not an inch of skin peeked out. Then she turned on the vibrator experimentally. It purred like a kitten. She turned up the speed. It rumbled. She slipped it beneath her jacket, then tipped it down onto her nipple and felt a jolt through her silk blouse and cotton bra.

A little sound escaped her, not quite a moan, almost nothing more than drawing in a sharp breath. She flipped off the vibrations.

She felt his eyes on her for a moment. "My breasts are small," she told him, God knows why, "but my nipples are very sensitive."

"Do you like them pinched?"

"Sometimes. Not now." Having her nipples pinched or sucked hard made her a little crazy. She wanted to be only half crazy right now. Oh wait, she was *totally* crazy for agreeing to this at all.

Yet it was so hot and unique and exciting. No date, no dinner, no wine, no small talk. Just lift your skirt and start doing yourself with your vibrator.

"Are you ready?" she asked.

He cupped his cock through his pants, squeezed, then tipped his head to her. "Hell, yeah."

She raised her skirt. She hadn't worn nylons, just thick socks for the boots. Her thighs were bare, her skin heated, almost rosy.

"Nice panties," he said.

"What color and texture?" She didn't think he'd actually looked.

"Green, like your eyes. And a pretty little red flower embroidered in the front." He smiled. "The material is silk or satin, hard to tell without touching it."

All right, so he could look and drive at the same time. She wanted him to touch. But she meant what she said, this was one-time only . . . unless she changed her mind. "Guess you're a decent multitasker."

He settled deeper into his seat, guided the steering wheel with one hand. The road wound higher into the mountains with gentle curves and twists.

"Give me more." His slacks outlined his cock. Big. Obviously hard.

She dialed up the speed on the vibrator once more, then laid it against the crotch of her panties. "Ooh." She felt the buzz right up into her belly.

"I picked a good model?"

"It's decent." More than decent. It was phenomenal for something so basic.

She traced her pussy lips, then slid along her cleft. The thin scrap of material didn't hinder the sensation a bit.

The best though, was sitting opposite him, her legs spread, her skirt hiked up, and his glances flickering to her every few moments. Hovering. Then back to the road. The color of his skin deepened, a dark flush, and something that smelled potently male drifted in the confines of the car.

"Put it inside your panties," he directed.

"No." The vibration was oh-so-hot, but he couldn't see her pussy. Just as he seemed to enjoy a little tease, so did she.

She let the toy delve deeper, hit her clit. Sensation shivered through her, and she moaned, leaning her head back against the side window, holding the vibrator with both hands.

"Ooh, that's good," she whispered, closing her eyes. Keeping it still, she rocked against the stem, her bottom undulating on the seat. "Oh yeah."

"Take off your panties."

She cracked one eye open. "You're interrupting my flow here." Then she cranked the speed and rode the thing.

So damn good. She was slippery and hot. She wanted to tell him to pull over and then drag him into the bushes. She needed his cock in her mouth, her pussy, in her, all over her.

She didn't have to open her eyes to know she mesmerized him. "Oh yeah, oh please," she chanted and rocked, tension rising up through her chest and down her arms, her legs tensing. Concentrating solely on her clitoris, she molded the hard plastic to her little button and held on.

"Oh God, oh God." Her body shivered and shimmied, trembled, jerked. She moaned and cried out, aware of him watching, wanting, until the moment when nothing else existed but her clit and the toy. Something exploded deep inside and shot out. For an instant she couldn't hear a thing, didn't know where she was, she was simply a starburst of sensation.

She came to herself with the hot sun beating down through the windshield, and his even hotter gaze on her.

"Sweet God," he whispered, then gave her his profile once more as he negotiated a steeper curve.

Flipping the vibrator off, she let it fall from her fingers to the floor of the car. She'd come harder than she could remember in a long time.

"Gee, that was good," she quipped. Then a dirty, naughty, outrageous thought came to her as to how she'd pay him back for getting her to diddle herself right here in his car. "And you didn't get anything," she teased.

Kyle rubbed his cock. "I can get off now, if you'd like."

Josie laughed. "Too messy, and you'll get us killed on this road."

They'd neared the summit, and Josie hadn't noticed that he'd already almost gotten them killed. Kyle's cock was as hard as a spike. She'd ridden the vibrator and all he could think about was pulling over, throwing the toy out the window, and driving hard inside her. When she came, she'd moaned and writhed and gave voice to her pleasure, the sound so sensual he'd felt it like a touch.

Fuck. That was hot.

And he hadn't even seen her pussy yet.

"You're wet."

She glanced down at her panties, then quickly back up at him, and watched his eyes as she slowly traced her fingers over the damp silk.

"You're gonna kill me doing that." He didn't know how he managed to stay on the road.

When she slipped her hand inside the elastic, her fingers moving, twisting, testing, he felt himself going mad.

Then quick as a blink, she leaned forward and ran her wet finger across his bottom lip.

He almost lost it.

"Taste me," she whispered, slipping a finger in his mouth.

Holy hell. She was ambrosia. Sweet, hot, all woman. Just like she smelled. Then she licked the rim of his ear.

"You need to get back in your seat now." His voice broke between the words, and for a moment he couldn't even breathe, he wanted her so badly.

"Spoilsport," she muttered, but sank into her seat. "This was your idea, you know."

He laughed, still feeling light-headed. "I know. And it was one of my better ones." He chanced a glance her way. "I've never seen anything better."

Her eyes glittered. "And you can't touch it."

"Not today."

She smiled low and lazy, leaning back against the door once more, her skirt now pulled over her knees. Yet in that position, her legs were still spread. He could still smell her. She could still make him insane.

"Maybe never," she teased.

At least he hoped to hell she was teasing.

Her lips tipped in a sultry smile. "You need a souvenir."

His souvenir was on his mouth. He could smell her, taste her, dream of her, whack off to her later.

She shifted, wriggled, then finally held up her green satin thong, the crotch damp with her delicious juices. She laid the pretty lingerie across the console between them.

"Here's what you're going to do." She paused dramatically.

"I'm all ears." She probably wanted him to masturbate with them like a horny teenager.

"I want you to wear them to work tomorrow."

He barked out a laugh. Couldn't help himself. "You're kidding, right?"

"No more than you were kidding about the vibrator."

She didn't really expect . . . He glanced at her. She arched a brow perfectly. Oh yeah, she expected it.

"They won't fit," he said.

She stretched them out, the little red flower prominent on the front. "It's a thong. All it has to do is cover"—she pointed at his cock, making it jump—"that."

"It'll show if I bend over." He'd seen countless women's thongs above the waistline. It seemed to be a fashion statement these days, as common as plumber's crack.

"So don't bend over." She was relentless.

"You're joking."

She shook her head. And smiled. "I did what you wanted. Now you do what I want."

Tit for tat. You couldn't outsmart a woman, at least not this one. He grabbed her damp panties. He'd be able to smell her on him all day. He wanted her all over him now, and he couldn't have stopped himself from lifting the satin confection to his nose anymore than he could have cut off his right hand. For one brief moment, he closed his eyes and drank in her scent. Then he concentrated on the road before he lost control.

She was silent for a full ten seconds after. Then she gathered her equilibrium. "And you're going to meet me at the end of the day so that I can make sure you wore them."

Hell, yes, he'd meet her afterward. He shoved her panties in his jacket pocket. "You're going to owe me big time."

She merely laughed. The husky sound reached up into his chest and stole his breath.

He'd wear them because he'd never passed up a challenge from a beautiful woman. The next time, he'd turn the tables. And she'd better watch out.

4

ERNIE was gone. She was manager. Yesterday she'd masturbated in a client's car.

Life had definitely changed.

It was wild. Josie hadn't expected Kyle to agree to putting on her underwear. She figured he'd refuse because wearing panties would compromise his masculinity. Except that he'd agreed, and she'd told him they had to meet afterward. God, they had a date. That wasn't supposed to happen, either

The whole thing was escalating without her even trying. She wasn't supposed to love masturbating for him as much as she had. Gee, she wasn't supposed to do it at all. Duh. She'd like to be able to say that it was due to her turmoil over Ernie, that his illness had her all wigged out, doing crazy things.

It didn't, however, make her spread her legs for a man. It didn't make her love masturbating for him. She was afraid she'd get hooked on the game, or worse, get hooked on Kyle.

As she headed to the ladies' room, Andrew Ronson waylaid her before she made it. He was maybe five-foot-eight, but in her high heels, she was slightly taller.

"What do you need, Ronson?" What was he doing here so early? It wasn't even nine o'clock, and for some reason, she wasn't prepared to deal with him yet. She'd sidetracked herself with all these thoughts of Kyle.

Three or four years older than her, Ronson wasn't a bad-looking guy, with fine blond hair and extraordinary, almost turquoise eyes. When he'd started at Castle a couple of years ago, she'd managed a side view of his eyes to see if he wore colored contact lenses. He didn't.

"So, Connor's little pet got the job."

Hell. She knew *that* was coming at some point. Still, she hated having people think she got where she was because of who she was related to. Ronson had been the original lead on last year's Dominican project. She was to be second, since it was complex enough to require two program managers. In the end, though, Connor had given the lead to her, probably a sink-or-swim test. Ronson had been flaming over having to play second, but he hadn't done much beyond giving her a bunch of shit about it.

This time, though, he was *pissed*.

Best to nip this crap in the bud. She got right up in his face. "I got the job because I can do it." Not because her cousin's husband was CEO or that her father was on the board, but because she was *good*.

He raised one edge of his lip in an unattractive snarl. "Sure you can do it. You just can't do it better than any of the rest of us."

"Hell, yes, I can," she snapped, hands on her hips, then immediately felt like she was engaging in some childish game of no-you-can't/yes-I-can. "My family has nothing to do with it."

He smiled, all smarmy. *Gotcha*. She'd fallen into the trap.

"Your family has everything to do with it."

"I've been here longer," she stated.

"I've got more experience," he challenged.

"A couple of years, big deal." There'd been major delays on his last two projects. He'd said it was the customer's fault, changes they'd wanted, contingencies they'd added, but that wasn't supportable in the end.

She sure as hell wasn't going to start listing all his faults. She was the manager now; she had to be the adult. Arguing with him in the hallway wasn't going to cut it.

"Ronson, let's meet in half an hour." She'd been busy setting up meetings with all her new employees. This was just pulling in Ronson's time slot a bit. "Ernie's office," she added. She wasn't ready to call it her own yet. "We can discuss your grievances and go over your projects at the same time. Kill two birds with one stone."

His weird turquoise eyes were blazing, and he had a helluva lot more to say. But for the moment, he realized he would only come across looking like a jerk if he didn't agree to the meeting.

"Sure. Whatever," he said.

Josie sidestepped him with a smile, heading to her original destination, the ladies' room.

Ronson's beef made her think of Trinity and that bimbo Inga Rice, who had given her such a hard time at work back in the spring. Same thing; Inga thought she should get the job, but Trinity got it because she was "daddy's little girl."

Now Josie was "Connor's little pet."

That bastard Ronson. Okay, she wouldn't get mad, but she didn't get this job because of her family. Or because Connor had favored her. She got it because she worked hard. Right out of college, she started in program management. She knew her stuff. Connor had given her a chance to prove that. In fact, Faith's father, Jarvis, hadn't believed Josie could handle lead on the Dominican job. See, family didn't think you were special just because you were born into their midst.

She now had a lot more empathy for Trinity's plight, and a lot more admiration for how she'd solved it, too. Not to mention that Trinity had gotten her man in the end. Jeez, that reminded her. She, Trinity, and Faith had to go shopping for Trinity's wedding dress soon. The wedding was in April, and eight months seemed early to Josie, but Trinity insisted she was already behind schedule. Then there were the bridesmaid dresses to choose at some point after that. Ugh. Shopping sucked. As did bridesmaid dresses. It was nice to be asked, though. Josie had never been in anyone's wedding party. Faith didn't have a wedding, just a trip to city hall. Still, despite the honor, Trinity damn well better pick something that didn't look Cinderella-ridiculous. Of course, with Trinity's elegant fashion taste, Josie shouldn't worry.

Feeling bitchy about shopping helped put Ronson's comments out of her mind. Not that she had a whole helluva lot of time to dwell on them anyway. She had back-to-back meetings with Ronson and Eastman, then individual conference calls with Jenkins and Walker. They went as expected, with Ronson giving her the most crap about which of her projects she and Ernie had decided to hand over to him. He questioned why this job and why that job, then criticized the work she'd already done. Par for the course; she'd known he was pissed, and she took his crankiness with as much equanimity as possible. Being a manager was not so easy.

Then Human Resources had dumped a stack of résumés on her desk. She read so many, the words all blended together until the applicants began to sound as if they'd all been using the same template off the Web. HR had already weeded out the total losers, but beyond that, no one stood out.

Finally, at three o'clock in the afternoon, Lydia wanted her piece of the pie. Seated in the chair opposite Ernie's desk, now

Josie's desk, Lydia twirled a thick lock of hair around her finger. "You know, I really feel that I'm being undervalued."

What? Josie managed to keep her incredulity to herself. "I can assure you, Lydia, that we all have the utmost appreciation for your effort on our behalf."

Lydia's face turned slightly petulant, a pout on her lips. "Then why am I the lowest paid admin in all of FI&T?"

Because she'd been at Castle the least amount of time, only two years, and due to her age, she had the least experience. Josie didn't know how to articulate that without ruffling Lydia's feathers. She was used to saying it like it was, but with employees, you had to watch each word to avoid misinterpretation. Fact was, when you were twenty-five, you didn't want to hear that all things came with age. You wanted it now. You *deserved* it now. But you sure as hell weren't going to get it now. Josie had heard it all herself and argued just as vociferously. Until the shoe was on the other foot. Now she wasn't willing to argue Lydia's salary issue with HR her first day on the job.

When in doubt, stall for time by saying you'll find out. Maybe that wasn't the best choice, simply the one that came to mind. "I've just taken over the job, Lydia. Why don't you let me have time to evaluate the situation and your performance?"

Lydia's jaw dropped. "I've been picking up after your butt for two years." Her lips slapped together when she realized she was talking to her boss. "That came out wrong."

It sure did. Josie understood there would have to be a transition period. She wasn't going to hold it against the girl right now. But damn, she needed a supervisor training course on how to handle this employee relations stuff. PDQ.

So okay, she needed to give a positive stroke here. But how, without making a promise or giving false hope? Lydia *had* always been a hard worker and efficient, just a teensy bit overemotional.

"You're right, Lydia, you have cleaned up after me and the guys, always going the extra mile." A very good stroke, if she did say so herself.

Lydia sniffed, but looked a little more pleased. "Thank you."

"I'll have to check the salary charts with HR and see where you fit in there." And *that* was totally noncommittal. Just the boss getting up to speed.

Lydia nodded. "Okay." Then she stood. "I used to screen all Ernie's calls. Do you need me to do that?"

"No."

"The phone guy will be in later to change over your extension."

So far, Josie had been forwarding her calls to Ernie's phone. "Thanks." She paused. Think positive strokes. "You're very efficient. I really appreciate the help."

Lydia blinked, assessed, as if she thought Josie was blowing smoke. In the end, she nodded, then flipped her hair over her shoulder and marched out the door.

The salary issue did bear more consideration. She needed to know how much everyone in the group made, just so she could head off the next person who walked in her door trying to manipulate her into giving them a raise. *She'd* certainly never talked salary info with anyone. But she wouldn't put it past Ronson.

Hell, she hadn't even talked to Connor about her own raise commensurate with the additional responsibilities of being manager. Was that stupid or what? She'd been thinking more about Ernie. And Kyle.

Kyle. She was supposed to meet him, but she hadn't even thought about where or when. Or even what she'd do once they were together.

What did she *want* to do?

She rose and shut the door, getting a little rush of pleasure out of the act. She had an office. Cool. She tried not to think about Ernie.

Back at the desk, she stared at the phone without picking it up. She had a couple of guy friends she dated. Well, not *dated*. They were . . . buddies. Rick and Paul. She got horny, she called one of them. One of them got an itch, they called her. It was the safest sex without actually having a relationship, and she had no problem calling to say "Hey, do me."

Calling Kyle made her hesitate. Kyle was different. Sure, he was mixing business and pleasure, but beyond that, she had a mess of indefinable emotions roiling around inside. Jeez, really, she needed to get laid. If she'd taken care of pleasure, she wouldn't have to worry about mixing it with business.

"Will you get over it?" she whispered, flipping open the SMG file and calling his number.

He answered on the fourth ring, just before she would have gone to voice mail. "Hold a minute." He rustled, and then there was a distant "Thanks, Kisa."

So. Little Miss Snowflake had wandered into his office. She wondered how many times that had happened today. "What's she wearing?" she asked when he came back.

He fell right in line, not even asking who the hell was on the phone. "Leather pants and a tank top."

"Leather? At work?"

"We don't have a strict dress code."

But he'd worn a suit, even for the quarry tour. "Bra or no bra?" she went on.

"Bra. But it's gotta be thin lace because I could still see her nipples."

"Horn dog."

He gave a half snort, half chuckle. "It wasn't like I could help noticing."

"You were probably focused like a laser beam." It was all in fun. She liked teasing him. She wasn't at all jealous of Little Miss Snowflake.

"I think you have a fixation on Kisa." A dry note tinged his voice.

"I'm just noticing *your* fixation." She liked that he played along with her teasing. "Did you show her your thong?"

He laughed. "No. I haven't bent over once today. And I didn't ask to see hers, either."

Hmm. "So you're wearing my thong? Honestly?" She didn't believe him.

"Of course," he shot back.

"Prove it," she said just as quickly.

"I'm ready, willing, and able to meet anywhere you want."

"Yeah, and you'll probably sneak into the bathroom before you leave work and put it on to try to fool me."

"I would never lie to you."

"Men always lie." It was just a matter of degree and how bad the fallout would be.

"Do I detect a note of cynicism there?"

"Just reality. A little lie is not always a bad thing." Connor probably told Faith white lies about nonessential things. It saved Faith's feelings and was perfectly acceptable.

"You'll have to tell me the story sometime."

"There is no story." Just her asshole professor in college. She'd put that whole episode completely behind her. Months later she realized she hadn't been in love with Ian at all. She'd been bowled over by him. Of all the students he mentored, she was *special* amongst them. She'd *meant* something. He knew she could do *extraordinary* things. Yeah, and after he'd screwed her over, he'd moved on to screw another *special*, gullible little cream puff in his next class. Whatever.

"Josie, did I lose you?"

Thank God for bad cell connections. "Yeah," she lied, "you cut out for a few seconds." Damn. All the teasing spark had melted right out of her. She should have kept her mouth shut and her thoughts toned down. This whole thing was a bad idea. It could blow up in her face, get her fired.

"Where shall we meet so I can prove I'm wearing the thong?"

"You know, I've been thinking—"

"Don't think. You need to know. You need the comeuppance after yesterday."

God. She needed something to take her mind off Ernie, Ronson, Lydia. She could remain in control. "All right, where?"

"Your place."

"Forget it." Not that she wasn't capable of kicking him out when she was ready for him to leave, but . . . well, just but. "And don't say your place, either."

"Then I'm open to your suggestion."

It had to be somewhere he could strip completely to give her the full effect. So not a car where all he'd be able to do was unzip his pants. She wanted maximum visual impact. There was always a hotel room, but then she'd be tempted to do other things. She needed privacy as well as protection from the big bad wolf. Where, oh where?

A dressing room. Yeah. What could happen in a dressing room other than making him prove he'd followed her instructions? There was this little lingerie shop her mother was fond of in Stanford Shopping Center. Josie didn't buy, but she'd tagged along. Once, she'd seen a man and woman enter the dressing room together. The saleslady hadn't said a word, as if it were done all the time. In fact, the guy kept coming out and choosing different things for his girl-friend to try on.

"I've got the perfect place." She told him how to get there and exactly where to meet her. In drive time, it was probably equidistant between his work and hers. All right, slightly more favorable to her, but it was such a good idea.

She'd pretend she was trying stuff on herself and make Kyle strip down to his, no, *her* skivvies.

THE small lingerie shop was tucked away in a barely noticeable tributary in the Stanford Mall. Kyle was fifteen minutes early, the evening commute traffic out of the city having been astonishingly light. August could be like that, with lots of people on family vacation before school started. Come Labor Day, the roads would be hell again.

A tasteful display filled the front window, black fishnet stockings draped over a white velvet pillow, a gold Mardi Gras mask, sequins glittering in the spot lighting, a silver satin . . . What did they call that thing, a bustier? Or maybe a corset? Holy hell. Was that a riding crop peeking out from beneath it?

Maybe this wasn't just a lingerie shop. What did Josie have planned for him? His heart picked up the pace as he contemplated just how kinky she could be and exactly how she planned to verify he was wearing her scrap of clothing.

He'd put them on this morning, feeling idiotic. She'd wanted to one-up him, push his masculine limits. She'd lost control yesterday, and she wanted it back any way she could get it. Despite knowing her only a handful of days, he'd figured that out. In an odd way, being cognizant of that gave him the upper hand. She thought she was leading, when actually she'd turned control over to him. She couldn't offend his masculinity at this point by virtue of the fact that she was playing along with him. Each new adventure entangled her more.

Then there were the panties themselves. Her scent was all over them, all over him. Closing his eyes, he felt her hand on him, heard her voice once again in his ear. The satin cupping his cock kept her image on the edge of his consciousness all day. The vibrator between her spread legs, the total concentration on her face as she came, the throaty, sexy cry that fell from her lips. He wanted her in the green satin again, and this time, he'd be the one to make her come.

He wandered inside, half expecting to find an assortment of canes, whips, and chains lining the walls.

Not so. Artful lighting enhanced an eclectic assortment of female frippery. Lace, satin, silk, bras, panties, thongs, stockings, corsets, every texture imaginable in all the colors of the rainbow. Lush blue carpet cushioned his footsteps, instrumental mood music played low, and the light scent of vanilla perfumed the air.

"May I help you?" The clerk smiled. With hair an attractive shade of gray and laugh lines at her eyes and mouth, Kyle didn't think she'd been the one to put the riding crop in the window.

He pointed toward the front of the shop. "I'm interested in the silver garment in the display."

"Oh, the bustier. They're right over here." She bade him follow her with a wave of her hand.

The bustier closed with a row of hooks and eyes down the front and was held together by laces along the back. The satin glimmered. It would push Josie's pert breasts high, show them off to advantage.

He figured his hands could damn near span her waist so he chose the smallest size. She was tall but lithe. "And the stockings in the window?"

The saleslady opened a drawer in a grouping of three five-foot bureaus lining the wall. "How tall is your lady friend?"

He tapped his hand to his nose. "About here."

She perused a chart on the package, then drew another pair

from the drawer. "I think this will be appropriate. But if not, you can exchange them."

He wouldn't have to. He'd get Josie to model them when she arrived.

The shop's door opened, and a bell tinkled. He hadn't noticed the sound when he entered, nor did he have to turn now to know it was her. He recognized her scent. Sweet, flowers. And hot, aroused woman. She'd been fantasizing on the drive over.

He felt the cool slide of her fingers lacing with his. "Hi, honey."

Her breath on his neck trickled along his nerve endings. "Yeah, baby, I was picking out some things for you to try on."

Her eyes widened at the endearment, then sparkled, and her mouth curved with more than a hint of laughter. Unaccountably, that near smile made him hot. Her lipstick was pink, her cheeks and eyes dusted with makeup, and she had on another of her pant-suits like she'd worn at their first meeting. The tailoring fit her curves, yet the lines were almost manly, as if she was trying to hide that she was a woman working a man's job.

She would look all woman in the silver satin. He glanced at the saleslady. "I think we need some black panties to match the stock-ings." Then he glanced down at Josie. "Or do you want to skip the panties, baby?"

"Oh no," she said, her lips again flirting with that almost smile, "we definitely need panties." She pointed to the rack he stood by. "I want those."

She held one up by the hanger for him to see.

Nothing more than a triangle of sheer black fabric, silky to his touch; the thong looked as if it were held together by string. What was the point in wearing it at all?

Except to drive a man mad.

"Our dressing rooms are in the back." Their clerk led the way, then pushed aside a long curtain disguising a surprisingly large dressing area. She turned to Josie. "When trying on the panties, please do be sure to keep your own in place."

"Of course," Josie said, then grabbed Kyle's hand. "Come on, honey, I want to model them for you."

She wanted him to go in there with her? Kyle glanced at the saleslady. She simply smiled. "Call out and let me know if you need another size."

The mirrored walls reflected them all as the woman hung the bustier and thong on two of several hooks and laid the stockings on a small glass table next to a gold padded chair. Then she closed the curtain behind them.

Kyle moved to the chair.

"Not so fast, buddy boy." In the mirror's reflection, Josie jutted one hip, and arched a brow. "I sit." She lowered her voice. "You strip."

So that was her plan. He wondered how far the salesclerk had gone. Before he let Josie sit, he crowded up against her back, letting her feel the heat of his body, the hardness of his cock. He liked the picture in the mirror, how petite she seemed in front of him, the smile playing on her lips. He breathed her in, parting the hair at her nape to reveal the creamy, sexy skin beneath. He wanted, needed a taste. Holding her still, he licked her right there, then blew warm air.

She shivered against him, and when he raised his gaze to hers in the mirror, her green eyes had turned the color of a queen's emeralds.

"Stop that," she whispered, then turned and lightly pushed him out of her way.

Josie sat and leaned back in the gold chair, crossing her legs, her shoe swinging. Fluttering her fingers, she reasserted control. Or so she thought. "Show me what you've got."

He unbuckled his belt.

"No, no, no, you are not just going to drop your pants for a second or two. I want everything off, jacket, shirt, slacks." She shot him a saucy grin and leaned forward, voice lowered once again. "Everything except your panties."

Oh man, she was laying it on. The lady was into payback. "Yes, ma'am." He hung the suit on a free hook, loosened his tie, and unbuttoned his shirt. Finally, he toed off his shoes and peeled off his socks.

Then he prepared himself for whatever comeuppance she planned to dish out.

HIS eyes were a smoky blue under the dressing room lights. Hair dusted his tanned chest, trailing down his defined muscles and flat abdomen, tapering to a thin line that disappeared beneath the waistband of his slacks. Josie's mouth watered. She didn't like excessively hairy men. She wasn't attracted to pasty white skin. Kyle had just the right amount of everything. Especially the bulge in his pants.

When she'd seen him eyeing the lingerie, picking things out for her, she'd gotten wet. When he called her *baby*, she'd actually lost her breath. She didn't go in for silly endearments like sweetheart or darling or honey—that had been a tease for him—but low and husky, his voice made the pet name sexy, hot.

She finally found her own voice. "What are you waiting for?"

"For you to tell me exactly what to do."

Oh yeah. Just as he'd told her what to do yesterday. She wondered if he'd actually be wearing her panties. "Take off your pants. Now." She paused, tipped her head. "But do it slowly."

He revealed a centimeter at a time. Green satin. Then a glimpse of red, the little flower. She covered her mouth. His image would be reduced to the ridiculous. She'd have a leg up on him. He might even decide to call it quits and return to business only. Men could be so touchy about their masculinity. If he balked, it didn't matter to her. Getting back to all business was fine. Even if he did make her as hot and wet as Little Red Riding Hood running from the Big Bad Wolf. She'd long since figured out there was a sexual undertone to *that* fairy tale.

His zipper undone but a hand blocking her full view, he hesitated, caught her gaze, his eyes a blazing blue, and she knew he'd back out, wouldn't show, wouldn't give her that last inch.

He fooled her. Grabbing his slacks at the waist, he shoved them down, then kicked them aside.

Good God. A wave of heat flushed her whole body. The crown of his hard cock burst above the satin's elastic top, the embroidered flower stretching over his length. The material could barely contain his cock and balls.

"Is it so tight it hurts?" she whispered with a touch of awe. God. How could he be so gorgeous?

He laughed. "It hurts my pride more than anything." Then he lowered his voice to match hers. "But the way you're looking at me makes it worth it."

"How am I looking at you?"

"Like you could eat . . . me . . . up," he said, his voice husky.

Even as she watched, come pearled along his tip. Her tongue slipped out; she licked her lips. He was right. She could eat him up, all of him.

It was like looking at a sleek, powerful swimmer in his Speedo.

Or Superman in his tight super-suit. Everything was there right before her eyes. She could almost taste the bead of come, and her mouth watered. Her stomach tightened with need. If she'd thought to emasculate him, she'd done the opposite. Her thong somehow enhanced his maleness, brought out the potent animal in him. Not that she hadn't known that was there. He oozed masculinity from every pore. She could smell it, taste it, feel its vibration in the air, and she wanted it badly.

She wanted to touch him, cup him in her hands, drink that tiny drop of his male essence, close her eyes, and savor the hot saltiness.

It wasn't as if she meant to, but suddenly she was on the carpeted floor at his feet, his cock right before her. She couldn't breathe, she needed him so badly.

"Don't," he said, and his voice seemed so far away.

She looked up. "Why?"

He didn't say anything, just stared down at her.

Eyes locked, she leaned closer, breathed in that musky male scent. Then she put out her tongue and unerringly found the tip of his cock. He tasted like sweet cream with a dash of salt. She licked him all over her lips.

A growl rose up in his throat.

"This isn't fair," she whispered. "You weren't supposed to look so good in them." She wasn't supposed to succumb to the need to touch and taste.

"I didn't look good in them until you got down there on your knees."

She nuzzled her face against the smooth material and the hardness of his cock. This wasn't going as she'd planned. He was supposed to beg to get out of them because he felt ridiculous. His eyes, however, weren't begging for *that*. Taking her hand, he folded her palm against his cock.

Sliding her thumb across the slit, she stroked him. Then she slipped her fingers beneath the elastic and touched flesh. Hot, hard flesh. He groaned and tangled his fingers in her hair. She ached to take him with her mouth, and yet she loved the pleasure of caressing him with her panties still wrapped around him. Holding on to his thigh, she tightened her grip. She'd gotten just a hint that day in the elevator. Time stopped, and all she could hear was his breath, her own, and a low rumble of need in his chest.

"Christ, you're going to make me come."

Then his body jerked, and she covered his crown with her other palm as he bathed her hand. He made barely a sound, but his fingers stroked through her hair. So much come, it dribbled down the front of the thong. Looking up, she found his eyes on her, and just as she'd made him taste her fingers after she'd masturbated, she put her palm to her mouth and licked him from her hand.

"Damn you," he murmured.

"Now give me my panties back."

He gazed down at her forever, his eyes totally unreadable.

"Everything fine in there? Can I get you anything else?" Damn. The saleswoman. Josie had somehow forgotten where they were.

"We're doing great, thank you," Kyle said, not a hitch in his voice, not one single giveaway that he was standing behind a flimsy curtain, naked except for a pair of her soaked panties. "Could you bring us the red bustier from the same rack?" he called. "And perhaps some matching panties or a thong. I'd like something frilly for her to try on."

"Certainly, sir."

"Thank you."

He'd done it again, gotten the upper hand. She was the one down on her knees, not him. His musky, distinctly male aroma, the taste of him . . . it fogged her brain. She'd stroked him; he'd come in her hand. It was nothing more than teenagers did in the backseat of Daddy's car, yet she salivated for his full cock in her mouth, his touch on her, fingers, lips, tongue, everything.

Taking her hand, he pulled her to her feet. Naked but for the slip of green satin, he was undeniably magnificent, even after he'd orgasmed. He stole her breath all over again. Which made her realize she hadn't said a word for long, long moments.

"I've decided you should wear my thong home," she directed, hoping it would reclaim some of her control.

His lips twitched. "It's wet."

"Exactly." His come had soaked in, creating a patch of dark jungle green amidst the brilliant emerald. She handed him his pants.

He gave her a full-blown smile. "I think you have the makings of a dominatrix."

"Here you go, sir." The saleslady was once again outside the curtain. Josie couldn't answer him.

Kyle stuck his hand through—"Thank you"—and came back with a delicate red corset and several pairs of panties. Then he lowered his voice. "For you."

Josie took the fripperies. Her pupils were wide, her breathing fast, her lips still glistening with traces of the semen she'd licked and sucked from her fingers.

His cock had surged once again when she'd done that. Here was a woman so sensual, so tantalizing beneath the tough business facade. He would have more of her, here, now, later, often.

"Your turn," he whispered. Then stepped into his pants and zipped. His feet and chest remained bare, and she seemed mesmerized by his nipples.

"My turn for what?" Her eyes were slightly unfocused, as if she were still in the moment when his cock was in her hand, when she had total control of him.

"Your turn to model lingerie for me." He had a little payback in mind. His own orgasm had been too incredible to let it go at that.

"But *you* were supposed to model for me."

"Which I did." He grabbed his dress shirt, pulled it on, but didn't button it yet.

She hung the panties and corset on the hooks. "I didn't intend to try anything on. All these things were just window dressing."

"Not in my mind. I want to see you in them. Now take off your jacket." He flicked the one fastened button at her midriff.

Then he did up his own shirt.

She stood still, watching, until he unzipped again to tuck in the tails. Then, belt buckled, he raised an eyebrow and fluttered his hand. Finally, he put her fingers to the one button. "Do it."

Josie swallowed. She had a beautiful throat, long, slender, a pulse beating. Undoing the jacket, she pushed it aside. Her nipples beaded against the white blouse. He'd yet to see her naked. Even yesterday while she masturbated, he hadn't glimpsed her sweet pussy.

He slung his tie around his neck, then sat to put on his socks and shoes. "Josie." Just her name.

She pursed her lips. "Whatever."

Yanking off the jacket, she hung it on the hook beside his. Her tight nipples told the real story, and her scent permeated the cubicle. Hot, wet woman. She wanted this. She just didn't want him to know how much.

His shoes done, he leaned back in the chair, toying idly with the end of his tie.

She pulled her blouse from her slacks with little artfulness and slipped the buttons loose, then went to the cuffs and undid those. With fast movements, she had the blouse off and on a hook, revealing her white, unpadded cotton bra with a pink flower in the center between the cups. When she reached behind to unsnap it, her small breasts thrust high, nipples stark against the white. Kyle felt yet another surge in his pants. If he wasn't careful, he'd need relief all over again, when right now he wanted to concentrate solely on her.

"At least try to be sexy," he drawled.

Something flared in her gaze. "I *am* sexy."

She sure as hell was, sexy and delicious, but she wasn't about to give up an inch of her power if she could help it. Power to her was making him the one out of control. She'd wanted him to wear her underwear simply to see if he would. To gauge how far she could push him, how much he was willing to do to have her. Wearing panties under his clothing wasn't his usual fare and didn't do anything for him sexually, but neither did it challenge his manhood. He'd done it solely to let her *think* she could lead him around by his cock.

She'd learn he liked the lead equally as much as she did.

She shimmied the straps down her arms, then let the garment drop to the carpet. "I *am* sexy," she whispered this time, running her hands up her smooth abdomen to cup her breasts.

She plumped them in her hands, then pinched her nipples, making the tiniest, sexiest little sound of pleasure. Her chin down, she looked at him through her lashes, searching for his reaction. He gave her none, yet he was dying to stroke himself. He sat, legs spread, hands on the arms of the chair, and simply said, "More."

The *more* was up to her. He didn't care what it was. She grabbed the silver bustier, his first choice. Wrapping it around her body, it fit snugly with each hook and eye she fastened until her breasts swelled above the tight top. Just a hint of rosy nipple peeked out.

"There. Satisfied?" She challenged him with one hand on her hip, and a slight purse to her lips.

"Most women would have undressed completely, then put the

bustier on."

"I'm not most women." She arched a brow, shot him a glare. But that pulse beat at her throat, fast and strong. She got off on sparring with him.

"Well, now I'm telling you to take your pants off."

Josie glanced quickly at the curtain.

"Nervous?" He was well aware that his voice might carry beyond their cubicle. If the saleslady stood at the head of the hallway leading into the dressing area, she'd hear every word. It turned him on, made him want to push Josie past the hint of inhibition in her glance.

"Of course I'm not nervous." When she loosened her belt and unzipped her pants, he knew she damn well wasn't going to back down from any challenge he issued.

She flipped off her low-heeled pumps—she'd worn them without socks or nylons—then bent, sliding the slacks down her legs. Gorgeous long legs, smooth lickable skin, the globes of her ass framed by a high-cut white cotton thong. When she stood, the stitched flower at the waistband matched the one on her bra. Holy hell, the woman was perfect. Lithe, toned, enticing.

He said nothing, simply handed her the thigh highs.

Peeling back the small bit of tape, she upended the package and shook it. Fishnet spilled out into her hand. She held it a moment, stroked a finger along it. "You know, I've never worn these things before."

"I'm glad you'll wear them first for me, then." She was green satin and white cotton, now he'd make her decadent, naughty fishnet. He was going to enjoy this transformation.

"Put your foot here." He patted his knee.

She eyed him, as if wondering what he could possibly be calculating. He'd never met a woman who so easily expected an agenda in whatever anyone else did. Or maybe she just let her suspicion show more than most.

Then she put her foot on him. Her warmth spread up his leg straight to his groin. Her scent intoxicated like a shot of tequila thrown back in one swallow. She accordioned the stocking in her fingers, slipped the tip over her toes, then slowly slid it up her long, long legs. At the top, she patted the lace into place and put her foot back on the carpet.

"Lovely," he whispered, his eyes on her panties as the cotton grew damp. She had perfect thighs, perfect everything. "The other one."

She repeated the procedure. By the time she was fully encased in fishnet, he was hard, ready, amazingly recharged by the scent of her, the sight, the need to taste that sweet triangle between her legs.

"Which panties do you want me to try on?" she asked, when it appeared he couldn't say a word.

Kyle perused the row of colorful lace and silk on the hooks. This one, that one . . . ? He glanced to the thong she already wore, then pointed at the center of the pink flower. "That. I like the contrast of white cotton, bare ass, and fishnet." A decadent combination. Hot woman, demure lady.

Then he tipped her pump to the side with his foot. "Too bad you weren't wearing high heels. Nothing like stockings and spike heels."

"Sorry," she said dryly. "What you see is what you get."

Damn, how much he wanted what he saw. He rose from the chair to stand behind her. Her hair smelled of spice and citrus.

"I like it," he whispered, capturing her gaze in the mirror. "A lot." Grazing his finger along the top of the bustier, he teased her, then slid a hand down the smooth satiny front to the elastic of her thong. "More than a lot."

He brought his body flush to her back, his cock riding the low curve of her spine. He dropped a kiss on her luscious nape, then watched the trail of his hand in the mirror.

"What are you doing?"

He tickled beneath the elastic waist. "Same thing you did to me."

She captured his wrist. "No way. This was my gig. I got to do what I wanted, not you."

"Correction. You did what you wanted, now it's *my* gig. And this is what I'm doing." Lightning quick, he tunneled between her plump pussy lips to all the heat and damp within.

She sucked in a breath, arched against him. "No."

"Yes." He pinned her against him with one arm and teased her clit. "You know you need an orgasm." He let his voice feather across her ear. "Look how wet you are." He withdrew, tracing her mouth, leaving behind a glimmer of her own moisture.

Her eyelids fell, her breath puffed, and her ass undulated against him. "This is bad. That woman might come back."

"This is good. And I don't give a fuck if she's standing right out there." He licked the rim of her ear. "Neither do you." His hand trailing once more to her panties, he stopped just at the edge. "But if you're worried, we don't have to do this."

She focused on his eyes in the mirror for one long moment. "You know damn well I'm not going to tell you to stop now."

But neither did she beg. Kyle didn't care. He simply hitched her closer and dove into her thong. She gasped as he entered her with one finger, sliding as deep as the position would allow.

"Like that?" he asked, gliding out to stroke the hard button of her clit.

She merely whimpered, squirmed, then dug her fingers into his arm where he held her. Leaning her head back into his shoulder, she caught his gaze in the mirror through the slits of her eyes. "It's fine. Whatever. If you want to go on, go on."

"You love it. If I stopped, you'd beg."

"No, I wouldn't." Above the line of the corset, her flesh was tinged with pink.

She wouldn't beg no matter how badly she wanted that orgasm. She wouldn't give him the power. Kyle didn't need it. He only needed to get her off, not for the advantage, but for the heat, the desire, and the beauty of it.

He rode her clit until she had to close her eyes again. Until she couldn't hold back her moans, and the breathy sounds slipped from her lips. Until she writhed in his arms, moved with his rhythm, put her own hand over his and helped him.

"Sir, are we doing fine in there? Anything else I can help you with?"

"We are absolutely fine," he said as he worked the gorgeous woman in his arms.

Josie bit her lip, but didn't say a word, didn't stop him.

"Well, then," the woman said on the other side of the curtain, "I'll give you a few more minutes."

"Thank you for your consideration." He slid deep, back out, pulled Josie high against him and shot her into oblivion with one last tiny circle of her clit.

She bucked, shook, and climaxed hard, pulling him forward until he was bent over her, his hand trapped between her tight thighs as she rode out the orgasm.

Finally she sagged, and he let them both fall gently to their knees on the carpet. He gathered her onto his lap, stroked the hair from her face, and placed a chaste kiss on her forehead.

It was the best fucking orgasm he'd shared in more years than he could remember. And he didn't have a clue why.

BASTARD. He'd made her lose control again, and it was too damn good. He stood in front of the mirror knotting his tie while she struggled to get all her clothes back on. Her legs felt weak, her head light, and she wobbled as she stepped into her shoes.

That's exactly how he made her feel: off balance, all wobbly. She was supposed to have come out of this the victor over him. Instead, he'd given her a cataclysmic climax to which her body still thrummed.

He gave the tie a last pat into place and pulled on his suit jacket. "Which one do you want?" He held up the silver bustier, then the red one.

Josie flipped the price tag. "Two hundred dollars?" She puffed a breath out and looked up at him. "Forget it."

"I liked you in the silver. With the stockings."

"I do not have two hundred bucks to spend on something like that." She yanked her jacket up her arms.

"I'm not asking you to pay for it. It's a present."

"I don't accept presents that expensive." Which her mother thought totally appalling. After all, a woman was worth as much as a man was willing to spend on her. And usually more. Josie had never liked the obligation. A man could think he owned you if he gave you lots of pretty things. That made it too easy for him to take something away, like your sense of self-worth. You were special only if *he* thought you were special. She wouldn't depend on a man, and she wouldn't owe him anything either.

Kyle tipped his head to one side. His eyes seemed bluer, maybe picking up the blue stripe of his tie. Dark-haired guys weren't usually blue-eyed. They were either brown or hazel, and certainly not that deep shade.

Then he sighed. "Fair enough. How about the stockings?" He flipped over the package she'd stuck the fishnets back into. Reading the price, he held it up for her to see. "This okay?"

She felt kind of stupid making a fuss about it, since it didn't seem like a big deal to him. "Yeah. That's fine." Jeez, twenty bucks for a pair of nylons with holes in them. "Thank you," she added, then started gathering all the hangers off the hooks.

"I do think the saleslady will clear those up for you."

She considered, then put them all back except for one pair of frilly, excessively girly panties. She was just full of ideas these days, and she was having a brilliant one right now.

Outside in the main shop, the saleslady beamed, even if they weren't carrying the expensive corset. "Oh, you've found what you wanted," she said, the smile in her voice, too.

Okay, so she probably hadn't heard what was going on in the dressing room for—Josie glanced at her watch—good God, half an hour.

"The stockings were amazing," Kyle said. If Josie could see his eyes, she knew they'd be sparkling. He handed the package to the woman, who headed back behind the glass-topped sales counter.

"And don't forget this one, honey." Josie held up the frilly underwear, then batted her eyelashes at him as she laid the hanger on the counter beside the stockings. "They looked perfect on you." Then she winked at the saleswoman. "They were a tad small, but then he's such a big man, I don't think they make them large enough."

Kyle started coughing, covering his mouth, and dammit, his eyes were *still* sparkling. Oddly enough, the clerk didn't lose one centimeter of her smile as she rang everything up.

Outside, Kyle grabbed her hand and pulled her around a corner. "Naughty little bitch," he said, just before his mouth came down on hers.

Oh my Lord. His mouth. Heaven. She'd never been a smoocher. But God, she could make out with this man for hours. He tasted of breath mints, his lips were warm, his tongue expert. The kiss lasted fifteen seconds, but it left her dizzy. And wanting more.

He shoved the bag of lingerie into her hands. "Payback is coming," he whispered.

She knew she was doomed. "You have to wait a week," she

said, trying to sound haughty and in control.

Kyle settled back against the wall, pulling her with him so that she leaned against his chest. "You can't wait a week."

Josie's eyes flared wide. "Oh yes, I can."

"All work and no play makes Josie a very dull girl," he quipped. She was anything but, especially with that whole panty thing back in the store. She deserved a lot of payback, and he knew the statement would get her going.

"I don't work all the time."

"You said you don't date. That sounds like a lack of play."

"I might not date"—she lifted her chin with an arrogant set to it—"but I play."

He snorted. "A vibrator doesn't count."

She pressed her lips together, narrowed her eyes, as if he'd insulted her. "I do have *friends*."

"Friends?" This was interesting.

"Men friends."

He let his smile grow slowly. "You mean"—dramatic pause—"fuck buddies?"

Her face colored. He couldn't imagine why. He'd had his share of casual relationships based solely on sex, at least in the beginning, though he'd found the majority of women ended up wanting to "move to the next level."

"Yes, fuck buddies," she said, with that haughty tilt to her chin once again. "What of it?"

The truth was, he admired it. The woman had goals, determination, savvy, smarts. Nothing was going to get in her way, least of all her own needs. She had an itch, she got it scratched.

"More than one fuck buddy?" he wanted to know.

"A couple." She shrugged eloquently. "If one's busy, I've got a backup plan." She suddenly smiled brightly.

God, the idea was hot. He liked the edge of vulnerability in her need to justify it, too. She wasn't all brass balls, as she tried to pretend. He wanted in on the game. "Make me your fuck buddy."

She pressed her lips together primly. "I think what we did tonight qualified." Then she smirked. "But I'm still not seeing you more than once a week."

"Because you have to keep your other buddies happy, too?" He didn't like *that* idea quite so much.

"No. Because I need my sleep." She put her hand to his chest and slowly pushed away from him, her eyes on his. "Which is why I'm leaving now."

She was a challenge, and he had to admit that made him more intrigued, kept his blood running hotter. Like a diamond, she had many different facets he wanted to explore.

And he'd make sure he was the only fuck buddy she had.

6

HER mother was the only one for whom Josie would miss half a morning's worth of work. A summons from Dora Tybrook was akin to a royal command. This time Jose was to pay homage at the country club. Her mom had a nine thirty tennis match.

Her sunglasses shading her eyes, Josie sat on a sideline bench, her bottle of water warming in the morning sun. It promised to be a scorcher today.

"Yay," she cheered as her mom won another point. Josie had never been into tennis. She didn't work out, she simply worked hard, walked fast, went to a coworker's office instead of picking up the phone to call, took stairs instead of elevators—unless there were too many floors and she was in a hurry, as she had been that first day at Kyle's office.

Heh. Sometimes a moment's decision changed *every*thing.

She'd never before considered turning a customer or even a

coworker into one of her play buddies. All right, call it what it was, a fuck buddy, just as Kyle said. She'd felt a momentary blip of embarrassment that she'd been found out, then gotten over it. She didn't mind the terminology, but neither did she advertise that she had "friends with benefits." Most people got on their high horse about it, but it kept her sane. She wanted sex, but didn't want the fuss that went with a relationship.

She met a guy, got the hots for him, and if things worked correctly, they developed an understanding where either one could make a booty call when their hormones were raging. They drifted in and out of her life just as girlfriends came and went. She never had more than a couple of buddies at one time, not as in two guys doing her at once, but as in two separate and distinct play relationships going concurrently.

Okay, there had been a couple of times that she'd been with two men together, but while she'd thought it would be double the pleasure, it was actually double the work. That might have been the guys she chose to do it with, though. Anyway, variety in both what you did and who you did it with kept a girl from entangling herself in messy emotions. It also kept her in the driver's seat, with the added advantage that it was a helluva lot better for all concerned than trolling bars. In addition, sex was the only arena in which her "buddies" entered her life.

Yet here she was considering Kyle as a new playmate. A key customer contact. A business associate. Mixing two separate parts of her life. Crazy

He was so tempting. He played the game with her, even one-upped her. She *loved* games. She often set up scenarios with her buddies, such as a quickie in the backseat at a mall parking lot. Or they'd role-play, and she'd have him pick her up in a bar where they pretended they didn't know each other. It was a turn-on with the bartender trying to listen in on what he thought was a stranger hookup. Josie adored her games, but she liked them safe. She needed to be on top, in charge, and in control.

Kyle wasn't safe. Maybe that's why she wanted him. He was older, he didn't let her have control, at least not for very long, and he kept her riding the edge. Maybe she *liked* giving up control once in a while. That was a novel concept.

Her mother dashed at the net and missed, the ball flying wide past her. Her lips tensed, and under her visor, her eyes narrowed. Dora Tybrook hated losing, whether it was a point, a game, a match, or an argument.

"Break," she screeched out, and jogged over to Josie's bench, perched on the edge, crossed her legs daintily, and slugged back three gulps of water.

"Was there a reason you called me here, Mother?"

"Of course there was." But she needed another chug from the bottle before she could speak.

At fifty-one years old, Dora Tybrook was in exceptional shape. She moisturized three times a day and had never smoked a cigarette in her life because it might ruin her skin. She played tennis four times a week, had a personal trainer with whom she spent at least two hours a day at the club, and followed her dietician's regimen of healthy eating.

Josie thought her mother was too thin, and honestly, her black hair was a tad too harsh, making her look closer to fifty-five than fifty-one. Not that Josie would *ever* say that. Upon pain of death.

"You need to talk to your father," her mother said, slipping her sunglasses on beneath the visor. "He's been nitpicking my expenses again. I get enough of that from Connor. I don't need it from your father as well."

Growing up, it had seemed that's what marriage was all about, one nitpick after another, on both sides. It took Connor and Faith to make Josie see that marriage didn't have to be that way.

"Your expenses are your own fight, Mom. I told you I'm not getting in the middle of you and Dad."

"Then at least speak to Connor for me so he'll stop ragging on your father."

Ragging? Connor and her mom had been battling expenses for over a year, almost since the day Connor started at Castle. Both her parents were on Castle's board, but her mom, well, let's be honest here, she was a great one for finding the flimsiest excuse for calling something a company expense. Such as her spa fees. After a grueling *(hah!)* board meeting, she needed a massage to release all the tension. *Gee, wonder why Connor had a problem with that,* Josie thought.

"Connor does not rag, Mom. He simply follows company policy."

"Policy, schmolicy." Her mother flapped her hand. "That's the other thing I want to talk about. Are you sleeping with Connor?"

"What?" Her blood skipped simmer and surged straight to boiling point. "Of course I'm not sleeping with Connor. He's married to Faith."

"Don't get all in an uproar." Her mother shrugged as if she didn't even see the insult. "You know Faith hasn't lost all the baby fat, and there was that fuss last year about Nina and Connor."

Yeah, a fuss her mother had created right to Faith's face. "Mom. I am not sleeping with Connor. He loves Faith to death. He loves the baby. And Faith is not fat." Josie wanted to smack her mother. Faith was gorgeous, the baby was beautiful, Connor absolutely adored them both, and Josie *hated* that her parents still denigrated their perfect marriage.

Her mom let out a heavy sigh. "I'll take your word for it. But I've heard all the rumors flying about why *you* got Mr. Masters's job." She smiled. "Not that I ever considered that the scuttlebutt had any validity, of course."

"Of course not." That was the thing about her mom. She could be clueless about a person's feelings, but at least she said it to your face instead of behind your back. "I got the job," Josie went on, "because I was the most qualified."

How could the gossip start flying this quickly? Not that her mom didn't have her ear constantly to the ground, trying to catch every rumor.

Dora held up a finger. "Hold that thought." She tossed her sunglasses aside and popped up to play another point.

Josie used to get mad and stay mad. But her mom was her mom. You couldn't change her. You either cut yourself off or you let most of what she said just roll off your back. Except that comment about Connor. That was going too far, but Josie didn't have any brothers or sisters, and disowning her mom or her dad was a thing of last resort. She was used to them. They thought the bigger the fight, the more it showed how much they loved each other. You didn't fight with someone you didn't love, right? Josie knew that was a load of dysfunctional crap. She didn't need a psychiatrist to tell her it was part of the reason she steered clear of a real relationship requiring real commitment. The other part was having the first man she gave her heart to walk all over it.

Lost in thought, Josie missed her mother's next point until she was once again back on the bench. "I knew it was just gossip about you and Connor. But, Josie, you've got to do something about this nasty talk." She finished off her bottle of water.

"And just what am I supposed to do about it, Mom?" She hadn't even known there were rumors.

"You have to quit."

Josie laughed, and really, she meant it. "I am not quitting my job. I love it."

"I don't know how you can love getting all dirty and grimy. I never remember you playing with toy trucks in the sandbox."

Her job was so much more than playing with sandbox toys, but her mother was disappointed she hadn't turned out like Trinity Green, pretty, socialized, First Lady material. Or at least the wife of a governor. Except that Trinity had shown them all and taken a position as a lowly supervisor at her father's company. Good for her.

"So," Josie said, "I'm not talking to Dad or Connor about your expenses, and I'm not quitting my job. Is there anything else you wanted to tell me to do before I go back to work?"

Her mom huffed out an annoyed breath. "You don't have to get snippy. I'm trying to help. I love you, and I don't like to hear people malign you."

Josie believed her. "I'm sorry. But I can't do anything except ignore the talk."

"Talk can damage your reputation." Her mom pressed her lips together. "You have to figure out who started these horrible rumors and have the person fired."

"Mom, you can never find out who started it. Someone always heard it from someone else." But Josie did have her suspicions. Duh. She *knew* who'd done it. Ronson. But fire him? First, she'd never get proof. Second, she couldn't fire someone right after she got the job. That would do more damage to her reputation than any silly gossip about her and Connor.

"Then I suggest you watch your back, because someone doesn't like you." Her mom gave her a long, assessing look, then glanced at the court. "Okay, must get back to my game." She air-kissed Josie's cheek, jumped up, fluttered her fingers, and served.

Josie was back at Castle before she realized her mother had never even congratulated her on the promotion.

Not that she needed the kudos.

"You got a package." Lydia tossed her the envelope as Josie breezed past.

She caught it by clasping it to her chest. "Thanks."

Things with Lydia seemed fine after their salary discussion, yet the girl had been late this morning. Was it the start of some passive-aggressive behavior?

Whatever. Josie didn't consider herself a hard-ass. She was flexible. She figured Lydia would make up the time.

In her office, she flipped the lightweight padded envelope onto her desk. There was no return address, no company logo. After hanging up her jacket, she ripped open the end and shook out the contents.

Her panties fell into her hand. She glanced up quickly to see if anyone noticed. Ernie's office, *her* office, looked out into the bullpen. Lydia's reception desk was off to the left, beside the common area with the copier, fax machine, printer, and filing cabinets. Beyond that lay the maze of cubicles. Lydia was on the phone. Eastman was walking down the corridor, his face buried in a report.

Josie turned and briefly held the panties to her nose. Just as Kyle had. They smelled of him, sex and sweet come.

Opening her bottom drawer where she kept her purse, she had to laugh as she dropped them in. Good God, she was becoming a panty sniffer. Then she peered inside the envelope. A note had snagged on the inside Bubble Wrap.

"Your scent drove me mad. Thought I'd return the pleasure."

Oh boy. She was in big trouble. Because she loved that he'd sent her the panties. Her come, his come, sex all over them. He had such a dirty mind. She'd always been into the physical side of things, but he had such a nasty, imaginative brain that he brought far more to it than simply the sex act itself. He made her hot, wet, and bothered, even when he was miles away in San Francisco. He lit a fire in her. He delivered the unexpected. None of her younger buddies had done that. She lit her own fire, then called them to put it out.

It was risky. Kyle could get the upper hand, but the idea of play-ing naughty games with him was irresistible. She wanted the chal-lenge. She hadn't had a clue how much she'd craved something different, but now she needed it.

Besides, Kyle was the perfect cure for the shitty mood her mom had inspired.

Rounding her desk, she closed her office door. Once back in her seat, she fed his number into her cell phone's memory and called him.

"YOU are a naughty man, and you need to be punished."

It took little more than her voice, and his cock got instantly hard. "They've got your sweet cream on there, too, so I'm not the only naughty one."

"How do you know I'm talking about the panties?"

"Just a wild guess." He paused. "You put them to your nose and smelled me on them, didn't you?"

"I took them to the bathroom and washed them thoroughly."

"Liar."

She laughed, a little too harshly, and for the first time, he noted a thread of something running through her voice. "Bad morning?"

She came back after a brief moment. "Nothing I can't handle."

"Want to tell me about it?"

The pause was even longer this time. "It's not about your proj-ect, don't worry."

"I wasn't."

He realized how stupid it was asking her to tell him her trou-bles. With her opening line, she'd told him she was looking for a little fantasy, not reality. "So you want to punish me. I think I pre-fer it the other way round."

"No way. I'm in charge."

He had no doubt she was. "How about we share that role?"

"You can't share it," she scoffed. "Then no one's in charge, and the project goes to hell."

"I was thinking more in terms of one time I get to be in charge, the next, you call the shots."

In the silence of his office, his door closed, he could hear her thoughtful puff of air. "Hmm," she murmured. He could even hear her mind working. "So you have to do anything I say when it's my turn?"

"Yeah." He let her savor the triumph a moment before adding, "And you have to do everything I say when it's mine."

"No pain," she said quickly.

"Not even a little spanking?"

She drew in a tiny breath. "Have you ever spanked anyone?"

"Not enough to leave marks."

She harrumphed. "I don't like humiliation either. Or water sports."

He laughed outright. "I promise none of that."

"Maybe. I'm thinking, I'm thinking."

"Slave for a week, then the other gets a chance."

"A whole week?" She let incredulity slip into her voice, teasing him, he was sure.

Kisa knocked, then stuck her head in without waiting for an answer. "I'm making a lunch run. Vould like you something?" She smiled, fluttered her eyelashes. "Anything at all?"

"Nothing, thank you." Then he thought of Josie hearing every word. "But I *really* appreciate the offer, Kisa," he said with extra emphasis.

"Bastard," Josie murmured in his ear. "Ever played slave for a week with Little Miss Snowflake?"

He laughed. "No."

Kisa looked at him oddly. As if she'd never heard him laugh

before when he had just as much humor as the next guy. He waved his fingers at her in a polite get-the-hell-out gesture.

"But you want to, don't you?" Josie went on.

Kisa gave him a smile, then shut the door, leaving him alone again. "I want to play it with you." He had the feeling Josie's fantasies would be infinitely hotter and kinkier than anything Kisa could imagine. "Now where were we? Oh yeah, you're going to be my slave for a week."

"We're only going to do it once a week, so a *whole* week consists of one date."

He snorted. "Only one date in seven days?"

"If we do any more, you'll become obsessed with me. It's for your own good."

He loved that she was such a spitfire. A hot little number. And always pushing to retain control. "You mean you're afraid you'll become obsessed with me."

"Hah. You don't need to worry about that. I've *never* been obsessed with a man."

There was enough emphasis on *never* to make him wonder. "Then neither of us has to worry."

"Right. And the first week is mine because you usurped my challenge while we were in the dressing room."

"Usurped it? I wore the damn thong. *And* I gave you a great orgasm."

"I didn't tell you that you could touch me. So you took over the challenge and therefore the next one belongs to me."

"Wrong. I wore your panties, and I got damn near naked in a dressing room to prove it to you. Plus, I let you jerk me off."

"You *let* me?"

"As I recall, I said not to, and you did it anyway." He'd been afraid he'd blow sky-high with one touch. But she didn't need to know that.

Still, she wouldn't concede. "You loved it."

"And you loved it when I fingered you. So we're even on that score, and it becomes my challenge." He had plans for her, and he wasn't giving them up.

"You're pushy," she huffed, but he knew it was to hide her laughter.

"True. Which is why I want a date tomorrow night."

"That's not a week. Next Wednesday." The fact that she was now bargaining over the actual day said he'd won the challenge.

"Your place?" he pushed.

"No."

"Mine?"

"Hell no. I'll send you an e-mail when I've decided where we'll meet." She hung up without saying good-bye and before he could say *he'd* choose the place for *his* challenge.

Christ, he loved it. She wasn't easy. She could skew logic any way she wanted, but he could skew it more effectively. She was delightfully kinky. An affair with her would prove to be more fun than he'd had in years.

He hadn't looked forward to a date since . . . well, hell, since the blush of new love with his ex before they were married.

Of course, that made it sound like his entire marriage had been a nightmare. He'd adored Marianne. She was year younger than him; they'd met at work and dated for two years. The sex between them had been good; fucking hot, in fact. And kinky. They used to sneak into work early and fuck on his desk just for the fun of it. On their honeymoon, she'd blown him in front of the open hotel window, lights on. She'd loved doing it in risky places as much as he had. He loved masturbating for her, shooting his load on her pussy or her breasts, watching her get down and nasty with a toy. They eventually moved on to other companies as a hedge against getting laid off at the same time, but she'd still sneak in after hours for a fuck. He loved that. He loved her.

Then she wanted a baby, and things changed. He'd wanted a child just as much as she had, but when she didn't get pregnant right away, the focus of their love life rapidly went from just-for-fun to having a purpose. Lovemaking became urgent. She'd call him up, say her temperature was right, they'd meet at home and fuck. No foreplay, no fun. The joy went out of it.

She started hanging out with some girls from work, and their talk was all about marriage and babies. They began ragging on her about the naughty sex the two of them had. That was when he'd gotten pissed, referring to her friends as the MAGS, Mothers Against Good Sex. The MAGS claimed that's why Marianne didn't get pregnant, because he wasted his semen in her mouth or on her breasts. So she decided that he could only orgasm inside her. He could accept that, but he hated the intimate details she shared with her friends and the way those bitches turned a beautiful, fun, adventurous love life into something unhealthy.

Things went nuts when Marianne learned she was the one who had internal issues that were making it difficult for her to get pregnant. It wasn't him at all. She, however, didn't want to admit to the problem, claiming the doctor was full of shit. If she'd been obsessed before, she moved into maniacal after. She decreed that he could ejaculate only when it was her fertile time of the month. That way his body would build up lots of sperm, and they'd have a better chance. He was allowed orgasms three days out of the month, and then he had to perform like a stud horse. Secretly, he hated her fertile period. Sometimes he'd watch porn on the Internet and jack off because he was going insane. She'd caught him, and they'd had a helluva fight. That was the end of it. He couldn't take anymore. They'd had five great years and two really shitty

ones. She'd gotten remarried three years ago and adopted a couple
of kids from China.

He'd learned that sex was fucking important. He wanted a
woman where anything goes, risky places, a dirty mind, sex for
sex's sake.

Josie Tybrook was exactly what he was looking for.

A week? She must have her head somewhere the sun don't shine.
How was she supposed to get through a week without a taste of
him?

By Saturday, she regretted not playing on Friday. By Sunday,
she was a little wild, wanting to call him and beg. Kyle made her
think about sex, sex, sex, even when he wasn't around.

The worst was that a booty call to one of her buddies wouldn't
cut it. It felt like cheating, though she and Kyle hadn't talked exclu-
sive. She had to admit she didn't like the idea of him taking out
Little Miss Snowflake despite how often she mentioned it to him.
No reason . . . just . . . she didn't like it.

Monday was a bitch at work. She couldn't *ever* remember thinking that regarding her job. But she was a woman ruling a bunch of
men now, men who had once been coworkers. Being manager was
totally different from being one of the guys. She could feel how
they shut her out. When she entered a room, they stopped talking.
They didn't come to her with their issues like they used to. They'd
done that even when Ernie was the boss, wanting to bounce things
off her, to make sure they didn't sound like idiots before they went
in to Ernie.

And Ronson? Jesus. The staff meeting had been a disaster. He'd
been openly hostile and antagonistic, calling her ideas stupid, though
he had stopped short of calling *her* stupid.

Her career as a manager would go down in flames if she didn't figure out how to handle them all, and blaming everything on Ronson wasn't going to fix it. He had a job site he was heading off to next week. Maybe things would settle down, and they could start off on a new foot come the following week.

Why did that feel like putting off the inevitable?

Wednesday morning, after going over purchase requisitions and another slew of résumés in which she found little to spark her interest, she decided to take the bull by the horns.

Punching in Ronson's extension, Josie felt her heart rate rise. Which was ridiculous. She wasn't scared of the damn man.

"What?"

She'd called him enough to know he always answered with his name, letting his caller know immediately that they had the right number. She also knew her extension would have shown on his caller ID. So he was being rude on purpose, to her specifically.

She badly wanted to slam him down. "I need to see you in my office."

"You mean Ernie's office."

"I mean *my* office."

"I'm busy."

It took two deep breaths to calm down. "Ronson, get in my office, now."

He hung up, didn't slam the receiver, simply disconnected without a word. She had no clue if he'd show. Or what she'd do if he didn't. At what point was she supposed to write him up for insubordination? Where the hell was the supervisor handbook?

It took him five minutes to make a ten-second walk.

"Close the door," she told him.

He did, then stood there, arms folded over his chest, a smirk creasing his lips.

And she'd had it. "What is your beef? I got the job, get over it or quit."

"You'd like that, wouldn't you." He punctuated his remark with an ugly sneer.

She hated being seated while he was standing, as if that gave him the advantage over her. Standing up, though, was like admitting she was down in the first place. So she remained butt-in-chair and let him have it. "I don't really give a shit. You do good work, to a point, but your attitude sucks. You want me to write you up, I'll write you up. It's up to you. Just start acting like a human being again."

"Teach you all that in manager training school?" He'd hit a nerve, and his smug smile said he knew it.

Why the hell was he being such a dick? He hadn't been this way before. "And you know," she told him, "you can cut the whole gossip mill, too. Everyone knows I didn't sleep with Connor to get this job." Yes, she'd verified that rumor had been floating around. It wasn't her mother's imagination.

"That wasn't me. I didn't spread rumors. I just told the truth about your lack of experience."

"Creating dissension is—"

"Speaking the *truth*," he cut her off. "Everyone knows I can do this job better. I've got more experience on much larger projects. I've been a lead for a lot longer. I should have had it. I *deserved* it." His eyes blazed, yet at the same time it sounded oddly as if he were repeating something someone else had told him over and over. "*You* got it because you're family."

It didn't matter who had been giving the pep talk about how great he was. She deserved the job, too. "I got it because you're late on projects and come in over budget, and if you do that with your own jobs, you've got the potential to overlook it with *all* the jobs."

"Listen, you bitch, you don't know a thing about—"

This time she stood. "What did you just call me?"

He seemed to realize he'd gone too far. His eye twitched at the corner. He opened his mouth, slapped it shut. Finally, he narrowed his eyes and his lip curled. "Don't like it, fire me. See if I fucking care. Because I'll bring a reverse discrimination suit so fast your head will spin."

Just as he hadn't slammed the phone down, he didn't slam the door as he left. He hadn't even yelled.

This *really* wasn't like him. He'd never been such an asshole. He was actually a pretty nice guy for the most part. So. What to do? Write him up for calling her a bitch? If she let him get away with it . . .

Aw hell. She wouldn't let it be said that she ran to HR at the first whiff of a problem, especially since she'd only been a manager for one freaking week. She could handle this. She'd figure out what the hell was going on with Ronson. She knew damn well it had to be more than just the fact that she got the job instead of him. Once she figured it out, she'd fix the problem.

7

AT quarter to four the next afternoon—thank God it was finally Wednesday—Lydia entered Josie's office, a plain manila envelope swinging in her fingers. "You've got another package," she sing-songed.

"It's work." Josie went to snatch it out of Lydia's hand.

Lydia backed up. "No return address. No company logo." She returned to singsong mode. "It's from a secret admirer."

Josie rolled her eyes. "Give me a break. And give me my package." She held out her hand.

"If it's not a secret admirer, then you'll open it in front of me," Lydia challenged.

Yeah, right. It might or might not be from Kyle. She couldn't take the chance. "I'm sure it's something highly confidential from a customer, and it would be a violation of ethics to open it in front of you."

Lydia laughed like a giddy child. You really couldn't get mad at the chick. She was too sweet. Then she shook the package right by her ear. "There's something in here."

"It's probably some defective parts being returned to me."

"Hah. It's . . ." Lydia wriggled her eyebrows. "I'm thinking . . ."

"Don't think too hard or—" Josie stopped herself before a totally bitchy comment came out. Lydia wasn't stupid; not at all. "If it was from a secret admirer, it would be flowers or a card, not an envelope that makes noise."

"Let's see who's right." Lydia's brown eyes gleamed.

The girl wasn't going away, so Josie put on her most stern face. "I am your boss. If you don't give me that package right now, I will fire you."

Lydia pouted. "Before you were my boss, you would have shown me."

Before she was the boss, she didn't receive naughty packages at work. She didn't receive presents at all. Flowers and candy weren't her thing. Honestly, while she might have joked a few times with Lydia, she never revealed secrets. She held her hand out and waggled her fingers.

Lydia grumbled under her breath but handed over the package. "If it's something fun, will you show me?"

Josie relented. "If it's something fun." Of course, that would depend on the definition of fun. If it was from Kyle, dirty, naughty, exciting, and hot didn't necessarily mean *fun*.

"Close the door," she said with a smile as Lydia walked out.

The girl smirked, grabbing the handle and swinging the door shut behind her.

Josie's heart raced as she picked up the envelope. It was the package, it was the surprise, it was him. Though the label was computer-generated, she knew exactly who'd sent it. What did he have for her this time? The anticipation sent jolts of excitement through her.

In a strange way, it felt like Kyle was courting her, plying her with little gifts, making sure she knew she was on his mind even if he hadn't called her. It was the oddest sensation, because Josie actually liked it.

She'd never been courted before. Not even in college. She'd simply been overwhelmed by Ian's personality.

She ripped open the envelope, tipped it, and a string of beads fell out onto her desk. Graduated in size, from seed pearl to perhaps half an inch, they were attached by a string that ended with a loop instead of a clasp.

Body beads.

She puffed the envelope open and out tumbled the note. "I want these in you when I see you. Go to the ladies' room now. Touch yourself while you insert them, but don't you dare climax."

She shivered. The challenge didn't start tonight. It began now. He was already ordering her around. And she liked it.

Stuffing the beads in one blazer pocket, she shoved the letter in the other. She didn't trust Lydia not to snoop. As she passed Lydia's cubicle, the girl raised her brows devilishly.

Josie honestly didn't know what to say. She liked Lydia, but they'd never been friends. Josie didn't even talk about man stuff with Faith and Trinity. She wasn't one of those women who got together with her female friends and gossiped about sex. Or men. Or anything. She wasn't programmed that way, never had been. She'd learned very young that girls—and women—could be pretty judgmental and it was best to keep as much as possible to yourself if you didn't want any backlash later.

So Josie simply scowled in her best mean-boss imitation, then mouthed, "Nothing fun." The beads were . . . sexy. Not fun. At least, not yet, though they certainly had potential for later.

Lydia's laugh followed her all the way to the restroom.

That was the really good thing about working in a building housing mostly men—the ladies' room was empty.

"I cannot believe I'm doing this," she muttered as she closed the stall door. Yet she touched herself the way he'd instructed, and God, she was wet. She caressed her pussy lips, then slowly slid the beads inside, one at a time, largest last, feeling each as it entered. By the time she was done, her clit was an aching nub. She touched herself, rubbed lightly, put her head back, eyes closed, and imagined Kyle's tongue on her. She barely held the moan in check.

Never in her entire working life had she masturbated on the job. But, oh God, she'd been missing something. The fear that the ladies' room door could open at any moment added another level of excitement.

When she stood, the little plastic circle at the end of the string dangled like a clit ring. She pulled up her panties.

When she moved, she felt the beads inside, tantalizing her. The ring itself, trapped within her thong, gave the slightest friction, just enough to keep her on edge.

She washed her hands, straightened her jacket, fixed a tiny smudge of makeup under her eye. She didn't wear much, just something to lengthen her lashes and add color to her lids.

As she returned to her desk, she was the picture of professional. But inside, she was burning. Wet. Ready to jump him the moment she saw him. Such a new feeling, this physical ache, the tantalizing need to . . . fuck. Right now. At work.

Thank God Lydia wasn't at her desk as Josie passed or the girl would have known something was up.

In her office, her cell phone beeped. A new message. As if he'd known exactly when she would receive his toy and that she would go to the restroom because he'd told her to.

"Since you never picked a meeting place, I chose it." He rattled off an address in that melting hot voice of his. "Meet me at six thirty." Nothing more, just as she'd done to him.

Despite what she'd told him on the phone the last time they spoke, a week ago, she purposely hadn't chosen. She'd left it all up to him. If he wanted the challenge, he had to make the moves. That wasn't the same thing as fobbing off responsibility for her actions.

God, she had so much work to do before she could leave. Taking her seat, her mind ran through all the tasks on her over-full plate. A frisson of pleasure shivered through her as the change in position thrust the ring against her clit and the beads shifted deliciously inside her.

Screw all the work she had piling up. She wouldn't be one second late for her date.

FOLLOWING the Internet map she'd made, Josie was five minutes early. Yeah, she'd punched the accelerator on her little hybrid, screwing up her gas mileage, but her body was running on high octane.

Her map led her right to the parking lot of a luxury airport hotel in the heart of San Jose. The planes flew overhead with a deafening roar, shaking her tiny car. A hotel room. He'd take her all the way tonight, and God, her pussy needed it. The beads had worked her to the point of no return. Then again, he might have her meet him in the bar and tease her to death without giving her any relief. Or, he could have her pick up another man. A couple. Or a woman.

What if he picked up a woman and made Josie watch? God only knew what he had planned.

She wondered what her limits were. She hadn't shown any before, but then her lovers were basically unimaginative. The more she pondered all the possibilities, the hotter she got.

Her cell rang.

"You're late," he said.

His voice trickled down her nerve endings. She glanced at her watch to find she'd been sitting in the car for six minutes. Good God. "I'm in the parking lot. You didn't tell me where to meet you."

He rattled off a room number, then *poof*, the connection vanished.

So. Definitely a room. He could still have someone else waiting for her. How did she feel about that? Excited. Nervous. Could she do it? Did she want to? That was the nature of a challenge, to keep the other party guessing, hold them right on the edge, scare them, tease them, thrill them.

She'd just never had anyone do that for her. She was always the doer, the planner.

Inside, thick walls and dual-paned glass masked the roar of jet engines. The lobby was sumptuous, with cushy chairs, sofas, and marble floors that flowed into lush carpeting. She waited in line at the elevators, but after the fifth floor, the elevator was empty all the way to the fourteenth. She leaned back against the wall, stretched, let the beads work their magic. God, she didn't care what he was about to make her do, she just wanted a damn orgasm. If she gave herself one now, she'd be able to think, to fight back if she didn't like his game. As it was, she'd do anything.

Yet Josie didn't get herself off. Instead, she let the need build as she negotiated the corridors to his room.

It took him forever to answer her knock. When he bade her enter with a flourish of his hand, she was relieved to find the room empty.

She was his for the night.

It was your garden variety hotel room with bureau, desk, a couple of chairs like the ones in the lobby, and, of course, a bed. A very *big* bed high off the floor covered with a thick comforter, lots of small pillows, and a bolster that stretched the entire width of the mattress. The air was scented with something subtly floral.

Without saying a word, he sank into the chair he'd placed only a couple of feet from the end of the bed.

"Naked," he said. "Now."

She stripped too quickly. Giving him a seductive tease felt uncomfortable. She wasn't a sexy, sultry babe who knew all the right moves. She worked in the dirt; she was one of the guys.

Yet his nostrils flared, and his eyelids fell to a hooded gaze as she stood bare before him.

"On the bed," he ordered, pointing with his steepled fingers.

She did that, too, artlessly, scrambling on her hands and knees, then rolling to her back, her legs parted slightly.

He rose, leaned close, and flicked the ring of the beads. Though he didn't touch her, she felt his heat, and the beads seemed to ripple through her pussy.

"Good girl," he whispered. "Spread your legs wider."

She did, his gaze on her making her feel . . . vulnerable.

Closer still, braced on one hand, he swooped in and breathed deeply. "You smell good."

She could hardly breathe, his mouth so near he could lick her. If she raised her hips, her pussy would kiss his lips.

He backed off before her body could react on its own. "Touch yourself."

She slid her fingers through her dampness.

He grabbed her wrist and sucked her finger. A guttural sound rose from his belly. "Wet," he whispered. "I knew you would be. So fucking wet."

She'd never had a man treat her with such sensuality, relishing scent, sight, taste.

He left the bed, went to his briefcase, and flicked open the lid. He withdrew something, but with his back to her, she couldn't see. He turned, came close, and tossed the thing on her belly.

Rope.

Her skin heated, her pussy tightened, yet she felt a hitch of fear in the pit of her stomach.

He tapped her ankle. "Wider."

She spread-eagled herself before him. Her blood rushed in her veins and pounded against her eardrums.

"Arms over your head."

She'd never been tied down. She wasn't against it in theory, but her whole body tensed as she stretched her hands up to the headboard, touching it with her fingertips. Somehow tying her down was worse than the thought of him loaning her to another man. She almost laughed, because that thought was ass-backwards for most people. And yet . . . she gulped in a breath, held it, swallowed, then exhaled long and hard.

Kyle tipped his head to one side. "Do you trust me?"

She didn't know him well, so how could she trust him? In the bedroom, he was an unknown quantity. But logic said her client wouldn't do anything to jeopardize the job, least of all cause physical harm to his project manager.

Get a grip. They were playing a game.

"The question is," she said, "do you trust me when it's my turn?" She was so damn pleased with how steady and natural her voice came out.

"Payback's a bitch," he whispered.

"Go for it," she said in kind. She was *not* going to lose a challenge over a few skittish nerves.

He swiped the rope off her belly and uncoiled it, perusing it for a moment. Then he held up a finger. "Don't move." He disappeared into the bathroom.

"You are crazy," she muttered to herself.

He returned with some washcloths crumpled in his hand. Tossing the bunch on the bed beside her, he selected one, then grabbed her foot and wrapped the terry cloth around her ankle.

"What are you doing?"

He glanced up, a smile dancing in his eyes. "Just making sure you don't chafe your skin if you decide to struggle."

She huffed out a breath. "I'm not going to struggle."

He knotted the rope around the material. "Let me rephrase. When you're orgasming so hard you shake and buck uncontrollably, I don't want you to hurt yourself."

"I don't get *that* out of control." At least, she hadn't before.

"There's always a first time." He backed off, made a grab from his briefcase, and returned with a knife in his hand. A sharp knife. She felt her eyes widen. He looped the rope over the blade and sliced it cleanly.

Down on the carpet beside her, he secured the end to a bed leg. Yanking on the cord, he tested the tightness. "Okay?"

"It hurts." Not too bad. She could handle it.

"Liar." He kissed her big toe, then rose, trailing his hand across to her other ankle and tugging her legs wider. Stopping for a moment, he gazed directly at her exposed pussy. "Beautiful. But a picture is worth a thousand words."

"You are not taking pictures of me like this."

He wrapped her ankle. "I'm not?" His voice changed subtly, deepened, hardened.

"No, you are not."

The rope knotted, he secured her to the bed. "You shouldn't make demands when you're all tied up."

She flapped her hands at him. "I can just as easily untie them."

He moved swiftly, crawling up her body, holding her down with his bulk and grabbing both of her hands. Before she could wriggle away, he had a washcloth around her wrists and the rope wound securely, binding her hands together.

"And how are you going to get yourself untied?" he asked, his eyes glittering, lips curved in a wicked smile.

Still holding her bound wrists, he rolled to the side, rose, and secured the end of the rope to the middle post of the headboard.

Fear thrummed through her. So did excitement. She was totally vulnerable. He could do anything he wanted. Give her to anyone. Take a photo and expose her on the Internet.

Do you trust me?

She shivered as if a breeze had blown across her body.

Yes, he could do anything. Or he could make her climax uncontrollably, over and over, as many times as he wanted. She was totally at his mercy.

"I don't think I like being tied up," she whispered.

"I know. That's why I did it." He went to his briefcase one last time. Once again by her side, he held something behind his back. "You're going to like this even less."

He laid a blindfold made of soft cloth across her eyes. It was everything she could do not to shake it off.

It wasn't a matter of trust. It was a matter of the game. She'd tested him, forced him to wear women's panties, and dammit, he'd won. She couldn't let him make her beg.

But she had a hard time breathing.

She'd made herself this vulnerable to Ian, and he'd trounced her badly. The fact that it had been emotional trust versus physical didn't matter. Kyle held all the cards. He could have her fired. He could ruin her. He could do *anything* to her. Or worse, he could do nothing at all, simply leave her there with no sexual relief.

He moved away and said, "I'll be back later,"

Josie almost screamed.

When the door snicked closed, she yanked and pulled on the bonds, thrashed her head trying to dislodge the blindfold. Then she lay quiet a moment listening. Was he standing there watching? Laughing at her? Was he going to leave her alone with her own thoughts to drive her crazy all night? Alone to show her he didn't want her, didn't need her, that she wasn't special and didn't matter? Maybe he'd even find another woman to slake his appetite with, then return in the morning to tell her how much better the other slut was.

Drawing in a deep belly breath, she let it ease through her body, spreading out to her limbs. He was teasing. This was a game. He wouldn't hurt her. He wouldn't humiliate her. She was allowing the inability to move and the darkness behind the blindfold to get to her. She was fine, it was okay.

If she remembered that, she would win his challenge.

HAD he gone too far by leaving the room? Kyle ordered two glasses of wine down in the bar.

He'd never tied a woman down before. He'd figured that Josie Tybrook would find it one of the hardest challenges to face. She wasn't a woman who liked giving up control. She needed to win. She'd bring him to his knees if she could.

Still, he might have waited a few dates before going straight for the jugular with her. Then again, anything else he could have done to her wouldn't be as much of a challenge. She'd set the tone of the game by making him wear her panties. He was upping the stakes, escalating dramatically. He couldn't wait to see how she'd try topping this one.

Unsure what she'd drink, he nevertheless didn't figure her for a champagne woman, so he'd chosen a vibrant chardonnay, one he liked as well. Especially since he wouldn't mind licking it straight off her body.

How long should he leave her up there to stew over what he had planned for her? He glanced at his watch and when twenty minutes had passed, he decided that was long enough. Besides, he didn't have any plans. He was going to wing it.

He scented her arousal the moment he entered the room again. A subtle musk he recognized from the car, the dressing room, and earlier tonight when he leaned over her.

"That wasn't funny." A tremor running through her voice belied the casual words.

Silent, he placed the two glasses on the bedside table.

Twisting as far as the bonds would allow, she turned her head to the sound. "Cat got your tongue?"

Heading round the end of the bed, he stopped between her spread legs. The toggle of his beads lay against her plump, aroused pussy.

"Are you alone?" An edge of desperation slipped through her words.

The silent treatment had always driven him to distraction. His wife had been a master at it. His intent now wasn't cruel and unusual. He didn't remove the blindfold, simply told her what she wanted to know. "I'm alone."

Kneeling on the bed, he flicked the small ring. She bit her lip. Crawling closer, he stuck his finger through the plastic ring, then raised his hand, pointing toward her breasts, and slowly pulled, gliding bead after bead over her clit.

She writhed on the bed.

"You like my gift?"

"Yes." She gasped as he changed the angle, sliding the beads in all her moisture, torturing her.

"How much do you like them?"

Her body trembled, her breath came fast, threaded with a moan. "God, they make me crazy. I wanted to play with myself right there in the women's room when I put them in."

Good. Very good. Exactly what he'd wanted. He massaged her clit with one bead after another until they pulled free at last. Her body jerked once, just before he tossed the beads aside. Her skin was tinged with pink, warm to the touch. Lean thighs, flattened stomach, small breasts trimmed with pert nipples, and a gorgeous pussy lightly dusted with hair.

"Do you want an orgasm?"

She exhaled in a rush. "God, yes."

He pulled away. "Not yet."

She groaned.

At the bedside table once again, he lifted the glass of tart wine to his lips and drank deeply. Then bending over her, he lightly kissed her lips, letting her taste.

"Like it?" he asked.

She nodded, and he held his hand out to drizzle the cold liquid down her hot pussy lips.

She squealed, then bucked.

Setting the glass down, he knelt beside her, parted her sweet pink lips and sucked the wine from her moist center. Her struggles rippled through her body, and if she could, he knew she'd have held his head to her clit until she climaxed. Hard. Forever. Instead he licked all around, above, below, her lips, her opening. And never gave her what she truly wanted.

"Do you want me to beg?" Her breath hitched, she moaned, then tossed her head to dislodge the blindfold. It stayed.

He rose long enough to say, "No."

"Bastard." She wriggled, tried to undulate against him to get what she needed. "Those beads, they made me crazy."

He flicked her clit with his finger. "It's not just the beads. It was being alone up here for twenty minutes wondering." He brushed his lips along her belly. "All tied up." He bit her nipple lightly. "Thinking, wondering, hoping, praying."

She moaned and writhed. "I knew you'd come back and do exactly this. Tease me."

"What did you want me to do?"

"I wanted you to get me off."

He held her chin between his finger and thumb. "What was the worst thing you imagined I'd do?"

She shuddered full body though he touched nothing more than her jaw, not even his length along hers. "That you wouldn't come back," she whispered.

Of all the things he'd considered, that one had never occurred to him. Where the hell would she get an idea like that?

He laughed, making a joke out of it, though he knew there was something true to her core in that fear. It would bear examination later.

"No such luck, sweetheart." Straddling her, he leaned in and rubbed the zipper of his pants across her lips. "You have to take care of this massive hard-on because I sure as hell am not going to do it myself."

"You have me tied down. I have to do whatever you want."

Unzipping, letting the sound ripple over her nerve endings, he fished his cock out of his pants. Pre-come already bathed the crown. Smoothing his fingers over it, he then stroked her lips until she opened, licked, sucked, took his juice on her tongue.

"You're going to swallow all of me, baby," he crooned. "Every last drop." He stroked himself, squeezing more from the tip, then trailed his fingers across her cheek to the edge of the blindfold, teasing her but keeping it in place. "Right?"

"I have to do whatever you tell me."

Bracing himself on one hand above her, he stroked his cock along the seam of her lips this time. "You're going to have to take it deep, down your throat. I want that, I need that, nothing else will do." Yet he caressed her lips gently, giving her only a taste of what he had planned for her.

He'd had a vague idea of multiple orgasms throughout the evening, until her body simply couldn't take another moment, until the pleasure was so intense, it was almost pain.

Yet her secret fears changed everything. This wasn't about her orgasm; it was about showing her how badly he wanted her to give *him* one.

"I'm going to fuck your mouth until you give me everything I want," he whispered. "You will take me until I can't hold back, until I flood you so full, you can't hold it all."

She licked him. Heat and sensation rocketed through him, the muscles of his arm spasming as he held himself above her.

"You're going to take whatever I want to give, aren't you?"

"Yes." She punctuated with a kiss and a suck.

"You can't stop me."

"No, I can't."

"Suck me," he murmured.

Holding his cock for her, he slid between her parted lips. Then he fucked her mouth. Her tongue swirled and caressed. When he backed off, she followed. She couldn't direct him or hold him, she could only submit, and yet she somehow took him.

"Oh God, yes, that's so fucking good. Suck it, baby, yeah." Finally, he loosed his own grip on himself, cupped her head, held her, jammed one hand on the mattress by the side of her, and simply pumped. She took all of him, swallowed him whole, owned him for those few moments in her mouth, until heat swept down through his body, his extremities, and blew his world apart.

Her name on his lips, he filled her with his essence, gave her everything, and for a moment lost all that he was to her.

8

GOD, that was amazing. Josie had only just caught her breath after taking all of him.

Somehow that felt like a metaphor for more than just his come shot. It was the hottest damn thing she'd ever done in her life. Though totally immobilized, she'd taken him, fucked him, owned him. And loved every second of it.

His hair was soft at her throat, his breath warm against her neck, his clothing rough along her bare skin from torso to thigh. Subtle aftershave tickled her nose, and something else, a salty male scent that made her mouth water. His taste lingered on her tongue, her lips. With the blindfold, everything was more potent, visceral.

His fingers trailed down her abdomen, leaving tingles and shocks in their wake. He tunneled through her pubic curls.

"No." She stopped him with her voice.

"Why not?" He rumbled against her throat.

"Because."

She didn't need an orgasm. His was enough to satisfy every longing. How that could be so, she had no idea. A climax was a woman's divine right, yet . . . she felt utterly replete as never before. Not even with two men. She needed only this moment with Kyle's body next to hers.

Later, probably not tonight, she'd want the orgasm.

"Because why?" he insisted.

Because she'd claimed him in some elemental way. She was tied and blindfolded, yet she'd been the one in control. She had the power. He'd been completely hers. He'd fucked her mouth, but *she'd* taken him. She made him need that release, and she was the only one who could give it to him. No one else would do.

Maybe saying all that would not be such a good idea. Men didn't like to even think they could be owned. On a normal basis, she wouldn't want to own him either. It was a thing of the moment. "I'm tired," she said instead.

He raised the material he'd draped over her face, just one corner so that she could only meet his intensely blue gaze with one eye. "You're kidding, right?"

She shook her head.

He whipped the blindfold off and tossed it aside. "Screw that, sweetheart. I'm going to make you come so hard you faint."

"I don't think so."

Hovering over her now, he smiled, wickedly, diabolically. "Another challenge, I see. That was probably your intent all along."

"I could take it or leave it," she answered mildly, then yawned for emphasis. Inside, her body quivered. Now she was starting to want.

"Bitch. You want to make me beg to go down on you."

Bitch? Ronson called her that, and it irked her. Kyle used the term, and it made her hot. "I'm tied. You can do anything you want." Okay, maybe one orgasm would be a good thing. Since he was insisting.

He crawled down her body. "What if I brought you to the brink, then stopped?"

If he brought her that close, she'd go off on her own. "Whatever. I told you I'm tired."

He licked her belly button. It tickled. Reaching up, his eyes on her, he pinched her nipple. Hard. An exquisite bolt of electricity streaked through her body. She trembled, and only his body between her legs held her down.

"Tell me you want it."

She swallowed. According to her mother, it was a woman's prerogative to change her mind as often as she wanted, so yeah, Josie wanted that big O. Now. But she didn't have to let him know how badly. "It's totally up to you."

He pinched her nipple again, letting her writhe a moment beneath him. "Naughty, naughty. Admit you want it."

Oh God, that was good, as if her nipples had a direct line to her clitoris. "Admit you want to do it badly," she countered.

"You are one tough woman."

"I always win." Now *that* was a big lie. She wasn't winning in her new job. But who cared about that when she had this delicious man between her legs? If she was going to mix business with pleasure, she'd sure as hell make the most of it. "You want to do it, do it. If you don't, let me up so I can get dressed. It's getting late."

No way was he untying her, she knew. Then again, he might not do anything since she was being so bitchy.

"Ask me nicely," he said.

She considered. "If it would make you happy, I'll allow you to lick me."

He laughed, his abdomen rippling, his breath rushing across the hot skin of her belly. "You don't give a guy an inch."

"Hah. You're way more than an inch, and I gave it my all."

He licked her hip bone. "So you did. But you still have to beg."

"I can easily take care of myself later."

"It's better when someone else does it for you."

She simply raised an eyebrow.

"No way." He stroked her inner thigh. "You'd rather masturbate than have a man go down on you?"

"A vibrator gives a very intense orgasm. Especially when a girl makes a lot of noise while she's doing it. Wailing makes the inevitable explosion all that much harder."

Smoothing his fingers through the curls at her apex, he teased just short of the mark. "Let's test your theory. I'll get you off, then you do it yourself. We'll see who's better."

What a challenge. "I didn't bring my vibrator."

He grinned, then rose slowly, backed off the bed, and turned to his briefcase to rummage a bit.

He'd thought of everything, dammit. "Are you going to get naked?" she asked.

"No," he said, without turning. "You're more vulnerable if I'm fully dressed."

Funnily enough, all the vulnerability she'd felt had vanished. Sex with him was too much fun. "Bastard," she said, just so he wouldn't figure that out. "My hands are tied, so how can I use the vibrator?"

He moved swiftly, brandishing the toy like a sword. It was the same one he'd had her use in the car.

"Hmm," she murmured. "Didn't we already determine I can do extremely well all by myself? I mean, you watched it."

"I wasn't rating the orgasm at the time. This is a better test."

"What if I lie about it?"

He crossed to the bed, laid the vibrator beside her, and untied her right wrist, leaving her other arm immobilized over her head. "Your body can't lie."

He was right, it couldn't. Besides, she'd get two orgasms for the price of one, and she'd still be running the show. "Will you put a pillow under my head so I don't strain my neck?"

"Sorry. I didn't realize." He pulled one of the small cushions from the head of the bed, put a hand beneath her nape, and settled her gently.

"Thank you. Do I have a time limit?"

"No." He tipped his head. "Do I?"

"You can take as long as you want." How could she lose?

He folded her fingers around the vibrator and, eyes on her, rotated the switch at the base to high speed. The buzz worked its way up her arm.

"Go for it," he whispered, his eyes a blazing blue.

She wasn't quite at the right angle because usually when she spread her legs, she bent at the knees as well, which served to tip her pelvis and part her lips. The thought gave rise to a brilliant idea.

"Since I have only one hand, I need you to open my pussy."

"That seems like cheating."

"Not at all. I just need you to expose my clitoris."

He gave her a knowing half smile. Okay, yeah, she wanted his fingers on her for a moment, the heat of touch versus the cold plastic.

She puckered up. "Pretty please with sugar on top?"

"Cheater, cheater," he chanted, but leaned over to glide his fingers over her skin, the pads rough, tingling. Sliding along her pussy, he searched for her clit, finding the nub, rubbing. "Is that it?"

She sucked in a breath, held in a moan. As if he didn't know. "Yep, that's it."

Grabbing the tip of the vibrator, Kyle guided her down to meet his circling finger. They touched at the same time, and Josie jerked.

"No fair coming yet. Not while I'm touching you, too."

Kyle recognized the moment sensation took over. She closed her eyes, her body flushed, her teeth nipped into her lip. Fingers tensed, she grasped the rope holding her arm over her head, and used the leverage to arch into the vibrator. Her hips rose, fell, rotated.

And she talked to herself. "Yeah, oh God, please." Panted, chanted again, then pushed the side of her face into the pillow.

Kyle propped himself on his elbow beside her, her sweet, musky scent perfuming the air. Sipping wine, watching her pleasure herself, holy hell, life couldn't get much better. He was already hard again, but not so close to the edge he couldn't enjoy the show. "That's it, baby, ride that vibrator."

She drove the tip down her slit and inside, humping it, filling the room with the slip-slide sounds of her pussy.

"Oh yeah, baby, you're so fucking perfect." Beautiful pink pussy, full lips, tight, plump clit, and all that cream.

Her legs trembled against the bonds, her body rose and fell with the vibrator's rhythm, then she held it still, right on her clit. Her breath sawed through her lips as she shoved her head back into the pillow, then a low keening welled up from her throat. She bucked, cried out, panted, then wailed loud enough to wake the neighbors beside, above, and below their room. The hot, over-the-top sound wrapped around his cock, going on forever, her orgasm hard.

As if she couldn't take another moment, she tossed the vibrator, hitting the wall, and collapsed into the bed. There she lay, her breasts rising and falling, until finally she turned just her head and slowly opened her eyes to gaze at him. Her lips curved in the sweetest of smiles.

"Top that," she whispered.

He wasn't sure he could. He wasn't sure that women really did need men. They could get their sperm from a bank, and their orgasms from a piece of cold plastic.

"It was only so good because I was watching," he said in defense.

She laughed, closed her eyes again, and relaxed into the pillow. "I wasn't even looking at you."

So true. "I guess I have my work cut out for me."

"Yes, you do." She flapped her free hand. "Better get busy. Or I might fall asleep, and you'll never win."

They hadn't established any parameters. "What do I get if my orgasm is better?"

"The pleasure of giving it to me."

"Wench," he answered mildly. Crawling between her legs, he lapped at her juices. So sweet. When he touched his tongue to her clitoris, she bucked.

"Hey, not fair," she muttered. "I made myself all sensitive."

He sucked the nub, swirled his tongue, then jabbed lightly with the tip. She writhed sinuously and started that sweet croon of hers. "Oh yeah, baby, oh, God."

His hand on her abdomen right above her mound, Kyle stretched her skin, pulling her pussy wide, fully exposing her clit. He went at her with lips and tongue and fingers, two inside her as he sucked.

Josie wanted his cock. Inside her. Now. Deep. Hard. She'd lied. There were things a woman couldn't do for herself. Hot, hard flesh beat cool plastic every time. But this was just his tongue, his mouth . . . Oh God. Sensation shot out from her clit, shivered along her limbs, shuddered deep into her belly, tingled at the tip of her breasts.

"Yeah, yeah," she whispered.

He grabbed her butt, held her firm, made her take everything he wanted to do to her. Jesus, that was the difference. If it got too intense with a vibrator, you backed off. You couldn't help yourself. Kyle wouldn't let her go. When she wailed, he sucked harder. When she bucked, he plunged his fingers deeper. When she tangled the fingers of her free hand in his hair and yanked, he growled, the vibrations shimmying through her. He met every sway and dip of her body, rolled with her.

Wrapping her hand around the rope, she strained closer, her hips rising, rotating, her whole body rocking. She heard herself wail, out of control, and it only made the sensations hotter, harder, brighter. Stars shot back and forth behind her closed lids, then they exploded like fireworks.

And still he wouldn't let her go. When she reached the pinnacle at which she would have tossed the vibrator and rolled into a ball, he circled her clit, kept his tongue right there no matter how hard she tried to buck him off. She rode the wave until she didn't know her name or where they were. Until she no longer felt the mattress beneath her, just the never-ending quake of her body. Until his mouth and her pussy seemed as one.

He retreated only when a tear leaked from the corner of her eye. She felt it run down her temple into her hair. The pleasure was almost pain, intense, glorious, infinite.

This was what they meant by died and gone to heaven. Especially as Kyle soothed her with light kisses, on her mound, her hip, her thighs, caressing her with his fingers. Then he crawled back up to lie beside her. That was another thing a vibrator couldn't give you, the sweet aftermath.

"Well?" There was a wealth of cocky in his tone.

She cracked one eyelid. And glared. "You win." Good God, she didn't want to move. "Maybe you should untie me now." She was beginning to feel vulnerable all over again.

Her eyes closed, she could feel every shift of his body as he untied her feet and hand. Cupping the back of her head, he held the glass of wine to her lips and helped her drink. She gulped, the alcohol going immediately to her head.

Then she curled into a ball and turned away from him. She loved oral sex, and most of her lovers had been adequate at it. Honestly though, some of her own self-generated orgasms were better. Not so with Kyle. Silver-tongued devil.

She had to lay quiet for a moment and think about what that meant. Or what it changed.

Leaning over her, he stroked the hair back from her forehead. "Best ever?"

She liked the way he smelled, that barely there aftershave, a slightly sweet yet tangy scent she couldn't identify. It came back to her at the oddest times. In meetings, or when she was on the phone with a customer. In her bed late at night.

"It was good." Best ever? God. Yes. It was. How could that be? She was thirty years old; she'd had several lovers. She'd actually been in love once. How could that orgasm have been the best?

"Liar," he chided softly. "A woman doesn't cry out a man's name like that if it wasn't the best."

She had cried out his name. Most of the time in the throes of ecstasy, she couldn't remember her partner's name. It didn't matter. It was just physical. But she'd used Kyle's name.

"It was just sex. I told you screaming and crying makes it better." But why his name? "So you've got a clever tongue. Big deal." Oh boy, it had been a terribly big deal. Her ears were still ringing.

He laughed and rolled her into his arms. "Have it your way. But I won."

He had. Hands down. Her body would never be the same. She'd expect, need, crave one of those climaxes every time. She'd like to say it was only because she'd made herself come so hard first, that she'd set up the next explosive orgasm for him. Yet she'd done all that with other men before. Something was different with him.

Her body would turn against her, make her need to have him around more than once a week, for more than just an evening. Maybe even all night. For a lot of nights.

Really, that wasn't a good thing. Not at all. Needing and craving led to obsession. She so wasn't going there ever again. Once was enough.

KYLE watched her drive away, then went back into the hotel to check out. It had been better than a clever tongue. It wasn't just sex. It had been more than proving his touch was superior to her vibrator.

He was having feelings about her now. Strong emotions. They felt good. He wanted to enjoy them. He wasn't sure, though, if that was a good thing in the long run.

BRIGHT and early Thursday morning—God, her body felt good upon waking even though she'd left the hotel just before midnight—Josie pulled into Castle's parking lot. She turned off the engine and the auto locks popped up. Chuck Eastman yanked open her car door and climbed into the passenger seat. His knees almost hit his chest, and he had to bend his head so it didn't scrape the roof. "I want to talk to you now."

No. Not now. Josie was still in overload from last night with Kyle. Maybe that was why she wanted to bash Eastman's face in for having the nerve to get in her car uninvited. She needed a little calm right now. She opened her mouth after a deep breath. "I'm not even inside yet. Couldn't we at least wait until we've got our coffee?" There, that sounded polite instead of a PMSing woman who was up, up, up one moment and mad as a stampeding buffalo the next.

They were an hour early, and only a quarter of the parking

spaces were filled. Eastman shoved a big hand through his thick brown hair and glanced at the main lobby doors of Castle Heavy Mining. "Trust me, you don't want to have this conversation inside where it will end up being official."

Oh God. A headache built behind her eyes. She had so much crap to do today. Three of her projects still required a lot of oversight despite the fact that they'd been passed on to Ronson, Jenkins, and Walker. It took time for another program manager to come up to speed. She'd also managed to find two job candidates and had HR hustle them in for first-round interviews. Today. And Eastman, well, despite being six-three and a big, buffed guy with loads of rippling muscles, he could be a bit of a melodramatic pantywaist.

"Spill, Chuck."

"Lydia pinched my ass."

She laughed. Then immediately slapped her hand over her mouth.

"It's not funny." He glared with Neanderthal eyebrows that stretched all the way across his forehead. "She pinches hard."

"I'm sorry." God, she was going to make a total mess of it if she wasn't careful. "It was shock laughter. I simply couldn't believe what you said."

Jarvis Castle arrived in his big old boat of a car, then walked to the front doors. Like the Mona Lisa's, his eyes never left Josie where she sat in her car. Good God, why did the old man have to be in so early and what must he be thinking?

"But it's true," Eastman went on. "And this is the third time. I thought about going to HR, but I figured I'd give you the benefit of the doubt first."

Meaning, he'd see if she had the guts to do anything about it. First, it was Ronson giving her shit and claiming reverse discrimination, then Lydia wanting a raise, and now sexual harassment in the workplace. Ernie hadn't even been gone two weeks, and the place was going to hell.

"I will have a talk with Lydia and make sure it never happens again."

Eastman glared at her for a long moment. His lips worked as if he had a lot more to say. Instead, he relented. "Okay."

Thank God. Crisis averted. She was sure Lydia hadn't meant a thing. She was just a kid, and Eastman did have a very pinchable ass. Not that she was making excuses for Lydia's behavior.

Inside, Josie got her coffee, then cleared her desk, which was the main reason she always arrived early when she wasn't on a job site. She liked to answer her e-mails and take care of niggling crap that seemed to require extraordinary amounts of time when people were interrupting you every few minutes. She waited until after eight, giving Lydia time to settle in herself, then buzzed the girl's phone.

Lydia bounced in a few seconds later.

Josie motioned with her fingers. "Close the door."

Her face lighting up, Lydia shut the door and threw herself into the chair opposite. "You got me my raise."

"No, I did not."

Her smile was quickly replaced by a frown. "Did you even try?"

Dammit. She couldn't get a word in edgewise. "I didn't call you in here about your salary. It's about Chuck's ass."

Lydia stared at her.

Shit. Josie heaved a great sigh. "I mean it's about you pinching Chuck's butt."

Lydia huffed. "I didn't pinch his butt."

"He says you did."

"I tapped him." Lydia rolled her eyes. "He was in my way."

"Three separate times?"

Her lips twitched. "I don't know about three times."

"Lydia, whether it's a tap or a pat or a pinch, you can't touch your male coworkers in those areas. In fact, you shouldn't touch them at all." There, that was safe.

"This is about my raise, isn't it?"

Josie resisted her own eye roll. "What does pinching Chuck have to do with your raise?"

"I didn't pinch him, I only tapped him, and you're just going to use this as an excuse to write me up so you don't have to give me a raise."

"He believes you pinched him, not tapped him, and you shouldn't tap him ever. And no, I'm not writing you up. This is just a warning, and not even a verbal warning, which would go in your record"— she hoped she was right about the procedure—"but only between you and me. *Unless* I get more complaints." She let out a rush of air after that lengthy dissertation. "Got it?"

Lydia scowled. "Yeah, I got it. I'm not getting a raise."

"Like everyone else, you'll get a raise when your review time comes." Jeez, she should have said *that* when Lydia first tried to railroad her. "Just don't do anything else that will have to go in your file."

"Things used to be fun when Ernie was here. Now it's like some Nazi concentration camp." Lydia stood and flounced to the door, her short skirt swinging. "I won't ever touch a guy around here again." Opening the door, she whispered, "Nazi," and was gone.

"That went well," Josie muttered. She wondered how Ernie would have handled the whole thing. Hmm, Ernie wouldn't have had the problem in the first place. Her employees were testing her, seeing how far they could push her limits. Sort of like Kyle.

That was all it took. Her total inability to determine how to subdue her staff gave rise to a damn near Machiavellian plan for her next challenge with Kyle. Oh yeah. This was gonna be good. He wouldn't know what hit him.

After a morning of Lydia's pouting, it was about eleven when Josie figured out that maybe Connor would have all the answers. Not about doing Kyle, but about Ronson, Eastman, and Lydia.

She stopped on his doorsill. "Hey, you."

Connor wasn't alone. Faith cooed to her little guy cradled in her husband's arms. Seeing Connor hold the baby so tenderly with that gooey look on his face always gave Josie a shock. He was transformed from tough guy to sap. Okay, that sounded totally negative. Faith and little David transformed Connor into something lovable.

"Hey, Little D, your auntie Josie's here." Faith smiled and waved the baby's fist at Josie.

David was so tiny, his hands almost too small to wrap around her finger. Josie had been terrified to hold him in the hospital in case she squeezed him too hard or, God forbid, dropped him.

He wasn't any less fragile now, like a porcelain doll. Breakable. She'd never played with dolls when she was a kid. She'd played with dump trunks even if she hadn't had a sandbox in which to put them. Still, Josie rounded the desk and made appropriate noises. "He's a cutie." Though his face was a tad smooshed.

Faith laughed. "It's okay. You don't have to lie for the doting parents. I know you're not a kid person."

"I swear it, he's adorable."

"But you're very glad he's ours and not yours."

Josie let her glance slide from Faith to the doting daddy. Connor's face shone, like an angel or something. As Josie's mom had said, Faith hadn't lost all the baby fat, but so what? She'd never been the model-thin type anyway, and now she was beautiful. Motherhood and wifehood or whatever the hell it was called . . . love gave Faith everything she needed. Her happiness glowed from within and made her absolutely gorgeous. She was meant to be a mother; she was meant to love her fabulous husband. She was meant for this life.

Josie grinned sheepishly. "Yeah, you're right, I'm glad he's yours." She was meant to be a career woman. Babies made her jittery, but she bent over to do the obligatory coochy-coo thing, eliciting another laugh from Faith.

With Little D still in his arms, Connor glanced up at Josie. "What'dya need, sweetie?" The endearment rolled off his tongue. Josie was pretty sure he didn't even hear it. He was . . . different around Faith and the baby.

"I was just—" Just what? Wanting to dump her problems in his lap? Whine about her crappy employees who were making her new job miserable? Tell him she was failing? No way. "I want to ask for your approval on attending a supervisory seminar to bone up on my managerial skills. I found one in the city. It's a couple of days next month."

"Yeah, sure, fine. Everything happened so quickly with Masters that we didn't have time to plan." He bent down and kissed his son's nose. Faith smiled.

Josie's heart turned over, a one-second roller coaster ride. She didn't want what they had, but there was something about the beauty of it, the level of emotion that almost seemed to shimmer around them. When she was twenty-one, in college, falling hard, she could have dreamed about having this.

"The commute's a bitch," Connor added, "so get a hotel."

"In San Francisco?" Her voice rose to a squeak. "That's astronomical in the summertime." And not much better in the winter. "I am not getting the company to pay for that."

"Josie"—Connor stared her down—"get a hotel room. I consider an hour and a half drive each way four days in a row to be too much wasted time."

Well, he was the boss, and the drive *was* horrendous. "Fine. I think they have a conference rate."

"So be it." The baby burped, and Connor rose, handing him off to Faith. "Wish I could take you to lunch, baby"—he kissed the tip of Faith's nose just as he had the little tyke's—"but I've got a meeting at the country club."

"That's okay, honey. I came to have lunch with Daddy. I want to take advantage before I start day care in the fall." Faith had been a kindergarten teacher, but she was opening her own day care facility once the school year started back up.

She turned to Josie. "You wanna go with us? Daddy would love to see you."

Jarvis Castle loved Faith to death, but he wasn't so big on the rest of the family, especially Josie's own father. They were third cousins, and, well, let's just say that Jarvis Castle didn't give a fig for the Tybrook family tree. Not to mention the fact that he would probably grill her on why Chuck Eastman was sitting in her car at a little after seven in the morning. "Thanks, but I'll pass."

She backed toward the door as Connor headed for the coatrack to pull on his suit jacket. "I'm having lunch with Kyle Perry, by the way," he said. Behind him, Faith reached up to straighten his collar.

Josie's blood pressure spiked. "Did he say something was wrong with the job?"

"No." Connor eyed her. "Is there?"

"No, no. Of course not." Though she was fighting with the company they'd chosen for long-belt replacement. "Nothing I can't handle."

"You working well with him?"

"Yeah, he's great." In and out of the sack. She willed a flush not to rise with that inane thought.

"Is that a generic 'great' or do you really think he knows his stuff?"

Why the hell should it matter to Connor as long *she* got the job in on time and on budget? He hadn't figured out something was happening between them, had he? Connor was pretty astute, and he read people well. But honestly, she hadn't shown a thing. "He's very competent."

"Good." Then he gathered Faith beneath his arm, kissed the top of her head. "Walk me out, baby?"

Faith jiggled her thumb and pinkie in the universal "give-me-a-call" gesture. Josie tipped her chin in the affirmative. Maybe a call to Faith would give her an inkling of what was on Connor's mind and why he'd be having lunch with Kyle.

Jeez. Connor had lunch with customers all the time. He wanted an update on the project, wanted to show his interest, yadda yadda. She was just being sensitive because she was diddling Kyle.

See, that was another of the reasons you shouldn't mix business and pleasure. You started reading things into everything anyone said to you, as if you had "slut screwing client" written on your forehead.

Whatever. Josie was too far gone to give Kyle up now, no matter what Connor's agenda was for today's lunch.

9

KYLE drove through the country club gates, heading for the main parking lot in front of the clubhouse and restaurant. Sumptuous digs, the place was way above his normal fare.

Being the daughter of a Castle board member, it wasn't above Josie's, but then he didn't get the impression she was into the country club scene. Kyle grinned. The woman could be down and dirty with the best of them, as she had been last night, tied to the bed and wailing her lungs out as she went over the edge.

A woman didn't let loose like that for just any man. Kyle didn't consider himself the world's greatest lover, but what they'd shared last night was damn spectacular. Special. Above and beyond. The lovers he'd had since his divorce had been great. With Josie, though, the sensations had been more intense, and he hadn't even fucked her yet. He had no easy answer for why that was so. Was it the power struggle? The need to subjugate? The games they played?

Some things simply defied rational explanation. He wanted her; that's all that mattered.

Connor Kingston rose politely as Kyle entered the dining room and the maitre d' led him to the table. The CEO of Castle Heavy Mining had called on Monday and suggested lunch this week. It just so happened that Kyle had to be in Watsonville on Thursday. The country club was on the way.

They shook hands, and Kyle tucked his tie to his abdomen as he sat.

"A cocktail?" Connor asked.

"No. Meeting afterward. Thanks."

The tablecloths were white, the cutlery silver, and the glass crystal. Patronage varied from middle-aged women in golf wear to men in business suits. Everything was so damn quiet, the voices barely above a hum, that he could hear the light clink of bone china.

"How's the project coming?"

Kyle perused the menu. "Right on track." He considered complimenting Josie, but wondered if it would come across sounding like favoritism. Then again, he gave credit where it was due. "Your program manager has everything under control. I'm surprised how quickly she picked up our manufacturing model."

"Josie gets a bad rap for being family, but she's damn good at what she does." Connor buttered a slice of sourdough.

"Family or not, you'll get no complaints from me. We're on time, and as we did the tour, she had some astute suggestions."

"Good. Her promotion to manager shouldn't interfere with her performance on your project." Connor brushed bread crumbs from his fingers. "She told you about the change, right?"

"Yes. I haven't had a problem with that to date," Kyle assured him.

"We at Castle are devastated by Ernie Masters' illness." It didn't sound like a platitude, but heartfelt.

"I'm sorry to hear that. I didn't know he was ill." Kyle had met him only one time, but had deemed him a nice enough guy.

"Cancer." Connor toyed with the stem of his water glass, his lips set in a grim line. Obviously Ernie Masters wasn't coming back.

Kyle wondered how that made Josie feel. She hadn't talked about it. Then he remembered the odd tone in her voice mail telling him about the promotion, and again when he congratulated her over the phone. It made sense now. She hadn't liked the reasons she'd gotten the job. He'd be willing to bet—no, he *knew*—that she even felt guilty about it, too, as if she were getting ahead based on someone else's misfortune. She tried to pretend she was a hard-ass, but she was hiding a soft core.

"Ernie and I both agreed Josie was the best choice to fill his slot," Connor continued.

"I'm sure it's the right decision." In that, Kyle was totally truthful. He was hot for the woman, but he also valued her expertise.

The waiter arrived, took their orders, moved on.

"You didn't invite me to lunch just to discuss the project." A phone call would have sufficed. Kyle leaned back, folded his hands over his stomach. "Something else on your mind?" He mentally hitched himself up. He didn't think this had anything to do with Josie, but his irrational gut was waiting for Connor to say that fucking the program manager wasn't appropriate.

"I'd like to offer you a job."

Kyle almost laughed. He was good at what he did, but he hadn't expected this. Thinking too much about Josie, perhaps, and missing the subtle nuances. "What job did you have in mind?"

"VP of FI&T," Connor supplied. Josie's group. Furnish, install, and train. "With your manufacturing and mining background, it's an excellent fit."

Vice president. Damn. The timing was perfect, just when he'd decided himself that a move was necessary for his career growth. But he'd be Josie's boss. Still, he asked for more details. "How much travel is involved?"

"We've got clients throughout the North American continent and South America. On average"—Connor tapped his fork on the table-cloth, giving himself a moment to calculate—"I'd say you could con-sider two to three weeks per quarter, unless a huge problem arises."

It got better and better. Two to three weeks per quarter instead of per month. It was only due to the retrofit at Coyote Ridge and the Watsonville issues that he'd been in town for the last two weeks. With the recent acquisition of the new quarries up in Wash-ington, he'd be away more than he was at home.

He wanted the better position, more responsibility, less travel. He was ready for it. He just didn't want to be Josie's boss.

There were other considerations, too. "You're a family-run com-pany. What kind of autonomy do you give your VPs?" He wasn't about to be micromanaged.

As if there was a joke in there somewhere, Connor smiled. "I've got my own job. I won't need to do yours."

"Number of employees in the group?"

Connor rattled off departments, head count, budgets, duties, et cetera. Kyle had more employees reporting to him now, but they were spread out over the various mines and quarries in SMG's list.

Then Connor got into salary, bonus programs, benefits. "We're instituting employee incentive stock options, too, something that's not just for family."

Kyle liked everything he heard. When his team went out for proposals on the upgrade, he'd investigated each of the contenders. He'd liked what he learned about Castle, their management style, executive team, mission statement, company policies. He'd be an idiot not to consider the opportunity.

"What would be your expectations on transition time from SMG?" Kyle wasn't going to walk out with no notice and leave SMG in a bind. He might not see any opportunity for advancement there, but neither would he screw them over.

"As SMG will remain our customer, I'd expect you to take adequate time to help them over any and all hurdles."

He wanted the job, he wanted the new challenges. There was only one problem. Josie Tybrook. She'd be his direct report. If he took the job, he'd have to end it with her. He knew he could separate business from pleasure, the work day from the evening fun, but continuing the relationship could be construed as unethical. Nor did he think Josie would easily separate him being her boss versus her lover. She'd already had a problem with the fact that he was a customer. She'd flip out if he were her supervisor.

Dammit, he *wanted* this job. Which meant he'd have to give her up.

The thought started an ache in his left temple he had a hard time ignoring. "It's a great offer. Castle's a good solid company. Mind if I take the weekend to think about it?"

"I'd think there was something wrong if you jumped on it," Connor said. "Decisions like this aren't made lightly."

No, they weren't. It was, though, a damn good indication of Kyle's emotions about Josie Tybrook. If it weren't for her, he'd have agreed to take the job right now.

Spying their meals arriving from the kitchen, Connor laid his napkin across his lap. "I'd like to keep this confidential until we come to an agreement."

It made good business sense to announce only once all terms had been agreed to and accepted. "No problem."

After that, the conversation turned light. Connor brought out the baby pictures. He was a proud father, a loving husband, a man one could respect. A man one could work well with.

Kyle had a lot to consider.

Back in his car, his cell phone beeped. He'd left it on the console. Flipping it open, he had four messages, two from Watsonville, one from Coyote Ridge, the last from Josie.

His heart skipped a beat. If he took the job, their games were over. He dialed in, listened to her voice.

"I've got big plans for you, buddy boy. Here's the scoop. You are not allowed to have an orgasm until our next meeting. You are not allowed to whack off. You are not allowed to do it with another woman. You will hold your load until I say you can release it." Her voice dropped. "If you do get off without me, you forfeit a turn. Got that?"

She had such a nasty mind and a sexy voice. Did he detect a question there, as in, was he seeing another woman? She could be testing the waters, expecting him to deny any entanglements. They'd joked about Kisa, but he'd never flat-out stated that Josie was the only woman he intended seeing for the duration. The possibility existed that Josie could be jealous, perhaps even proprietary. He found he liked the idea.

He had the weekend before he needed to make a decision on Connor's offer. In the meantime, there was no reason he couldn't have her one more time. Besides, he had to go up to Washington State next week for some site inspections. He didn't want to wait to see her until he returned. They needed to step up the one-week limit she'd put on things and make a date before the weekend was out.

Maybe she'd make him change his mind about taking the job.

KYLE called her back three hours after she'd left her dictatorial queen-bee message. Josie closed her office door, leaning against it with the cell to her ear.

"I'm out of town next week," he said.

Which totally blew her plans out of the water. Dammit.

"So," he went on, "it's got to be this weekend." He paused, letting that sink in. "Or you'll have to wait for your challenge until I get back."

It sounded like an ultimatum. It felt like escalation. "You just can't wait more than a week for an orgasm."

Her stomach hitched. What if he had some other little plaything to take care of him on the road? Maybe the darling Little Miss Snowflake accompanied him on business trips as his secretary and more.

Even if she hadn't said all that aloud, in her own mind, she came off like a shrew.

"What I can't wait for," he said, "is your hand, your mouth, and your pussy all over my cock. I want all that right this fucking minute."

Oh. God. Yes, please. He disarmed her with that one sentence, a reaction that was actually kind of scary. "Sweet talker," she muttered.

He smacked her a little kiss over the phone.

"All right. Saturday." She knew what she was going to do, just not where. "I'll have to call you back with the location." A little feistiness was in order, too. After all, it was *her* challenge. "So keep all of Saturday free, day and evening."

"What about the night?"

"I turn into a pumpkin after midnight."

She wasn't spending the night with him. She wasn't sleeping with him. She never stayed over at a lover's house, and no one stayed at hers. You slept with a guy, and they got all proprietary. There was the whole morning-after routine, too. Really, what did you talk about? Your life? Your dreams? With Kyle, they could talk about work, the project . . . no, no, no. She was already mixing business with pleasure, she wasn't about to muddle up her real life with his as well.

"Fine." He laughed. "I will block out nine a.m. to midnight just for you and be at your beck and call, to answer your every whim and desire."

She toed the carpet with her shoe, hugging the phone to her ear. "You don't have to go overboard."

"I have only one condition."

"It's my challenge. No conditions."

"If I'm at your beck and call, there's a condition."

She puffed out a breath. "Fine. One condition only."

"You do have to let me shoot my load before it's over."

"I have every intention of that." Oh boy, did she ever.

"Thank God." He sighed.

She felt the sound like a caress along her thighs. "You really don't trust me, do you?"

"I admit I had vision of you putting a cock ring on me and not letting me take it off."

"Oh man." It was just the thing. "Why didn't I think of that?"

"Holy shit, I shouldn't have said anything."

She laughed and did a Snoopy dance over to her desk, then threw herself in her chair. "This is marvelous. I love it."

"Please don't." But she heard the smile in his voice, the male satisfaction.

"You know you want it, that's why you brought it up." It would go so perfectly with her other big plan for him. Oh yeah. "I have to go shopping after work," she whispered to him. "And you are going to love it."

He'd trussed her up like a Christmas goose. He deserved everything she planned to do to him.

SHE waited beside her white hybrid car, a black canvas bag slung over her shoulder.

She'd called him Friday afternoon with the place, instead of keeping him in suspense until Saturday morning, and she'd chosen the middle of the day. As before, she didn't tell him what, only where and the time he should meet her. Being a sunny, gorgeous weekend, the traffic was a bitch even it wasn't a work day. At a little before noon, everyone was heading over the Santa Cruz mountains to enjoy the sun and the ocean, and the address she'd given him was right on the way.

He'd finally found the place in the half-full lot of an Indian casino he hadn't been aware existed in the Bay Area. What did she have planned this time? Strip poker? Her games kept his heart rate up and his cock hard determining ways to turn the tables on her.

First, though, he had to discover how she'd try to take him down a peg. He'd figured that's what all her games were about. Taking him down. Hence the panties, the dressing room of a lingerie shop, and how quickly she'd glommed on to the cock ring idea. He deserved comeuppance for tying her down. That would set the tone for most of their subsequent battles, he was sure.

What he'd liked, though, was that so far they'd both won. No matter who was in charge, they both ended up on top.

As he climbed from his car, she crooked a finger at him without saying a word. She wore a tie-dyed, wraparound skirt that swung around her calves and revealed a tasty bit of thigh as she walked. Wending her way through the parked cars, she crossed the newly macadamized lot to a series of trendy storefronts opposite the casino.

She chose a set of green glass doors that masked any view of the inside. PARADISE arched in a curlicue font across the front window, accompanied by painted palm trees and brilliant birds-of-paradise.

Inside, the lobby walls were sponge-painted to look like fake rocks in varying shades of gray and black. Recessed lighting in the ceiling centered on palm trees in pots and gleamed on the black-

and-green mosaic floor. Mist puffed from jets along the baseboards to complete the steamy, jungle setting, yet underlying it was the scent of chlorine.

The young woman at the counter wore tight leopard skin, heavily outlined eyes, and a deep red lipstick that looped too far outside the true lines of her lip. "May I help you?"

"We'd like a private room." Josie pulled out her wallet.

Kyle still hadn't decided what the place was. Perhaps a spa or sauna, his and her massages.

"I have the coupon from the website, too"—she laid it on the counter—"plus we'd like the free extra half hour since it's before five."

She was born into wealth, yet she watched every penny. She wouldn't let him buy her an expensive corset, and she used Internet coupons. As if she had to earn everything rather than be given it. In a regular family-run company, she would have had the manager's job without question, and yet she seemed to work hard to deserve all she had. Right down to the economy car she drove. She probably lived off her salary, not her family money. She worked off her reputation, not her family name. Being accepted for her accomplishments was more important to her than all the wealth and comfort her family could supply.

The leopard woman rang up the charge. "Would you like any water?"

"No, thanks." She hugged her magic canvas bag tighter, her body language indicating she'd brought her own bottles.

"Then follow me."

The woman was leopard from head to foot, with thin spike heels that wobbled as she walked. In flat sandals, a spandex workout top, and a quarter the amount of makeup, Josie outshone Ms. Leopard by a mile. He admired the sway of her ass in the wraparound skirt.

Down the hallway, the chlorine aroma intensified. Unlocking a door, the lady snapped on a light. "No bubbles or lube in the tub, please. The towels are right up here." She pointed to a wire rack above the light switch.

"Thank you." Josie motioned him inside as the woman left them, closing the door.

Fifteen by fifteen, the room had two levels. Surrounded by wood decking, a recessed hot tub sat up a short flight of stairs, its water already rumbling and frothing. At tub level, exactly opposite the door through which they'd entered, lay a thin mattress covered in a jungle-print sheet. The lower level was perhaps a couple of arm lengths wide. The floor they stood on was concrete, with a shower at the far end, just below the hot tub.

Josie hit a switch, and the overhead light flipped to a black light. Jungle images glowed in fluorescent color: insects, birds, palm fronds.

With that mattress, the room was made for illicit activities. "You bad girl," he said. "How did you know about this place?"

She gave him a look and shook her head, rolling her eyes. "I like a good soak." She arched one brow. "Now strip, slave."

Hanging her bag on a hook beneath the towel rack, Josie pulled out a couple of water bottles and fed them through the railing surrounding the tub, setting them on the deck within easy reach. Then she stood, arms akimbo, hands on hips.

Kyle kicked off his flip-flops, yanked his T-shirt over his head, draped it over one of the hooks along the back wall, then popped the buttons on his shorts.

He was naked beneath. Beautifully, magnificently naked and hard already. Josie heated on the inside. Oh, the naughty things she had planned for him. "Now get in the shower."

He turned on the tap, holding his hand under until the water warmed, then stepped beneath the spray.

"Soap up," she said.

From a wall dispenser, he filled his palm. Josie leaned against the wall just beyond the fall of water. "I want to see you clean everything."

"Yes, ma'am."

He soaped his chest, which was covered with the lightest dusting of hair. He lingered over his nipples, his eyes on hers. Then he stroked down his stomach and grabbed his cock. It grew in his fist as he pumped, gaze still on her.

"You better not come," she admonished.

"I won't. This is nothing."

Oh, it was something, all right. Gorgeous and suckable. She pulled the tie on her skirt and let it fall, then slowly stepped back to hang it on a hook next to his clothing. She left her sandals behind, too, then rolled off the spandex bodysuit.

In the black light, her white thong and bra glowed. She stripped those off as well.

"You going to help me wash?" he asked, still stroking himself.

"Oh yeah, I am." He had no idea the things she was going to put him through. She climbed beneath the water, which he'd left on the cool side. That was fine; once in the tub, they'd heat up fast. "I'm taking over."

Pulling his hand away from his cock, she smoothed the soap all over his shaft, balls, and back to the sensitive bit of flesh before his ass. Even in the dim lighting, she saw his pupils dilate with the slight pressure she exerted.

She leaned in to bite a nipple and loved his involuntary shudder.

"We have to make sure you're very, very clean." She tipped her head back to meet his gaze. "So turn around, grab the railing, and spread your legs." She gave him a wicked smile.

He visibly suppressed his own smile and followed her

instructions, presenting his back as he wrapped his fists around the railing and looked out over the bubbling hot tub.

"Spread 'em," she said, like a cop getting ready for a pat down. Then she pumped soap from the dispenser.

Right up against his side, she pressed close, put her lips to his ear and whispered, "You're going to like this, prisoner." His butt cheeks were smooth as she caressed them.

He turned his head, eyes glittering. "Oh please, Officer, don't hurt me."

"Shut up and take it, big boy."

She slipped along the crease of his ass, and probed lightly. His nostrils flared.

"Spread 'em wider," she whispered.

His gaze focused on her, he did exactly as she instructed. Fascinated by the flicker in his eyes, she slipped her finger deeper. She'd never done this to a man. In a way, it was a violation, yet she knew some men loved the feeling, the pressure against the center of their sex. She just hadn't figured he'd like it, and the fact that he did, that it actually made him a little wild, was infinitely more powerful. This was submission, and yet it was more. Pure heat, pure sex, pure pleasure. Only a truly sexual being would allow this, like this, want this.

Kyle was all that and more.

His fingers tightened on the railing. "Shit. Fuck."

She knew she'd found the spot. She washed him, cleaned him with soapy fingers, and drove him bonkers. Grasping his cock with her other hand, she found him magnificently hard, his balls tight. He shuddered in her grip.

"That's enough for you," she whispered.

Withdrawing, she washed her hands, then soaped herself as he watched over his shoulder. He didn't say a word, but in the black light, his eyes blazed a hot, glowing blue.

"You're mine," she said, rinsing off, "to do with as I wish. You don't have a say in it at all." She tipped her head. "I shouldn't have promised I'd let you climax."

"Bitch," he murmured.

In a way, it was the highest of compliments. She had him in the palm of her hand. She knew just what to do to him. She'd have him begging, on his knees, metaphorically tied up, wound up, crazy.

"Get in the hot tub," she ordered.

He turned, brushed against her, his body hot despite the luke-warm water. "Enjoy this," he told her, "because you will pay more than you can imagine."

Josie almost shuddered herself as images fluttered through her mind. She was diabolical. Kyle, she feared, could be infinitely worse. Yet she laughed. "You're going to beg me to do this to you again and again. I'll always be the one in control."

Stepping away, he stroked a finger down between her breasts. "You'll be dying to give up control to me."

He took the stairs gracefully, padded the two steps to the edge of the tub, then climbed down, his lower half disappearing below the water. Stretching his arms out along the rim, he leaned back and, with merely a look, dared her to take him.

She wondered if she'd bitten off more than she could chew.

10

JOSIE had that deer-in-the-headlights look as she climbed into the tub and sank down across from him.

Kyle splashed a little water at her. "Aren't you forgetting something?"

"What?" Her tone came across slightly belligerent.

He'd bested her even as she'd stroked inside him. Expecting him to balk, she didn't quite know how to handle the fact that he found ass play by a woman equally as pleasurable as fucking, though he hadn't indulged in it frequently. Marianne had never wanted to play that way. Here, now, with Josie, his cock was damn near purple under the water, and his balls ached with need. He forced himself to ratchet down, and the heat of the tub was helping.

"The ring?" He let the question lay between them.

He recognized the moment she came to her senses, her eyes widening, lips pursed. "Shit."

"Don't tell me you forgot it." He clucked his tongue, shook his head, chiding her. "And here I was so looking forward to it." The truth was, a cock ring was exquisite torture. It made him feel like his head was about to explode, but he couldn't come. When it was released . . . holy hell, look out.

"You know, this is *my* challenge." She gave him a pout. "So stop ordering me around."

"I'm not ordering. Simply asking." He raised both hands. "No harm in that, is there?" He also loved a woman's touch as she put it on him.

"You're too hard for it anyway. The package says you have to put it on . . . before."

He reached over, yanked on her arm, and pulled her close. "I have a will of iron, and it's gone down a bit." He wrapped her fingers around his cock. "See?"

She blinked, opened her mouth.

"Cat got your tongue?" He adored teasing her. She was so easy to tease, yet so feisty. In a second, she would start giving him hell again.

"You're still too big."

He was a man, he liked hearing that. "It will get even bigger with a cock ring." Gazes locked, he reeled her in, settling her on his lap, his cock between her legs, her hand still on him.

"Stop directing the action." She squeezed him gently.

"I'm just helping." If she wasn't careful, he'd fuck her right in the water.

Slowly unwrapping her fingers one by one, she let him go. "I don't need help."

Leaning in, he took her tight, beaded nipple in his mouth and licked, punctuating with a little bite. She sucked in a breath.

"You like that kind of help." Then he tunneled a hand into her hair and pulled her down to capture her mouth with his. "I'm willing to do whatever you want." He licked her bottom lip. "I'll play your clit like a maestro. I'll lay you back and lick you till you scream." Her mouth opened beneath his, and he showed her exactly how good his tongue could be. "I'll bend you over the side of the tub and drive deep inside you." He made love to her mouth, sliding a hand between her legs at the same time, testing her, finding her pussy slippery with juice. "Whatever you want," he finished, backing off, letting his words, his kiss, his touch work their magic.

Her breath puffed from her lips, her eyes dilated. He snugged her closer, his cock almost touching her pussy. She shimmied away, then shoved off with one hand on his thigh and floated through the water to the other side of the tub.

"I've got your number, buddy. And I'm not falling for your games." She tapped her chest. "*My* show this time." Then she raised a brow. "After all, I paid for the hot tub."

"I would have paid for it."

She rolled over, floated to the steps, and climbed out. "It's getting way too hot in here." Padding down to the lower level, she retrieved her canvas bag from the hook, rummaging in it as she returned to the wood decking by the tub. "Ah, here it is." She held up the prize.

A circular leather strap with snaps, two smaller strips of leather, also with snap closings, attached on the bottom side.

He laughed. "What the hell is that?"

She tipped her head, sniffed primly, and shot him a most offended glare. "It's a cock-and-ball harness, which"—she batted her eyelashes—"the saleslady assured me is much more effective than a cock ring." She smiled wickedly. "See, you put the big strap around the base of your cock and these"—she indicated the shorter pieces of leather—"you wrap around your balls individually." Josie tipped her head, laughter dancing in her eyes. "Sort of like a bra that lifts and separates, as that old commercial said."

"You expect me to wear that? It sounds like a torture device."

"You *will* wear it."

Kyle stared at the thing, then raised his gaze to hers. "Are you putting it on me?"

Her smile grew slowly, until she became a female version of the devil incarnate. "Oh yeah. I can't wait to truss *you* up."

Payback's a bitch. "All right." He rose, water running off his body. "I hope you got extra large."

She laughed. "Extra small will work just fine."

The woman knew how to cut a man down to size, so to speak. He stood on the lowest step of the tub while she sat on the seat.

Grasping his cock, she lifted her face. "Ready?"

"Maybe you should suck it first."

She flexed her fingers around him. "No. It's got to fit before you get really hard." She winked. "And we know what my excellent cock sucking will do to you." Folding the band of leather around his base, she snapped it in place. "Okay?"

He had room to grow, for sure.

"Okay, now for the hard part." She cupped his balls, then rolled and snapped closed first one leather strap, then the second, effectively pocketing each nut.

"Shit."

"Is that a good shit or a bad shit?" She stroked each ball in turn, then licked the crown of his cock.

"Most definitely a good shit." She touched him; he hardened. He felt the familiar build in his balls, the surge in his cock. The leather bindings put him on edge, like getting a jerk off from a female bodybuilder with a relentless grip. Head back, eyes closed, he savored the sensations.

"Perfect," she purred to his cock. "I think you're ready."

"For what?" He had an inkling.

"Step out." Grabbing a towel, she dried him, starting at his chest, working her way down, fluffing his cock, then squatting to dry his legs. Finally, she toweled herself off. "On the mattress."

Steam rose from the water, leaving the room humid and warm. He lay flat on the thin bed, cock rising straight up.

"Oh no, not on your back, buddy. Hands and knees."

He chuckled. "You're really putting the screws on, aren't you?" But he rolled to his hands and knees, his cock brushing the sheet, and when he looked up, he was reflected in the mirror on the back of the door. The railing separating the two levels looked like bars over his face.

She rummaged in that canvas bag of hers once more. And came out with a monstrous double-headed dildo.

"Jesus," he swore.

She grinned. "Think you can take it, big boy?"

"I'm not so sure."

She crawled toward him, and even in the mirror's reflection, he detected an unholy glitter in her eye. "Ever had anyone do this to you before?"

Should he lie, let her believe he'd never allowed such a thing? Say yes, but let her think he'd hated it? Or tell her the truth, yes, he'd done it, and hell yes, it was fucking good.

"You're my first."

She bit her lip. Smiled. He'd said just the right thing.

"You are so going to be at my mercy."

He relished her utter concentration in lubing up the toy. "You ever done this to a man?"

Right behind him, she eased a finger down the crease of his ass, oiling him there as well. "No."

"You'll be very careful, won't you?"

She leaned down to nip one cheek of his butt. "I'll be gentle."

The cock ring tightened around him as she tested the fit of his ass with the lightest of probes. Christ. He held his breath, flexed his hands supporting him on the mattress.

"Is it okay, baby?" she purred in his ear.

"Yeah." More. He needed more. Easing back, he let her know he could take it, wanted it.

In the mirror, she held his hip, leaned over, concentrating. Such a fucking incredible sight as her litany of words washed over him. "It's okay, baby, you can do it, you'll love it, I promise."

She no longer punished him or challenged him. She simply took him. He closed his eyes, groaned. She crooned as if she thought she'd hurt him.

His cock swelled, but the ring kept him in check. He rocked, helping her fill him, forcing her to give him more.

Finally, inevitably, she looked up, met his gaze. "That's so good, baby," she whispered as she fucked him. Without the ring, he would have come, whether she touched him or not.

"Christ. Give it to me." He arched and pushed back.

She was right behind him, her head rising above his in the reflection. Then she reached around and stroked his cock in her fist at the same time. He thought he'd die. He needed to come, but couldn't.

"You want this, baby, don't you? You love it." She urged him higher, her voice taking him to the edge.

"Fucking amazing." He could manage only those words, nothing more.

Then he reared back on his haunches, taking the dildo deep, and she was right behind him. He could feel her fist against his ass, holding the toy, keeping it steady for him. Bending slightly to the side, he wrapped his arm around her shoulders, pulled on her hair and dragged her face up for his kiss. He devoured her mouth as she consumed him with the dildo. She rocked her hips against his ass, shoving harder, deeper, faster, until finally she was pounding him, fucking him.

He'd never had anything like it with another woman. Her taste on his lips, the reflection in the mirror, her hand and body an extension of the dildo deep inside him, as if they were one, her, him, the cock between them.

Then she reached around, yanked on the leather ring, sending the snaps flying, releasing him in a mind-altering rush, and he came harder than ever before in his life, until all that existed was the gut-deep explosion, and her voice, her touch, her body wrapped around him.

JOSIE lay cradled in his arms without quite knowing how she got there. His body was sticky with sweat, warm, salty, and he smelled deliciously of come.

In a sort of haze, she remembered him taking care of the dildo, then crawling back to where she lay curled in a ball.

She'd fucked him. That was the only word for it. He'd kissed her, and she'd gone wild. Bracing herself on one hand, she pumped her hips against his ass, the dildo trapped in her fist between them, her body driving it home.

She'd never tasted such power with a man before. She didn't believe it could be duplicated. He'd shouted through his climax, and she'd felt . . . full. She hadn't gotten off herself, yet she'd been closer to him than to anyone ever in her life.

She shuddered with the immensity of it. For one moment, she had been a part of him. She'd watched it in the mirror as the power washed over her, inside her.

No man had ever given her such a gift.

When she bought the dildo, she couldn't have imagined it would be like this.

"Want to get in the tub?" he whispered in her hair.

She didn't want to move or open her eyes. It was too much, too good. If she spoke, she'd destroy the moment. Ruin the memory. If they got in the water, she'd make a joke or laugh, blow it all off as nothing.

Instead she lay in his arms, savored the scent of his sex, put her tongue out to test the saltiness of his skin, and kept the moment alive. Her thighs ached pleasantly, as if she'd had a hard workout. They didn't speak again. He simply stroked her hair with his thumb.

She hadn't subjugated him at all. He'd carried her off with him into some orgasmic never-never land. A part of her wanted to stay there forever.

Not a good feeling to have, not at all. She was letting her emotions get away with her, going deeper. The downward spiral had to stop. She thought about how she could leave without saying anything. Without looking at him. Without admitting how much it had meant. Until his breathing changed and his body relaxed against hers. His foot twitched. His hand fell from her hair. He slept.

It was cowardly, but Josie slowly eased away. God, he was beautiful. His body was perfect, his features strong, the slightest shadow of a beard on his chin, though she hadn't felt it when he kissed her. A shimmer of semen marked his belly. She wanted to lick it off. He lay with one leg bent to accommodate the shortness of the mattress, the other stretched out at an angle, his foot on the decking. An arm rested against the wall.

She rose slowly, then hung on to the rail so she didn't slip on the damp stairs. After dressing quietly, she then grabbed the canvas bag. She'd put her keys and wallet in there. She left the dildo behind for him.

She couldn't talk to him about this now. She needed time to think. She needed to put it in its proper place, give it perspective. It wasn't *that* important. It was just fun. Yes, she needed to get to a place where she saw the act for what it was. Just sex.

Instead of some defining moment of her life.

A phone was ringing. For a moment, he thought he'd fallen asleep at his desk. Then he felt the mattress beneath him, the muggy atmosphere around him, his lassitude, the ache in his muscles, and he remembered everything.

The phone continued while he rose, gathered his equilibrium, then eased down the stairs to answer the insistent ring.

"You have ten minutes left." A disembodied female voice he assumed belonged to the leopard woman.

"Thank you." He hung up, leaned against the wall a long moment.

Where was Josie? The room was empty, her clothes gone. She'd left while he slept.

Climbing the stairs once more, he slid down into the bubbling water. He could afford five minutes before getting dressed. He closed his eyes, and let the heat of the water soothe his muscles. His body ached pleasantly. That was fucking good. More than good. Mind-blowing.

He wished she'd stayed. He wasn't a wham-bam-thank-you-ma'am type. He liked the long minutes afterward as you slowly came down off the high. Besides, he'd wanted to taste her pussy, feel her body shudder when he tipped her into oblivion with his tongue.

She, however, had to maintain the facade of the game. Perhaps she didn't have an inkling how extraordinary it had been. Maybe she didn't even know exactly what she'd given him.

But he knew. For those few moments, when she'd crooned to him, taken him, she'd given herself. He didn't believe Josie Tybrook had ever called a man *baby*. In that moment, she'd lost herself to him. He'd be damned if he'd let her take it back. Because of course, she'd try. He knew that.

He knew something else. He wasn't giving her up for a job. But neither was he giving up the job opportunity Connor Kingston had laid in his lap. He'd ended his marriage five years ago, and ever since, he'd been skimming the surface of life with casual sexual encounters that lasted a few weeks or months. He was ready for the VP slot, but he was also ready for more than a few hot interludes with Josie. He was ready for a relationship, maybe even heading toward a commitment.

He wanted both, the job *and* Josie. Nothing would stop him from getting what he wanted, not even Josie herself.

HE'D given her a piece of himself on Saturday. Josie didn't know what to do with it. She didn't want him to think he'd get a piece of her in return. That was the thing that bothered her.

She didn't have time to think about that right now. The day was blowing up in her face. Lydia was late. The Monday morning project meeting didn't accomplish a damn thing, though at least Ronson was in South America and she didn't have to deal with his sarcasm. Hey, there was a bright spot. But she had three interviews with candidates for the next Program Manager position, and she didn't even have her questions prepared. That was bad, considering she'd never done job interviews before. Not that she couldn't handle it, of course, but she needed some more prep time.

She looked up at the tap on her door frame.

"Got a minute?" Douglas Sarcose headed Human Resources. A tall man with a bushy head of prematurely salt-and-pepper hair, he'd been with Castle for six years. In his early forties and married to a pretty wife Josie had met at company functions, he was father to three primary school–age kids. She'd always found him to be soft-spoken, competent, and fair.

"Sure, come on in." Josie waved him to the chair opposite.

He closed the door. "Great."

Josie liked him. She just didn't like him showing up in her office for an impromptu, closed-door meeting. "Is this about the interviews I've got today?"

"No."

Damn. She didn't know what to say to that. "Okay."

He steepled his fingers and stared at her over them. "Chuck Eastman came to see me this morning."

Her stomach sank straight to her toes. "Was it about Lydia? Because he told me about that, and I had a discussion with Lydia last week regarding her behavior."

"A verbal warning?"

"Well, yes. Since this was the first time anything like this was reported. She said it wouldn't happen again." After she'd pouted and hadn't taken the whole thing as seriously as she should have.

"You didn't send over any notice of a verbal warning to be added to her file."

"Yes. Well. Since it was the first time, I decided it didn't need to be documented."

He breathed in, let it out slowly, his gaze focused. "This isn't the first time."

Shit. "Oh?" She felt, and sounded, like a total idiot.

"If you'd come to me, I would have told you that Ernie had written her up a couple of times for the same kind of behavior with various male personnel."

"Oh."

"Sexual harassment isn't taken lightly around here, Josie."

"I know, but—"

He held up his hand. "I'm not done yet."

She felt like a recalcitrant child.

"Before you make decisions like this, you need to consult me and the employee files. In fact, I'm surprised you haven't already been over to HR to go through all the personnel files. That should have been your first order of business."

"Yes, well, I . . ." Goddammit, she'd fucked up. She wasn't an idiot, but she hadn't thought things through. She hadn't had *time*. Because she was too busy thinking about Kyle. How had she not noticed that Lydia had a sexual harassment problem? She felt totally clueless. Her job did take her out of town a lot, but if you kept your ear to the ground, these things got out. "You're right. I'll take care of that this afternoon." Shit. She thought about all the interviews. "Well, at least by tomorrow."

"Connor told me you're going to a supervisory training course up in the city. Where's your requisition on that? It has to be one of our approved courses."

Dammit. "Oh, sure. Sorry. I'll fill that out and get it up to you. I'm pretty sure it's approved because I remember a Castle contingent attending last year." She'd remembered it and looked up the course on the Internet instead of going to HR.

"I'm not trying to get on your case. I know you've been thrown into this with Ernie being sick. But we are human *resources*. So use us. Ask us for help. You don't have to go it alone. We're in this together." He sounded like a twelve-step program.

"Thanks. I appreciate it."

"And I will have to call Lydia in for a talk."

"Sure. I'll let her know when she gets here."

He raised one brow, but didn't comment.

When he left, she felt like laying her head down on her desk as if it were a chopping block. She'd been dumb, hadn't used her brain. She didn't want anyone else to know she was an idiot, either, so she hadn't gone to HR for a thing. Probably because she wouldn't dream of going to them to complain about someone else. She'd always handled her own problems. If someone got uppity with you, you slammed them down. End of story. Going to HR was the coward's way out.

The problem was, when you became a manager, HR was a fact of life you had to deal with.

All right, lesson learned; she wouldn't cry over spilled milk. And gee, were there any other clichés she could think of?

She grabbed the stack of interview résumés just as her desk phone rang. "Josie Tybrook here."

"We're up shit creek right now." Though he didn't identify himself, she recognized the voice of Todd Adams, Coyote Ridge superintendent.

Her stomach had dropped to her toes with Doug's visit. Now her heart quickly followed. "What's wrong, Todd?"

"We've got less than half a silo of glass sand left, and the covered hoppers are lining up for loading. Gate-to-gate time is in the shitter. And the dryer isn't here yet."

She pinched the bridge of her nose as an ache shot straight to her forehead. They'd sent the drum out on Saturday. It was to receive a special cured coating that would help to retain its heat rather than bleeding it off into the atmosphere during down times. The sand plant ran seven days a week but didn't load on Sundays, and they'd paid the coater a premium to pick up, coat, cure, and reinstall the dryer by Monday at nine. It was now ten.

Why the hell had Todd waited until ten to call her?

"I'll get right on it," she said, "and have an answer back to you in fifteen minutes."

"Fine." He was gone.

She grabbed the Coyote Ridge file, looked up the vendor's number, and dialed. Dammit. This wasn't like her. She should have been on the phone with the coater to verify the delivery the moment she walked in the door this morning. If there was a milestone, she was on it. How could she let this happen? Where was her head?

She knew. It was at the hot tubs with Kyle. It was analyzing her thoughts about him ad nauseam. To the exclusion of everything that was important.

Ten minutes later she was back on the phone with Todd. "There was an accident on southbound 17 causing a nasty backup on the highway, but the truck is about fifteen minutes out now, and the coater has agreed to drop the premium for the weekend service."

"Fine. Great. But why the hell didn't someone call?"

"I should have checked when I first came in. It won't happen again, Todd."

"Good." And again, he was gone without another word.

She deserved the rudeness. Production was king, and her ineptness had just cost them. Granted, she couldn't do anything about an accident on the freeway, but if she'd given Todd a heads-up, he could have rerouted the trucks. She'd *never* had to apologize to a customer for a mistake. What was that principle she'd heard about in some college business course? You were promoted to the level of your incompetency. Good at one thing, you naturally moved up the ladder. Until you failed. That was her, for God's sake.

Okay, okay, calm down. Things weren't that bad.

Then another thought struck like a tanker. Soon Kyle would be calling when he heard what an idiot she was.

KYLE'S flight landed earlier than expected, his rental car ready to pick up, and by ten o'clock Monday morning, he'd been on his way to the first of the sites he was visiting, this one outside of Pleasant Lady, Washington. The plant was a new acquisition for SMG.

He plugged in his hands-free, voice-activated phone and said Connor Kingston's number.

The call went straight through. Kyle identified himself and cut right to the chase. "I'd like to accept the job if we can agree on salary, benefits, and the option package."

They'd already discussed his desired salary range, and Kyle had done his homework on the other executives. Despite the fact that Castle was a family-controlled corporation, there was a fair amount of disclosure in their annual report. As Connor said, their executive pay was industry standard, though in Kyle's opinion it was actually a bit better. For the most part, people stayed at Castle. The last VP of FI&T had moved on only due to family considerations; aging parents back East.

"I'll e-mail you the offer I've come up with." Connor ran down the basics over the phone.

It was exactly as Kyle expected. "Then consider this a verbal acceptance unless I see something unexpected."

"Welcome aboard."

"I'd appreciate it if you'd keep a lid on it until I return on Thursday. I need to let my bosses know, then get out to the Coyote Ridge plant. I want them to hear from me that this isn't going to make any difference to the upgrade."

"Of course. And I'll need a start date, too."

"Done. I'll have that for you on Thursday after I discuss the transition."

"You'll be a great addition to the family."

Family? Did Connor know about Josie? Hell, no. He meant the Castle family, the company, the dynasty. It was going to be good. Kyle had never worked for such a closely held corporation before. He was looking forward to it.

There was one other thing he needed to do before Connor made an announcement. He had to tell Josie. She wasn't going to like it. He was sure she'd fight him every step of the way. He'd be her boss, but he would make her see how well this could work.

It came to him then what his next challenge for her would be. To let him into her house. No hotel rooms or cars or hot tubs, but her house.

When he told her about the job, he didn't want her to be able to run away.

11

JOSIE held out her hand for the woman to shake. "It was a pleasure meeting you. I'll escort you back to HR."

"Thanks. And if you do have any questions, please don't hesitate to call." Bertrice Denton smiled. "I think Castle Heavy Mining would be a great company to work for."

"Thanks. Castle *is* a great company." There, that was noncommittal. Josie didn't want to make promises.

Bertrice was qualified, but a little overly eager. At twenty-eight, she'd been a project assistant, then a project manager in microwave communications. She was pretty, with shoulder-length red hair, but her attire was a tad too sexy. In a man's world, you had to dress down to their level in order to fit in. Josie didn't want any more butt pinching episodes on her watch. Bertrice did have the experience and the college education, and of the three candidates, Josie had interviewed, Bertrice was the pick of the litter.

Outside Douglas Sarcose's door, they shook hands again. "Doug can tell you everything about Castle's benefits package."

Josie's cell phone vibrated as she exited HR. She fished it out of her pocket, then glanced at the number. Oh God, oh God. It was Kyle. He was calling to ream her a new asshole for screwing up the dryer. She wasn't ready. Of all the people in the world, she didn't want Kyle to see her as incompetent.

She couldn't avoid it forever. "Hello," she said, veering off to the lobby doors. She'd rather talk to him outside. In the sun. Away from eavesdroppers.

"You walked out on me while I was sleeping."

It was so not what she expected, she laughed in giddy relief. "That's what women say."

"I've never walked out on a woman while she's sleeping."

Wandering to the picnic tables on the cafeteria side of the building, she wondered briefly how many women he'd been with. "You were too peaceful to wake."

"I'd rather you'd stayed. I wasn't done with you yet." He paused, a laugh filtering through his breath. "I still have that dildo. All clean and tidy. I think we need to use it on you."

"Depends on where you put it." The picnic tables were empty since lunch was long over.

He chuckled. "My turn, I get to use it where I want."

She wondered if she'd like it *there*, but her stomach was churning, and she couldn't put off what was really bothering her. "Did Todd call you?"

"About the dryer? Yeah."

She'd checked; they were up and running now but three hours off schedule. "I'm really sorry for the oversight."

"It was a traffic accident, Josie. I don't think that was your fault unless you were the one who caused the accident."

"I should have checked the status."

He waited a beat before answering. Josie steeled herself for his castigation. "Todd is a big boy, Josie. When he's got a problem, he knows how to dial his own phone, which he did. You're our project manager, not our bumboy."

He was letting her off too easy. Probably since she was fucking him. "I don't want special treatment because we're—"

"Your standards are too high. I'm not displeased with your level of service, and neither is Todd. He called, you acted, crisis over."

"But the lost production time, the gate-to-gate interval—"

"Josie, shut up."

She stopped. Swallowed. Did she feel worse because it was Kyle she'd let down? Or was she maybe, perhaps, likely overreacting? Everything else about her job was taking a beating, so it was possible that she'd gone a tad overboard on this. Whatever the reason, Kyle's words took the bite out of it. Which, come to think of it, was frightening. She didn't want to have to turn to the man for approval of her every move or need him to tell her it was okay—whatever the *it* of the moment happened to be.

"Now, are we done talking about the project?" he asked.

She didn't have any further updates. Everything else was on schedule. "Yes."

"Good. Because I've only got a fifteen-minute break between meetings up here, and I don't want to waste them talking about a problem which is already solved."

"Where are you?" She'd forgotten to ask on Saturday.

"Washington State. I'll be back on Thursday."

Thursday. Three days. She wanted to see him now. Things were definitely escalating, so it was damn lucky he was away.

"We need to talk about our next challenge before I get back."

The sun heated her through. Or maybe it was the idea of their next little playdate.

"It's my turn," he stated when she didn't answer.

Oh. Yeah. She'd gotten her turn at the hot tub. "I realize that." He'd already tied her up, what more could he do? Use the dildo on her?

"And my challenge is that we meet at your house."

She almost dropped the phone. "No."

"Yes."

"I told you we weren't doing it at your place or my place. That's off-limits."

"There was never a limit on the challenge. And mine is that you let me into your house."

"I don't have a house."

"You live with your parents?" Incredulity slipped into his voice.

She snorted. "I have a condo."

"Then we'll meet at your condo."

"The challenge is supposed to be about sex."

"It *is* about sex. You're going to let me fuck the hell out of you in your condo."

She didn't want him in her condo. It was nothing much, and she wasn't so big on expensive furnishings. Some people—like her parents—might consider it pathetic. Letting a man into her space was . . . well . . . "It's not a good idea."

"Afraid to let me come over?"

"I'm not afraid of anything."

"Then accept the challenge."

She drummed her fingers on the picnic table, refusing to answer, thinking.

"You don't accept, you forfeit a turn."

"This isn't fair."

"You made me wear your underwear to work and you fucked me in the ass with a dildo, Josie." He paused to let that sink in. "I think this is an equally fair turnaround."

Dammit. He was pushing, asking for more than she wanted to give. If she said that, he'd simply deny it. She never should have used the dildo on him. Instead of being subjugated, he was thinking it meant some kind of ownership.

"Payback's a bitch," he whispered across the line.

"All right, fine." She would not let him think she was afraid. "But I don't cook, so I'm not making you dinner."

"I'll bring takeout."

"No food. This is just about sex."

"Eating can be a very big part of sex. Besides, you're going to need your strength for what I have planned."

"I'll eat before you get there." Now she sounded childish.

"Have it your way."

"And after this, we institute a new rule. Our homes are *not* part of the challenge."

ONCE is all it would take. He'd fuck her so well, she'd beg him to spend the night.

Kyle realized he was getting cocky. Josie wasn't easy. She wasn't a pushover. He'd have to work double-time for every foothold he got in her life. But he would wear her down. Persistence was his middle name.

The question was whether he should tell her about the job before or after he'd fucked the hell out of her.

KYLE got in late Wednesday night. The trip had been nonstop meetings and inspections at the Washington sites. Everything had checked out perfectly. His job was done.

His first priority on Thursday morning was his resignation. It went well, and Kyle didn't expect any counteroffers. He gave three weeks, but his boss told him it wasn't necessary. So be it. That confirmed that opportunities for his growth at SMG were nil. They agreed on the end of August. Before he left his boss's office, they'd already decided on two candidates for a suitable replacement. He offered his continuing cooperation with any transition. Very civilized. For his successor's benefit, he wrote up detailed trip notes.

With Todd, he needed a face-to-face. They'd worked closely on the retrofit, and he wanted to make sure the man knew he'd still give Coyote Ridge 100 percent support even when he'd moved over to Castle. In Kyle's opinion, it was unethical to jump ship and let Coyote Ridge sink. He wouldn't do that to Todd and Will or their crews. Not that it was possible with Josie on the job. Her consternation over the dryer drum clearly indicated her level of commitment.

He could have sworn she was ready for him to verbally beat her up over it. The woman was a perfectionist.

By the time he made it out to the plant, a hot afternoon wind was blowing across the sand. The fine dust caught in his eyebrows, and he could taste it on his lips. He donned his hard hat and steel-toes before climbing out of the car. The hum of the dozers filled the air as he went in search of Todd. Kyle found him in the weigh master's office.

His first order of business: "How's the dryer?"

Todd's smile was slow to grow, but finally it stretched across his face. "I'm predicting it'll cut our energy bill by a quarter. And when we've got the automatic temperature gauges on the furnace itself"— he whistled long and low—"look out, baby." Todd removed his hard hat. "But you didn't come all the way out here just to ask about the dryer."

"No." Kyle did likewise, setting his hat on the counter. "Let's talk in your office."

Todd had a cramped room the size of a closet at the back of the weigh master's office. Not that its size mattered. He was rarely in it anyway.

Throwing some manuals onto the floor, he cleared a chair for Kyle, then shimmied behind his desk. There was barely enough legroom.

"I wanted to give you personal notice that I'm leaving SMG."

"Fuck." Todd slammed his hard hat down on the desk. An old-fashioned guy, he cleaned his language up around the ladies, but behind closed doors, he let loose.

"That's why I'm here," Kyle went on. "I want you to know I'm still supporting the retrofit. I'll be working for Castle now."

Todd stared, scratched his head. "You're kidding."

"Nope."

"You going to be a project manager over there?"

"Nope. I'll be VP of the group."

"Fuck no." A grin spread across Todd's face. "They shoulda made you fucking VP at SMG. What's-his-face sucks." Todd never called Kyle's boss by his name. He was always what's-his-face or who-the-fuck.

Kyle had to admit there were some good reasons for that. "I'll keep those comments confidential."

Todd smirked. "I don't give a rat's ass if you do or not." The man could definitely be outspoken, which was one of the reasons he hadn't made it beyond plant superintendent. Then again, Todd liked it right where he was. "Seriously, though," he went on, "congrats. I mean that. You deserve it. I'm glad someone's finally giving you your due. They sure as hell didn't appreciate you here." He leaned over, stuck out his hand. "It's been a pleasure working with you."

Kyle didn't want to get into the trials and tribulations of working at SMG. This wasn't a bitch session for him. Instead, he simply shook Todd's hand. "Thanks."

"But I'm all about me-me-me." Todd stretched back in his chair, clasped his hands behind his head. "So who the fuck is taking your place?"

"He's"—meaning their VP—"got some good guys in mind. You're not going to be disappointed."

Todd snorted. "I'll believe that when I see it."

"And with me there, you've got a big in over at Castle. The upgrade will get top priority." With the automated ticketing system, Castle was stepping into new territory, and it behooved both parties to make sure it was a success.

"The chick hasn't been doing so bad."

"Josie's been doing a good job, and you know it."

Todd grinned. "Josie, huh?"

Kyle was sure there'd been no special inflection in his voice. But it was a reminder to be careful in how he spoke about her and to her at Castle. "Yeah. Josie." He raised a brow. "You want me to call her Miss Tybrook?"

"Just screwing with you." Todd rubbed the side of his nose. "She jumped on the dryer quickly enough. I was sort of surprised how responsive she was."

Kyle allowed himself an inner smile. Hell, yes, the woman was responsive, in ways Todd had no clue about. "We'll make a good team, I'm sure. Castle's a good outfit."

"Kingston was all right, too." Todd tipped his head, shook it slowly, regarding Kyle a long moment. "You know, you're really making the right move."

"I believe I am."

"Well"—leaning in, Todd slapped the desk—"if I'd known, we'd have had cake and ice cream for you." Then he stood. "Will's going to want to know all about it." Then he shook his finger like a gnarly old woman. "But don't you think about stealing him away."

"Not my intention."

He spent the rest of the trip glad-handing the well-wishers. He'd worked with them all in one aspect or another, more so than any of his other operations. They were a damn good group. It was the one part of SMG he wasn't glad to leave behind.

An hour later, nitpick details on the upgrade having been discussed, he was back on the road. Josie's turn now.

She answered her cell on the first ring. "Josie Tybrook here."

So professional on the outside. So hot and nasty on the inside. "You didn't leave me your address on my e-mail."

"I expected you to change your mind," she said, a trace of snootiness in her voice.

"Wrong. I've made up my mind. This is what I want."

"Fine." She rattled off her address so quickly he didn't catch it.

"Repeat, please."

She sighed. "I'm in Los Gatos."

This time when she said the address, he got it. When he stopped, he'd punch it into the GPS. "When will you be home?"

She sighed again, heavier this time. "Midnight."

He laughed out loud. "You're an obstinate little bitch, aren't you?" He waited for her to freak out over the term.

"Oh, you have no idea how much of a bitch I can be." Laughter laced her voice, which was preferable to heavy sighing.

There wasn't a woman, or man for that matter, who wasn't capable of being a bitch when the circumstances were right. With Josie, he didn't believe bitchy was her natural state.

But if he wasn't careful, she'd be sure to give him a really good taste, especially after he told her about the job. "Seven sounds better than midnight. That's when I'll be there. You'd better be there, too."

It would be like her not to show up until midnight to teach him a lesson. She was a feisty little thing. He liked that about her.

She snorted. "Any more orders, *master*?"

"Not right now. Wait until later."

"Fine. Over and out."

Oh yeah. He'd have some orders for her all right. He'd make sure she loved every one of them.

EVERYONE thought Los Gatos was ritzy and expensive, and it was, if you lived close to town. Out by the freeway, the houses were quite a bit cheaper, but the neighborhoods were less cutesy, more tract-home type. Still, she liked her condo. In the three years she'd lived there, the trees had grown up, making it feel less like a concrete jungle. With as much as she traveled, her mom couldn't figure out why she even had a place of her own. If she was so about saving money, she could have lived at home. Josie wanted the investment. She wanted to be a homeowner. She *didn't* want to have to come home to her mother.

Her place was your basic two-bedroom, two-bath upstairs and large L-shaped kitchen, dining room, and living area downstairs. She had her own washer and dryer and a gas fireplace. What more could a girl ask for?

As she looked around, though, Josie figured she could have asked for a new sofa. Her mother had given her one from the pool house, and it was showing the wear: a tear in the flower-print arm, one side sinking too deep when you sat. All right, so she wouldn't let Kyle sit. She moved a pillow to mask the hole.

Then she saw every spot on the carpet, every mark on the walls. The condo was clean. She didn't leave junk lying around, but she wasn't a neat freak, either. New carpet and paint were on the list of to-dos, but she hadn't gotten to it. Just as she hadn't found time to put up pictures or paintings. Faith would have made the place cozy, and Trinity would have been the essence of elegance. But she wasn't Faith and she wasn't Trinity.

Jeez, what did she care what some man thought anyway?

The clock caught her eye. Okay, she did have *one* thing on the wall. Good God, it was already six thirty. Grabbing the newel post, she flung herself up the stairs. She had to shower, put on at least a tiny bit of makeup, decide what to wear. She didn't even have anything sexy. Except the stockings he bought her and those frilly girlie panties she'd embarrassed him with. Wait. What about that silk robe Trinity bought her for her birthday? She'd never even taken it out of the box.

Thank God she was a quick change artist. By six fifty-nine, she was showered, dressed, and made-up, even if her hair was still a tad wet. She fluffed it in the bathroom mirror, then rushed into the bedroom for those high heels she had stuffed at the back of the closet. The bell rang just as she was stepping into them.

"Nice," Kyle said when she answered the door.

A bottle in his hand, he stood in the recessed stoop surrounded by a few potted plants that she actually did remember to water. His eyes traveled the lapel of her robe, the opening stretching all the way down to her navel. Though at that point, only a sliver of flesh was revealed. With the flare of heat in his gaze, her nipples peaked against the silky fabric.

Circling his fingers in the air, he indicated she should turn. She gave him a full three-sixty view of the short, white silk robe that barely covered her ass, and the seam of the fishnets down the backs of her legs.

"You dress up nice."

It was his tone, not so much the words, that heated her. She liked the little things he said to her. "Thanks." Stepping back, she let him in, closed the door.

"Nice place," he said after a cursory look around.

"It is not nice. It's adequate and needs work, but whatever."

He turned, tipped his head. "Why don't you accept compliments?"

She huffed out an answering breath. "You said I dress up nice. I accepted that."

"Yes, but—"

"Is that champagne?" She shut him up by pointing to the bottle in his hand. Really, she didn't want to get into some bizarre discussion right now. She was nervous enough that she'd let him into her house.

"Yeah, champagne. Already chilled." Allowing himself to be distracted, he held it up.

She liked that he'd chosen something middle of the road, not terribly expensive, but not cheap either. "How thoughtful." She noted that he'd taken her at her word and hadn't brought takeout.

"I don't figure you for a champagne girl in the main, but I determined this to be a special occasion."

Because she let him come to her house? That was a comment best not acknowledged. "I even have some champagne glasses around here somewhere." Trinity did love her champagne cocktails, so Josie kept the glasses on hand.

Her high heels tapped on the linoleum kitchen floor as he popped the cork behind her.

"Another nice view," he murmured as she reached for two flutes on the top shelf.

"Don't let it foam over," she said, glancing over her shoulder. She loved his understated compliments.

He held the bottle aloft. "Perfect job." Taking the first glass, he tipped it to the side, pouring slowly, expertly, without creating a head. "My ex loved champagne," he offered when she raised a brow.

Somewhere along the way, she remembered he had said he was divorced. Five years ago, or something close to that.

He traded glasses with her and filled the second one, then set the bottle on the counter. Tapping his glass to hers, he saluted. "Here's to a gorgeous, hot, sexy woman."

She smiled and sipped, unsure what to say to that. Compliment him back maybe?

"And here's to the new job I've accepted." He didn't drink, waiting for her reaction.

Her stomach plunged. A new job? She wouldn't see him anymore. "What about the project?"

"Todd is your main contact now anyway." His gaze remained unreadable.

"Oh. Well. Todd's great." She sipped cautiously. "Where are you going?" It wasn't her business. He could be moving away. But if he wasn't . . . Where moments before her stomach had dropped to her toes, her heart now started to beat faster. Seeing him wouldn't be mixing business and pleasure anymore. She could actually call him up and tell him to meet her for a lunch quickie. Or after work. Anytime. No restrictions. No fear that someone might figure out her latest fuck buddy was also her lead project contact. Wow.

She was so busy thinking about all the possibilities that it was a few moments before she realized he was staring at her intently. He hadn't answered her question.

She took a step back. "What?"

"Connor offered me VP of FI&T at Castle."

Horror washed over her, goose bumps pimpling her arms beneath the silk. "You're not taking it, right?"

He blinked. "I've already accepted."

"But—" She stopped herself right there. She would *not* tell him she didn't want him to take the job. She wouldn't even ask why he hadn't discussed it with her first. They were booty buddies, playmates. He didn't owe her anything. She didn't *want* anything. Yet she couldn't help the anger bubbling up. "So tonight was one last fuck for the road before you told me?"

He set his champagne on the counter. "I did just tell you. *Before* I fucked you."

"Well, good." Dammit it all to hell. "I'm glad. Because I'm not fucking my boss."

"I'm not your boss yet."

Hands on his hips, he was blocking the way out of the kitchen. She turned in a tight circle, barely restraining herself from slamming the stem of her glass onto the countertop. Instead, she set it down very, very carefully.

"When did you know about this?" Connor hadn't said a word to her about a job offer. But he had asked a couple of times what she'd thought of Kyle.

"I had lunch with him last week."

That lunch. She'd wondered why Connor was meeting with him. "So you knew on Saturday."

"I had an offer, but I hadn't made the decision."

Why did it feel like betrayal? For God's sake, why did it *hurt*? "Oh, so then Saturday was the last fuck. And what was tonight supposed to be?"

His nostrils flared slightly. She was starting to piss him off. Good. Because she was pissed.

"I have no intention of letting tonight or Saturday be the last time."

"Oh, *you* don't. What about my intentions?" She tried to step around him, and the heel of her shoe caught on the edge of the carpet. She pushed past, kicked the damned high heels off, then turned on him in the center of her living room. "I am not fucking my boss. And that's that."

It was bad enough that Ronson—and everyone else, for that

matter—thought she'd gotten the manager job because she was family. She would not, under any circumstances, let it be said that she kept it because she was doing Kyle.

"May I remind you," he said, "that I haven't actually fucked you yet."

Semantics, dammit. "Well, now you won't get to."

He breathed in, deeply, as if striving for patience. "No one has to know. We can be as careful as we are now."

"That is *not* acceptable." He was crazy. "People *always* figure it out."

"We are not ending this just because of a job."

Who the hell did he think he was? "Then maybe you need to tell Connor you're not taking it." Jesus God. She didn't mean that. Okay, she didn't mean to *say* it. She opened her mouth to take it back, but once it was out, it was out.

"I want this job. I want you. We'll have both."

"That," she said, turning and heading to the stairs, "is the dumbest thing I've ever heard." She grabbed the railing. "This is *my* career, *my* company. I will not jeopardize it for a simple fuck."

God, she had to get out of this stupid outfit. She needed real clothes, not sexy bedroom things which put her at a disadvantage. She bounded up the stairs.

He followed. She should have known he would. Kyle wasn't about to let it go. He wanted to win.

But she needed to. Because she was the one with the most to lose.

12

AT the top of the stairs, Kyle grabbed her arm, hauling her around to face him. "This isn't a simple fuck."

Josie shoved her hair out of her face. "It's just a game." Her breath puffed after her sprint up the stairs.

All right, he should have done her first, then told her during postcoital bliss. But he'd been thinking about it on the drive over and not telling her right away seemed like deceit. On Saturday, his decision had yet to be made, but tonight, he'd already committed himself to Castle Heavy Mining.

He leaned down, in her face, his voice low. "Saturday was more than a game. It was fucking fantastic. I know it. You know it. Admit it." He wasn't giving her up.

She backed up against the wall by the bedroom door. The tie of her robe came loose. All that gorgeous skin beckoned. He could barely keep from touching far more than her arm.

"As I recall," she said, her smile taunting, "I didn't even come."

"And it was fucking hot without the orgasm, wasn't it?" He damn well knew he was right.

Her breasts rose and fell with her quickened breath, and she pushed back at him, ignoring what he said and cutting right to the quick. "I will not fuck my boss. I won't have an affair with my boss. I will never give my boss that kind of control over me."

That was it. She figured that if they had a personal relationship, he'd use it against her in the business arena. "Two separate things."

"*Not* two separate things." She put two fingers to his chest and shoved. He didn't move. "Get out of my house. Because if you don't, I'll sue my *boss* for sexual harassment."

Her anger was a living, breathing thing that seethed in the air around them. He hadn't figured on that. He'd only imagined a little cajoling, some gentle convincing. It was going to take a helluva lot more than that. "So sue me," he whispered.

Don't do it. Don't touch her, a voice in his head shouted at him. He ignored it. Capturing her chin, he took her mouth, kissed her hard, forcing her lips apart. Then he trapped her against the wall with his body, bracing himself with both hands beside her head.

She bit his lip, lightly, not enough to hurt, just a warning. He took her deeper. Sliding his hands down to her bottom, he lifted her, rocked his hard dick against her. She squirmed, her throaty little noises filling his head. He left her mouth to bite down on the side of her neck, sucking her skin. She could have stopped him then, said something, kicked him, anything. Instead she tunneled her fingers beneath his belt, flexing them against the crest of his ass.

He dropped a hand to take her nipple between his fingers. "You want this."

She gasped, arched into his touch. "Fuck you."

Her body said it all. "Tell me how badly you need it." He wanted the words. He wanted her to remember in the middle of the night. He wanted her to know exactly what she'd be missing if she turned him away.

"I don't need a damn thing from you." Yet she raised one leg, curled it around his thigh, and rode the ridge of his cock between her spread legs.

Grabbing her by the butt cheeks, he hauled her higher, pulled both her legs to his waist, and pumped against her. "You're dying to have me inside you." Christ, he needed to be inside her in the worst way. They'd played too long, too many times, now he'd go completely nuts if he didn't get inside her.

She clasped him closer. "My vibrator's just as good and hard."

He pulled away from the wall, taking her with him, turned and went down to the hall carpet, laying her flat on her back. "Your vibrator can't do this."

He would force her to see what they'd be missing if she shut him out.

Stroking the silk robe aside, he took her nipple in his mouth, tunneling into her panties at the same time. She was wet, hot, pulsing, and she dug her fingers into his scalp as he nipped the pearl of her breast.

"It vibrates harder and faster than you can," she taunted.

He crawled down between her legs to find her pussy encased in the frilly panties she'd had him buy. They weren't her at all. She was naughty, sexy, green satin and long, long legs. He tore them off and tossed them over the banister.

"You're dying for me to lick you." Her scent surrounded him, her taste beckoned.

"Let me get my vibrator, and we'll compare again. You'll lose this time."

He flicked her little button with his tongue, then sucked her into his mouth.

She made a noise, a hot little sound that was half moan, half groan, all woman. "Fine. Whatever," she said, a hitch in her voice. "You want to get me off, fine. It's not like I'll be throwing my vibrator out or anything."

Yet she writhed against his mouth, shoved her fingers through his hair, and hung on. He sucked, licked, took her pussy with his tongue. He'd make her beg, scream. The tremors started in her legs, rode up her torso. She released one hank of his hair and clenched a fist around a stair rail. Her body rocked in time with his tongue. When she let loose, she wailed. He loved the sound, kept at her until she rolled to her side, tried to shove him away and close her legs against him.

Kyle wasn't having it. He sank his fingers into her hips and held her body to his mouth. Josie thought she'd die. The orgasm went on and on until she couldn't tell where her pussy ended and his mouth began. So good. So bad. Too much.

"Please. Stop. God." She put both hands to her mouth and hiccupped.

At last, he relented. She was aware of him shoving a hand into his pocket, retrieving something, a condom packet. Rolling to her stomach, she pulled her knees beneath her, heading for her bedroom.

"Oh no you don't." He was on her, pulling her beneath him, forcing her to her back, facing him. His blue eyes glittered. "I'm going to fuck you, and you're going to look at me while I do it."

She wanted it. Wanted him. Yet she couldn't cave in and let him win. "No."

Braced above her on one hand, he met her gaze for one long moment. Her stockings were halfway down her thighs, she'd lost the panties, and only one arm remained in her robe. He was still completely clothed.

"No means no," he whispered.

God no. No meant yes. At least this time.

Please, don't stop. Do it. Take me. Just don't make me say it.

He read everything in her eyes. "Oh no, sweetheart, you have to say it."

She didn't want to capitulate. She wanted to be able to throw it all back at him when it was over. "If you're going to do it, just do it. I can't stop you anyway."

His eyes traveled her face, landed on her lips, then trailed back up to meet her gaze. "That's too easy. Tell me yes or tell me no, but mean it."

She didn't want to choose. "Why do you have to get all chivalrous now? It's *your* challenge. I have to do whatever you want."

"My challenge is that *you* make the choice."

"Damn you." She couldn't think. He stole her breath. Her body clamored for him. One fantastic orgasm wasn't enough. Her pussy craved him, his cock, everything.

He waited.

She let her breath out in a whoosh. "All right, fuck me."

"You could be a little more romantic."

"I am *not* romantic."

He came down flush on top of her and put his mouth to hers. Gentle. Sweet. He took just her lips, licking, kissing, tasting, angling his head one way, then the other. Long, slow, infinitely sweet, achingly hot. His shirt caressed her breasts, his pants stroked between her thighs. She sifted her fingers through his hair and held him to her.

It was too goddamn romantic. She didn't kiss like that. Didn't want to need it, didn't want to like it, love it, or want it.

She just needed to get it over before it started to mean something. "Fuck me now," she whispered against his mouth.

He pulled back, his gaze shifting over her. He had such damn beautiful eyes. Then he went back on his haunches, unzipped his pants, and rolled on the condom.

Coming down on top of her once again, he stroked the head of his cock from her pussy to her clitoris. "Is this what you want?"

"Yes."

He eased in an inch. "Tell me how good it feels."

Amazing. Momentous. Beautiful. "It's fine."

In. Out. With short bursts of his hips. His eyes on hers. "Perfect."

"Okay." The best ever. He was big, his tip filling her.

"Want more?"

Why couldn't the man just do it, like every other man? "More, please."

He gave her another couple of inches. It wasn't enough. Her hands over her head, she stretched, rose to meet him. "Take me," she murmured.

Holding her hips, he drove all the way home. She cried out, it was so damn good. Everything about him was so damn good.

"Love it?" he asked.

"Like it," she conceded.

He began to pump. She spread her legs wider, wrapped her thighs around his butt and clasped her ankles. He put a hand beneath her and angled her higher. With every thrust, his body rubbed her clit.

Oh God. Oh God. So good.

"Just good?"

Damn, she'd said that aloud. "Good is a damn good fucking word." She wanted this. She wanted him. Climbing higher, reaching for that pinnacle, finding it, and tossing herself off the other side, she knew only one thing.

He was too damn good to give up. Even if he was going to be her boss.

Oh God. She was totally screwed.

KYLE took off half of Monday morning from SMG to attend Connor Kingston's staff meeting. It was his introduction to the management team. Due to his work with Castle on the Coyote Ridge project, most of the executives were familiar to him. All good men, in his opinion. He knew that Josie wanted to be the first female VP. He had no doubt she'd make it, too. A more determined career woman he'd never met.

Right after the exec staff, Connor called a brief meeting of the FI&T group. At most companies, they'd send out an e-mail announcing a new hire with a few details on his or her background. Not so at Castle. Kyle was now part of the family.

Fifteen or so people crammed the conference room. "Several of you have already met Kyle through the SMG project." Connor gave an obligatory nod at Josie and the other department heads he'd dealt with. "He comes to us with several years of experience in the mining industry, bringing a unique hands-on perspective to how our equipment works in the field. We'll save all the introductions for next week, when he starts officially." Then he turned the floor over to Kyle.

"I'm excited to be joining Castle. It's a solid company, and I look forward to working with all of you. Over the first few days, I'll be meeting with all department heads to get fully on board with the workings of the group." Short and sweet. "Any questions I can answer now?"

Leaning against the wall by the door, not a single muscle twitched on Josie's face. She'd been polite but nothing more. He hadn't seen her since that cataclysmic event in her upstairs hall. Their next date was hers to plan, hers to challenge, and though he'd wanted to see her that weekend, she'd refused, insisting they wait the requisite week. She wasn't about to allow him an extra foothold, but at least she hadn't ended their relationship entirely. Despite himself, he was looking forward to whatever she threw at him next.

A dark-haired girl raised her hand. Young, mid-twenties, long hair, a pretty smile. Kyle gave her a nod.

"How are you on granting extra personal time if someone's already used theirs up?"

Josie jumped in. "Lydia, that's between you and your manager. *And* on a case-by-case basis." She was polite, yet a slight thread of annoyance ran through her voice. He figured Josie was Lydia's supervisor.

"Thank you, Josie." Then he turned to Lydia. "She's hit the nail on the head. I wouldn't get between a supervisor and an employee unless some mediation was needed."

The girl merely grimaced and subsided back into her chair.

"Anyone else?"

He had four basic areas of control: subcontract purchasing, instructors, installers, and program management. Josie's department was key in bringing all the other groups together, controlling the timeline and the milestones. She'd get the most recognition if things went well, and the most grief if everything tanked.

He was just about to wrap it up.

A tall guy, big enough to have been a wrestler in a past life, raised his hand. Kyle gave him a nod.

"How are you on sexual harassment?"

Josie sighed, shook her head, but said nothing.

Kyle maintained his expression. "I suggest you use your current company policy as your reference point on that."

What he planned with Josie was not sexual harassment. It was mutual. But was the guy implying something? It wasn't possible he could know about their affair.

"As you well know," Connor said, "we have policies, Chuck." Oddly enough, he turned to encompass the girl Lydia in the look. "And we have zero tolerance." Then he glanced around the group at large. "People, these questions are too specific for this forum. If you've got real problems here, I have an open door policy. Come see me."

Both Chuck and Lydia's questions were out of line for the situation. It gave Kyle pause. What had he gotten himself into?

JOSIE set her notepad on her desk, holding it down with one finger as if it were a snake that might crawl away. Her eyes closed, she breathed in deeply, out.

What a disaster. Lydia had asked about personal time, which most likely had something to do with why she was late twice last week, then again this morning, slipping into the meeting as if she didn't think anyone would notice. Then Chuck made that remark about sexual harassment. She was surprised he hadn't come right out and said Lydia pinched his ass.

What were they thinking?

What the hell would Kyle be thinking?

She and Kyle were not committing sexual harassment. They were doing something else; she just wasn't sure what that was. But her life did feel as if it were spiraling out of control. Instead of paying attention to the meeting, she'd been thinking about his hands on her, his cock inside her, his tongue shooting her to the stars. He was going to be her boss, for God's sake. She had to at least stop craving his touch while they were at work. She had to practice that, master it.

"What was that all about?"

Despite her jumble of thoughts, she didn't even jump. She knew eventually Connor would come looking for her, after he'd shown his soon-to-be VP out the door.

She turned, stepped around him, closed the door. "Did Douglas talk to you about Chuck and Lydia?"

"Yes. I thought the problem was resolved."

"It is for now. Lydia's been written up. But Chuck's still pissy." In fact, they were both still pissy. "I believe he said that in the meeting to get Lydia's goat because he doesn't think she's taking it seriously enough." She waited for Connor to say none of this would have happened under Ernie's regime.

"Josie, these are just growing pains. It's always more difficult when someone from within is promoted to manage the group rather than the new manager coming from the outside. Especially with Ernie going the way he did. Emotions are high."

He was making goddamn excuses for her. She wanted to scream. The worst was that Kyle had seen the shenanigans, too. They'd humiliated her in front of him. Maybe they'd done it on purpose. The thought only now occurred to her.

She wouldn't voice it to Connor. "You're right. Things will settle down. I've got the new hire starting next week, then we won't feel so overloaded. I believe Bertrice will work out."

Connor put his hand on her shoulder. "I have faith in you, Josie."

If she were a different person, she'd be choked up at the sentiment. Instead, she laughed. "You've got plenty of faith." Her cheeks colored as she suddenly heard the double entendre. God. "I mean, speaking of Faith, your wife insists I meet her and Trinity at the bridal shop at four thirty this afternoon. May I request half an hour's worth of personal time?" There, she'd made light of Lydia's silly comment.

He gave her a drop-dead wicked smile. "I'll have to look at

your personnel file and make sure you haven't been taking too much personal time, but otherwise, I approve the half hour off."

She saluted. "Thank you, sir."

He jutted his chin and stared her down. "And do not take my wife out drinking afterward."

"You're dying for me to drop her off tipsy and you know it." Faith had mentioned that she got frisky when she was tipsy.

Connor winked and was gone. She didn't envy them marriage and children, but their devotion never failed to make her feel a little gooey, as Trinity so eloquently put it.

All right, she had to deal with Lydia and her tardiness problem before it became chronic. Josie was headed for the door just as her cell phone rang.

She knew it was Kyle, as if she now had radar where he was concerned.

"Is there something I need to know about your department?" he asked as soon as she'd identified herself.

Damn them both. She closed her door. "Lydia and Chuck are having a little spat. Nothing I can't handle." Right. She was handling the whole department so well. At least Ronson wasn't there to further humiliate her. She was sure he would have gotten in his licks if he was.

"Are they sleeping together?"

She laughed. Although maybe under the circumstances, that wasn't so laughable. "No." She told him about the ass pinching.

"You're kidding, right?"

"I wish I were. I think Lydia's learned her lesson, though. She can't get away with something just because she's a woman."

She wondered if she should tell him about Ronson's reverse discrimination threat, then decided against it. She didn't believe Ronson would do it; he was just pissed right now. By the time he returned from South America next week, he'd be fine.

"Well, it's certainly going to be fun over there at Castle."

"Oh yeah, we're just a barrel of laughs."

"Have dinner with me."

He switched so fast, she could barely keep up. "Tonight?"

"Yes, tonight."

"I have a date."

He paused. A very long pause. "With whom?"

They didn't have a relationship, but she didn't see any reason in letting him think she had a date with another man. "My friends Faith and Trinity."

"Is that Faith Kingston?"

"Yeah. Connor's wife. My cousin."

"All in the family," he murmured. "Tomorrow night, then."

"Tomorrow is not Friday. Our next date is on Friday." It wasn't really a date. It was sex. That was all. She had to keep this thing in perspective, no matter how well he fucked.

"What happened to Thursday? Our last date was a Thursday."

"And I want Friday. I have something special planned." Actually, she didn't have even an inkling of a plan. But so what? He'd conned her into agreeing to a continuation of their little games despite the fact that he would soon be her boss. There was no way she could see him every day and resist. But that didn't mean she had to roll over and let him control *everything*. "So it's Friday or nothing."

"All right, Friday. What are we doing?"

"That's on a need-to-know basis only. You don't have a need to know yet." Then she realized she was doing this all on work time, when she should be taking Lydia to task yet again. "This is not a business call. You have to wait until after five."

"It is a business call. I needed to know what that was all about in the meeting today."

"We've passed that now and have moved into personal."

He started to say something, and she heard the telltale silence indicating he had another call coming in. "I'll let you go," she said

"It's only Kisa. I'll call her back when we're done."

"Ooh, Kisa," she cooed. "You'd better take it. She might be offering herself to you now that you won't be working at SMG anymore."

He gave a definite snort. "You're jealous."

"Of course I'm not." She liked to tease him, that was all.

"You'd freak if I really asked her out."

"It wouldn't bother me in the least." Of course it wouldn't. She and Kyle weren't boyfriend and girlfriend. They'd never put any ties on each other. Except for the night he'd tied her up. If she had any emotions about Little Miss Snowflake, they were simply that the girl was so obvious.

"You're trying to sidetrack me from the real issue here," she went on. "No personal business during work hours. Those are the rules." She could not allow him to call her up any time, especially once he was actually working at Castle. That would be a disaster. Eventually someone would overhear. "Business only during business hours. Got that?"

"Loud and clear. You're a hard woman."

"Actually," she couldn't resist, "you're a hard man. Now go talk to Little Miss Snowflake." She cut the call before he could say another word and set her phone on the desk. That's when her diabolical plan started to take root. What if her next challenge wasn't about her at all? What if it was about the naughty Little Miss Snowflake? What if she challenged him to ask the girl out?

There were two advantages to that. First, it would prove to Kyle that she wasn't jealous. Second, it would state unequivocally that they didn't have a relationship per se. After all, they were just . . . fuck buddies. There was a third advantage, too. If she decided she wanted to see one of her other friends, well, the stage would already be set. He couldn't get all huffy and dictatorial with her. It was a great plan. Totally brilliant.

Except if he decided he wanted to see Little Miss Snowflake on a regular basis. Or if he fell in love with her and chose to see her exclusively.

Dammit. She'd hung up on Kyle because they weren't talking business and here she was mooning over him and Little Miss Snowflake. Work. That's what she needed. She opened her door. "Lydia, we need to talk."

Lydia dragged her feet as if she had a ball and chain attached. "What now?" she whined.

She'd never noticed Lydia was such a whiner. Maybe she hadn't been, not for Ernie. Josie herself might be the one who brought it out in her. Dammit, she was still pissed that the girl had humiliated her with such a stupid question in Kyle's introductory meeting.

Lydia closed the office door behind her—at least she didn't slam it—and flopped onto the chair. "If this is about Chuck, I apologized and told him I'd never do anything like it again. I didn't even say he was a prima donna, either. So I don't know why he had to go and bring it up in the meeting." Lydia's eyes were red-rimmed, as if she'd been crying. Maybe she really had learned her lesson.

About the pinching anyway. "I didn't want to talk about that. I wanted to discuss why you were late this morning. And last week, too. That's not like you."

Lydia's lip trembled, and her hands suddenly became of the utmost importance. "I . . . well . . . it's just that . . ." She burst into tears. Horrible, great sobs. Lydia never did anything quietly.

"I'm not going to write you up again, Lydia." Oh jeez. Josie wanted to roll her eyes, but resisted. "I just wanted to talk about it. If there's a problem."

The girl hiccupped, gasped, and wiped at her eyes, which only smeared her mascara all over. "I'm pregnant."

Total paralysis. Physical and mental. If there'd been an earthquake, Josie would simply have sat on her ass right through it. It wasn't shocking that an unmarried twenty-five-year-old woman was pregnant. It was shocking that Lydia would tell *her*, and look at Josie as if she expected her to do something about it.

Finally, *finally*, Josie found her voice. "I really don't know what to say to that, Lydia." Didn't she have a best friend to tell? Or a mother? A father? Anyone? Gee, how about the boyfriend who'd knocked her up?

Josie hadn't known Lydia was even seeing someone. For a person who didn't mind sharing intimate details about her life, Lydia had been oddly mum on that subject.

"He's married," she whispered.

"Oh no." A horrible thought occurred. "It's not Chuck, is it?" Or, good God, Ronson?

Lydia managed a disgusted yet tear-streaked face. "Of course not."

"It's not someone you work with?" Please, please don't let it be.

She shook her head. "He's a friend of my brother's." She sniffed, swiped at her eyes. "Do you have any tissues?"

Josie started to shake her head, but Lydia pointed to the right side of the desk. "Ernie kept a box in the bottom drawer."

She cried to Ernie a lot? Josie opened the drawer. Sure enough, there at the back, behind the hanging folders so that Josie had missed it, was a box of tissues. Half empty. She handed it to Lydia.

"Thanks." She blew hard, pulled out a couple more, wiped beneath her eyes. "She treats him like total crap, won't have sex with him, calls him a dirty rotten bastard all the time. But they've got two little kids, and he's not going to get a divorce."

Oh gee, what a story.

Lydia gauged the look. "I know you think that's what all married men say to get a girl to sleep with him, but honestly, I know that's what she's like. He used to talk about it with my brother, before, you know"—she dipped her head, sniffed again—"we did it."

Josie sighed. "So what does he say?"

Lydia's mouth drooped. "I haven't told him yet. I only just peed on the stick last week. And it's been hard just getting out of bed every morning." Hence her tardiness. "I don't know what to do." She glanced at Josie.

Don't look at me. Thank God she managed to trap *that* thought inside. She had no idea this was what being a manager was all about. People had all sorts of shit they wanted to dump on you. The box of tissues in Ernie's desk was evidence of that. She thought of all the crap he was probably having to deal with while knowing he was dying. Her appreciation for him rose, as did her guilt. She hadn't given the guy his due. She didn't think Ernie would have looked at Lydia and told her to handle her own problems, don't bring them to work, yadda yadda. Oh no, Ernie would have shown compassion.

Josie wasn't sure she knew the meaning of the word. "Maybe you need to talk to a professional. You know, they have this program here where you can call a counselor. It's all confidential and everything." Josie remembered getting a flyer about it. What the hell was the program called? She could get the info from HR.

"What would *you* do?" Hope glimmered in Lydia's eyes.

"Do?" For a moment, Josie didn't even understand the question. Or rather, her brain simply stopped functioning.

"Yeah. Would you have the baby? Keep it? Give it up for adoption? Get an abortion?"

She felt the quagmire sucking her down. "I'm not equipped to advise you."

"I don't want advice, Josie. I just want to know what you'd do."

"I . . . well . . ." She sounded like Lydia when the girl first sat down. "I wouldn't have gotten pregnant in the first place." It didn't sound holier than thou. It simply sounded stupid.

"No. You'd never make a mistake."

Was that sarcasm in there? Josie wasn't sure. "I make lots of mistakes, Lydia." She took a breath. "But if it did happen to me, I don't know what I'd do. Honestly."

Lydia lifted her chin, swallowed.

"So I really think you need to talk to someone impartial, who's not going to judge you or tell you what *they* think you should do or want you to do. Because whatever you do has to be your decision since you'll have to live with it the rest of your life."

Yeah. Talk to someone else, not me. I'm like Pontius Pilate washing my hands.

But honestly, she couldn't offer a single ounce of advice. Even if she'd simply been Lydia's coworker instead of her boss, she wouldn't have known what to say.

"So would you like me to find the number for that counselor program?" she offered, knowing it wasn't enough.

Lydia slowly shook her head. "No." She patted the tissue beneath her eyes, managing to get most of the wayward mascara, then dabbed at her nose. After one last sniff, she went on. "I think I know exactly who to talk to." Rising from the chair, she put the box of tissues on the desk. "Thanks." When she disappeared through the door, she looked almost like herself again.

Josie laid her head on her desk, closed her eyes, breathed deeply. What the hell was Lydia thanking her for? She hadn't been able to offer a single word of good advice.

God, she so sucked at being a manager.

13

BRIDAL shops made Josie nervous, almost as much as babies did. There was all that shocking white, the satin, silk, and lace, the gauzy material, the beadwork, frills, and flounces, everything so girlie. Not to mention the estrogen overload.

Trinity didn't have a dressing room, she had a dressing *area*, surrounded by mirrors and lush cream carpeting. There was not one salesclerk, but two. They'd brought out the silver coffeepot and bone china cups, the tea cakes and the shortbread cookies. Everyone—except Trinity—perched on little round chairs with wrought iron backs. Verna poured. The closest thing Trinity had to a mother since her own had passed, Verna worked for Trinity's father as his secretary. In her mid-fifties, with hair a silver-gray, Verna had been with Trinity's family company since her twenties. She'd watched Trinity grow up and seen her through the trials and tribulations of her divorce. Now she could finally see Trinity happy.

Verna handed Faith the first cup, then poured one for Josie. Faith had left the baby with the sitter. While she loved the little guy dearly, she wasn't one of those mothers who couldn't let her baby out of her sight. She insisted that at least once a month she and Connor have "date night."

Pretty, blonde, and blue-eyed, Trinity turned on the dais before the three angled mirrors and smoothed the satin dress over her butt. "Does my behind look big?"

Josie almost snorted her coffee out her nose. "Your butt could not possibly look big." True, Trinity had stopped being such a fussy eater, but she was by no means big in any way.

The satin draped her perfect figure, falling in elegant rivulets to pool on the carpet. The form-fitting bodice gave her cleavage and showcased her tiny waist.

"It's very elegant, Trin." Faith's bone china cup clinked on her saucer.

With the wedding in April, Josie still thought it was way too early for the whole shopping folderol, but Trinity was in her element. She was in Love with a capital L. Scott was a great guy, even if he was a little older than Trinity. Okay, a lot older, like fifteen years. He had two college-age daughters, for God's sake. They'd be in the wedding party also, which meant another shopping extravaganza for the bridesmaid dresses. Jeez, getting five women to agree on something that major . . . It didn't bear thinking about.

Josie's fiasco of a day didn't bear thinking about either, but one bad thought breeds another, and there it was in the front of her mind. First the meeting, then that disastrous conversation with Lydia. And the way the job she'd loved had suddenly started to suck.

"Are you all right?" Faith set her cup and saucer on the table.

"I'm fine." Except for the panic attack that suddenly threatened. And she was *not* the panic attack type. "Why?"

"You looked like you were about to choke."

God. Now her turmoil was starting to show on her face. "Work stuff."

Faith tipped her head, her hair falling across her shoulders, shining with natural highlights of gold and red. Her eyes round, her voice hushed, she said, "You *never* have work stuff bothering you. Not ever."

Faith was more intuitive than Josie had given her credit for. "Being a manager isn't as fun as I thought it would be."

"What's wrong?"

"People."

"Yeah." In the midst of stripping down for another dress to try on, Trinity stopped to add her two cents. "If we didn't have to supervise people, the job would be so much easier."

Trinity got her first job at the beginning of the year, Accounts Receivable Supervisor working for her father. She'd had one helluva time in the beginning. Josie remembered hours of consultation over dinners at Vatovola's, Trinity's favorite restaurant.

Verna nibbled on a shortbread biscuit. "So what's gone wrong?"

Josie didn't know Verna well. Trinity and Faith would forgive her idiocy, but she wasn't so sure about Verna's reaction. Of course, the salesladies would hear, too.

What the hell, she needed advice. Or at least to talk her thoughts out before they drove her nutzoid rumbling around inside her own head.

"The whole thing went to crap the very first day Connor promoted me." As Trinity got herself strapped into another wedding gown, Josie gave them the rundown, from Ernie and Ronson, to Chuck and Lydia, minus any names, of course. She even included how she screwed up getting the dryer back out to Coyote Ridge.

When she was done, Josie leaned forward on her chair. "You know, Trinity, I owe you a big apology."

Trinity sucked in her stomach and smoothed the dress over her breasts, gazing at her reflection. "Whatever for, hon?"

"I didn't take your problems with Inga Rice seriously." Inga was one of Trinity's employees. "I thought you were making a mountain out of a molehill, but now, when I'm faced with the same kind of crap, I realize I did you a misdeed."

Hands on her hips, Trinity gave one of her pretty musical laughs. "Besides Faith, you're the only person I know who would apologize for a teeny-tiny thing you thought *months* ago. Especially when you didn't even say it out loud."

"And we never would have known if you hadn't just told us," Faith added.

Verna nodded. "That Inga can be a real bitch."

"Besides, what you told me to do back then was right," Trinity went on.

"What did I say?"

"I can't remember, but whatever it was, it was right."

They all laughed.

"So here's what you should do." Trinity sucked in a breath when the helper girls got the last of the seed pearls done up. "This one isn't going to work." She grinned at them all in the mirror. "I don't think Scott'll have the patience to get all these teeny-tiny pearls undone," she whispered loudly.

Kyle would have all the patience. He was into teasing, keeping her on edge. Dammit, she needed to stay focused. She needed her friends' advice.

"Okay, where was I?" Trinity flapped her hand. "Slam down the guy making you miserable because you got the job."

"I did. I just don't think I've heard the last of it yet."

"Then that's all you can do," Verna said. "He'll either stay or he'll quit, or if he goes too far, you'll have to fire him, but you can't let him get to you." She smiled. "I do know that's easier said than done."

"Have you talked to Connor about all this?" Faith asked.

"He knows some of it, like the sexual harassment thing, but not the rest. And don't tell him, okay? I don't want him to think I'm a total screwup."

Faith zipped her lip. "You know what happens in Vegas stays in Vegas," she quipped. "He thinks you're doing a fine job. He always knew you would."

It was kind of weird. She'd never known exactly why, but Connor had gone to bat for her with Jarvis, and she'd always be grateful to him for that. "Yeah, but I can't go running to him with every little issue."

Faith patted her knee. "That's what we're here for, so you did the right thing. And what you told that girl was actually quite marvelous."

Josie snorted. "I fobbed her off, told her to go find a friend to talk to."

"Isn't that exactly what she *should* do? Just like you're coming to us?"

"Well, I guess, but—"

"Shh." Faith shut her up with a Dr. Evil hand gesture. "You are always the hardest on yourself. As far as I can see, you did everything right."

"Yeah," Trinity seconded, as she slipped into the third dress on her rack of maybes.

"You talked to the butt pincher. You didn't ignore it."

"But I should have checked with HR first."

"Shoulda, woulda, coulda," Trinity said. "Didn't." She shrugged. "Big deal."

"But—"

This time Verna shushed her. She was starting to like Verna a lot. "Honey, only God doesn't make mistakes. You really have to start believing in yourself."

"But I do." At least, she'd thought she did. Until she'd lost control of the department and started thinking that perhaps she'd been promoted to the level of her incompetency. So yeah, even her own belief in herself was in doubt.

"The point is," Verna stressed, "you dealt with the issue. It's resolved. Unless *they* act up again."

"You can only control what *you* do," Faith added. "If they want to act like babies, you can't do anything but deal with the aftermath."

"See," Josie said, "that's the whole problem. I want them to act like adults and they don't."

"Believe me, they never will." Trinity turned on the dais. "What do you guys think?"

She was gorgeous. The cream satin sheath, overlaid with a delicate lace, left her shoulders and throat bare. Tight over the hips, the dress then flared, cascading down to a two-foot train in the back. Elegant, tasteful, nothing overdone, just like Trinity herself.

"Oh, that's the one your mama would have wanted to see you in." Verna wiped at her eyes.

Faith gave a little *ooh* of total approval. Josie wondered if she missed not having the big wedding, the dress, the photographs. On second though, nah. What Faith and Connor had was perfect.

"What do you think, Josie?" Trinity waited, as if Josie's opinion really mattered.

She'd never had best friends before. Despite being related, Josie hadn't been close to Faith until a little over a year ago, right after she'd married Connor. And with Faith came Trinity. She'd never been in anyone's wedding, never been asked for her opinion on the perfect dress. She'd never had friends to talk over her problems with. So she'd never talked. It would be great if you could see all the answers clearly—even all the problems—by yourself. But you couldn't.

For the first time, Josie began to see all the things she'd missed, such as having best friends to tell her she wasn't a total screwup. Friends. They were as important as a career. And to have good friends, you had to be one.

"I love that dress, Trinity." Josie beamed a huge smile. "Bet there's never been a prettier bride to walk down the aisle."

JOSIE had dropped off a slightly tipsy Faith at her house, then headed home herself. The scent of bread pudding in brandy sauce still lingered in her nose—Trinity had gotten her hooked on the stuff. She'd clambered into bed, turned off the light, and rolled over when her cell rang on the bedside table.

She flipped open the phone and spoke, knowing it was Kyle. "Are you peeping into my windows to see when I go to bed?"

"I'm like a swami. I sensed you were fantasizing about me licking your pussy, and I had to call."

"I was not thinking any such thing." Actually, she'd been planning his next challenge. Bits and pieces of it had come to her throughout dinner while the conversation flowed over her. "I was thinking about sucking your cock." Oops, she shouldn't have said that.

Because he immediately took her up on the invitation. "Let me come over."

"Are you going to be this pushy when you're actually working at Castle?"

"Only in non-work hours."

She doubted it. The man would probably try to cop a feel in every nook and cranny he could find. She didn't trust him. Yet she felt herself inexorably pulled in. As if he were the mesmerist he claimed.

"It's a work night. I need my beauty sleep. Hang up the phone." She should have cut the connection herself.

"You at least need an orgasm so that you sleep well."

"I don't need you here for that."

"I don't have to be there. You can do it for me right now."

"Over the phone?" Not that she hadn't done phone sex before, but with Kyle it was yet another escalation in a long line of them. "No."

"Yes." He groaned. "Don't make me jerk off alone."

"Are you stroking your cock?" She said it with an appropriate level of disgust, yet she was already getting hot and wet beneath the sheet.

"I've been stroking it the whole time." His breath picked up the pace.

"You're such a perv." She wanted to touch herself, too, except that would be giving in.

"All night I've been imagining my face buried in your pussy and your lips wrapped around my dick."

A perfect sixty-nine. "We agreed to once a week."

"That was for a date." She could hear the stroke of his hand in his voice now, the slightly harsh breath, the space between his words. "But we can have phone sex any time." A pause, a groan. "Except during work hours."

The sounds he made shivered over the air. God, she wanted to touch herself. She wanted to ask him how good it felt with his hand on his cock and her voice in his ear. "No phone sex." But would he notice if she gave herself one tiny orgasm?

"Killjoy."

"We had rules for this whole thing." She wanted to break them all, except that would give him the power, especially after she'd failed to call quits to their arrangement when he took the FI&T job.

"Come with me, Josie," he murmured, voice guttural, intense, drawing her in.

She pinched her nipple and moaned.

"That's it, baby. Touch yourself. Tell me how wet you are."

"I'm not touching myself." She slipped her hand down, tunneling beneath the elastic of her panties.

"Liar. I'm so fucking hard knowing you're fingering your clit for me."

She did just that, shooting an electric shock straight up inside. "I'm lying here listening to you be a total perv, that's all." Yet she dipped her finger down to her pussy, so wet, gliding it back up. In her college dorm room, she'd learned to masturbate without making a sound, her roommate fast asleep, never the wiser.

"I want you here, now, riding my cock."

"I'm going to hang up now." She pushed her head back against the pillow, arched her body into her hand.

"Don't go yet. Hear me."

"I'm going to fall asleep if you don't hurry up." She kept her breath normal, steady, and just the effort in that drove her higher, closer to the pinnacle.

"Christ, you know how to torture a man."

"You called me, remember. I'm not doing a thing." Except getting herself off, his voice, his breath, the man himself pushing her as much as her own touch.

"Ah fuck." He groaned, then let out a gust of breath. "Fuck, fuck."

She could hear him, she was with him, right there. Oh shit. She almost cried out, almost moaned and thrashed as his groan washed over her, then his low cry brought her to the edge and dumped her over. Oh God, oh God. The need for silence, the effort of holding it in intensified the orgasm almost as much as wailing. She rode the crest forever until she heard his long, satisfied sigh.

"Fuck, that was good. We can do this every night."

"It didn't do a damn thing for me."

"You had the best orgasm since I fucked you on Thursday, and you know it."

True. Admitting it, though, would put him on top again. Since he would soon be her boss, he'd have all the power anyway. He kept drawing her in, slowly, inexorably. She hadn't called either of her other buddies in weeks. Every occasion she did Kyle, each time she talked to him, even if she just freaking saw him in a meeting, she took another baby step in the wrong direction. Wrong for her career, wrong for her desire to keep her relationships on a friendly, casual, emotion-free basis.

There was a way. She'd thought about it, planned how to make it happen, considered the consequences, decided it was worth it in this little game they had going.

"Cat got your tongue?" Kyle murmured.

"I don't have a cat," Josie answered literally.

"Then maybe you're just overcome by your climax and can't think right now."

"Oh, I can think, all right."

Kyle had to admit he was having trouble thinking. Aftershocks still quaked lightly through his body. Damn, she'd been quiet, barely a quickened breath, but she'd come, he knew she had, no matter how much she wanted to deny it. He'd bet it was fucking good for her, too. Phone sex had never been so hot, maybe because she fought him as well as herself.

He'd left the window open and the night breeze trickled over his nerve endings, almost like fingers. Her fingers.

"I've been thinking about our next date."

Good. She'd called it a date. "And?" He rose, headed to the master bathroom to wipe the semen off his stomach, the phone still to his ear.

What he wouldn't give to have her here, watch her make a feast of his dick.

"It needs to be Friday," she said, her voice slow, lazy, satiated after the orgasm she wouldn't admit to.

"You already told me that." Clean now, he padded to the closet. "Tell me something I don't know."

"Are they giving you a going-away party?"

Grabbing his robe off a hook, he chuckled. "I do believe it's a lunch. Kisa asked me where I wanted to go." He said the girl's name with a purse to his lips, knowing it would set Josie off.

It did, right on cue. "Oh, Little Miss Snowflake is giving you your own little party. How sweet."

"I thought so." In the dark, he allowed himself a feral grin.

"What about after work? Drinks with the group?"

"Not if you and I have a date." Opening the sliding glass door, he stepped out onto his deck. The night sky was filled with twinkling stars.

"I've decided that your Friday *date* is going to be with Little Miss Snowflake."

Sitting, he slouched, laying his head back on the chair to stare at the sky. This was a new game he hadn't figured out yet. "So you want me to tease her into thinking I've got the hots for her?"

"Since you won't be working there after Friday, now you can do her."

He took in a deep breath through his mouth and shot it out his nostrils. "There's one small problem with that."

"What?"

He believed he knew what Josie wanted. A declaration. "I don't want to do her."

"Liar. You loved her hot thigh-high boots."

"Just because she looked hot in them doesn't mean I want to do her."

His denial didn't seem to be working with Josie. Obviously she wanted something else from him. "Why don't you want to try?" she asked. "Because she's a lot younger than you, and you think you can't get her to put out?"

"I could get her to put out." He was stepping right into her net, but he wanted to be absolutely sure what the trap was. Why the fuck did she want him to do Kisa?

"I think you're afraid you can't. I think you're worried Little Miss Snowflake is all talk and no action where you're concerned. She's just a tease."

He didn't think the girl was a tease at all. She'd asked him out for an after-work drink more than once. He'd refused. She was too young, too needy, and assuredly looking for a lot more than casual sex. All that was in addition to the fact that he preferred understated women.

"All right"—he shrugged—"have it your way. She's a tease." He paused to give a piercing stare, as if she could see him. "What exactly is your challenge?"

"Ask her for a drink." Josie chuckled like a woman with a very naughty secret. "Then take her out to your car, and get her to blow you."

"You're crazy." She pissed him off. Badly. Why the hell did she want to fob him off on another woman? To prove he couldn't get it up for anyone else but her, that she had him pussy-whipped? "Fine. You want me to get her to blow me, I will. But lady, you're going to pay for this one."

She'd never know whether he did or not. He'd simply go home and call her after an appropriate amount of time.

"And I want to be at the bar to watch you work your magic."

Damn her. "Are you going to follow me out to the car, too?"

She huffed a breath. "No, she might notice that. I wouldn't want to screw this up for you."

"What makes you think she won't recognize you in the bar?"

"I only met her once, and she was too busy bantering with you to actually notice me. To be sure, though, pick a place that's dark. I'll get there first and sit way in the back."

Sonuvabitch. She'd really been working this one out.

Why the fuck was he going to play this particular game with her? He should tell her to get lost, call the whole thing off, this bizarre relationship that wasn't a relationship at all.

Jesus. That's exactly what she wanted. He'd gone from being her client to her boss, and she was trying to get *him* to end it. He wasn't letting her walk away. He'd gotten her to invite him to her home, then fucked the hell out of her until she'd agreed to keep on seeing him outside of work. He'd make her stick to that.

She'd issued a challenge, and he wasn't about to be the first to back down. She'd asked for a show, and she would get a goddamn good one.

"You're on."

GOOD God. He'd said yes to her challenge.

It wasn't until the moment he'd agreed that Josie realized she was hoping he'd tell her to forget it. That he didn't want Little Miss Fucking Snowflake, he only wanted Josie. Sure he'd *said* it, but he'd given in way too easily. It was debilitating to know she wasn't above craving a little ego boost.

Dammit, despite his denials, she'd *known* he had a thing for Little Miss Fucking Snowflake.

It didn't matter. The episode would put the relationship in perspective for both of them. This was just sex. Pretty soon they'd get tired of the game and mutually decide to move on. Her career would be back on track without any emotional entanglements.

Truthfully, it didn't bother her one teeny-tiny bit—as Trinity would say—if he decided to move on with Little Miss Fucking Snowflake.

Hah. She could even call herself Cupid.

14

ON Friday, Josie counted the hours, the minutes, even the seconds. She hadn't talked to Kyle since Monday night. Tuesday she'd sent him an e-mail instructing him to e-mail her with the time and place of his rendezvous. She hadn't heard from him on that, either.

He was going to back out. She knew it. Heh. She'd win. The next challenge would be hers all over again, and this time . . . well, she wouldn't pick something involving another woman.

She celebrated her soon-to-be victory by inviting Lydia to lunch. Okay, it wasn't a celebration. She'd put off talking to Lydia all week. What would Ernie have done, if Lydia had told him at all? Should she tell HR? What if something happened to Lydia, and Josie hadn't told anyone? What if she told, and Lydia had a nervous breakdown because everyone suddenly knew her secret? Being a boss was a bit like being a priest. You didn't tell unless your employee said you could. God. Too many decisions.

For a brief moment that morning, she considered asking Kyle.

Their games aside, she admired him and respected his opinion. But jeez, she couldn't tell him *that*. Especially not after she'd told him he had to get Little Miss Snowflake to blow him.

Instead, she decided on steak at the Outback. Lydia ordered a salad and barely touched it. Josie didn't mention Lydia's problem at all until they were walking back to the car. She'd found a shady tree to park beneath and stopped by the hatchback without hitting the automatic lock remote.

"You okay, Lydia?"

The girl hadn't been late a single day since she'd burst into tears in Josie's office. "I'm fine."

"Did you talk to someone? If you didn't, I can give you the number for Employee Assistance." She'd at least uncovered the name of the company-sponsored program and gotten the phone number. "Or you could call Planned Parenthood. They have counselors for this sort of thing." Unplanned parenthood. She had looked the website up on the Net and browsed a bit. They could give Lydia advice about her options.

"Do you think I should have an abortion?"

The blood drained right out of Josie's head. She felt dizzy and close to passing out. "I can't advise you, Lydia. I'm your boss."

There would be legal ramifications. Besides, she wasn't qualified.

"What would you do?"

Jesus. She could not have Lydia and her baby on her conscience. "I honestly don't know what I'd do, Lydia. I would never want to have to make that choice."

Lydia pursed her lips, to keep them from trembling, Josie was sure. She stared at the concrete. "I know you wouldn't want to. I don't want to." Then she raised her dark brown, puppy-dog-sad eyes. "But I'd really like to know what you'd do."

"Why me, Lydia? You must have friends you can ask."

"Because I've always admired you."

Jeez. There wasn't so much to admire. Josie struggled for everything she'd gained. All her life she'd worked harder, faster, to be better, so that she'd stand out and be noticed. Connor was the first one to really give her a chance. Everyone else thought she had everything handed to her because she was Dora and Preston Tybrook's daughter.

She'd believed Lydia thought the same. Yet Lydia turned everything around on her. Josie stepped close, dropped her voice. "I think that I would have the abortion." She felt the oddest tingle in her eyes, as if she might actually cry. "But I don't think I would live with it well." She put her hand on Lydia's shoulder. "I don't think you would live with it well, either." What she didn't say was that even knowing that, she still would have the abortion.

God, that said something terrible about her as a person. All her childhood fears of not being good enough or lovable or special suddenly rose up inside her.

Lydia swallowed. Her eyes shimmered, but not a single teardrop fell. "Thanks."

Josie wasn't sure what she'd done. For a moment she was terrified of the consequences of those few words, like the ripple effect, where they spread out and suddenly the whole world was changed. And not for the better.

They were silent on the way back to work. In her office, she checked her e-mail. There was one from Kyle. He was taking Little Miss Snowflake to a dark bar in one of the hotels by the San Francisco airport. They'd be there at six.

Good God. She'd forgotten she'd have to get all the way up the Peninsula on a Friday evening during commute traffic. Idiot.

Cancel, cancel, cancel.

She could say she'd changed her mind. Or she could tell him about Lydia, how the lunch experience had soured her. She certainly would not mention that she didn't feel like watching Little Miss Fucking Snowflake suck up, so to speak.

She started typing a reply. "Something's come up at work, can't make it."

He'd ask what. Or he'd suggest he go it alone with the woman.

She deleted the line and started over. "I'm sick. We'll have to postpone." Then she'd postpone forever. Woman's prerogative to choose a new challenge.

God, she wished she'd never issued the damn challenge in the first place, but if she backed off, he came out on top. Numero uno. He'd win. He'd probably even think it was because she didn't want to see him flirting with the Snowflake. She didn't care at all, of course, it was just this whole Lydia thing getting her down. But she'd never get him to believe that now.

She deleted the line again. Dammit. She had no choice. She'd started it, she had to follow it through.

She typed. "Make it six thirty." And hit send.

That was that. She'd keep it in mind for the next time: don't start something you might decide later you don't want.

At five, she made a quick repair to her makeup. Casual Friday meant jeans and a T-shirt. She wished she'd worn something sexier. Such as what, she had no idea. Why hadn't she planned better this morning when she left the house? Fine. Whatever. She was imagining Little Miss Fucking Snowflake in sexy thigh-high leather boots and low-cut spandex top, and *that* made her feel . . . less.

On the road by ten after five, the traffic was at least cooperating. With it being the last week before Labor Day, lots of people were on kiddy vacation before school started again. She made it to Millbrae and the airport hotel ten minutes early.

He'd chosen a luxury hotel amidst an array of motels convenient to the airport. There were no shady nooks to park in, and it wouldn't be dark for another two hours. If Kyle took the Snow-flake back to his car, they'd be getting nasty while it was still light. Would they have driven separately? Or maybe he planned on getting a hotel room for the dirty deed.

Josie's breath hitched in her chest. She hadn't contemplated that possibility.

"What do you care?" she whispered harshly to herself, then yanked on the door handle and climbed out of the car.

The faux marble lobby was awash in people, suitcases, luggage carts, and bellhops. There was some sort of convention, with a *lot* of women dressed in varying amounts of pink, from full pink suits, to pink blouses, to just pink shoes. The mélange of perfume gave her a headache. She followed the sign to the bar. Just as she'd instructed, it was intimate and dark, with candles flickering on the tables. A fair number of businesspeople were seated at them, and again, a lot of pink ladies. She found a lone table in the back corner, ordered a German beer, and sat back to wait.

Kyle arrived. Alone. Josie's heart kicked up. His gaze roamed the room, passed over her as if she didn't exist, and landed on a table being vacated by two businessmen. He wore a dark suit himself, white shirt, red-and-black tie. God, he was lip smacking. So, too, thought the pink ladies as they gawked.

He gave his order to the waitress. She was quick to bring the drinks. Two of them. A cocktail tumbler with amber liquid for him, and a glass of blush wine.

Josie's heart beat in her ears. Maybe he was waiting for her to vacate her table and join him, blowing the challenge out of the water. She waited, her breath fast. He twisted his glass on the table. One minute, two. Josie started to rise.

Little Miss Fucking Snowflake sashayed through the door. Her black leather skirt barely covered her crotch. Josie was sure her butt cheeks would be clearly visible from the rear, just as the tight, stretchy sweater top barely contained her nipples, and gee, she was either cold or totally happy to see Kyle. Dammit.

Josie sank into her chair and picked up her beer glass. She almost slugged down the remainder, managing only at the last second to daintily sip. She didn't want Kyle to know . . . what? That the Snowflake bothered her? Ridiculous. She couldn't care less. For God's sake, she'd arranged the whole thing, so of course she didn't give a rat's ass.

She sat back to watch. If she'd been worried the girl might recognize her, forget it. The Snowflake didn't spare a glance for anyone else in the bar, not even the pink ladies who regarded her outfit with awe.

She giggled at Kyle. Yuck. Taking the seat right next to him— not across, of course—her bare leg brushed his knee. Kyle slid her wine in front of her. She left a big, red lipstick mark on the edge of the glass. Josie wondered how much lipstick she'd leave on his . . .

Stretching back in her chair, the girl raised her arms to flip her long hair out from behind her. Her breasts thrust out, and the bottom of her tight sweater rode up. She pulled it down. Kyle's eyes followed every move.

For the very first time, Kyle glanced at Josie, his grin feral. Some bizarre emotion rode through her like a tidal wave, up into her throat, hitting her so quickly, she felt choked with it. Her pulse pounded erratically, and her gaze seemed to glaze everything else over like a microscope lens, leaving only Kyle and Little Miss Fucking Snowflake in sharp focus.

If he touched the bitch, Josie wouldn't be responsible for her own actions.

KISA had flounced into the bar sprinkled with a liberal dose of overwhelming perfume. She'd managed to catch a ride with him to and from the going-away lunch and finagled the seat next to his for the meal itself. Her thigh had rested against his most of the time. Kyle hadn't wanted to issue the invitation for drinks, but he'd done it for the sake of the challenge.

The hotel bar danced with conversation, and Kisa's breasts jiggled as if she were moving to music. He'd always figured them for the real thing. She laughed, low and husky, at something he said. That was another thing he figured about Kisa, her laugh got huskier for the effect she knew it had on a man. With Josie in his life, he wasn't one of those men.

In the corner, Josie was doing a damn good job of pretending disinterest, yet her glance flitting about the room bounced back to his table again and again. She fidgeted with her beer glass as if she didn't know what to do with her hands. She garnered her own measure of interest from a table of businessmen. Not that she gave them an iota of attention. Despite her apparent nonchalance, she focused on every touch Kisa put out, every laugh, every move the girl made.

He was driving her fucking crazy. He knew it, felt it pulse in the air. It turned him on like nothing ever had. She'd asked for it, gotten it, now she didn't know what the hell to do with it.

The evening was a crapshoot for how it would play out, but one thing was for sure, he would somehow turn it to his advantage.

KYLE didn't touch the girl; he didn't have to. The bitch did all the touching for him. A flirty swipe of her fingers across the back of his hand. Leaning forward so he could see down her top, leaning back so he could admire her nipples. Her leg bouncing right next to his, stroking him with her calf. Each word out of her mouth was said with an enticing little pucker of her lips.

Josie burned. It couldn't be jealousy. She'd never been jealous of anything or anyone. Maybe a bit with asshole Ian, but nothing this intense. She wanted to jump up, dash across the room, and smack the glass out of the girl's hand. Rip her hair out. Josie's chest was so tight, she couldn't breathe, she couldn't think. The thought of that woman putting her hands and her mouth on Kyle made Josie's bile rise. A tremble started in the center of her chest and worked its way out.

When Kyle stood and held out his hand, Josie knew she was going to lose it. When the Snowflake took it and rose, she thought about murder and how she could hide the body. When they left, she wondered how she could hide two bodies. Ready to pour the last of the dregs into her glass, her hand clenched so tightly on the bottle, she was afraid she'd pulverize it back to the sand from which it was made.

Good God, she was jealous. She really was.

"Can I get you another beer?"

She hadn't noticed the waitress approach, wasn't aware she'd actually finished her whole glass. Another one? No way. She wouldn't be responsible for what she might do. "Just a ginger ale, please."

The waitress darted away, and it was all Josie could do to stay in her seat. She wanted to follow them. The need seethed in her. Whose car would they use? How fast would it take the bitch to get in his pants? God. When her ginger ale arrived, Josie grabbed it and gulped half of it down as if she were an alcoholic coming off a year-long dry spell.

Not once since college. *Ne-ver.* She'd learned her lesson. Jealousy was unknown. She hadn't even remembered what it felt like. So why now? Why Kyle?

"Hey, little lady, you look lonely over here by yourself."

She turned just her head. *Little lady?* The guy was middle-aged, but good looking. *Really* good-looking, with salt-and-pepper hair that had once been black, Richard Gere–bone structure, and a Mr. Universe body. He was tall, too, and she liked tall men.

He took a step back at whatever he saw in her eyes.

"Get," she snarled, "lost." Her mother would be appalled at her rudeness. In other circumstances, so would she. Especially since the guy was a hottie. But if he didn't leave, she'd do something bad.

Because not only was she jealous, she was pissed. If the man wasn't careful, she'd take it out on him. Holding up his hands in surrender, he backed away from the pending gunfight at the OK Corral. Smart dude. He slid down into his chair at a table with three equally handsome older guys. Guess hot men just naturally gravitated together or something. He leaned in, murmured something, and they all looked.

Josie narrowed her eyes to threatening slits.

The only thing that kept her at her table in her dark corner was the tiny higher functioning part of her clearly Neanderthal brain. She was overreacting. She'd asked for this herself. She didn't care what Kyle did with Little Miss . . . Snowflake. She wouldn't even *think* the adjective.

Her guts ached, and her temples throbbed, but God forbid she should need a man, depend on him, or allow herself to be hurt by one ever again. This was just some freaky thing brought on by her problems with Lydia, the confrontations with Ronson, screwing up on the dryer for the sand plant. And Ernie. God, *especially* Ernie.

"You're okay," she whispered, then quickly glanced around to make sure no one saw her talking to herself. The spoken words calmed her slightly. Yep, that's what this was, a mini-breakdown. Short in duration. She'd be over it soon. At least she didn't fear committing murder anymore.

But what the hell was taking Kyle so long? He was a fast shooter with her, for God's sake. She couldn't stand it. She would have left if she didn't think he'd call her on it later. She wanted to get this over and done, then she'd go home and pass out. Emotions were freaking tiring.

She didn't look at her watch, but she felt every second ticking by. The pink ladies chattered away, creating enough noise to cause an echo. She wanted to put her hands over her ears and shut it all out.

Then he stood in the bar's entryway, his suit jacket buttoned, his tie perfect, not a hair out of place nor a lipstick smudge on his collar. She felt sick all over again. Making his way to her table, all the pink ladies' eyes followed. So did the gaze of her *friend* and his cohorts.

Kyle pulled out the chair next to her. "Did you order me something? I'm parched."

Asshole. She smiled sweetly. "What would you like, honey?"

He gave her a crooked half smile in return. "A beer. Like you had."

So he had been watching her. A bit, anyway. But Jesus, why didn't he just tell her what had occurred out there? She couldn't stand not knowing. "What happened?"

He signaled the waitress. "After my beer."

He was such a damn tease. "Fine. Whatever," she snapped, hating the bitchiness in her tone. She modulated it. "I'm patient." Like hell. "I can wait."

Leaning back, folding his hands over his stomach, he gave the waitress his order, then glanced at Josie. "You want something?"

God, yes. "A Kahlua and cream, please." Smooth, dark, rich. Something to soothe her, because her emotions sure as hell were ruling her head right now.

Why? She didn't get it, despite her little pep talk to herself about how Ernie and everything was affecting her.

Kyle merely watched her. That set her on edge, too.

Their drinks arrived, though it wasn't anywhere near fast

enough. She sipped, savored, which made her think about how she savored his come. How Little Miss Fucking Snowflake probably savored it. Unless she was too fastidious to swallow. Hmm, no, not a possibility.

He slugged back a swallow of beer.

"So?" she said.

He sighed, tipped his head, met her gaze. "Do I get points for trying?"

Her heart started to beat faster. "Depends. Tell me the whole story." Her voice cracked.

"She flirted."

"Duh. I noticed." She sipped her Kahlua to keep her hands busy.

"We went out to my car."

"Saw that, too. Don't keep me in suspense."

"She balked when I asked her to"—he dropped his voice to a murmur—"blow me." His eyes glittered in the table's candlelight.

"No way."

"She wouldn't do a thing."

"I can't believe it." He hadn't done it. He had not done it. She wanted to curl up, hug her knees, and breathe through the rush of relief. If she'd been standing, her legs would have collapsed.

He leaned in, forearm on the table, and lowered his voice once again. "I was so fucking hard with you watching us. My balls ached. I needed it bad."

"But she must have seen your hard-on." The sips of Kahlua were a lifeline. Otherwise her fidgeting would have given away her state of confusion.

"I kissed her by the car. She *knew* how horny I was."

Eww. He kissed her. Josie felt sick. She wanted to scream. She thought about feeding his body parts through a wood chipper.

"She didn't taste good. Not like you." He laid a finger on her lips, traced them, then put the tip to his own mouth and licked off the vestiges of Kahlua. "She didn't smell as good as you, either."

She sucked in a breath, needed more. "Did you at least get her into the car?"

"No. I told her I needed some TLC. She laughed and told me to take care of it myself."

"That bitch." Oh God, she could have wept with sheer relief. "She's a cock tease. She meant to get you all hot and bothered, then drop you flat."

"Yeah."

She could breathe. She could laugh. She wanted to dance. "I'm sorry. Poor baby."

He took her hand in his, placed it palm down on his thigh, and forced her to rub the muscle. "My ego has been thrashed. I need to be taken care of."

His hard-on was clearly visible as he unbuttoned his suit jacket. "I haven't come since Monday night. I was saving it, and now I'm so fucking backed up, I ache."

She eased off a micron. "You were saving it for Little Miss Snowflake?"

"I was saving it for *tonight*."

There was a read-between-the-lines message in there. He was saving it for Josie. Then she sniffed. She could smell the bitch's perfume on him. Leaning close, gazing into his eyes, she knew he could be lying. He might very well have let the woman suck him off, then gone to the men's room and straightened everything.

Josie didn't care. She wanted to believe. "Is it dark out yet?" The bar was windowless, all inside walls.

"Not quite," he said.

"Is the parking lot crowded?"

"Lots of people coming and going." He took her chin in his hand, held her. "But I thought of somewhere."

He'd been thinking. About her. Not the Snowflake.

Her hand still in his, he rose, pulled her with him, then fished in his pocket for some bills to toss on the table. Her boot heels were too high, and she stumbled following him out. She was aware of all the pink ladies, watching everything, how he'd met with one woman, left with her, and now was back for seconds.

"Where are we going?" she asked when he had her in his car. His house? She would have gone without a fuss.

Instead, he took the airport ramp.

"Put your hand on my cock."

He was huge. His body surged up as she stroked him through his pants. He couldn't have come with the bitch, couldn't be this hard if he had.

"It's for you," he said as if he could read her mind. "I didn't even want her." He reached across, lifted her chin. "Watching you watch us is what made me so fucking hot."

At the moment, she didn't care if he was lying. She pulled away as they came up to the short-term parking gate. There could be cameras.

He grabbed a ticket, threw it on the dash. "I thought about it all week. You sitting in a bar watching her hit on me." He glanced in the rearview mirror as he negotiated a turn in the parking garage. Then he smiled. "It made me fucking nuts."

He found a spot in a corner, a terminal entrance far behind them, a wall on his side, another in front, isolating them. "You owe me," he whispered, "for doing what you wanted."

"But you didn't do it," she answered right into that glittering blue gaze of his.

"Which is why you owe me even more."

Then he leaned over the center console, gathered her hair in his hands and pulled her head back, taking her lips, kissing her hard, openmouthed. He tasted of beer and man. He didn't taste of *her*, that bitch.

"Now suck me." He never lifted his lips from hers.

She crawled down his chest, pushed aside his jacket and tie, yanked his shirt from his pants, and unzipped him. Come pearled on the tip of his cock. A man had never tasted better. He groaned, the sound vibrating against her ear. She kneaded his balls as she licked him, caressed him, stroked him, sucked him. He was full, hard, his orgasm building. She felt him shift and tipped her head to find his gaze pinning her, his fingers sunk into the headrest behind him.

"Take your hands away," he ordered.

She did. He surged, filled her, fucked her mouth. She took all she could, everything, closed her eyes to let his scent surround her. Grabbing her head, he shouted, thrust one last time, and unloaded hard, so much she could barely contain him.

Finally, there was nothing but his harsh breathing. She soothed him with light licks, fingers stroking his thighs, her tongue cleaning up the tip of his cock.

"Come here." His voice was a guttural rasp as he pulled her up by the arm. "Kiss me."

His lids rested at half-mast, his head back, a deep breath expanding his chest. She smoothed a hand down the white fabric of his shirt and leaned in to lightly brush his lips with hers.

"More," he whispered.

She opened her mouth, stroked him with her tongue, let him taste himself. It was unique, erotic, beautiful, frightening. He folded his arms around her until the kiss ended, and she rested against his chest.

"Either you recharge fast or she really didn't blow you."

When she tried to look up, he held her head to his chest. "She wouldn't," he murmured. "She was a tease, nothing more."

Nothing. It was scary to realize she wanted him to mean that Little Miss Fucking Snowflake was nothing special to him.

He slid his hand down her back, stroked along the crease of her butt, then rounded her thigh and tunneled between her legs. The jeans didn't let him in. When he went for the zipper, she pushed his hand away. "Not now."

She wanted to savor his come, his kiss. Her own orgasm was secondary to the power she got from a man flying apart in her mouth. Especially Kyle; maybe *only* Kyle. Like the night he tied her up in the hotel room, or at the hot tubs. Everything seemed to be about *him*. What did that mean? She shoved the question aside. It was too unsettling to think about.

Tipping her chin, he kissed her, lightly, ending it with a swipe of his tongue across her lips. "I'll let you get away with that this time. But you owe me an orgasm."

"Sure."

She'd planned on teaching him a lesson, that sex between them was casual. She wanted to believe she knew that, too. Yet lying against him, his arms around her, his scent filling her, his taste lingering on her tongue, she realized she'd learned something else altogether.

Kyle might be her boss, but he was a man first. And it was the man she wanted. She closed her eyes and admitted the worst. Not only did she want him, she needed him.

Suddenly, he held the power. She could no longer walk away from this thing between them no matter what happened at work.

KYLE drove her back to her car in the airport hotel lot. "Spend the night with me."

She hovered in her corner of the car. "No."

Fuck. He knew she'd say that so why bother asking? She was

willing to give him to another woman, what the fuck did she care about spending the night with him? He'd had a great orgasm, a few moments of bliss as she kissed him, but she'd withdrawn, and his anger boiled to the surface.

"Tomorrow night." He was a glutton for punishment.

She just looked at him. Far away from a parking light, her eyes lay in shadow, unreadable.

"All right," he said, "then I'll see you on Tuesday."

"Yeah. Fine."

He wondered if that was better than, *Fine, whatever.* With Josie, he couldn't tell a thing.

Kisa was so much more transparent. He'd walked her to her car, she'd tried to kiss him, he extricated himself quickly. Leaning against the driver's door of her car, she'd told him how she'd dreamed of sucking his dick for months. He'd had a hard-on, but it was all about Josie, the avid way she'd watched, the tense lines of her body. Josie was jealous; he knew it in his gut. Kisa's voice had droned on at him. She wanted to touch him, taste him, take his come down her throat.

What he'd wanted was Josie taking his cock in her mouth, swallowing him whole. He'd gotten rid of Kisa, sat in his car for fifteen minutes, then went to the men's room to gauge what Josie would read on his face and body. He quite clearly remembered saying "You're pathetic" to the reflection. Unlike Snow White's mirror, it hadn't answered him back.

"My challenge next," he said, keeping his voice low.

"But she didn't do it."

"I had no control over what she would or wouldn't do. But *I* did what you wanted." He angled up against the door. "In fact, you owe me big time to make up for my ultimate humiliation." He might as well play it up for what it was worth.

Josie gazed at him with those unreadable eyes. "All right. Your challenge."

She'd agreed too easily, but he refused to let the new game backfire on him. He'd figure out the perfect challenge to show her she was his. No more Kisa, no more fuck buddies. Josie loved to have control, but from now on, he was going to be in charge.

He wasn't about to let another man touch her, not for a long, long time. If ever.

15

SHE'D had an awful weekend. How many times had she picked
up her cell phone to tell Kyle she'd changed her mind and wanted
that orgasm badly? Way too many to count. Even a hot mastur-
bation session with her vibrator on Saturday night hadn't relieved
her tension. Rick, one of her buddies, had called; she'd turned him
down. Only Kyle would do. Gee, wasn't that a terrifying thought?
For God's sake, he was her boss. How was she supposed to separate business from pleasure?

Since Monday had been the Labor Day holiday, on Tuesday
morning Josie and her staff gathered in the conference room for the
weekly update meeting. Walker and Ronson were back in the office
and Chuck had flown out to Arkansas. Jenkins was out on-site for
the second week in a row.

Josie sat at the head of the table, with Lydia to her right, pen
poised for note-taking. When Lydia had arrived this morning—on

time—Josie'd asked how she was doing, and Lydia said fine. That was all. If she'd made a decision, she wasn't sharing it.

It was Kyle's first day, along with Bertrice Denton's. Bertrice sat next to Lydia, and Kyle, the last to arrive, ended up at the far end of the table, opposite Josie.

"You all know Kyle Perry." She indicated him with a flip of her right hand. He wouldn't attend the PM staff meeting on a regular basis, but he'd wanted to get up to speed on everything outstanding in all the departments.

Ronson and Walker had been on job sites, but she'd introduced them this morning. Kyle had laughed at something Walker said, and she'd thought of him laughing with Little Miss Snowflake on Friday. He shook Ronson's hand, and she'd remembered how firm his grip was, yet how gently he could play her clitoris, how hard, fast, and orgasmic. She had a bad feeling she was going to have a naughty image of him every time he did or said anything. Working with him would be torture.

Especially when she realized that she hadn't asked him if he'd see the Snowflake again. Just to prove he could have her after all.

God, her jealousy was like a cancer that permeated every nook and cranny of her life. That thought made her think of Ernie, and a guilty flush rose to her cheeks. How could she even *think* to compare her situation to Ernie's?

"And our new program manager"—Josie put out her left hand—"is Bertrice Denton." Though she wore a business suit, Josie still felt the woman dressed too sexy, the skirt too short and too many blouse buttons left undone. But whatever.

Josie had chosen a couple of new jobs coming down the pipeline from Marketing and planned to brief Bertrice on them after the meeting.

The whiteboard on the wall detailed the open projects with milestones and status. Josie pointed to the first on the list, Walker's

Washington job. "You should be near to closing this one out, right?"

Walker skimmed the flat of his hand over the spiked hair of his old-fashioned crew cut. He'd spent six years in the Air Force and kept the hairstyle. He was in his mid-thirties, and he'd called Castle home for three years. He flipped a page on his clipboard and ran down the list of remaining items with military precision. "Just mice nuts," he said in conclusion. "I'll have them closed out by Wednesday." At the whiteboard, he ticked off his milestones in red marker.

"Go ahead and update us on the rest of your projects since you're already up there." Normally they would only discuss problem areas and roadblocks, but a full rundown would give Kyle a better feel for everything.

Walker was meticulous yet brief. Chuck was traveling and unavailable. Jenkins, on speaker, tended to concentrate on the minutiae and required prompting to keep him on track. Despite that, he did good work. Josie covered the particulars on the Coyote Ridge Sand Plant, her only open project since becoming manager. After the debacle over the dryer, things had settled down nicely, and the programming on the new ticketing system was actually ahead of schedule. Kyle asked a few questions throughout the discussions, but even when he merely listened, Josie was always aware of him. It wasn't easy separating between boss and lover. She kept wondering what he thought of her management style: did she sound stupid or snippy or know-it-all?

Would she have felt that way with any new boss?

Ronson was last, due only to the fact that his first job was fourth on the list. "VIM"—Venezuela International Mining—"is on target." Ronson had returned from Venezuela on Saturday. "I'll have to go back down at the end of the month, but probably for only a week."

Josie prompted him with a couple of questions. He gave her

sparse answers. Rather than pull it out of him now, since the meeting was already running over, she decided to go over the file with him later.

"What about Alta Vista?" It was a Mexican project she'd passed onto him after taking over from Ernie.

Fair-haired and fair-skinned, two bright spots of color rose in Ronson's cheeks, punctuated by a gleam in his turquoise eyes. "The job's a fucking mess."

Josie glanced at Kyle. He was studying Ronson, his face a mask, expression indeterminate.

She didn't bother to correct Ronson's language. It wasn't as if they hadn't all used the word at one time or another.

"What seems to be the problem?" She remained rational, giving him the benefit of the doubt, yet something in the pit of her stomach started to rumble.

"Harvey didn't know he needed to schedule in the training for the first week of October." Harvey Toffer was head of Castle's customer training department. "Now he's got a conflict with Lurient Mining."

"As I recall, Lurient was supposed to be the third week of October."

"Well, you recall wrong. There's a conflict."

Her heart rate jumped up a notch. She didn't like his tone, she didn't like his attitude. Lurient *was* supposed to be the third week of October, but she wasn't going to argue in front of Kyle. As it was, she felt his glance flick between the two of them. It had been Chuck and Lydia last week, now it was Ronson. Kyle would start wondering if she could handle her department.

Josie picked up her pencil and jotted a note on her pad. "All right. I'll set up a meeting with Harvey and we'll figure it out."

Ronson's nostrils flared. "It doesn't take a fucking meeting."

There was a breath of nervous silence. Kyle sat back in his chair, turning his pen around and around in his fingers. Next to Ronson, Bertrice, their newbie, pushed back slightly from the table as if afraid she'd get caught in the cross fire. Lydia stopped writing, glancing between Ronson and Josie.

"I said we'll have a meeting with him, Andrew." She tapped her pad. "Next issue."

He shot her a sullen, narrow-eyed glance. Then his lip twitched in a snarl of a smile. "You've got the wrong boom length on the dragline system for Huntington."

"I did not have the wrong boom." In that moment, she hated him. He wanted to humiliate her in front of Kyle, make her look inept, stupid, and worthless.

"Oh yes, you fucking do," Ronson shot back. "Want to see the spreadsheet *you* put together?"

"Stop being an asshole, Ronson."

"At least I'm not a fucking idiot like you," Ronson shot back.

"We will end this meeting now." Kyle rose.

Good God, what must he think of her? Dammit, she *wasn't* sure she was right and Ronson was wrong about the boom, but with a red haze in front of her eyes, she wanted to beat Ronson to a bloody pulp. Another part of her simply wanted to crawl beneath the table. She hated this overwhelming need to impress Kyle.

She hated more that Kyle had to come to her rescue in the middle of *her* staff meeting. God, she wanted to make Ronson pay. Damn him.

On the conference phone, Jenkins cleared his throat and brought her back to the moment. Ronson had stormed from the room; the others were filing out, except Kyle and Bertrice, who still wore a wide-eyed expression of horror. What a way to start.

Josie hit the speaker button and picked up the receiver. "Jenkins, we've got your updates. Unless there's anything else, we'll see you on Monday." He was flying in late Friday night.

"Sure thing, Josie. You know he's an asshole. Ignore him."

She glanced at Kyle. He studied her with a steady, dark gaze. "Thanks, Jenkins. Have a good week. Talk to you later."

Kyle would call her on the carpet now, tell her she'd handled the situation like a petulant child.

Instead, he flipped his wrist and glanced at his watch. "I've got a meeting in three minutes with Toffer. I'll let him know about the Lurient issue."

What did that mean? That he didn't think she could handle the problem? Everything was a fucking mess. "Fine. Thanks. I'll check with him later."

She'd also check on the goddamn boom for Huntington. She crooked a finger. "Bertrice, let's go over the projects I'm assigning. In my office."

"Sure."

Kyle stopped at the door. "Ladies." He waved Bertrice through first.

Was he watching Bertrice's ass in that tight suit of hers? Josie felt the color rise in her face. She was losing it. Completely. She'd let Ronson belittle her in front of the entire group, resorted to name calling, and now this, jealous of the new girl.

Her day couldn't get any worse.

Kyle tapped her arm. "We need to talk after I'm done with my meeting. I'll give you a call."

Oh yeah. It could get a lot worse.

KYLE wasn't sure why, but Andrew Ronson had it in for Josie. His meeting with the head of Customer Training might enlighten him somewhat.

Harvey Toffer was a genial guy in his early forties with red hair that reminded Kyle of Bozo the Clown. He was competent, at least as far as Kyle could ascertain on such short acquaintance.

They met in Harvey's office, which was overrun by binders and folders that seemed to multiply like rabbits as the discussion progressed. He'd ask a question, Harvey would pull down a binder. Instead of putting it back, he'd set it on the floor or a chair, even the top of the trash can when he ran out of room elsewhere.

But he found every answer he was looking for.

"Tell me about Lurient," Kyle said. "I understand there's a conflict on the dates with Alta Vista."

Harvey leaned back and steepled his fingers over his belly. "All right, I got my wires crossed on that. Lurient wanted to pull in the training two weeks early so I scheduled them. I didn't realize we already had Alta Vista that week."

"I'm not sure how that happens. Isn't there a master schedule somewhere that you and the project managers work from?"

Harvey seesawed his head. "Yes, yes. I missed updating it. After Andrew brought it up, I checked my e-mails, and I saw I'd missed that one from Josie." He frowned. "It was the day Ernie left. We were all a bit muddled." Then he raised his hands. "But it's not a big deal. Andrew sent me an e-mail last week, so I checked with Lurient. They say the second week of October will work just as well." He made a face. "I told Andrew that this morning."

True, Josie could have checked the training schedule or followed up with another e-mail. However, he also knew the project had been turned over to Andrew fairly soon after she'd been made manager, so the responsibility became his. To use Josie's vernacular, whatever. Andrew had deliberately made it sound as if the date conflict was unresolved.

He was trying to sabotage his boss in an open forum.

After the update meeting with Harvey ended, Kyle returned to his office. As VP, he'd gotten a second-floor corner with windows on two sides overlooking the side parking lot and a row of hedges separating the facility from a warehousing outfit next door. His chair was leather, the desk expansive, and the six-man conference table made of oak.

He didn't have a dedicated secretary, but he could use any one of the AAs. They had four in the group, including Lydia Gomez. One of them had kindly left him a company directory. He looked up Andrew Ronson's extension.

Five minutes later, the man entered his office.

"Shut the door."

Andrew had a paunch on an otherwise slight build. After closing the door, he sat in one of the two chairs in front of Kyle's desk, pulling his pant leg up slightly and crossing an ankle over the opposite knee.

Kyle didn't give him a chance to say a word. "First, you don't use *fuck* in a meeting."

"Josie's heard the word *fuck* before."

"I don't give a shit. It's unprofessional. You use it in meetings, it'll slip in with customers. So don't fucking use it."

"Yes, sir."

He didn't like the man, and he didn't give a damn that he was coming across as an autocratic asshole. Andrew Ronson needed a wake-up call.

He gave him one. "Second, keep a civil tongue when you're addressing your boss."

"Just like she keeps a civil tongue?" Andrew's lip curled in a snarl.

Kyle leaned forward, narrowed his eyes. "You do not shit on your boss in the presence of others. You save it for an appropriate time and place. Got that?"

"Yes, sir." The *sir* was not a compliment.

He wasn't about to have a mutiny on his first day, but in a war zone, he'd take Josie's side. With him, she had a proven track record. Andrew was an unknown. "This is your only warning, because I'm not getting a good impression."

Andrew clenched his teeth. His jaw worked. "I've got it."

"Thank you for your time." Though Kyle knew he'd created an enemy on his first goddamn day, he smiled genially as the man left. There'd been no help for it. Whatever the underlying reasons—which he still needed to learn from Josie—he didn't tolerate bad behavior. If you didn't act immediately, the problem escalated out of control.

He'd left Josie alone all weekend. Though God help him, he'd picked up his cell phone several times wanting to make contact, to hear her voice. This morning, she was as cool as ice introducing him around. The first emotion she'd shown was with Andrew. He wanted to know what was going on, with the department in general and Andrew Ronson in particular. And after she blew him in the short-term parking at the airport, he badly wanted to know where things stood between the two of them.

As he reached for the phone, though, Connor Kingston entered for a chat.

Damn. What he wanted from Josie would have to wait.

KYLE had said he wanted to speak with her after his meeting with Toffer, yet Josie'd received neither a call nor a message. She'd seen Toffer in the hall half an hour ago.

She headed down to the cafeteria. There was a full-service grill featuring burgers and hot meals, made-to-order sandwiches, a coffee bar with a do-it-yourself espresso machine. Crock-Pots of beef stew, today's special, bubbled on the counter, perfuming the air with a spicy, mouthwatering scent. There were several tables inside and picnic tables out on the patio, but not many were taken. The rush hadn't started yet.

Josie kept her lunch in the refrigerator. She brown-bagged it every day unless she was at a customer site. When she'd first started at Castle after she'd graduated college, the habit absolutely appalled her parents, her mom in particular. They weren't trailer trash, after all. But Josie wasn't going to live by their rules. Buying lunch was expensive, even with subsidized cafeteria prices, especially as she'd been saving for a condo. Plus, you generally ended up with less healthy meals, or eating too much. She wasn't going to let being a manager change the way she did things. Besides, she could eat at her desk and get some work done, too.

She had a lot to do since she'd be out of the office tomorrow for a trip to Coyote Ridge. The load-out upgrades were being installed. Then Thursday and Friday she had supervisor training up in the city. It wasn't a good time to be gone, with Kyle starting and Bertrice to babysit her first few days. Not to mention Ronson being such a dick. He was the reason she needed the damn supervisor training in the first place. Still, it was bad timing.

She grabbed her bag from the fridge, peeking inside because she'd forgotten what she'd made. Salami, cheese, and an apple.

"So now you have the new boss in your pocket, too." Ronson, voice low, her ears only.

Dammit, what had Kyle said to him? She crumpled the edges of her bag together, a particularly apt epithet rising to her lips. Being a manager, though, she had to learn to think before she spoke. Calling him an asshole in the meeting was bad.

He leaned in. "Guess we know whose cock you've been sucking."

Jesus. A lump jumped to her throat, and her heart turned over, beating furiously. He couldn't know. It wasn't possible.

He smiled, a malicious turquoise sparkle in his gaze. "I admire how fast you work. He's only been here a day, and already you've got him eating out of your hand, taking your side."

She could breathe again. He was merely trying to rile her. He didn't know anything. "Why don't we go to HR and you can reiterate your comment?"

"You've got them all in your pocket because you're family. I'd end up getting the shaft."

She marveled that they could speak so softly, appear so mild to the few people scattered about the cafeteria. It wasn't full-on lunch hour yet. "What's up with you? I don't get it. If you hate it here so much, why don't you quit?"

He leaned close enough for her to smell his sweat. "Because I want to make your life a living hell."

Why, dammit? Not that *why* really mattered. With the heels on her boots, he was only slightly taller. She raised her chin. "Then we're both going to be in hell because I'm going to make you fucking miserable until you leave with your tail between your legs."

He laughed softly. "Using the word *fuck* is unprofessional. I might have to report you to your boss."

So that was one of the things Kyle had said to him. "Are you declaring war, Ronson?"

"You bet your fucking ass, I am. Make sure you keep it covered, sweetcheeks."

Then he walked away, disappearing around a corner. Obviously he'd only entered because he saw her and couldn't resist the chance to shovel a little more shit in her face.

Dammit. Why did Kyle have to involve himself? He'd made everything ten times worse.

She didn't find him in his office until after lunch. Closing the door, she shut herself in with him. "Why did you talk to Ronson? I could have handled the problem on my own."

He sat behind his desk, elbows on the arms of his chair. "Have a seat."

"I don't want to sit. I'm pissed." She realized she wouldn't have said that to any other boss, but dammit, Kyle was different. *They* were different.

"Andrew isn't just *your* problem. He became my problem in that meeting."

She hated his calm, level tone when she couldn't even get a semblance of order on her emotions. She paced to let off some of the steam. "He pointed the finger at me for all the issues, not you."

Kyle cocked his head. "I would appear weak in front of the whole group if I let him get away with that shit in a meeting. Even for you, I'm not letting them think I'm a pushover."

For her? "You ended up making me look weak instead."

"You did that to yourself."

His words sliced like blades. She didn't even have a comeback because he was right.

"Whatever the issues are"—he went on slicing and dicing her—"you don't let yourself get pulled into name calling in front of your subordinates. When you stoop to his level, it diminishes you in their eyes."

She wasn't a crier, the furthest thing from it, but her throat clogged and her eyes ached. His first day, his *very* first, she came off looking like a total fuckup. She didn't want him getting this view of her. She could blame Ronson, but she didn't have to rise to that dickhead's baiting. It was too damn demoralizing for words.

She didn't even have a lover to whom she could run after work and spill all her troubles. Kyle was it.

"You've got a huge rift in your department." He didn't have to add that she'd only been managing the group a month. "Why?"

"I don't know." She hated admitting it. "Other than the fact that Ronson wanted the job." Should she mention he'd threatened her with a lawsuit? She decided to lay it on the table so it didn't come back to bite her ass later. "He might be trying to push me into firing him so he can call reverse discrimination. Or something."

Kyle shook his head. "A suit will never fly in the long run, but it'll be a pain in the ass having to deal with it. We need to effect some sort of reconciliation."

How was she supposed to do that when they'd declared war on each other down in the cafeteria? All right, *that* she wasn't going to tell Kyle about. "I'll take care of it."

"Sit down, and we'll strategize together."

She rubbed her temple where it had begun to ache. She hated how bad she must look in his eyes. It didn't matter whether they were fuck buddies or not, she'd have hated it with any boss.

"I don't have the time right now." She didn't want to reveal any more of her deficiencies.

"Josie, we need to talk."

"I said no," she snapped, the sound harsh in her throat. She certainly wouldn't have said *that* to any other boss. "I have a meeting with Walker," she added, as if that would somehow mitigate it. Of course, Walker didn't know about the meeting.

"You put it off too long, it'll blow up in your face." He didn't say that it meant things would blow up in his face, too, because he was her boss, but that was the fact. It would reflect just as badly on him.

So she gave him what she could. "I'll be at Coyote Ridge tomorrow, then supervisor training, so I'll be out of the office the rest of the week. It'll give us time to cool down, plus I can talk it out with the experts at the training."

"It's a start." He rose. "Where's the training?"

"In the city. Thursday, Friday, and a half-day Saturday."

"On Monday, I want a solution."

"Fine. You'll have it." Dammit, she wasn't an idiot, and she didn't need his hand-holding. She would figure this out.

"And we need a resolution on the Huntington boom," he added.

Thank God she'd looked it up. "They changed the requirement, so the order is good. Ronson didn't see the notations I made about it in the customer file." Or he'd simply ignored them for a chance to make her look bad.

"I appreciate your checking."

Yeah right, like she *wasn't* going to research it?

She left his office pissed, at him for his high-handed meddling, at Ronson for being a total dick, but mostly at herself for acting like the idiot she so badly didn't want to be.

ANYONE else, Kyle would have called both parties into his office and told them to work it out. Now. Josie, however, wasn't just anybody to him, and he couldn't run the risk of alienating her further. As it was, he'd said enough to send her running. She'd refused his advice, preferring to talk it out with the *experts*. Obviously he wasn't one. He knew something she couldn't refuse. His next challenge.

At five on the dot, he called her cell.

She picked up. "I haven't left the office yet. This is still work time."

"Then call me back when you have."

She was a feisty handful. He waited two hours before she returned his call. "I am off the clock, you are not my boss now, so I don't want to talk about anything to do with work."

"I don't want to talk about it, either."

"Fine." Irritation sizzled through her voice.

"You're in the city Friday night, right?"

She hesitated. "Yes." He could almost hear her brain working overtime trying to figure out what he had planned.

"There's a place up there."

"What kind of place?"

"Let's call it a sex club." He'd never been, he'd only heard about it. But he wanted to try it. With her.

"No way."

"Oh yes. We will be attending on Friday night. Late. I've heard the action at the club doesn't really start jumping until midnight."

"I've got training in the morning."

"I'll have you back by morning."

The bleat of a car horn filled the silence on her end. She was parked now, minus the drone of the moving vehicle.

She'd fed him to Kisa on a silver platter. Now the tables would turn. "You will do everything I say."

This time she was quick to answer. "I'm not fucking some skanky guy you pick out just so you can get your kicks."

It was the furthest thing from his mind. She was his. "I won't make you fuck a skanky guy."

Another long silence, then finally. "Are you going to fuck some skanky girl?"

"I won't fuck any skanky women." *Go on. Ask me. Beg me not to fuck anyone at all.*

She didn't beg. "I reserve the right to say that something is going too far."

"Other than fucking a skank, which I've already agreed I won't make you do," he murmured, "what's going too far?"

Click, click, click went the wheels in her head. "I won't know for sure until you try to make me do it."

"That's leaving the field wide open."

"Take it or leave it."

"Aren't you forgetting it's my challenge?"

She sighed heavily. "I don't want to be compelled to do something distasteful."

"It was distasteful for me to be rejected by your Little Miss Snowflake. My ego has been mortally wounded."

"You"—she laughed with an edge—"are full of crap. You enjoyed every minute of that entire evening."

He enjoyed making Josie hot and bothered. "You win. I will not choose any skanks for either of us to have to get nasty with. You get first right of refusal."

He could hear her humming under her breath. "All right, fine, whatever," she said. "You can call me and tell me what time to meet you and where."

"I'll pick you up at your hotel."

She huffed. "Fine."

"And when we get there," he said, "there will be no huffing. You will enjoy what I make you do. Got it?"

"Yes, sir." She punctuated that with another huff and hung up.

Kyle had to laugh. She was a firecracker. She thought he'd make her perform with a stranger. Or watch him perform with some hottie. It was obvious she didn't like either option.

Good. Before long, he'd get her to admit their relationship was more than just sex.

16

JOSIE had lain awake all night, and on the drive over to the Coyote Ridge plant, her mind was awhirl. She was damn lucky she didn't have an accident because she sure as hell wasn't paying attention to the road.

All right. She'd set him up with Little Miss Snowflake, but the wench hadn't come across with the goods. Now he was dying to prove he could find another woman to take him to heaven. Josie had fallen into her own trap. She now *hated* the idea of any woman touching him, let alone sucking him. She was even past the point of being okay with a kiss. It had to be her or no one.

More than anything, she'd wanted to stipulate they couldn't touch or be touched by anyone else, but that would have revealed way too much. If he knew how she felt, he'd have all the power.

Hell, he already had all the power.

The sand plant was fine; the installation went off without a hitch. On the way back over the mountain highway, she was *still* running through all the different scenarios Kyle could pull on her. Of course, she should have been thinking her way out of her Ronson problems, but whatever.

Her cell phone rang, and she knew it was Kyle. She already had her Bluetooth in.

"Josie Tybrook here."

"Hey, Josie, how goes it?"

So much for her internal radar. She didn't recognize the voice. Thin, soft, a little gravelly, she could barely hear it over the road noise. "I'm sorry. I'm having trouble hearing you. Who is this?"

"Ernie," he said louder, though his voice still sounded weak. "Your old boss?" he added, as if she'd forgotten she knew someone named Ernie.

"Ernie, how are you?" Good God. She hadn't even called to check on him.

"I'm okay. But I've been hearing stuff about you."

Her stomach did a somersault. "Like what?"

"Nothing bad, don't worry. Only that people are giving you a hard time."

Someone told Ernie about *her* crap? "Who'd you talk to?"

"Never you mind. But I feel badly I left you without any words of caution, not even a rundown of any personality issues."

He was sick. He had *that* to worry about, not her or the job. "Ernie, you don't owe me anything."

"I should have done more prep work with you."

"Ernie, please. You need to concentrate on getting well"—God, how trite that sounded—"and people from work shouldn't be bothering you."

"Listen, kid, I want you to stop by the house on your way back to the office."

So, he'd talked to someone who knew she was out for part of today. Duh. Everyone at work knew. "I really can't do that."

"I want to talk to you. It'll make me feel better."

She wondered if he was playing the guilt card on purpose. Not that it mattered. She'd do whatever Ernie wanted. "All right." She glanced at the dashboard clock. His house wasn't far out of the way. "I'll be there in about twenty minutes."

"Good. Glo just made my favorite, a red velvet cake. You ever had red velvet cake?"

"No, Ernie." Why did the thought of his wife Gloria whipping up his favorite cake make her want to cry?

"Then you're in for a treat."

After ending the call, she phoned Lydia to let her know she'd be later than anticipated.

Gloria answered the door when she arrived. Gray sifting through her brown hair, a little on the plump side, she had the facial wrinkles of a woman who laughed a lot. Or at least she used to. Josie remembered her as always having a smile, but now there were lines of strain across her forehead, grooves of sadness slashing down by the sides of her mouth.

"Josie, come on in." Her cheeks were still pink from the heat of the kitchen. "Ernie's in the family room. I'm cutting the cake. Do you want coffee or tea?"

"Coffee, if you've already got it made. But tea's fine otherwise." She wasn't fond of tea, but she wouldn't put Gloria to any trouble.

"It's already perking."

The scent began to drift into the entryway as Gloria led her to the back of the house.

Ernie lay on the brown-and-yellow plaid sofa in the family room, pillows stuffed behind his back, a blanket pulled over his lap despite the summer warmth. He looked smaller, his chest shrunken, yet his face was puffy, the lines filled out. He looked like one of those funny caricature sketches with his head too big for his body. A TV tray by his side bore the remote, a couple of paperback thrillers, his coffee mug, an empty water tumbler, a can of Ensure, and a profusion of pill bottles.

Josie swallowed hard, then leaned down to give him a hug, his bones fragile in her embrace. "Hey, you."

She couldn't say he was getting better. It was obvious Ernie was never getting better.

Oh God, oh God. She wanted to close her eyes and not see.

"Have a seat." He held out a hand, indicating the easy chair next to the sofa.

"Thanks." She sat, crossing her legs. "Now, you have to stop worrying about work or me or any of that, Ernie."

"I'm not worried, but I figured it's been a month, and you'd probably need to talk."

She smiled, shaking her head. "*People* have been calling you to say things are falling apart." She waved her index finger at him. "If I figure out who it is, they are in big trouble. Nobody should be laying this stuff on you."

Ernie just smiled. It looked odd on his overly round face, as if the skin was stretched too tightly.

"Here we are. Cake and coffee." Gliding in from the kitchen, Gloria handed Josie a plate off the tray balanced on her palm, then deposited a steaming mug on the coffee table. Removing the dirty glass, Ensure can, and the used mug from Ernie's TV tray, she gave him a fresh coffee cup and a plate of red cake with gooey white icing. There was no third plate for her, and she went immediately back to the kitchen, the clink of glass in the sink and running water filtering back into the family room.

The plate trembled in his hand as Ernie forked a mouthful of red velvet and savored, his eyes closed. "Yum. Yum." Two separate sentences, the same emphatic word.

It tasted like sludge, but Josie realized that was only her mood. "Good, huh?"

"Yum," she punctuated.

He moved like an old man, slowly, a little wobbly. She almost wanted to hold the plate for him.

"So, tell me all, baby girl."

He'd never used pet names on her before, yet despite the oddness, it was comforting and eased the tension that had been riding her chest. "You sure you wanna hear everything?"

"Everything." He slid another forkful into his mouth and closed his eyes as if he were already in heaven. His smile beamed. "Lay it on me."

She did. About Ronson sabotaging her in the staff meeting, Chuck and the ass pinching, Lydia's baby, the screwups, the indecision, the new girl. Everything except the part about fucking her new boss.

"Baby girl, you think you've got an insurmountable mess on your hands."

She nodded, and funnily enough, after getting all that off her chest, the cake tasted better. Delicious, in fact; moist, smooth, with orgasmic cream cheese frosting.

"Well, you don't," Ernie said

"What do I have, then?"

"Life."

"It was never like this when you were there."

"It was exactly like this." He waited, letting her absorb.

She remembered the box of tissues in his desk drawer, right where Lydia knew it was. How many times had Lydia gone into his office, closed the door, and asked for the box? Josie hadn't paid attention.

"You wanna know Ronson's problem?"

"Yes, please." She nodded eagerly as if she were talking to the oracle at Delphi.

"His wife. They've got three little ones, and she's constantly riding him that he doesn't make enough money, that he's away too much, that he leaves her to take care of all the really important stuff."

Ronson's wife sounded like a bitch. Josie had never met her. "So he wanted the manager job for the extra money and less travel in order to make his wife happy?"

"To make his wife start seeing him as a man worthy of her."

Wow. That was harsh. "He actually told you that?"

"That's my diplomatic version of it." He shook his head, eyes sad. "Sometimes a man's gotta get stuff off his chest."

She still had a hard time imagining Ronson admitting that aloud, though she could empathize with how helpless it would make him feel. "Why didn't you give him the job then?"

"Because my first loyalty is to the company, and Andrew is not a leader." He eyed her steadily.

"And I am?"

"You've got good potential."

"Why didn't you tell me that before?" She didn't need constant strokes, but once in a while, it would be nice to hear.

"I was a shitty boss." He set his empty cake plate aside.

"No, you weren't."

He smiled, shaking his head slightly. "You're a terrible liar, baby girl."

She really liked his name for her. Anyone else, she'd have hated it, even Kyle. He could call her baby, but that was it. "So what do I do about Ronson? He can't have my job, I'm not giving him a raise, and he's still going to have to travel."

"You're going to think like a woman."

She made a face. "Huh?"

"When he starts acting like an asshole, you're going to remember exactly why he's doing it. Because his wife is giving him hell at home."

She set aside her plate. "And then what?"

"Then you're going to say something like, 'Thanks for fixing that problem with the training overlap, Andrew. Thanks for noting that about the boom length. Good job.'"

Ernie's imitation of her made her laugh. "That's not going to work."

"Sure it is. Don't take offense, don't take blame, offer praise instead. It will defuse him. He wants you to react badly so he can feel justified in taking his anger out on you. If you don't let it get to you, however, he'll look like a putz for escalating."

She thought about exactly what went on. Ronson had been baiting her, but the nasty stuff didn't start until she got her back up. Right? It might have been yesterday, but just like seven witnesses gave seven different versions, she couldn't recall exactly how it went down. Ernie could be right. "It's sort of like training a dog."

"That's my girl, you got it."

"Except that it might already be past the point of no return." She dipped her head. "We sort of had a little gunfight in the cafeteria."

"Josie, Josie, Josie." He shook his head, a frown of overdone sadness on his face. "You have to learn to think before you speak."

"I know. It's a big fault of mine."

"Doesn't matter, though. Just pretend it never happened."

She huffed out a breath, jutting her chin forward. "You can't just pretend something like that away."

"You'd be surprised what you can pretend, baby girl." Then he lowered his eyebrows. "Unless it's your mistake. That goes for a boss, a subordinate, or a significant other. If it's yours, own up to it and apologize."

She leaned back in the chair and popped the footrest up. "You

know, Ernie, I underestimated you all these years. You're a verita-
ble fountain of knowledge."

He laughed, and God, it looked good, even if his face was puffy
with whatever drugs they had him on. "Baby girl, you underesti-
mate *yourself*. Now, Lydia or Chuck next?"

She wagged her head back and forth. "Chuck." Lydia was a
whole different bowl of goo.

"You handled it the best way you can. It'll blow over."

"Did you ever have that problem before?"

The smile was slow in coming, but it finally sparkled all the
way to his eyes. "Chuck likes to complain, and he wants his complaints validated. Lydia hasn't figured out where the line of familiarity ends." Then he shrugged. "You've discussed it with Chuck,
talked to Lydia about it, HR got involved. Issue over."

"It can't be this easy."

Ernie reached for his coffee cup, blew on it though it had already cooled, then sipped. "It's not easy. You'll get sick to death of
the crap that comes into your office. Some days you'll just want to
shout, 'People, get a life!' "

She already wanted to shout that from the rooftops, and she'd
only managed for a month.

He grinned. "Want your old job back?"

She snorted. "No." A very big 33 percent of her did. "Lydia,
though, I think I've said all I can say."

Ernie gazed at her for several seconds. "Lydia's a sweet girl,
but she's a bit of a drama queen. She doesn't need your advice because she'll figure it out on her own. She just needs you to listen to
her. She's a fine worker, but she needs babying. She wants to think
you love her and care about her."

"I'm not her psychiatrist, for God's sake." Or the girl's mother.
It seemed ridiculous. Josie would never have considered telling Ernie anything so personal. Should a boss have to listen to all this to

keep her workers happy? "I don't think you need to mollycoddle your employees."

"As a boss, you give them what they need in order to get the best out of them. Being a good manager is figuring out what that 'need' is and fulfilling it. Within reason, of course."

"So for Lydia, it's having someone listen to her and care about her?" It seemed too simple yet at the same time a bit terrifying. She couldn't sit and listen without needing to tell Lydia how to fix it.

Ernie gave a quick shake of his head. "You don't have to fix it for her."

"I did not say that out loud," she said.

"You're an open book. But *you*"—he pointed—"are doing fine." He leaned back against his pillows. "Just don't take everything so seriously. Mellow out, baby girl."

Ernie hadn't solved her problems. He could be right. He could as easily be wrong. What he'd said sounded so simplistic. Too easy. Still, she felt immeasurably better.

She stayed a while after that, told him all the latest gossip— except her own—laughed with him, talked with him, let him call her *baby girl*, and tried to pretend he wasn't dying.

On the way out, Glo gave her a long, tight hug. "You made him feel good, important. Needed." She patted Josie's cheek, and whispered, "Thank you."

It was four thirty. She debated going back to work or going home. She wanted some time to process everything Ernie had said, come up with a plan of action. Because no matter how many times Ernie told her not to take it all so seriously, she *had* to have an action plan. That wouldn't happen if she went back to the office. She'd get caught up in . . . stuff.

Then again, she would see Kyle. If she was going to take advice from Ernie, then maybe she shouldn't be so harsh when Kyle gave her advice. It was her ego getting in the way.

Home or the office? Eenie, meenie, minie . . . Kyle.
She took the freeway exit for Castle.

IN the chair opposite, Josie crossed her legs. Having been out at the quarry, she was wearing those sexy steel-toed boots again. They made it damn hard to concentrate on what she was saying.

Kyle rose, shifting to sit on the edge of his desk so he could see them better.

"And that's the plan," she said, giving him a pretty smile.

"That sounds more like doing nothing."

"No. It's letting bygones be bygones. If Ronson wants to continue it, he's going to have to act badly, and that will make him look idiotic."

"Josie—"

She held up a finger. He wanted to take the tip in his mouth, suck it. He simply raised one eyebrow, letting her go on.

"I want to try this. If it doesn't work, I'll rethink."

She looked calmer after her visit with Ernie Masters. She looked like the woman he met the first day—confident, competent.

"All right." He doubted changing her behavior would have an effect on Ronson. In his opinion, the man was too far gone. He was pissed at the world, not just Josie. But she'd come back from Ernie's all fired up. Kyle wouldn't put her down now.

Nor would he wait until the situation was a powder keg or a lawsuit waiting to happen. "You're back on Monday. We'll see how it goes in the meeting. I'll give you a couple of days to gauge the effect on Ronson, then we'll revisit the issue."

"Thank you."

He glanced at the wall clock. "It's after five."

She turned her wrist to confirm. "So it is. I've got work to do." She started to rise.

"Sit."

"I'm not a dog."

"It's after five, business is over. I want to know what you're wearing on Friday."

"To the supervisor's training?" A playful light flickered in her eyes.

"Friday night."

She glanced behind. "Your office door is open."

"I can close it."

"No, that would be even worse."

"Talk softly then." He kept his eye on the hall outside.

She rolled her eyes. "I haven't decided."

"Then I'll decide for you."

Lowering her chin, she gazed at him through her lashes. "Which is what you wanted to do anyway."

Of course he did. "I want you in all black. High heels, the fishnet stockings, short skirt, preferably leather, and a tight top. Lycra would be good. Something stretchy."

She made a face. "Eww."

"What is *eww* about it?"

"That sounds like Little Miss Snowflake's attire."

"Not at all." For a moment, he couldn't remember what the hell Kisa wore, only what Josie had done to him in the car, her scent, her taste.

"It is," she insisted.

He folded his arms over his chest. "Do I have to make this an order?"

The rap on wood startled him. Connor Kingston stood in the doorway. "Is she flouting orders already?"

Josie gasped, her eyes flew to Kyle's. She swallowed visibly.

Kyle merely smiled. "I think we're beginning to see eye-to-eye, but she certainly does have her own way of doing things."

"I'll say. But she's good."

Josie turned in the chair, bracing herself with one hand on the back. "You know, I'm right here. If you want to talk *about* me, I'll just leave."

Connor held up a hand. "No. I don't want to interrupt your meeting."

"We're done," she said, with an edge Kyle hoped Connor didn't pick up on. She turned back. "I'll be at the supervisor training Thursday and Friday, but I'll have my computer so I can check e-mails on break, and if there's anything urgent, you can leave me a voice mail."

That was his Josie, thorough, professional. "Sounds great. Have a good time."

She eyed him as if there was a double message in that, which of course there was, then she gave him a polite employee-to-boss smile and left.

As he ushered Connor in, he wondered whether she'd wear what he told her to. Or surprise him. Either way, she was his for the night.

GOD, that had been a close call. That's why she didn't want to even *talk* non-business with the man while they were at work. *Anyone* could drop in, or eavesdrop. What if Connor had over-heard Kyle detailing her clothes, for God's sake?

Of course, she stopped at the mall on the way home to find a Lycra top. She had everything else, except that the skirt wasn't leather the way he wanted. Instead, it was a short, pleated school-girl style. She liked the effect of it with the fishnet stockings, the good and bad girl all rolled into one.

That night, she stopped in the midst of packing her bag. "Why are you doing this, everything he wants, *anything* he wants?"

It wasn't like she had an answer, but excitement thrummed through her blood. Picking out clothing to wear for him tantalized her. In the store, she'd fingered the top, thinking of him, and she'd actually gotten wet. Stripping down in the dressing room to try it on, she'd touched herself. She hadn't played, but she stood in front of the mirror with her hand in her panties and imagined how hard he'd get watching her. She especially remembered the lingerie shop.

She left early Thursday morning to avoid the traffic. The two days of seminars were common sense, plus studying the applicable laws. God, there was a law for *everything*.

Nothing blew up in her absence, no emergency e-mails or hysterical voice mails. Not even from Lydia. Josie hadn't seen her on Wednesday when she'd returned to work. Okay, she'd pathetically rushed right to Kyle's office, so she hadn't spoken to Lydia about her *predicament*. Truly, was the girl's only need a shoulder to cry on and a boss who cared?

Who knew? Lydia was . . . different. Supervisory training hadn't offered any miraculous answers. Though Josie was glad to learn that her experiences weren't the wackiest. One woman had an employee who'd climbed under his desk and wouldn't come out. They'd had to call his wife, who had in turn called his mother.

After class ended Friday evening, the training group met for dinner in the hotel restaurant. Josie couldn't concentrate. Even making conversation with these relative strangers was damn near beyond her.

Kyle would be here in another two hours and thirty-five minutes. She wanted to soak in the tub with a glass of wine, shave, use a sweetly scented body scrub she'd purchased, then smooth lotion all over. She wanted to smell sweet for him, her skin smooth for his touch.

She'd never prepped like that for a man before.

By the time he knocked on her hotel room door, she had the jitters. That was something new, too. Men were just men, dates were just dates. Kyle was different.

He looked her over. "Hot." Then he raised a brow. "I think I like this skirt even better than what I had in mind. Lots of things are possible."

Her heart rate went up a notch thinking about the ideas running through his mind. Dressed in black jeans and a black, button-down shirt, he made her mouth water.

"Will you keep my card key for the room? I don't want to take a purse." She didn't want to lose it in a place like that.

"Good idea." He put her card in his back pocket. "A purse would get in the way." He held out his hand. "Shall we go?"

She could change her mind. She had no clue what he'd make her do. Or make her watch *him* do. Somehow that was the more horrifying prospect. She hated her jealousy all over again.

Putting her hand in his, she determined to get over it before she ruined the sexy thing they had going. "I'm ready."

The place wasn't far, and though it was well after nine on a Friday in the city, Kyle had no problem finding parking. Amazing. In San Francisco, people usually circled like buzzards searching for a spot, especially on the weekend.

Kyle came to her side, but she was already out. She'd never been one to stand on that kind of ceremony. "This is it?"

"This is it." Kyle nodded, gazing up at the elaborate plasterwork.

The facade was typical San Francisco, with a walk-up to a recessed doorway and curlicue bars over the long windows. She'd been expecting more of the discotheque look, with a crowd mingling outside. This was a quiet neighborhood street, the few shops on the corners long closed for the night. As they watched, a couple entered. Mid-thirties probably, the guy wore regular jeans, the woman a calf-length skirt, nothing out of the ordinary.

"It's not what I expected."

"They don't advertise what's going on inside," Kyle said. "No single guys, only couples or women. At the slightest hint of a problem, they boot the troublemakers."

She turned slightly, glancing at him from the corner of her eye. "So, you come here often."

He smiled, took her hand, and pulled her to the stoop. "I've only heard about it."

"Yeah, right. That's what they all say."

He squeezed her fingers. "I swear on a stack of bibles."

She stopped on the sidewalk. "You don't think we'll know anyone in there, do you?"

He glanced at her, shook his head, then let out a small, exasperated puff of breath. "I seriously doubt that Castle Heavy Mining is infested with perverts like us."

"But those people looked so normal." She considered that she and Kyle looked normal, too, but really, she couldn't see any of her coworkers entering a place like this. She couldn't imagine any of her friends attending either. Truthfully, she was the only pervert she knew. Except maybe Rick or Paul. But then if they saw her, it wouldn't matter. Besides, she didn't think they were this imaginative.

In the meantime, Kyle hadn't said a word, as if waiting for her to come to her own conclusion.

"Okay," she said. "You're right." She'd give him that.

They reached the top of the steps. This time she let him get the door for her. Inside was a small vestibule, the door opposite closing behind the couple they had followed in. To the right was a ticket window, as if they were doing nothing more than buying admission to a movie.

The man behind the Plexiglas, though, was more like what she'd expected; pitch dark hair, a stud in his left nostril, black nail polish, and a body thin to the point of boniness.

"You want Caligula, Tiberius, or Caesar?"

"Caesar." Kyle handed him some bills.

"Just go up the stairs until you get to the green door that matches the color of your hand stamp." Then he waggled his fingers.

They both stuck out their hands for a fluorescent green hand stamp that would get them into "Caesar."

"Here're the rules, dude."

"I read the rules on the website," Kyle told him.

"Yeah, well you're gonna hear the rules anyway. Watch all you want, but no touching unless invited. No drinking, no fighting. No cameras, no recording devices, no cell phones, no solicitation, and no giggling."

"No giggling?" Josie mouthed when Kyle glanced at her.

"You don't follow the rules," the kid went on, "have no fear, you will be tossed out on your ass. There're condoms all over the place. Use 'em." Then he raised a thin arm and waved them on. "Go forth and fornicate, my friends."

As Trinity would say, *ohmigod*.

INSIDE was a coat check room, but Josie hadn't brought a coat. Kyle led her up a narrow set of stairs. "They really have a website?" she asked.

"Yes, they really do. And it explains everything."

"What's Caesar?"

He raised her hand to kiss her knuckles. "Couples and single women only."

"Why no single men?"

"Because the place would be overrun with horny guys."

Duh. "What about Tiberius?"

"Mixed. Heterosexual, gay, lesbian, and transgender."

Okay, she would not make a remark about transgender. "What about Caligula?"

"Hardcore BDSM."

"Eww," she said on an out breath.

"We can watch, if you'd like."

She snorted. "No way."

They reached a landing with three doors: men's room, ladies' room, and a bright fuchsia door. Music pounded from behind the wood. "Tiberius," Kyle said, and turned up the next flight.

At the next landing, men's and ladies' again, and this time a fluorescent green door. Kyle opened it and held their clasped hands for the bouncer to identify their stamps.

The music was softer here than on the floor below, but was still rock and roll, though Josie couldn't identify the band. They entered into a great room. A disco ball twirled in the center of the ceiling, reflecting prisms of light across the walls and the few dancers. The parquet floor was ringed with tables and bar stools, with couples watching. A bar ran along the back wall.

"I thought there was no alcohol."

"It's probably just sodas, water, and nonalcoholic froufrou stuff." He leaned in, his minty breath washing over her. "Fucking is very thirsty work."

"You're bad."

"And about to get a lot worse," he murmured.

That she didn't doubt. "Yeah, well, you'll have to prove it," she said dryly, "because there isn't a whole lot going on right now." It was more tame than a country-and-western hot spot on line-dance night.

"We're early yet." Kyle touched her arm. "The place will be rocking in a bit."

"I was expecting . . . more," she mused, glancing around.

His mouth quirked. "What, you want sex on the dance floor?"

She shrugged. "At least a little nudity."

"Slut," he whispered into her ear.

"Well, if you're coming to a place like this, you want to see some hot action. Otherwise, what's the point?"

He tugged her down a wide hallway with institutional light gray walls and beige linoleum squares, almost as if it were designed for easy cleanup.

"Hot action coming up," he murmured in her ear.

Doors opened on either side, and she glanced in the first room. Video screens covered every wall, the sound of movie moans and groans overlaying the music from the dance floor. Two couples and a single woman were stretched out on beanbags watching a standard porn movie. Her knees bent and legs spread, the woman diddled herself beneath her dress.

"I didn't think women were into the whole visual thing?" Josie muttered against Kyle's shoulder. She wasn't so much, at least not in videos.

"That one obviously is."

The couples swapped oral, man on woman and woman on man. Now that was better than video and oddly exciting, not so much because the live performers were attractive—they were pretty run of the mill—but because she'd never watched another woman take a cock. The slow glide of her mouth down her partner's shaft shot a little bubble of heat straight to Josie's pussy.

"Good technique," Kyle said, pulling Josie closer and wrapping his arm around her waist.

She scented him like an animal scents her mate. He was hot, sexy, aroused where his body snugged against hers. Even as she watched, the couples separated, came together again, this time having switched partners. Good God. What if Kyle asked the woman to do him, too?

"I can suck better than that," she said, disdain dripping from her voice.

He nuzzled her hair. "Most likely."

She jabbed him lightly with her elbow. "Most *definitely*."

"Jealous?"

"Give me a break." Yes, terribly. If Kyle approached the woman, Josie might have to rip her hair out in a total bitch fight.

"Let's move on." He towed her away. "There's so much more to see."

In the few minutes they'd been in the room, the hallway had begun to fill up a tad, gawkers peering in rooms just as she and Kyle were doing.

Kyle led her through another door, on the right, shuffling up against the wall and pulling her to him. Back to front, he wrapped his arms around her waist and watched over her shoulder.

A black light made everything glow, the shag carpet a fluorescent blue and the walls a rainbow of color. For the center show, a woman splayed herself on a device that reminded Josie of a small mechanical bull. On a pedestal, the machine was low enough to the floor to allow the woman to quite literally ride it. Her skin was painted with flowers and swirls of color, and her body glowed as she bounced. Holding a handle in front, she rose and fell, revealing a large, black, ribbed dildo slipping in and out of her pussy. Throwing her head back, she moaned loudly and pinched her nipples. The small crowd gathered in the room murmured their excitement.

Kyle slid a hand down and palmed Josie's pussy through her skirt, then he delved beneath the material and stroked her clit. In his description of what to wear, he hadn't mentioned panties. So she hadn't worn any. It was so good, thank God she was leaning against him or she might have fallen. She wanted to close her eyes, arch into his hand, come hard, for him, only him. Everything came back to Kyle, and that alone was frightening. She was losing the game to him.

"Stop that." She swatted at him, pulling his hand away.

"Don't tell me," he whispered in her ear, "that watching her ride a massive cock doesn't make you hot."

It was his touch that made her wild. She tipped her head back against his shoulder. "It's . . . interesting."

"Want me to buy you one?"

"You buy me one and I won't need you anymore." She batted her eyelashes.

"You will need me badly before this night is over." He pinched her nipple hard enough to make her pussy wet. Wetter. He was right; she was turned on. The woman, the mechanical dildo, the people, and most especially Kyle's hard cock riding along her spine.

"Don't get your hopes up," she quipped. He was the one who would be dying for her. She'd make sure of it. "What else is there to see?"

He nipped her earlobe. "Let's find out."

Jostling them through the doorway, he pulled her along behind. She didn't feel they'd been here that long—and she'd specifically left behind her watch—yet the place was rocking now, as Kyle put it, more men than women despite the rule about couples and single women only. Nevertheless, a fog of perfumes floated on the air. Against the wall, a man allowed his zipper to be tugged down, his cock yanked out, and a female mouth descend upon him. The woman wore a silver-studded leather collar, and a big beefy guy held the leash in his meaty fist as he watched the two. "Take him deeper," he demanded, gently tapping the back of her blond head. "Suck him harder."

"You want that?" Kyle whispered. "To have me push you down on your knees and make you suck a cock for me?"

"Do not think you're *ever* putting a leash on me."

He smiled wickedly, all teeth. "My challenge, I choose."

She wagged her finger at him as he propelled her through the now crowded hall. "I do have my limits, and that's one of them."

Before she could even blink, he whirled her around and backed her up against the wall, towering over her. His eyes glittered. Holding her chin in his hand, he forced her gaze to his. "What other limits? Tell me now."

Don't touch another woman, don't fuck another woman, don't let her go down on you.

She couldn't say any of those things. It was debilitating to admit she felt that way.

"No leashes, because you don't own me and I'm not your little pet." She blinked. "But if you want me down on my knees sucking some random guy's cock, I can do that." It was absolutely true. She had no qualms about doing that if he wanted her to. If it made him hot, hard, irrevocably turned on, by her, by what she would do for him. She just didn't want him to want some other woman. Everything had to be about her. "As long as he's not skanky," she added so he wouldn't be able to see her thoughts written in her eyes.

He took her mouth hard and deep, stealing her breath, weakening her legs. For a moment there was only him and his kiss, his male scent, his minty taste.

Then he backed off, first his mouth, then his whole body slipping away.

"I may or may not decide to loan you out tonight." His eyebrows dipped devilishly. "We'll see how I feel later."

Her stomach fluttered. Would he really? How did it make her feel? Anxious. Hot. Terrified. Unbearably wet. "I'd rather suck you for them."

She could do another, but the thought of taking him while everyone watched made her light-headed. She wanted every woman down to the last one in this seedy, nasty place to know he was hers. To want and not have. To be jealous of *her*. Oh yeah. That she could do. Easily. Gladly.

Exhibitionism was something she'd never tried before, never thought she'd like. Now . . . maybe . . . yeah. For sure.

How badly she wanted to do *something* set her nerves jangling and a hoard of butterflies loose in her stomach. She'd never felt the need to claim a man before witnesses. Make him hers. Own him.

Kyle yanked her away into the wave of people. Where had they all come from? Out of the woodwork it seemed. More men than there should have been. Obviously some were sneaking in without a date. Kyle stuck his head into door after door. There was an orgy in one. All she could make out were heads and asses bobbing, a writhing mass of naked humanity on a pile of mattresses. She hoped they were all following the condom rule. In another, a woman lay on a bed, several men standing over her, jerking off, spraying her with their semen. The next room was a lounge, with sofas, tables, conversation, and only the smallest amount of sex, comparatively speaking; no more than a woman sitting on her lover's lap, her dress hiked, the rest obvious though not visible.

Finding a room that appealed to him, Kyle dragged her in. A large, round dais carpeted in plush blue sat center stage, spotlighted. People mingled. A couple was just stepping down.

Before anyone could take their place, Kyle forced her up.

"Strip off your shirt," he demanded.

"What?" She couldn't be sure she heard correctly.

"I want your breasts naked. I want these people to see how gorgeous you are." He stared at her a long moment in the hot lights beating down on the dais. "I want them to see what's mine."

Her heart pounded, and her body flushed. "No." But the hot glitter in his eyes made her want to do whatever he asked in front of this greedy, avid audience.

"Strip," he said again, louder.

The crowd picked up the word. "Strip, strip, strip." The chant filled the small room, bouncing off the walls, beating inside her chest. "Do it, do it, do it."

So many people, so many eyes. Yet his gaze was all that mattered, and it was all for her. Kyle made her special. Above and beyond anyone else.

Standing up on the dais, she wasn't just some consolation prize because Little Miss Fucking Snowflake hadn't blown him. In his gaze, she saw it, felt it. Kyle Perry wanted Josie Tybrook. He had *chosen* her.

She didn't do it gracefully. She wasn't teasing or sexy. She wanted to expose herself because he was proud enough to want to display her. She wasn't afraid of what anyone saw beneath the mask of her clothing, not with Kyle's hot, hungry gaze literally eating her up. The noise, the laughter, the people all faded away as she yanked her Lycra top over her head and tossed it to him.

Her nipples pebbled at the appreciative murmurs. Her breasts were small, her figure almost boyish, with barely there curves, yet Kyle's eyes blazed hot for her.

He stepped up beside her, then circled his fingers indicating she should turn. The lights were bright, the crowd in the room indistinguishable beneath them. They were mere shadows, faceless. There was only Kyle and the soft shush of voices around him. Hauling her up against him, he plunged his hands beneath her skirt and squeezed her ass, giving all a brief glimpse.

"Gorgeous," he whispered, his eyes smoking hot.

She felt gorgeous. No man had ever called her that before, not because she wasn't reasonably attractive, but because gorgeous applied to someone more feminine. Someone who cared what she wore and how her makeup looked.

All she cared about was the way Kyle saw her. All she wanted was to show these nameless, faceless people how she affected him, that he belonged to her as much as she belonged to him. The need was as frightening as it was exhilarating.

"Turn around," he urged.

She did, and he pulled her against him, her ass to his cock. Then he tipped her head back by her hair like a caveman. "Do you want this, Josie?"

She swallowed. "I don't know."

"You have to be sure. I don't want you throwing it back in my face later."

She didn't know exactly what he planned to do, nor did she care. Her breasts were bared, his cock hard against her, and she was hyperaware of the hushed crowd beyond the spotlight, their silence tense and avaricious. She rested her head on Kyle's shoulder, her eyes slitted against the lights above her. His scent filled her to the brim. "Yes, I want it."

Would he push her to her hands and knees and fuck her from behind? God. It didn't matter. She wanted every last damn person in that crowd to know he was hers in any way he chose to show them.

Kyle cupped both breasts and pinched her nipples simultaneously.

She moaned, closed her eyes, and rolled her head on his shoulder, the electric shock shooting down to her clitoris.

He slid both hands down her abdomen, his skin warm, the ridges of his fingers slightly rough. Over her hips, down her thighs, to the bottom of her skirt. Dipping his knees, he bent to grasp the hem, then finally he was beneath the material, his hot touch at the top of her thigh highs.

"I want them to see how hard you come for me," he whispered in her ear.

"I wanted to get *you* off," she murmured.

"You owe me this."

She couldn't remember why. Because he'd let her take him with the dildo? Because she'd forced him to wear her panties? A host of reasons. The crowd waited and wanted, their collective breaths held. She turned her head, her lips brushing his throat as she said, "Do it."

He never exposed her pussy, simply slid a finger between her lips, slipping in her dampness. He swirled over her clit, rubbing lightly, caressing slowly. She held on to his biceps to keep her legs from buckling beneath her. God, it was good. Her hips rolled to his rhythm.

"Let us see," someone called out.

Kyle didn't lift her skirt high enough for the full view. Instead he tormented them.

"Let me taste her." The voice was closer. Josie opened her eyes. A big bald head, two earrings in each lobe.

"Only I taste her." The growl in Kyle's voice was prehistoric. He put his hand to his mouth and sucked her juice from his fingers to prove his words. "Only I fuck her. Only I make her come." Then he was back beneath her skirt.

Oh God, his words shot her higher, the possessive grip of his hand at her waist, the play of his fingers, and his low, menacing growl.

"Come on, dude, share a little of the wealth." The bald guy waved his arms at the throng around him. "There aren't enough women." Then he lowered his voice. "And she's so fucking hot. She loves exposing it, man. Give her to me."

Kyle tensed against her back, but his touch never left her, his fingers never stopped making her crazy, driving her higher, closer to the edge. Then he plunged inside her with two fingers. "You want this fucker, Josie?"

"God no." She closed her eyes, rode his hand, lost herself in his touch, his scent, the gravelly pitch of his voice.

"Fuck off, man"—violence shredded his voice—"before I break your face."

She climaxed so hard, she screamed out his name. Every nerve, every cell was merely an extension of her clitoris as she flew apart. There were no lights, no crowd, no bald guy, only Kyle's hand on her body, his voice in her ear saying, "She's mine, she's mine, fucker."

When she came back to herself, she was wrapped in his arms, her face buried at his throat, her breasts smashed to his chest and his cock hard against her belly. She couldn't move, didn't want to. God, he smelled good, hot, primeval.

"Would you really have broken his face if he touched me?" she said against his skin.

"Fuck yes."

That word. So hot. So harsh. He pulled her head by her hair again—God, she loved that as much as she loved the hint of violence—and took her mouth. His lips devoured her. Then finally he rested his forehead against hers and closed his eyes.

Whether in reality he would have hit the guy or not didn't matter. She'd known Kyle such a short time, yet he'd gotten her to love committing naughty acts she thought she'd hate. Like tying her up. Getting her to masturbate for him on the way back from a business meeting. Making her come undone in the middle of a crowd. Threatening violence to a man who wanted her.

The only challenge she'd hated was Little Miss Fucking Snowflake. And that one had been her own.

Hated that one, but loved everything else.

God. *Love* was such a terrifying word. She wasn't in love, had learned long ago that it was just an emotional drug. Yet Kyle made her love all the things he did to her. She could become addicted.

Correction, Josie, you are addicted.

Addicted to her boss.

"I need to get dressed." She suddenly felt naked, as if he could see all her thoughts and feelings written in her gaze.

His hand still on her arm, he reached to the edge of the dais for her top. Getting dressed was so much more embarrassing than tossing off your clothes. You had the heat of the moment going for you when you started, but afterward, you were down off the high.

She didn't regret what she'd done. She merely felt vulnerable. The center of attention. She wondered how much she'd revealed in the moment of orgasm, Kyle's name on her lips.

He helped her ease the top down her midriff, then held out his hand for her. In the midst of a sex club, taking a man's hand in hers seemed terribly intimate. She faced the crowd again. It wasn't as large as she'd thought but just as greedy, watching them with fervent eyes. Kyle led her down the steps, and a path parted for them. The bald guy with the two earrings—and a chipped tooth she hadn't noticed—started clapping. Then it seemed everyone did.

"I need to use the restroom," she whispered to Kyle's shoulder. She needed to get hold of herself. Most things didn't ruffle her feathers, yet she felt completely ruffled. It had been too good. She'd liked it too much. What did Kyle think of her reaction up there? Did he believe it was more than another challenge, another game?

"I saw a sign," Kyle pointed off to the right.

He tucked Josie beneath his arm, folding her to his side as if she were something precious, and led her from the room. A short way down, the ladies' room sign blazed: A woman with a devil's forked tail snaking from beneath her skirt.

Very apt, Kyle thought.

Josie's fingers slipped from his grip. He didn't want to let her go, as if once she disappeared he'd never find her again.

The door closed in his face, and the crowd ebbed and flowed in the hallway around him. He was aware of voices, faces, the scent of sex, but the only real thing for him was the taste of Josie on his tongue.

Fuck. The sex on stage had been cataclysmically hot. He thought he'd get her here, she'd watch, ooh and aah, then freak. But not Josie. The woman constantly surprised him. He hadn't intended to do anything. He'd wanted to get her so hot and bothered with watching that she'd let him drag her back to his place so he could fuck the hell out of her. But something had happened to him when she'd looked up and said she'd rather suck him in front of everyone. *Him*, above anyone else. To her, it was probably some throwaway line, but he'd stopped thinking in that moment. Instead, he'd needed to see how far he could push her, how much she'd do for *him*.

He knew why he'd done it, but why had *she* climbed up on that stage for him? She was so quick to fight him, yet she'd stripped off her shirt in front of a room full of strangers after only one *No*.

It was too easy and too good.

Would she claim later that he'd forced her? Or deny how much she'd wanted it? Just as she'd denied being jealous of Kisa when he knew damn well she was.

One thing for sure, she'd loved riding the violent edge with him. She'd come when he'd threatened the beefy bald dude. She liked being claimed. She liked knowing that he'd actually beat the guy if he so much as touched her little toe. He just didn't think she was ever going to admit having feelings for him. She'd write off everything she did tonight as part of the game.

Jesus. How damn long was she going to be in that fucking bathroom? Every second without her grated along his nerves.

He tamped down his unreasonable ire. Across the hall, hooting and hollering rose. People crowded into another of the playrooms. The noise drew more, like locusts. Out of curiosity, Kyle sidled over and slipped in, just to the left, so that he could keep an eye on the ladies' room door as well.

A black spread draped across a tall bed, one of the old-fashioned kind you had to climb a small set of steps to get into. A man, on hands and knees, corset strapped tight around his middle, bared his ass to a woman in a tight, black leather cat-woman suit. With the head of the bed against the wall, she positioned him at an angle, his ass taking the brunt of the overhead lighting, his face slightly in shadow. Holding a dildo aloft, she displayed it for the throng. Thick, long, black, with a bulbous head, lube dripping down onto her hand.

Kyle thought of the day at the hot tubs when he'd allowed Josie to use the dildo on him. It had been hot, orgasmic, but it wasn't something he'd share with strangers.

So why did he make Josie orgasm in front of a crowd? How was it different? Fuck. It had to be the fact that in the one instance *he* was baring his soul (as well as his ass), and in the other she was exposed, even if he hadn't pulled her skirt to her waist. At any rate, it was shitty to say that what she'd done to him was any more intimate than the things he'd made her do.

Yet the feeling persisted that they'd shared something damn fucking amazing that day at the hot tubs, something that would be lost if witnessed by an audience of even one.

On the bed, the woman spread her partner's cheeks and took him with one hard thrust. Throwing his head back, he cried out, then grunted and pushed back hard.

Not the way Josie had done it, and Kyle far preferred her gentler touch, but this was about the show, not the intimacy.

He glanced at the women's room. Josie still hadn't come out. Had he traumatized her?

No way. She was a fighter. If she truly didn't want something, she'd slam him down.

A second man stepped up to the bed. Unzipping, he took out his cock, grabbed the other guy by the hair on his head, and made him take his dick deep into his mouth.

Okay. *Really* not Kyle's cup of tea, but it sure as hell was for the guy on the bed. He bucked and sucked, moaned and groaned. Tossing his short blond hair, writhing for his audience, he gave them the performance of a lifetime. In a short matter of time, less than a minute, he had the guy shooting in his mouth. Stepping back at the last moment, the man's finishing touches cascaded down his very willing victim's face.

Je-sus. Come dribbled over his lips. He licked it off. Kyle found it a bit horrifying, not that he considered himself homophobic. Even as he watched, the woman grabbed the guy's hair, pulled his head back like a horse rearing, and displayed his come-soaked cheeks to their audience. There was something almost familiar in the man's expression.

Something frighteningly familiar.

Holy hell.

The man was Andrew Ronson.

18

KYLE shoved through the gawkers for a better look. It couldn't be. Impossible. The odds against it were staggering. Yet on closer inspection, the man getting reamed up the ass was indeed Andrew Ronson.

Andrew put out his tongue and lapped up more dribbles of come from his lips. Then he opened his eyes, smiling for his audience.

And looked straight into Kyle's face.

He stared, as if he were placing Kyle. Like when you see the girl from the coffee shop in a bookstore miles away. You know the face, but you can't remember the place.

Then Andrew put it together, and his eyes flared with panic. If he'd been close to orgasm, he lost it. He tried wriggling away from his partner's relentless pounding. The woman grabbed his hip, forced him down.

"Take it, you little worm," Kyle clearly heard her say, then she looked right at him, a naughty smile growing on her lips. "You want him to blow you next, honey?"

"Thanks," Kyle told the generous woman, "but it's not my thing." Then he smiled so Andrew could see it, feel it, fear it. "I really appreciate the show, though. It's not something I'm going to easily forget Monday morning when I return to work."

Andrew whimpered, closed his eyes, then snapped them open again, perhaps hoping he'd only imagined Kyle standing there. Kyle was willing to bet a lawsuit the man's wife wouldn't approve of what he was doing.

Drifting back through the small enclave, Kyle never let his gaze waver. He sensed the open doorway and with one last pointed look at the tableau on the bed, he turned and exited.

Holy shit. He had to get Josie out of here before Andrew got his wits about him. His heart beat triple time. He'd been a total fucking idiot taking her up on that stage. Where the hell was his head? If the roles had been reversed, and Andrew had seen *them*? Fuck. He couldn't even think about the damage the man would have caused. She'd asked him if they'd be recognized, and he'd so glibly told her no way. He had his head up his ass. Okay, he hadn't expected Ronson, or the position the man was in, but he'd taken a huge risk without considering the possibilities. Scanning the hallway, he didn't see Josie. He hoped to hell she hadn't gone looking for him.

He grabbed the arm of a woman leaving the ladies' room. She looked pointedly at his hand, and he dropped it. "I'm looking for my girlfriend. Dark hair about this long"—he waved his hand at shoulder length—"green eyes, wearing a black top and skirt, fishnet stockings. Did you see her in there?"

The woman, middle-aged, wore too much makeup that emphasized rather than masked her wrinkles. "No," she said, "didn't see her. Sorry."

Kyle glanced back at the open doorway of Ronson's showroom. How much time did he have? Another lady exited, and Kyle held the door before it closed. "Josie, you in there?" he called.

Dammit, where was she?

"You know"—her voice suddenly at his ear, her sweet, womanly scent filling his head—"a girl's date shouldn't wander off to watch nasty activities without her."

He whirled, took her arm, propelled her down the hall to the great room by the entrance. "I thought you'd drowned in there."

She laughed, and he stopped long enough to look down at her. Her smile was sweet, genuine, not the shell-shocked expression she'd worn when she'd run to the women's room.

"I'm done here, let's go," he said.

"I'm just getting started. The girls in the restroom said there are all these themed rooms, a voyeur room, a whole bunch of stuff we haven't seen yet."

"I thought every room we'd been in was a voyeur room." He pulled her to the door again, and though she had long legs, she had to skip to keep up with him. He held her close so they couldn't be separated. "I'm ready to take you back to the hotel and fuck the hell out of you." True. He wanted that in addition to getting her the hell out of this place before she accidentally ran into Andrew.

Forget about what he'd done onstage to her; even being seen here would be bad for her. It was one thing for Andrew to have seen him. Kyle was fully clothed and in no compromising position other than the fact that he was at a sex club. But Josie? First, a woman couldn't get away with the same things as a man. He could simply laugh off the fact that he was a semi-pervert. Not Josie. There was a double standard. Second, Andrew would sure as hell put two and two together and realize Kyle and Josie were here *together*. He elbowed past a couple making out. No way in hell could he let Ronson see her.

Third, he now had a very large stick to hold over Ronson's head. He'd use it to get the man off Josie's back. Ronson had handed his own head on a platter to Kyle.

Josie, however, had other ideas. She dug her heels in when the door was in sight. "Hey. What's up with you?"

He sure as hell wasn't going to tell her. She'd freak. She'd call off the relationship. He couldn't let her do that. Instead he hauled her up against him. "If I don't fuck you within the next fifteen minutes, I will die."

She stilled in his arms, her hands folded to his chest. She searched his face. "Do it here," she whispered, "in front of everyone."

His breath caught in his throat. His cock was instantly hard, throbbing, and damn near painful. He would have done it, tossed her into a room and taken her like an animal, letting everyone within eye- and earshot know that she was his and his alone. Like a ram having won her after a long, bloody battle.

Except Andrew Ronson lurked somewhere. True, he might have hightailed it home in pure panic, but Kyle couldn't risk it.

"Not here," he said. "I'm taking you home with me."

She swallowed. "Home?"

As she said it, he wondered if *home* was perhaps the bigger battle. "Home," he repeated.

"But I have the class in the morning."

"I live near the Marina. I'll have you back in plenty of time. Tomorrow morning," he added, so she'd be in no doubt that she was spending the night.

"Kyle, that's not a good—"

He put a finger to her lips. "It's a perfect idea." He felt the ebb and flow of people around them. "Say yes."

After a moment that seemed to last forever, she mouthed the word he wanted. "Yes."

Kyle didn't hesitate a single second longer. He should have taken her to his home in the first place instead of some seedy, skanky sex club.

HIS house was gorgeous, with a back deck that overlooked the swan pond at the Palace of Fine Arts. In the near distance, the spires of the Golden Gate rose into the night, dark shadows against the sky.

Josie closed the sliding glass door to the outside, her reflection suddenly stark in front of her.

What the hell was she doing here?

She'd allowed him to make her come in front of a crowd, even suggested he do her right there in the club, yet the confines of his home were far more frightening. Intimate. The flat-panel TV was much larger than anything she could afford. Then again, she wasn't home much to watch. His chrome-and-glass tables and black leather furniture looked fairly new, or it never got used. That could be the reason there wasn't a single smudge or ring on the glass, a damn near impossible feat for a man. Okay, it was impossible for her, too.

Really, what *was* she doing here? It was midnight. She was usually in bed long before.

Kyle returned to the living room with a bottle of white wine and two glasses. "Cheers," he said after pouring and handing her the sweet stuff. A Riesling.

"So, what about the fucking?" It would be easier to get it over and done. No fuss, no muss, then he could take her back to the hotel. She didn't spend the night with a man.

"You're spoiling the mood." He sat on the sofa, patting the spot beside him.

She moved once again to the glass door. From the street she'd be clearly visible with the lights behind her. What she saw reflected, though, was a woman in dark, sexy clothing with wide, terrified eyes.

Until Kyle flipped off the lamps and plunged her into darkness.

"There, the view's better." His voice was suddenly behind her, close; then his breath sweet with wine; finally his body heat.

Brushing aside the hair at her nape, he laid his lips on her. Oh God, she simply wanted to lean into him, feel his body against hers, his lips cool with wine on her, smell him, bury her fingers in his hair as she held his mouth to her throat. Before, sex had always been about orgasm and satisfaction.

The last time she'd allowed herself to wallow in the texture of a man's skin, the scrape of his five o'clock shadow on her thighs, the warmth of his breath, his taste, his scent . . . the last time she'd allowed herself those pleasures, she'd gotten screwed. There was a helluva difference between fucking and getting screwed.

Her emotions about Kyle were escalating. Just the fact that she *had* emotions about him was terrifying. She'd been experiencing them for weeks now.

"You need to take me back to the hotel," she said, yet her voice was soft and dreamy.

"I'll take you to bed instead."

They hadn't done it in either of their beds. Doing it in *his* bed was a bad idea. "Listen, either fuck me now or take me back to the hotel. The wine is making me tired." And totally bitchy. Really, she hated being a bitch, but she felt him dragging her under.

His lips still on her neck, he slid both hands down her sides. Obviously he'd set his wine down somewhere along the way. She sipped hers and tried not to shiver at his touch.

"You're always rushing," he finally murmured, then he was bunching her skirt in his fingers and raising it. She was naked beneath. In front of the window, he trailed around to her mound, then tunneled one finger between her pussy lips and found her clitoris.

They were too close to the window, even in the dark. They'd be seen if someone was out walking their dog a final time that night. Yet she reached back, winding her arm around his neck and running her fingers through his hair. "Stop that."

She knew damn well he wouldn't.

"I haven't come yet tonight." He paused. "And you came hard."

She hated to admit how shattering that climax had been. "I can give you a quick blow job if you want."

He laughed. Nothing seemed to make him angry enough to take her back to the hotel. Instead he worked her clitoris, and her body writhed against him of its own volition. "Come to bed," he urged. "A blow job's not enough. I need to fuck you."

"No. If you want to do me, do it here." In front of the sliding glass door was better than the intimacy of the bedroom. Better? No, easier. Somehow safer.

His finger stilled, his caresses stopped. "In the bed, I can make you scream. Standing up, you won't come as hard." He simply wanted her in the bed, that was all. As if it were some sort of coup, one up on her.

"It's kinkier in front of the window." And less intimate for her. "That will make better orgasms for both of us."

His cock caressed the crease of her butt. He needed to come. A man could always be led around by his dick.

"Fuck me here and now," she said, "or don't do it at all. I couldn't care less." Her pussy ached for a major explosion, but her heart couldn't take it unless it was on her terms.

Kyle stepped back. She waited for the shush of his button fly. Nothing. Her skin cooled where he'd been touching her. In the window reflection, she couldn't discern his gaze behind her.

"I'm going to bed. You want to join me, I'd like it. If not, there's the couch, and I'll take you back in the morning."

Damn him. She turned on him. "What is so important about your fucking bed?"

He held out his hand. "Nothing. I simply want you in it."

"You'd rather sleep with me than fuck me?"

"I'd rather do both, but if all I get to do is sleep, that works for me."

She drew in a breath. The man made her want to scream. "I let you finger me in front of a pack of howling strangers. I don't know what the hell else you want from me."

"You, in my bed."

"No."

"Why?" He tipped his head like a dog searching for the source of an enticing sound.

"Because. I don't spend the night with guys. They want to own you in the morning." There, that was innocuous enough. It didn't come close to revealing any of the turmoil inside her. It wasn't that he'd want to own her, but that she might actually want to be owned by him. *That* was scary. She hadn't felt anything like it in too many years to count, and even then, the memory was bad.

His eyes glittered in the moonlight falling through the window. "I don't want to own you."

Josie stripped her Lycra top over her head. "Prove it. Do me on your living room floor, then take me back to my hotel."

Still, silent, Kyle watched as she undid her skirt and let it drop to the floor. She stood determined, naked but for stockings and shoes.

Christ, he wanted her badly. He'd been deep in her body only once, and while all the other sexual things they'd done were hot and orgasmic, he'd meant it from his gut that he'd die if he didn't get inside her. His cock was so hard, it pulsed, his need so great, he ached with it.

Yet she was *still* fighting him. If he gave in to her now, she would always win.

Then again, if he let her go without fucking her here, he had the sense to realize he'd never have her again. They'd be over.

"Turn around and get on your hands and knees," he told her, even as he searched in his back pocket for the condoms he'd carried tonight.

She smiled, knowing she'd won this round, and did exactly as he told her to.

He wanted Josie to remember what she'd done to him at the hot tubs. She'd taken him as they faced the mirror. He would do the same, though their reflections were wavery and indistinct in the door glass.

Going down on his knees behind her, he stroked his hand from her ass straight forward to her clit. "You're so damn wet."

She wriggled back against him, then glanced over her shoulder. "I could be more so."

He played her, slipped a finger inside her, then across her clit and back to the sensitive bit of skin just by her ass. "You wanna come first or when my cock's in you?"

"Both."

"Greedy bitch." He meant it as compliment.

She smiled, accepting it as such. "I'm a woman who knows what she wants."

"Yes, you are." Right now she thought she had his guts wrapped around her little finger.

Taking her hand, he put her index finger to her clit. "Work that little button while I get out of these clothes."

She moaned. "Whatever you say." Her breathing quickened.

He loved watching her masturbate. She had no inhibitions about it whatsoever. "But hell, don't come without me."

She laughed, sultry, sexy, ending on a gasp. Condom pack in hand, he shucked his jeans.

"Ooh, ooh, you better hurry," she cooed.

He sent his clothes flying across the living room. "You'll be punished if you don't wait." Moments later, he wore only the latex.

"Ooh, I'm so afraid."

He loved her laughter laced with heat and a moan. Then he climbed over her, his cock between her thighs, bobbing against her fingers as she stroked herself. Christ, it would have been so fucking good without the condom between them, but he knew she needed the security for now.

"You damn well better be afraid," he said against her ear, keeping his tone light. Then he pinched both nipples hard, the way she loved.

She rewarded him with a sexy rotation of her hips against him. "If you punish me like that, I can't help but be naughty."

This was how he loved her best, when she was laughing, playful, and sexier than hell. "If you rubbed my cock against your clit, that would definitely be naughty."

She clasped him close, sliding him through all her moisture, readying them both. He slapped her hip.

"Hey."

"You need to be punished." She needed to be his in any way he could have her.

"Not having this big fat cock inside me is punishment." Yet she rode him with her clit just the same.

All the laughter died as her orgasm rose. Her body tensed beneath him, her breath heightened, turning into gasps, then finally she shuddered, crying out.

He entered her before she came down, and she met him with the full force of her orgasm. He thrust, she pounded back, his balls slapping against her pussy.

"You love this, don't you?"

"Yes." She gasped, slamming back against him.

"You can't live without my hard cock inside you?" He couldn't live without being inside her.

"No." A moan threaded through her voice.

"You want it." She fit him so tightly, *he* had to have it.

"Yes." Her breath hitched, her body tensing around him, dragging him deeper.

"You need me." He held on to her hips and plunged.

"God, yes." In the door's reflection, she bit her lip, writhed against him.

"I'm all yours, baby."

"Yes, please, yes, please," she chanted, her rhythm perfect, matched to his.

The orgasm built deep in his gut, his balls, his cock. When she shouted "Oh God, I'm coming," he let loose inside her.

JOSIE woke to the floor hard beneath her despite the carpeting. His arm cushioned her head, and his body kept her warm. Still, he'd thrown a blanket over them, though she couldn't remember him leaving her long enough for that or to get rid of the condom.

Tilting her head, she could see straight out the sliding glass door. The lights of the Palace of Fine Arts flickered across the pond. The night carried the light shush of cars on the road and voices from far away, laughter, a horn. Kyle's breath was steady in her ear. She had no idea what time it was, only that the dawn hadn't yet arrived, the sky inky black except for the stars and the twinkling lights of the palace.

You need me. She'd answered yes. *I'm all yours, baby.* His words had made her come.

And now? She could have stayed in his arms until morning, except that she had to pee.

God, it was all too much. She had to get back to her hotel. The sooner the better. She had to accept that her emotions were all tangled up with his and find a way to exorcise them.

It was inevitable that he'd wake up. "Christ, this carpet is hard."

"Never fallen asleep after fucking a woman in front of the window before, huh?" She tried to make it a joke, but a thread of jealousy ran through her. How many women had he brought home? The thought made her shudder with too many unwanted emotions.

He stroked a finger down her arm. "I'm usually not an exhibitionist in my own neighborhood."

"Luckily no one saw you or the police would already have been here."

"Or our video will be on YouTube in the morning."

She laughed, but he hadn't answered her unspoken question. She wasn't about to ask again. "Where's your bathroom?"

He pointed to the left and the dark recesses of the remainder of his home. "First door down the hall."

She grabbed her clothes, found her shoes, and made her way through the dim light. A city, she realized, was never completely dark. In the bathroom, she took care of nature, then climbed into her skirt and top.

He was naked in the hall when she came out. "Let's go to bed." His voice was flat.

With the only light falling through the bedroom door, she couldn't even see his eyes or read his expression.

"You need to take me back to the hotel."

"In the morning." He put a hand to her elbow and tried to herd her into the bedroom.

"Now."

He stood, silent, tall, naked, warm, enticing.

You need me. Maybe she did. But she didn't want to. "If I have to, I'll call a cab."

"You didn't bring a purse."

This time she glared at him. "Then lend me twenty bucks." The more he tried to control her, the harder she'd fight.

"You agreed to spend the night."

She bit down on her inner lip harder than she intended. Dammit, he was pissing her off. "I said I'd come home with you so you could *fuck* me." She gave the word extra emphasis. "I never said I'd spend the night."

"That's not how I remember it."

"All right, I'm done playing your game." She narrowed her eyes and didn't give a damn whether he could see it or not. "If I have to walk, I will."

"Why are you such a hard-ass?" He puffed out an exasperated breath. "It's one fucking night."

It was more than she could give without—

What? If any other man had done this, she'd have spent the night, let him drive her home in the morning, then told him bye-bye-and-go-fuck-yourself in no uncertain terms.

Why couldn't she do that with Kyle? Because he was her boss? No, that answer was too easy.

"You're afraid you're going to like my bed too much and keep coming back over and over."

"Dammit, do not put words in my mouth." Even if they were the right ones, correct to a T.

He eyed her. "You want me to say it first?"

"*God* no." She didn't even want to *think* what "saying it first" could mean. He was between her and the outside door. She'd have to touch him to get by.

"I want you in my bed," he murmured, taking a step closer.

"Tonight. Tomorrow night. A lot of nights." He smelled so damn good. "I don't want to play any more games either."

She pushed up against the wall. "You're my boss. We don't spend the night together. We don't even acknowledge each other at work."

He didn't take back the distance she'd won. "We can be more. If you want."

She could hear him breathe, feel the tenseness of his body even two feet away. He wanted. She couldn't give. "There's too much inequity in our relationship."

For a moment, she was sure he'd push it.

Instead, he stepped back, turned and headed back to the living room. During the day, with noise all around, you couldn't hear a person dress, but in the quiet of the night, even a city night, she made out the rustle of his clothing. Then a light came on, streaming down the hall to land just short of her shoes.

She was still standing in the same spot in the hallway when he filled the entry. "Here's your card key."

She'd forgotten he had it. "Thanks."

"Ready?" He jangled his keys when she didn't move.

She didn't know what she was. He'd simply deflated her. Maybe she'd wanted a knockdown, drag-out. Maybe she'd needed a little more convincing.

Maybe she simply wasn't worth fighting for.

IT was dark, but the sunrise wasn't far off. Kyle sat on his deck, his feet propped on the railing, a steaming mug of coffee in his hands.

He couldn't quite accept that she'd walked out. Or rather, that she'd forced him to drive her back to the hotel in the middle of the night when his bed was soft and close by.

Perhaps some women were more like men, and sex was just sex, but he could have sworn the intimacy was there between them. Or it truly might be the job that bothered her. He'd fucked up by working for Castle, at least as far as she was concerned. Water under the bridge though. He couldn't quit on Connor now.

He'd made his bed. Now he had to figure out how to get her to lie in it with him.

19

MONDAY was another day. The morning Program Management meeting was at nine, at ten it was training considerations with Harvey Toffer, then the executive staff meeting at two. Once Kyle got the routines down, he wouldn't attend the departmental meetings; he'd simply set up one with his own staff to obtain the necessary updates and resolve any issues.

He did, however, have one issue that wouldn't wait. Andrew Ronson didn't answer his phone. Kyle left him a message. "See me, ASAP." He left neither his name nor his extension. The man would know what it was about.

A flicker of movement in the doorway caught his attention. Andrew.

"That was fast," Kyle said, genially. "I only just left you the message."

Andrew didn't utter a word nor twitch a facial muscle. He

looked like death, dark circles beneath his eyes, slightly red-rimmed lids, bloodless lips.

"Have a seat," Kyle invited

Andrew closed the door. Instead of sitting, he slid a paper across the desk.

Kyle read. *Subject: Resignation.*

"Sit," he said again, pointing this time.

As if his bones had gone soft, Andrew collapsed into the chair. "My wife doesn't know. My family doesn't know. It would kill them all, and I'd lose everything. My wife would make sure I never saw my kids again." He lifted his shoulders, let them drop, and stared at the top of Kyle's desk.

Kyle kept his voice even. "This wasn't what I'd intended. Blackmailing you into resigning isn't my style." Besides, there was always the possibility Andrew could get vindictive and, with nothing to lose, start bandying it about that Kyle had been at the club also. It wouldn't make or break his career, but it would be embarrassing.

Andrew swallowed, twice, as if it were painful. "What did you intend?"

"A little cooperation, like I asked you for last week."

"You mean all I have to do is stop giving Josie a bad time, and you'll keep what you saw to yourself?"

Kyle allowed three extra seconds for the idea to settle in. "Correct." He'd never intended blackmail. Even for Josie, Kyle wouldn't compromise his integrity, but he could do a little negotiation on her behalf.

Andrew stared, his vivid eyes going wide. "That's all?"

"That's all," Kyle repeated.

Andrew waited another beat, his hands gripping the armrests. "How do I know I can trust you?"

"You have my word on it."

"What if something else comes up?"

He had a feeling the man wasn't questioning his veracity, but was simply terrified. So he spelled it out. "My discovering you in a compromising position was probably a one-time thing, right, Andrew? If you've got anything incriminating on your computer, you'll delete it. You'll erase your Internet history. If you're hiding something somewhere, *anywhere*, you'll get rid of it. So there won't be a shred of proof to back up anything inflammatory that *someone*, myself included, might accuse you of." He leaned forward, put his elbows on his desk, and speared the man with his gaze. "If you don't stop this shit with Josie, I will simply fire you after proper documentation of your behavior at work. However, if everything goes smoothly from here on out, there'll be nothing negative to go on your file." He held out his hands, palms up. "See? Your personal life has nothing to do with your work life." He paused, eyed Andrew with a long, level gaze. "Nothing else is going to come up, is it." He didn't leave it as a question.

Andrew hung his head, staring at his pant legs. Finally he lifted his eyes to Kyle's, met him full on. "I'm resigning anyway. I've been dissatisfied with the job for a while. It's not just Josie getting the manager position. I'm done, ya know? I need to get out of here, start over, clean slate." He let out another sigh. "I was investigating better opportunities anyway, and I've got my wife's agreement on that."

Kyle couldn't be sure whether that was truth or the fact that Kyle knew his secret, especially since it sounded like he needed his wife's permission, not just her agreement. The threat Kyle's knowledge posed would forever exist in Andrew's mind.

"If that's what you want," Kyle said, "we'll give you references as per company policy." The guy was leaving; Kyle didn't need to screw him over at this point. He simply wanted accord in his department.

Upon Andrew's exit, Kyle punched in Josie's extension. She didn't answer, so he left a message. She didn't answer her cell either. What was up with that? Her cell was like another appendage.

He could only think she was paying him back for Friday night. Well, Andrew's professional demise at Castle just might get him back in her good graces. It was only after the thought lingered that he realized how pathetic it sounded. The woman had him by the short hairs.

THE conclusion from supervisor training? Confront issues head-on and right away. Don't pussyfoot. Or it'll all blow up in your face.

Josie could apply that to her relationship with Kyle, too, but she'd decided *not* to confront that head-on. He'd dropped her off at the hotel, kissed her goodnight, then she'd walked through a silent hotel lobby and taken the elevator to her room. She hadn't heard from him since. She hadn't called him either, and decided that she'd won the skirmish.

Leaving the restroom, she glanced at her watch. She'd have to see him in half an hour at the morning meeting. That's when she'd really know who'd won. For now, there was Lydia to deal with. Confront the issue. For Lydia, that was the baby, what she was going to do about it, if she'd need time off, yadda, yadda, any support her boss could give—within reason, of course.

Josie shuddered. She would have preferred confronting Ronson, but due to his long drive from Tracy, he wouldn't be in until just before nine. Hopefully there'd be no blowouts during the meeting. She really didn't want to have to deal with any crap in front of Kyle. There was a limit to how much she'd be able to control herself, and if Ronson made her look like a freaking idiot again in front of her boss—her lover—well, she might lose it and ream him a new asshole.

No, she wanted a nice, quiet, even-tempered discussion to work out their differences. *Make the problem joint rather than just the employee's. Talk about the behavior, not the person.* She kept repeating the training in her mind.

Until she passed Ronson's cubicle, and there he was cramming family photos, a mug, childish drawings, and other personal items into a box.

"What the—" She cut herself off before the expletive burst out. "Why are you here so early?"

"I turned in my resignation."

"Oh my God." Lydia poked her head over the top of the divider. She must have been kneeling on the desk to do it. Josie flapped her hand until the girl retreated, but the silence throughout the cube area was vast. She could almost hear the collective breaths held as everyone honed in.

Why did she always get in this position with Ronson? "We should talk."

He stopped, but he didn't look at her, as if he couldn't meet her eyes. "It's done. I gave notice to your boss already."

Huh? "To Kyle?" she asked, just to be clear, because that didn't make sense at all. "Why?"

He resumed his packing, opening the desk drawers. "Ask him."

She didn't like the sound of that. What had Kyle done behind her back? That issue, though, she'd address later. "I mean why are you quitting?" With no warning, no time to catch up on his projects or reassign them before he left.

Though she should have, she really didn't care about that.

His back to her, his shoulders tensed. Finally he turned. "You and I both know it's not working out. I'd rather find something closer to home that doesn't involve as much travel." He sighed. "I'm missing my kids growing up."

It sounded so much like the stuff that Ernie had told her, about his wife pushing him. Well, Josie couldn't offer him less travel or more money. A part of her, a very big part, was glad. Issue resolved by voluntary termination. Was there anything in the supervisory handbook that said you shouldn't be glad when an employee decides to quit because then you don't have to deal with the problem at all?

However, it did piss her off that he'd gone to Kyle instead of her, as if she were nothing. Hell, what was the point, though, in making an issue of it with him?

"Good luck, Ronson."

He stared at her a moment, as if he expected her to try talking him out of it, yet the look in his eyes was unreadable.

She watched him pack his last few items, then he handed her his badge. "You can have Payroll mail me my final check."

"Fine."

Feeling the entire group's eyes on her back, she followed him out, holding the door for him. Balancing the box on his hip, he popped his trunk lid, then dumped his stuff inside. He didn't wave as he drove away.

Josie remained in the doorway. She supposed she should have made him check out through HR. There was probably some sort of protocol to follow. But again, she didn't care. He was gone, and it was human to say that suited her. He'd made her manager days miserable.

Why hadn't Kyle told her what was going on instead of letting her find Ronson cleaning out his desk? The oddness of it unnerved her.

There was only one way to find out.

His office door was open, and Kyle wasn't doing a damn thing. His chair pushed back from the desk, one ankle balanced on his knee, and his hands stacked behind his head, he was sitting there as if he'd been counting the seconds before she arrived.

"What the hell is going on with Ronson?"

"I left you a message," he said almost conversationally. "You didn't answer your cell phone either."

"I was in the bathroom." She couldn't help the slight edge. "I actually don't carry it in there with me."

"I'll try to remember that. If you don't answer your phone, it's because you're in the ladies' room." He looked too damn chipper, a sparkle in his eyes and a snarky half smile on his lips. "Close the door."

"Fine." She did. If he got personal with her behind closed doors, she'd deck him.

"Now sit."

"I'm not a dog." She sat anyway, her anger rising.

"Josie, please, I have something to tell you."

"Why did Ronson give his resignation to *you*?" She didn't like that she'd been sidestepped as if she were insignificant. Though of course that was probably the exact reason Ronson had done it.

Kyle took two extra seconds to answer. "He and I had a little run-in Friday evening."

"Friday evening? You mean before you picked me up?"

"No." He gave her another two-second perusal. "At the club."

"At the club?" she repeated. Stupidly. Club? What club? Oh God.

He recognized the moment it registered. "Yes, *that* club."

"He *saw* us?" A wave of heat rose to her face. Her heart started to hammer in her chest.

"He saw *me*, not you. While I was waiting for you."

While she was hiding in the restroom. She thought she was going to hyperventilate. "Jesus, what's he going to do?" This was bad, really bad.

"Just what he did: resign."

"That doesn't make sense. You're the exec, it would look worse for you than for him if it were to get out." All the scenarios ran through her mind, morals clause in an executive's contract, et cetera. This could *ruin* Kyle.

"Would you like to know what he was doing when I saw him?"

She stopped, cocked her head, her voice barely there as she asked, "What?"

"On his hand and knees getting screwed by a dildo and sucking a cock at the same time."

"A *man's* cock?"

He raised one eyebrow. "Is there any other kind?"

"You know what I mean," she snapped. "Like a real one, not just a dildo."

He laughed, an almost involuntary sound. "Oh, it was real, all right."

"And he saw you?"

"Right at what I'd call a very auspicious moment." He shook his head, a slight smile creasing his lips, and oh yeah, that telltale sparkle glittering in his eyes. "You should have seen the look. Like the credit card commercial says: priceless."

"Oh my God." It came out as a mere whisper. Then she looked at him. He'd used it to get rid of Ronson, for her. "So you told him either he resigned or you'd tell?"

All the mirth died on his face. "No. I don't work like that, and you should know it."

"But—"

"I don't blackmail." He dropped his foot to the floor, rolled his chair to the desk, and eyed her with a steely gaze.

"I didn't mean it like that. I'm just shocked, that's all."

"I merely suggested that he should learn how to come to an amicable working relationship with you."

"Or what?" It sounded like blackmail to her.

"Or nothing. I didn't threaten him. He turned in his resignation."

"But you must have said *something*." Otherwise Ronson wouldn't have had a reason.

"I didn't say a damn thing. I told him he didn't have to leave. He just had to work it out with you."

"Well, I'm sorry, but that sounds like it had an 'or else' attached to it."

Kyle scraped a hand down his face. "All right. Let's put it this way. I saw him on Friday. This morning he came into my office to hand in his resignation. I took it. He's gone." He pulled a paper forward onto his blotter and tapped. "Now I have to take the resignation to HR."

She remembered the badge in her jacket pocket. Laying it on the desk, she pushed it across. "He's says they can mail his final check."

"Good. Then it's finished."

She gritted her teeth. "I don't like that you handled my problem for me." It was the second time he'd done so.

His jaw worked. "I didn't handle it. It was an opportunity that landed in my lap."

"You wouldn't have done this with any other employee."

He leaned forward. "I wouldn't have been at a sex club with any other employee. It's a mitigating circumstance."

He just didn't get it. He treated her differently. He fixed things for her. "You should have called me up here for the meeting with him." She drummed her fingers on the arm of the chair. "And dammit, Friday night you should have told me you saw him, not leave it until today." Would he have told her at all if Ronson hadn't resigned?

"I didn't want to worry you."

"Because you were going to take care of it." This time she

leaned forward. "When are you going to figure out that I can take care of myself? I can handle things *myself*. I don't need you to do anything for me."

He thought she was incapable, a screwup. The boss had to fix everything for her. It was because she was sleeping with him. He'd lost all respect for her.

Josie stood, her blood racing through her veins sounding like a freight train in her ears. "This isn't working."

"*What* isn't working?" Kyle remained in his seat.

"This relationship."

"We don't have a *relationship*. We play games." Now he stood, towering over her on the other side of the desk.

Despite herself she backed up one step beside the chair. "We *can't* have a relationship because you don't respect me at work. It was a bad idea to start with."

"I fucking respect you." His nostrils flared. "I wouldn't have let you handle the sand plant in the first place if I didn't."

"Then why can't you let me handle my own employee issues?" It *hurt*. "It shows you don't respect my judgment."

She wanted him to deny it, but he'd already done that. Yet she needed more, to know she was special to him, in bed, at work, anywhere, everywhere. That was the problem being with him. He turned her into a pitiable, needy woman.

"Your problem with Andrew is done, over"—he stabbed a finger across his desk at her—"but because I didn't call you in and have you be part of every second of what went on, you get all bent out of shape. You can't give a single fucking inch. Not in this, not in business, not in personal, not in anything."

Now *that* wasn't fair. On a work basis, their relationship was inequitable, but she knew damn well where he was going with this one. Pursing her lips, she crossed her arms. "So we're back to the fact that I wouldn't spend the night on Friday."

He shook his head in a decidedly disgusted move. "No. I'm on to how you have to fight about everything. You have to come out on top, no matter what. You can't take anyone's help. You certainly won't take mine. In fact, when I offer it, you shit on me."

"That's not true." She felt a twinge in her belly. She had gone to Trinity and Faith, even Ernie, with her problems rather than take them to Kyle.

"You're fucking high maintenance, you know that?"

"I am not." She raised her chin, but what he'd said stung. "I just want respect."

"You don't get it by fighting me every step of the way."

"I only fight because all you want to do is control me." She took a step closer, pointed her finger just as he had. "I will not let you ruin my job."

"I have no intention of doing that."

She ignored him. He was *wrong*. "Everything we do is escalating this thing. Someone is bound to find out."

"So let them find out. Big deal. If it's acknowledged openly, no one will care. It's the sneaking around that will sink us."

"*Ronson* almost saw us." She threw an arm out. "And look where we were."

"I admit it was inadvisable. We'll be more careful. But something like that would look a helluva lot better if people already knew about us."

"And what?" She shot out a breath. "I'm supposed to tell them I'm fucking my boss?"

He narrowed his eyes, his pupils mere pinpricks. "You tell them we're dating."

"We're *fucking*. Dating never works with your boss." Look what happened with Ian. He used her, stole everything, set her graduation back a full semester. She would not let that happen again.

"So we're *just* fucking." Kyle pierced her with his gaze.

She drew in a deep breath, held it, then let it spill back out. "Of course that's all we're doing."

He tipped his head. "You're scared to admit it might be more than that."

Her heart leapt to her throat. "I am not scared. I'm realistic and practical. I won't let what happens between us get in the way of my career."

Kyle was silent for a long, tense moment. "So you're saying the job is more important than a relationship with me."

She hadn't meant it that way, but that's what it ended up being. She couldn't deny it. "I told you all along that my job was the most important thing in my life."

He shook his head, grabbed a pencil from a holder, and twirled it on the blotter. "You're right," he said, staring at the whirling pencil. "It's not going to work"—he finally looked at her—"because you can't for one moment believe that I'm not trying to control you or judge you or otherwise treat you like a piece of dirt." He glanced at his watch. "You've got a meeting in five minutes."

With that, he dismissed her, closing the door behind her as she left.

What have I done?

Traveling the executive hallway, Josie couldn't quite believe it. She'd told him it was over . . . and he'd accepted. He wasn't supposed to agree so easily.

Her mom and dad always fought back and forth. That was their way, but they made up in the end. Neither of them said, "Okay, fine, you're right, we're done, let's get a divorce." They fought, they yelled, they did the silent thing, as if the battle was foreplay. Josie had hated the fighting, but she knew how it would end eventually.

"Hey, you okay?" Ryan from Quality passed her on the stairs.

Josie just waved her hand and smiled, then moved on without a word.

Kyle had let her walk out. Just like that. Over. Done. Didn't work. *You're too high maintenance.* High maintenance? Good God. *Her?* She was the least high maintenance of anyone she knew. Right?

Except for that one problem. She was like her parents, turning everything into combat. Right or wrong, she emulated what she'd been taught. It didn't help that she'd gotten trashed by her first—and only—serious relationship. Okay, so maybe she was a little scared, too, of getting hurt, of having her life blow up again. All right, she needed to face it: she was her own worst enemy when it came to men. That's why she always chose the buddy route. She didn't have to fight. She told them how it would be and maintained control of the situation that way.

Back in her office, her cell phone beeped with a missed call. Kyle. She'd already been on her way to his office when he'd phoned. There was another message from him on her regular voice mail, too. His voice actually made her ache inside.

So she had a little issue. He was going to let her walk out just because of that? She could stop fighting. She could . . .

Jesus H. Christ, what was she thinking? This wasn't about her fighting him or playing games or liking to have a bit of control. This was about her *job*. She couldn't compromise on that. She couldn't rush over to Connor's office and risk losing everything she'd worked for by admitting she'd been having sex with her boss.

And please, Connor, would it be okay if I kept right on fucking him?

God, she'd love to tell Kyle she was sorry, beg him to take her back, give in. She'd love to, but she couldn't lessen the importance of her job, or of how terrified she was of screwing it all up with one wrong move, or of how she needed to control her environment.

No matter how much she wanted Kyle, she couldn't change all those things that were fundamental to who she was.

"AS you all know"—Josie passed a glance around the conference room—"Ronson left the company today."

She was amazing, in Kyle's opinion: calm, cool manager all the way. You'd never know she'd dusted him off her hands not fifteen minutes ago.

"It puts us in a bit of a bind," she went on, "with Bertrice being new as well." She smiled for the latest addition to her entourage. "But we can handle it. I've already filled out a personnel requisition, which I'm sure Kyle will sign." She flicked the paper with her fingernail, sending it flying down the conference table to him at the other end. Then she smiled.

Sonuvabitch. Not a hair out of place, not a wrinkle on her brow nor a concern in the world. Just business as usual.

"Kyle and I were just in his office discussing how to divvy up Ronson's projects"—she didn't even bat an eyelash at the lie— "but don't worry, I'm going to be taking what I can until we've got Bertrice up to speed and another program manager hired. Luckily we've already been through the process, and I think there might be a couple of candidates amongst those I've interviewed."

He almost hated her. She wasn't high maintenance; she was fucking cold as an iceberg and just as hard.

He'd never meant anything more to her than any of her other fuck buddies.

She didn't give an inch, didn't bend a rule, especially the one about not fucking the boss. The price of being with him wasn't worth considering any other option.

Just like his ex-wife, where the baby was the all-important thing, no compromise, wouldn't even talk about adoption. She'd listened to everything the MAGS said and ignored what he'd wanted. Then *bam*, for husband number two, she was suddenly willing to consider all the other options. It had been years. He was no longer bitter. He was simply angry that Josie was of the same ilk.

They could have worked it out, but she was too damn scared to even try. Easier to cut and run. Now he had to see her every damn day and know he'd never get to touch her again.

Fuck, he wanted to touch her. Badly.

She leaned forward to address the speakerphone. Kyle could see down the unbuttoned lapel of her blouse. "Chuck," she said, "how are you coming on finishing up there?"

Chuck was . . . somewhere. Kyle realized he should care. This was his job, and like Josie, he needed to separate business from personal, yet he hadn't said a word since entering the meeting. Nothing to add whatsoever.

He needed to get his head out of his ass.

Plucking his pen from his shirt pocket, he signed the personnel requisition and sent it shooting back down the table to her. She was done. He needed to be done, too.

He just wasn't sure how, because she'd somehow managed to worm her way deep inside him, and he'd have to damn near cut his heart out to get rid of her.

20

KYLE hadn't said a word in the meeting, not one. He'd simply signed the requisition and flicked it back at her.

Josie had to stop thinking about him.

"Lydia," she called over her shoulder as she passed the girl's cubicle, "I want to talk to you."

Ronson was taken care of, even if Josie hadn't accomplished that. Now it was Lydia's turn. She was going to help that girl whether Lydia thought she needed it or not.

Lydia followed on Josie's heels. "Is this another closed door meeting? Because I haven't been late for over a week."

"Yes, this is a closed door meeting, and no, it's not about being late."

The door secured, Lydia flopped down in the chair, then rolled her eyes. "I haven't pinched anyone's butt, either. Well, not a male butt, at any rate."

"You shouldn't be pinching *anyone's* butt, male or female." Josie shot a puff of air out her nostrils. "No pinching period, got that?"

Lydia saluted. "Yes, ma'am." Then leaned forward in the chair, her eyes suddenly wide with an avid light. "Wasn't that a shocker about Andrew? Just to up and quit like that, no notice, nothing. His wife is going to squeal like a stuck pig."

"I'm sure he and his wife discussed it before he did it." Only what could Ronson possibly have told her? "My boss's boss saw me at a sex club?" Oh no, no, no. "That isn't why I called you in here."

"Oh God"—she rolled her eyes again—"what have I done *now*?"

Ernie was so right. Lydia was a drama queen. Still, Josie was going to try to give her the comforting shoulder Ernie thought she needed. "Nothing. I wanted to know how things were going with"—Josie shrugged—"you know, everything. To make sure you're okay."

Lydia cocked her head as if she were pondering the mysteries of life. Then something flickered in her eyes, and she brushed her long, dark hair over her shoulder. "Everything is fine."

Josie felt like burying her face in her hands and giving in to a few tears. It had been such a damn long day, and it wasn't even ten in the morning. She still had to meet with Kyle on how to re-assign Ronson's projects. How was she supposed to do that when he'd smell so good, she'd lose all her concentration? Or blurt out that she hadn't meant a word of it, and *please, please, take me back*.

Now Lydia was actually going to make her *say* it. The day couldn't get worse. "I was referring to the baby and what you de-cided to do. I want you to know I'm here for you."

Lydia's jaw dropped. Then she seemed to collect herself. "Oh. The baby. Yeah. Well." She cleared her throat. "That's all taken care of."

"Taken care of?" What the hell did that mean? "You, um, had the abortion?" But when? Did they do those things on the weekend? Because Lydia had been at work every day. At least Josie *thought* she'd been here on Thursday and Friday.

"Well, no." Lydia studied her fingernails. "What I mean is I found out I wasn't pregnant at all."

What? "But you peed on the stick." Awe and disbelief trickled through her voice.

Lydia huffed. "I read it wrong."

"Didn't you do it a second time?"

"Not right then." Lydia flicked her hair over her shoulder. Was that a nervous gesture? "But then I started my period over the weekend, so it was all just a big mistake."

"Why didn't you tell me?" She'd worried herself sick about how to help Lydia. She'd even told Ernie, for God's sake.

"You were gone to the supervisor's training." Lydia pursed her lips. "It wasn't like I was going to leave you a message on your voice mail."

"But you just said you started over the weekend. You could have told me when you first walked in this morning." Why was it pissing her off so much? Because of Kyle, and with her jumbled emotions, this was the last straw?

"Why are you making such a big deal?"

Josie resisted the urge to massage her temples. She wanted to do what Ernie suggested, figure out what Lydia needed, then give it to her, but she so sucked at pampering. "I'm trying to figure out why you're mixing your story up." *Good, Josie, when you look bad, throw it back at the other person.*

Just as she did with Kyle. Everything was his fault, not hers.

"Are you calling me a liar?" Tears welled in Lydia's eyes.

"No, I'm . . ." Now wait a minute. Something about Lydia's story *did* stink. The timing was all wrong. "Lydia." She waited until Lydia lifted her eyes. Were those tears real? "*Are* you lying?"

She opened her mouth, closed it. Hemmed, hawed, and finally, "Well, I *could* have been pregnant. I just didn't pee on the stick."

Josie felt her blood pressure rise. "So why did you tell me you had done the test?"

"Because . . ." Lydia shrugged. "You were ragging on me about something, and I just thought if you had something else to think about . . ." She trailed off.

"I was *talking* to you about your tardiness, and you made up a story to cover why were you late." She paused. "For work, I mean."

"Yes, but you were always picking on stuff, like when you didn't think I should have a raise." She sniffed. "And that whole thing with Chuck, which was really just in fun, and he didn't mind it at all until he saw me pinch Ryan over in Quality"—oh God, not another one!—"and realized that it didn't *mean* anything." Lydia dabbed her eyes.

Good God, the girl was the best actress Josie had ever seen, better than any on the silver screen. She'd been totally taken in.

Yet Josie felt something snap inside her. "How could you do that to me?"

For the first time, Lydia saw her own danger. She stopped dabbing and sniffing. "It was a little lie."

"A *little* lie?" Her blood roared past her eardrums. "Do you even realize how I felt having to admit that I'd get an abortion? Why would you even *ask* me that when it couldn't have meant *anything* to you?" She'd bared her soul, and for a moment she'd had to face the very nature of evil inside herself.

"I was curious," Lydia said, her voice very small. "You're always so together and perfect and on top of things. I wondered what you'd do."

"So now you know I'd be a murderer." It hurt even thinking it.

Lydia shook her head slowly. "No." She swallowed. "Now I know you're human, and you'd feel just as bad as I would, and I like you better." She smiled, a very small, almost frightened smile. "You're kinda special, I think."

A wave of heat washed down Josie's body, leaving her lightheaded. "I was never special"—it was less than a whisper, then she gathered herself—"and you're trying to schmooze me."

"Yeah, yeah," Lydia said. "I just felt you seemed nicer to be around knowing you were human and all." She sniffed. "I'm really sorry." The sheen in her eyes seemed almost . . . real.

Lydia was young and silly, but maybe she had something right. You didn't have to be perfect to be special. Is that what Ernie had been trying to tell Josie with completely different words?

It suddenly seemed cruel and mean not to accept Lydia's apology. "Yeah, well, it's okay." Opening the bottom desk drawer, she pulled out the box of tissues. "You had Ernie completely snowed, too, didn't you?"

Lydia grimaced. "He never kept on at me the way you did, though. I'd tell him something, he'd let me cry, then he'd just forget all about it."

Her extreme emotion about what Lydia had done was subsiding, yet Josie wasn't about to forget the lie. It wasn't personal, it was business, and Lydia needed to learn that. "You know, if your work sucked and I hadn't already lost Ronson today, I'd fire you right this minute for lying to me." She paused, letting the idea sink deep. "And if you pull any shit like this again, you are out on your ass. This is your one and only warning, and it's not going to be written in your file." She narrowed her eyes, stared Lydia down. "You just know that's how it's going to be."

Lydia nodded, twisting the tissues. "I'm sorry."

"And no pinching your coworker's ass. And God only knows what else, Lydia. You *lied* to your boss." She let that sink in a moment. "Don't *ever* lie to your boss. See, that's the problem. Now I can't trust anything you say." She shook her head. *This* was what Lydia needed, a lesson in what was acceptable and what wasn't. Ernie was sweet, but he'd been enabling the girl. "You're smart," she went on, "so I don't know why you thought you had to get by with lying all the time."

Lydia shrugged and raised her eyebrows. "I don't know. Ernie made it easy."

She felt a momentary blip of extreme anger. "Don't you *ever* blame anything on Ernie." She blew a breath between her lips and calmed down again. "Lying is *your* fault."

Lydia's face colored as she realized she'd taken Ernie's name in vain. "You're right."

"You better watch your own butt now." Josie reached across the desk, plucked up the tissue box, and threw it in the trash. "No more crying wolf."

Lydia stood. "I won't do it again."

"Yeah. Right." Josie snorted.

"I mean that. I really appreciate that you're not firing me."

Josie hoped she wasn't making a mistake. She flapped her hand, turned to the computer, and Lydia headed to the door.

"Wait," she said just as Lydia opened it. "Was it true about your brother's best friend?"

Lydia grimaced. "Well, his wife *is* a total bitch, but he'd never do anything with me. I'm waiting for him to see the light and divorce her before I tell him how I feel."

God. Lydia was so young. Hopefully, having been caught in her lies would help straighten her out.

"SO we have Nancy Fairburn starting next Monday." Josie sounded so damn pleased to announce the new addition to her people in the Monday meeting. In the three weeks since Andrew quit, they'd all pulled together and gotten through. According to Josie, even Lydia and Chuck stopped sniping. Bertrice was golden— Josie's word again, but Kyle agreed.

"You trying to stack the deck with all women, Josie?" Jenkins said over the conference phone.

"Nope." Josie smiled for her group, which today consisted of Lydia and Walker. Chuck was traveling, Jenkins and Bertrice were on speaker from their respective job sites. "She was simply the best qualified," Josie added.

Kyle leaned into the speaker. "Her level of experience will allow her to take over some of the more complicated jobs as easily as possible, which I'm sure you'll all appreciate."

"I want to thank you all for the overtime and the hard work." Josie nodded for both Lydia and Walker. "The worst is over."

"Rah-rah," Jenkins replied, in his usual laconic style.

They'd discussed bonuses for the department, and Kyle was pushing them through.

"So, let's get on with today's business." She'd e-mailed them the discussion points for the meeting earlier. "Let's start with you, Jenkins, since I know you've got a heavy agenda today."

Kyle listened. She handled it all efficiently, every point, every problem, every comment. There was no reason for him to attend the staff meetings now. After a month at Castle, he was up to speed. Lydia took detailed notes and e-mailed them to all attendees. Josie kept him informed of any changes or issues that came up during the week. By being here, he was micromanaging. Yet he couldn't seem to let go.

She smiled, spoke without artifice, came to him when the job required it, asked his opinion, took his advice. She was so damned professional about it all.

He didn't think she laid awake at night remembering, the way he did. He smelled her all over the house. When he closed his eyes, he felt the texture of her skin, tasted her sweet come. When he jerked off, it was to the image of her on her knees taking his cock deep into her mouth.

And there she sat at the other end of the table, ignoring him unless she needed something from him. As if they'd never shared a damn thing.

It drove him nuts thinking about her fuck buddies, wondering how often she called one of them. Or two of them at once. It made him insane thinking about her sucking another man's cock, letting another man lick her pussy, take her, fuck her. Jesus. His guts ached most of the damn time. He wanted to howl, but he wouldn't beg. She'd made it clear. After three weeks, it was even clearer. Josie Tybrook didn't need him. She was fine going on the way she had before she'd copped a feel off him in a crowded elevator. He would never be the same.

Half an hour after the meeting began, Josie tapped her pencil on the table. "Okay, thanks, Walker. We're done for today, you guys." She glanced at the conference phone as if Jenkins and Bertrice could see her, then smiled at her two present employees. "Lydia, if you'd get today's notes typed up and distributed, that would be great."

"Sure thing, boss."

Josie had reached stasis with Lydia. There'd been no more

incidents that required Human Resources' intervention, no more tardiness. How Josie accomplished it, Kyle didn't know. She told him only the things she thought he needed to hear.

Lydia leaned forward and punched off the speakerphone, gathered her notes, and followed Walker out the door.

Kyle found himself alone with Josie. Christ, the things he wanted to do, to say. "I needed to talk to you about the bonuses." It was a pathetic excuse for spending a few more minutes with her.

She cocked her head. "Yes?"

"Your office would be a better place." Kyle stood and held out his hand, indicating the door.

"Oh. Sure." Josie grabbed her yellow pad, pencil, cell phone, and coffee cup.

She needed a refill in the worst way. She absolutely hated being behind closed doors with him. He was so there, so male, so hot, and she was so damn needy where he was concerned.

You'd think after three weeks, she'd have gotten over thinking about him all the time, but no, not her. She knew when he was coming before she saw him, a sixth sense or the fact that he smelled so good, so unique, so different from any other man.

She entered her office, rounded the end of her desk, and sat while he closed the door. Pure torture. He always looked good, but today he was downright hot in a dark blue suit, white shirt, and navy-and-red tie.

Elbows on the desk, she folded her arms. "The bonuses? Is there a problem? I think I wrote up a good case for them." She wasn't kissing ass; her people deserved it. Her people. She'd started thinking of them that way instead of as Ernie's people.

Kyle watched her with those gorgeous blue eyes and got her all jittery. Why did he bother coming to her damn Monday meeting, and why the hell did he need to talk to her in person? They could have done everything on e-mail. Didn't he have one freaking idea what this was doing to her? He was always watching, judging her, yet he never showed a single emotion.

"Connor has endorsed the bonuses," he said.

"Oh," was the only answer she could come up with. He wanted something more, because what he said *definitely* could have been put in an e-mail.

Lydia passed by the office door, making a face of doom at her through the glass side panel. Darn the little eavesdropper, not that the girl could hear through the closed door.

Josie's cell phone started to vibrate on the desk, and she grabbed it. "Gotta take this." Yeah, right. She normally didn't interrupt a meeting by taking calls, unless it was an emergency, because it minimized the person with whom you were dealing. This time, she didn't even look when she answered. She needed a moment's respite from Kyle's steady, assessing gaze.

"Josie Tybrook here."

"Wanna fuck?"

Good God. Paul, one of her booty buddies. Her gaze flew to Kyle, and her cheeks heated, as if he'd know. "I'm in a meeting right now. Can I call you back?" Then, thinking, trying to make it *sound* like business. "Unless it's an emergency."

"It's an emergency, all right. My cock is so fucking hard and my balls are about to explode. Do a little phone sex with me so I can get off, then come over tonight, okay? Just say yes."

"I'm sorry, since it's not an emergency, I'll really have to call you back when I finish this meeting."

"Josie," he whined.

She realized Paul whined a lot. She realized, too, that it irritated her. She couldn't imagine doing him now. She hadn't been with another man since she'd met Kyle. She hadn't made a booty call, hadn't *wanted* to.

"I'll call you later," she repeated, a slight edge in her voice, then hung up. She wouldn't call, not ever again.

Kyle blinked, his expression deadpan, yet something flickered in his eyes, turning them an icy blue. "Business?"

"Of course."

He drew in a deep breath, let it out. "Because I know you'd never mix business with pleasure."

She let him have his dig at her simply because she didn't know how to fight him, or what she wanted out of a fight. "So," she said, trying to make her smile look real, "that's great that Connor's agreed to the bonuses. Was there something else?"

"Yes," Kyle said.

Dammit, Lydia passed by *again*, a different face of doom, a little more comical this time. Josie wasn't in the mood for her antics.

Her cell began to vibrate. Shit. Paul *knew* not to bug her at work if she told him she was busy, and she'd have to read him the riot act. She couldn't, however, resist glancing down. It wasn't Paul. It was Ernie. She'd talked to him two or three times since she'd been over there, but not in the last couple of weeks. Guilt assailed her. She'd been so busy. Dammit, she'd made too many freaking excuses.

"I really have to take this. It's Ernie." Her hand hovered over the phone.

Kyle nodded, smiled, but it didn't erase the frostiness in his gaze.

"Hi, Ernie."

"Josie?" A woman's voice. "It's not Ernie. It's Gloria. I just needed to let you know that Ernie's gone."

A great fist slammed into her belly. For a moment, she couldn't hear above the roar in her ears. Kyle shifted, leaned forward. "Ernie's gone?" she said.

"He passed last night."

"Passed?" It didn't make sense. Passed what?

"You were always his favorite, so I called you instead of . . . well, I don't know, Human Resources, I guess. I know his old boss isn't there anymore. Who should I tell, Josie?"

She couldn't get a word past her frozen lips, and everything just seemed to get blurry in front of her, even Kyle's face. Ernie was gone. Ernie had passed.

Ernie was dead.

She held so tightly to the arm of her chair that her fingers hurt. She was pretty sure Kyle said her name. Or something. And he was standing.

Finally, she managed a choked word. "I—" It was a croak. She started over. "I'm so sorry, Gloria." A deep breath didn't help.

"Don't worry." Her head still felt muddled, her mouth full of cotton. "I'll tell everyone for you." Oh, God, *how* was she supposed to tell everyone?

"Thank you, Josie. I'd really appreciate that." She marveled that Gloria could sound so calm. "We're having him cremated, and my sister will send you an e-mail with all the memorial information."

"Oh, great. Thank you." Her eyes ached, almost pulsing inside her head. She closed them, blotting out the sight of Kyle and everything but Gloria's voice. "I'll send it on to everyone here." What else was she supposed to say? "He was a wonderful man."

"Yes," his wife answered softly, "he was. I have a lot of calls to make. I'll talk to you soon. Bye now."

Okay, she should do something. Tell everyone. Lydia would cry. Someone should tell Ronson, too, because despite everything, he'd liked Ernie. Ernie had understood his problems, listened to him.

"Josie?"

She looked up and Kyle was still blurry, everything around him foggy.

"Baby," she thought she heard him murmur.

Then everything burst out of her, tears and pain and guilt, and she was clinging to him, feeling his arms around her, holding her, stroking her. He breathed soft words, called her sweet names.

Someone knocked on the door, opened it. Lydia, a box of tissues in her hand. "Josie threw out the box Ernie had in his bottom drawer," she explained to Kyle.

"Thanks." His voice rumbled against Josie's cheek. The door closed again. One hand left her back, then he folded a tissue into her hand.

God, it was embarrassing. What the hell would Lydia think? That she was fucking her boss, and he'd dumped her. Yet she couldn't stop crying.

"It's okay, baby." Kyle soothed a hand up and down her back.

Josie hiccupped, ineffectually tried to pull away. Kyle didn't let her go. He didn't give a damn what anyone thought, either. She needed him, that's all that mattered.

The cancer had gotten Ernie at last. Sad. He wasn't old; was darn near the prime of life. Yet Josie's reaction still managed to shock Kyle. With the cell in her hand, her face had gone dead white, and her eyes had clouded with moisture. He didn't think she was even aware she'd started crying right then on the phone.

"I'm sorry about Ernie," he said.

She cried harder, burying her face in the lapel of his suit jacket.

"He was a good man," Kyle went on.

"Very good," she whispered. "I should have . . . gone to see him . . . again," she said between sniffles and hiccups. "But I got so busy . . . after Ronson. I let . . . Ernie down."

"No you didn't. Nobody blames you."

Lydia passed by the door again, stopped, gave him a raised brow. He simply lifted his chin, nodded his head, and let her take whatever meaning she wanted. He was damn sure Lydia had never seen Josie cry either.

"I'm sorry, I'm really sorry. I don't know what's wrong with me. I'm not usually like this." She hiccupped again.

She was always trying to pretend she was a hard-ass, that she had everything under control, that she was emotion-free. But she cared. Her breakdown was all about her guilt, what she hadn't done for Ernie. She cared about her job, her projects, her employees, her family, the company. She wanted to be appreciated and valued. She wanted to give her all. He'd seen that the day she'd freaked out about the dryer at Coyote Ridge, though the full significance of it hit him only now.

She just didn't want to be hurt. He'd never given that enough importance. He'd simply demanded, that she spend the night, sleep in his bed, give him her emotions, let him win her challenges, let down her barriers—all the things he wanted, not what she needed.

He wrapped her in his arms, held her, stopped trying to minimize her grief or her guilt. "I'm here, baby. Go ahead and cry. I'll keep you safe."

She trembled against him and gave in to a new burst of tears.

Jesus, she was everything he wanted. He didn't give a damn that he was her boss, that she worried about her job, that she was scared of what people would say. None of that mattered, not his job, not her fear. Pulling her closer, hugging her tighter, he gave her the simple comfort of his arms.

Somehow, he'd figure out how to give all the rest of himself as well. Because he needed her.

21

"WOULD you look at the fu—" Todd Adams stopped himself, glancing at Josie. "The freaking gate-to-gate times." He pointed at the computer screen for Kyle's benefit.

The new ticketing system was off to a great start. They'd done a week of testing and debugging, and today was the final sign-off on the whole sand plant project. *Her* final project. Now it was manager all the way.

Ernie had passed almost a month ago—a day which Josie hated to relive. His memorial was a week later, the same day Nancy Fairburn had started. Despite her too-sexy attire, Bertrice was working out well, and the guys were accepting her. And Nancy? The woman was a lifesaver. She'd taken Ronson's projects all the way.

"Holy hell," Kyle muttered as all three of them gazed at the computer and those lovely, delightful, miraculous gate-to-gates.

"Your programmers are wizards." Todd nodded slowly, in total awe.

Josie noticed he said *your*, as in Kyle was now part of Castle's team, no longer a proprietary piece of SMG.

"It was all in your detailed description," Kyle said, playing along with the mutual admiration society. "Feel like doing a testimonial for us?"

"Fu—" Todd again cut himself off. Josie felt like telling him she'd heard the word *fuck* before, but she liked his politeness, too. "Hell, yes," he finished.

Work life was good. Except for the way her hair smooshed from the hard hat she'd worn during the inspection. Everything from the dryer to the load-out to the ticketing system worked like a perfect little fantasy.

"Ready to sign off, Todd?" Josie held out the clipboard with the final paperwork. Why did it feel so good, above and beyond any of her previous jobs?

"For sure." He took both pen and clipboard.

Josie fluffed at her hair and wiped the sand dust from her eyebrows. It had been windy, and she could taste the grit on her lips. But, as Todd signed with a flourish, she considered once again that life was good. The job had settled down, her new employees were working out, no more ass pinching, and she hadn't caught Lydia in another lie. She missed Ernie, but she'd said her good-byes at the memorial, and it was good to know he wasn't in pain anymore. Even she and Kyle were doing fine work-wise.

She chanced a glance at him. Dressed in jeans and a button-down shirt, he had the same smooshed hair that she did and grit in his dark eyebrows. They worked well together, were polite, diplomatic. He was on her side, listened to her ideas, backed her up, praised her when she deserved it. He even let her cry the day she'd needed to. Just as Ernie had let Lydia cry. What more could a manager ask from a boss? Not a damn thing.

The problem was that she wanted to ask a helluva lot more from Kyle the man, not Kyle Perry, her boss.

Todd handed back the clipboard. "I'd invite you guys out to lunch, but we've got a new customer coming in for a tour this afternoon." He glanced at his watch. "Hell, make that in half an hour."

Josie stuck out her hand. "It's been a pleasure working with you, Todd. If any issues arise, don't hesitate to call me. Just because you signed off doesn't mean we're dumping you."

"Thanks." Then Todd clapped Kyle on the back. "And you, bud, you're looking great. The job's obviously agreeing with you. Good luck. Don't be a stranger if you're over this way."

"Sure." They shook hands, then Todd herded them out to Kyle's car parked at the back of the weigh master's office.

It was the end of October but as hot as August. She could hardly wait for the air conditioning. Climbing in beside him, her skirt rode up to reveal the lace-up, knee-high, steel-toes Kyle loved. On the way, he hadn't even noticed them. That part of their relationship was done, over.

Except that she couldn't wipe out the feel of his arms around her. When she thought of Ernie dying, she remembered Kyle holding her as she cried, the two memories inseparable, tactile. It had been horrifying, excruciating, exhilarating, frightening. She'd completely lost it. Kyle was the one who had to tell everyone about Ernie, cramming the entire FI&T group into the conference room.

At Ernie's memorial, it felt as if half of Castle attended. Connor, Faith, Jarvis, VPs, right on down the ranks. Castle was a family, they'd lost one of their own, and the loss hit the company right in the heart.

"The meeting went well," she said, because it hurt to think

about Ernie, about Kyle, about what might have been but wasn't because . . . she'd wanted the job more than a relationship.

"You did a great job." Kyle headed out to the mountain road instead of the freeway.

Just like the first time. When he'd pulled out a vibrator and made her masturbate for him. "Thanks."

They were silent until the downhill side coming into Los Gatos.

"There's a folder on the backseat," he said, giving her a start. "Read it."

Sure enough, a blue folder lay there, one she hadn't noticed on the way. Reaching behind his seat, she scented him like the bitch in heat that she was. After Ernie, she'd started to realize how much she missed Kyle in her life. Prior to that, her *life* had been all work, but seeing Ernie's daughters and wife, she'd started to see that there was life beyond Castle, beyond a twelve-hour workday. Late at night, she missed something she'd never even had, rolling over in bed to touch Kyle, to savor his smell, his skin, falling asleep in his arms, waking up to his warmth. All night long. In her bed or his.

She didn't even feel the sigh until it rolled out of her.

"Open it," he said.

The folder sat on her lap. "Okay." Inside, letterhead from a company out in Tracy. She recognized it as a glass bottle manufacturer, a customer of SMG.

Her stomach plunged all the way to her steel-toes. It was an offer letter. VP of Manufacturing. Beneath that were two more offer letters, a firm over in the East Bay, another in the South Bay, Willow Glen.

A full-body flush rode through her, and she felt herself falling as if she were dropping off the top tier of the sand plant, bouncing from level to level until she hit the rocky bottom. Shifting in her seat, she stared at his profile a moment, taking him in. "You're leaving?"

"Yes. But I haven't decided which job to take."

Had her change in feelings been so obvious that he needed to physically distance himself from her? "Wow." She went for innocuous rather than show her true horror. "Three offers in this economy. That's incredible." It was sickening.

"I was motivated."

Good God. That bad. She'd never have another chance. She'd be stuck with her vibrator for the rest of her life. Worse, she'd have to go back to her fuck buddies, not that she'd heard from either Paul or Rick lately. Not that she *wanted* to hear from them. There was only Kyle.

"It'll be a long commute from the city," she said, amazed at how benign her voice sounded.

"I put the San Francisco house on the market. I'm looking in Los Gatos."

Where she lived. He'd be so close, and yet so far. The cliché made her want to laugh hysterically. "Connor will be sorry to lose you, I'm sure."

"I feel shitty about that, but I had to make a choice." He didn't look at her as they rolled down the hill into town. He hadn't looked at her since he'd told her to open the file.

Until now. "Kisa," he said, and she winced at Little Miss Fucking Snowflake's name on his lips, "would have sucked the hell out of my cock that night." He turned back to the road as they approached the first stoplight. "I told her no."

"Oh." She felt jittery, as if she were coming down off some drug high. "Why?"

"Because I didn't want her. I never wanted her. I wanted only you, and I was pissed as hell that you gave me to her."

The light changed; someone honked when he didn't move. He took off slowly, his gaze shifting from the road to her, back again.

He shrugged. "I didn't want you to know that no other woman attracted me, so I lied and told you she turned me down."

"No other man attracts me," she whispered, her heart climbing into her throat and almost cutting her off.

"We've both got control issues." He took the cloverleaf for the freeway. They'd be back at work shortly, off the next exit. "My ego was less important than my need to hide that I was hooked on you even then. Badly."

"Then why are you quitting?" Running away from her?

He shook his head. "I thought you'd see right away."

"I'm not so smart."

He laughed softly. "You're right. Sometimes you miss the subtle nuances." He turned to give her a pointed look. "Here's how it is. You won't have a relationship with me if I'm your boss or your client. So now I won't be either of those things. I'll just be some random guy working at another company."

They pulled into Castle's parking lot. "So I figure," he said, twirling the wheel into one of the few parking spots left this late after the lunch hour was over, "I'll take the job in Willow Glen."

"But that was the lowest offer."

"It's the closest to you."

She closed her eyes, felt his words wash over her, his warmth fill her. He stole her breath, her ability to speak, even to contemplate how much that one sentence could mean.

"You are more important than any job," he murmured.

He'd given her everything, risked everything, made all the changes, all the sacrifices. He'd sold his house, found another job, altered every facet of his life. For her. Because she was special to him. He didn't need to say it, didn't have to declare undying love. What he'd done for her was . . . everything.

She hadn't done a damn thing in return, hadn't taken one single risk.

The sun beat through the windshield. With the engine off and the air no longer blowing across Kyle's face, a bead of sweat dotted his forehead. But Josie didn't have him completely pussy-whipped. "No more games," he told her. "Your bed or my bed, and there has to be a whole night involved."

She gazed at him for long silent moments, her eyes that jungle green he loved. "That's not giving you enough," she finally whispered. "Nowhere near enough."

"I don't need anything else."

"Oh yes, you do." She grabbed the door handle. "There's something I have to do." Then she was out and jogging across the parking lot.

Damn. He'd just bared his soul, and she had something better to do. He gathered his briefcase from the backseat, shoved the folder she'd dumped into the side pocket. He'd planned the coup for damn near a month, interviewed his ass off in non-work hours, gotten a Realtor, scheduled a whitewash of the house, and actually done his job as well. He felt like shit dumping on Connor Kingston this way, but he didn't have a choice. He needed Josie. He'd do whatever was necessary to have her. The Willow Glen job would have to do; he was sick of driving.

Pocketing his car keys, he followed her inside, catching sight of her as she disappeared down the hall toward the executive offices. He climbed the stairs more slowly.

Whatever that cryptic comment meant, he wouldn't let her get away with it. She was his. Tonight, she'd sleep in his bed. Or he in hers.

He turned into the hallway to find her standing halfway down it. "Well," she huffed, "come on, what's taking you so long?"

Her skirt still swung about her calves from her fast jaunt up the stairs, those hot and sexy lace-ups getting him going. He'd been hard-pressed not to jump her in the car on the way over to the sand plant for the sign-off.

She crooked her finger at him. *What the hell.* Kyle followed.

He caught up with her at Connor's open office door. The man himself was seated at his desk, alone, miraculous in the mid-afternoon.

So, she was putting him to the test, forcing him to turn in his resignation. She didn't believe he'd do it anyway. Why couldn't she believe in him?

"Connor," she said, "I have to talk to you."

Connor turned his head slightly, gave her a suspicious look, then glanced at Kyle. Kyle simply shrugged an I-don't-know-what-the-hell-she's-doing answer.

"I looked through the employee handbook, and there isn't a thing in there that says you can't date your boss."

His heart jumped clear into his throat. She wasn't . . .

"So," she went on, hands on her hip, "I want to be completely aboveboard about this. Kyle and I are going to start dating."

Oh yes, she was. He wanted to shout. He wanted to pick her up and twirl her around the room.

Connor didn't even turn a hair at her declaration. "True, there's nothing specific in the employee handbook about not dating your boss. But you do realize people will be putting the two of you under a microscope looking for evidence of favoritism."

She shrugged. "They already say that now because my parents are on the board. It's nothing new. But I know"—she stabbed her chest—"and you know"—she pointed at Connor—"that I do a great job." She glanced back at Kyle, one eyebrow raised, a slight smile curving her lips. "Right?"

Christ. There was a whole hour before the business day ended and pleasure began. "Right." He patted his briefcase. "I've got the sign-off from SMG to prove what a great job you do."

"Good." She tipped her head at Connor. "Okay, that's all. Just wanted to get it out in the open, and now we've got tons of work to do before the day is over."

She turned on her steel-toes and marched for the door.

"Wait just one minute, young lady." Connor rapped his desk.

Josie's back tensed, and Kyle knew all the hairs on the back of her neck were rising. She *hated* those kind of terms. But she turned. "Yes, sir?"

"I was going to mention this to Kyle, but now seems as good a time as any. Swanson's going to be retiring next year." Swanson was VP of Operations. "And we've got our eye on Nichols to take his place, which means the Director of Materials position will need filling. Since you know materials inside and out, I think you'll be a perfect director when the time comes." He glanced at Kyle. "As long as your current boss is willing to let you go"—he turned back to Josie—"I'd like to move you into the purchasing manager position with the expectation of taking the director spot when Swanson retires."

She gaped. "But I've only been a manager for two months."

Connor nodded agreement. "True. But you've been through the fire, handled it well. With a little grooming over the next year, you'll be more than ready for the job." She'd be responsible for Shipping and Receiving, Warehouse, Purchasing, and Production Planning.

Josie opened her mouth, closed it, looked at Kyle, and he could have sworn her eyes glazed with a tear or two. She'd searched for years for a man who believed in her, and right here in this office, she had two. Not to mention Ernie looking down from above.

She was silent so long, Connor sweetened the pot. "Added benefit, working in Operations, there won't be any conflict of interest with dating your ex-boss. As long as you don't sign any of Kyle's purchase orders."

"Take it, Josie," Kyle whispered.

"And you won't leave?" she asked just as softly.

"I will never leave."

She sucked in a breath, then rolled her lips between her teeth, held them a second, then puffed the air back out in a rush. "Well, of course I don't even have to think about it. Yes, yes, yes"—she bounced on her toes—"I wanna groom for Director of Materials."

"Well, then start searching for your replacement," Connor told her.

She saluted. "I'm on it." No one stopped her when she marched out of the office.

Connor raised one mocking brow. "You realize you have your work cut out for you."

"Oh yeah," Kyle answered, finishing with a chuckle. "Do I ever know."

Connor gave him the nod. "Welcome to the family."

This time he meant more than the company family. Kyle thought about denying that, claiming his boss was moving them forward way too fast, but honestly, it wasn't damn fast enough. If he could, he'd move in with her tonight. "Thanks."

"I'm not even going to ask how long this has been going on."

"Thanks for that, too."

"Tell your girlfriend she better call my wife fast, because if I get home and I'm the one"—he tapped his chest—"breaking the good news, there will be hell to pay."

Hands on the doorjamb, Josie stuck her head back in the door. "I'll call her, dammit. Now"—she gave Kyle a look—"are you coming? We've got to figure out who's going to fill my spot." She disappeared again.

Connor shook his head. "Really, you don't have a clue."

Oh yes he did, and he wanted every delicious moment he could get. "Coming, dear," he called, then winked at Connor before following Josie out.

FOR the rest of the day, they didn't say a word to each other that wasn't business, but she was going mad for a taste of him. They went over the potential for promoting from within, which was Castle's policy where possible. She had a meeting with Swanson and Nichols to discuss her new job, yadda, yadda, et cetera ad nauseam.

At precisely five forty-five, she left Kyle a message on his cell. "I'm running late. Meet me at my condo in an hour."

She couldn't believe she'd walked into Connor's office and told him she'd been playing naughty with her boss. Okay, she hadn't *said* that, but Connor was no idiot.

Kyle had made the sacrifice by finding a new job. She could do no less than admit to everyone that she wanted so much more with him than to be his program manager. And Connor had given her a new job out of it. Woohoo, they didn't have to hide *and* no one could claim favoritism. Well, at least because of Kyle. As she'd told Connor, they'd always say it because she was family.

Kyle hadn't balked, either, when Connor welcomed him. Hot damn.

She had so much to do. Calling Faith in the car—her cousin shrieked with delight—picking up champagne to celebrate her new job and Kyle not having to hand in his resignation. There was one other must-do errand.

Of course, when she finally arrived home, Kyle was early—or she was a tad late—and lounging on her front stoop.

He was so damn beautiful. She couldn't wait to get him out of those jeans. Wow, wow, wow, how had she gotten so freaking lucky?

Why did it take her so long to figure it out? Ah, the mysteries of life.

She tossed him the little present she'd just had made for him. Catching it deftly, he opened his hand and stared at the silver key on his palm.

"Open the door," she said.

He thumbed over his shoulder. "This door?"

"Yeah, that door."

He didn't move. "And this is mine?"

"Yeah, it's yours."

"So I can come and go as I please?"

"It's stupid to make you stand outside if I get held up, don't you think?" She knew she was making light of it.

She knew he got it as he unlocked the door. Then, with a certain ceremony, he pulled out his own key ring and snapped her key in place.

It was warm out, but with the blinds closed and the drapes pulled, the condo had stayed relatively cool. She set her computer case down by the stair wall, but held on to the bag with the champagne. "You probably don't have a change of clothing for the morning, do you?"

"Ending up in a lot of dusty places, I always carry a change of clothing."

She was pussyfooting, not saying what she meant. So she grabbed his hand, yanked him over to the sofa, and made him sit. "Okay, here it is." She hugged the champagne bottle to her chest as she stood before him. "I've got this whole bad habit going about needing to protect myself, making sure no one ever gets one up on me, especially not my boss." Someday, maybe tonight after she'd had her way with him, she'd tell him the whole story about her asshole college professor. "But I'm so over that. I didn't even need Connor to give me the materials job"—she wagged her finger—"not that

I'm giving it back. But what you did, looking for a new job—nobody's ever done anything like that for me."

"You're worth it, you know."

"I didn't know that until you did it. And it kind of overwhelmed me." She shrugged, then flopped down on the sofa beside him. "You probably think I was all melodramatic and everything, marching into Connor's office, and I'm really not a melodramatic person."

"I liked it."

She finally relinquished the champagne bottle, setting it on the coffee table. "I wanted to show you I wasn't all talk and no action. That I don't want *us* to be a secret. That I don't care if people say you're playing favorites."

"Josie—"

She put a hand over his mouth. "You wanna spend the night with me?"

"God, yes," he said against her palm.

"I hated Little Miss Snowflake," she confessed.

"I know."

"You did not."

He raised one eyebrow. "Did, too."

"I'm glad you didn't touch her." She ran a hand down his shirt-front. "That you didn't *vant* to touch her."

He laughed at her bad imitation. He had the most gorgeous eyes she'd ever seen on a man.

"And I won't make you wear my panties or force you to let me use the dildo."

"Now wait a minute there, don't be too hasty."

She nuzzled his ear, drew in his scent, came alive with his close-ness. But he had to understand she was totally serious about him. "No more games, Kyle. I promise."

He pulled back, gave her a boyish grimace. "The panties we can skip, but I liked the dildo."

"You did?" He'd certainly seemed to have one helluva great orgasm.

"You damn well *know* I loved the dildo." He kissed the tip of her nose. "And for the next game, I get to use it on you."

Oh God, he was so perfect. "No way, next game is mine. You made me do the sex club, remember?"

"Oh, I remember." He held her chin in his hand. "Don't ever stop playing those kinds of games with me, Josie. Promise?"

"Oh yeah, I promise." She started planning the next game right then. "And baby, you better watch out."

"Payback's a bitch," he whispered. Then he paid her back exactly the way she loved.

Jasmine Haynes has been penning stories for as long as she's been able to write. Storytelling has always been her passion. With a bachelor degree in accounting from Cal Poly, San Luis Obispo, she has worked in the high-tech Silicon Valley for the past twenty years and hasn't met a boring accountant yet! Well, maybe a few. She and her husband live with Star, the mighty moose-hunting dog (if she weren't afraid of her own shadow). Jasmine's pastimes, when not writing her heart out, are hiking in the Redwoods and taking long walks on the beach. Jasmine also writes as Jennifer Skully and JB Skully. She loves to hear from readers. Please e-mail her at skully@skullybuzz.com or visit her website, www.skullybuzz.com, and her blog, www.jasminehaynes.blogspot.com.

BE ON THE LOOKOUT FOR THE NEXT EROTIC NOVEL BY
JASMINE HAYNES

Yours for the Night

AVAILABLE NOVEMBER 2009 FROM HEAT BOOKS

**Transformed into mistresses of the night, three women
discover that sometimes fulfilling your deepest desire is
the most dangerous thing you can do . . .**

Raised to believe that the only measure of self-worth is money, being a
courtesan gives Marianna Whitney value beyond her wildest dreams
in **"The Girlfriend Experience."** She discovers a world where she holds
the key to unlocking a man's fantasies—until one of her "dates" opens
her eyes to the delight of complete surrender to her own fantasy . . .

Devastated when her husband leaves her for a younger woman, all
Dominique Lowe wants is **"Payback."** Becoming a courtesan and having her pick of men is the perfect revenge. But when she meets a man
determined to resist her, she wonders what she'd be willing to give up
to make him hers . . .

In **"Triple Play,"** three divorces have taught forty-year-old Noelle St.
James that her sexual appetite is far too insatiable for any one man.
But even she is shocked by her newest patron, who wants to prove
that one man *can* give her everything she needs . . .

The novels of Jasmine Haynes are

"SO INCREDIBLY HOT."—*Romance Reader at Heart*